SUCCUBUS FOR HIRE:

THE

BILLIONAIRE'S

HEIR

SUCCUBUS FOR HIRE:

THE

BILLIONAIRE'S HEIR

MICHAEL DON ANDERSON

CRIMSON WEREWOLF LIMITED • USA

Dedication

This book is dedicated to powerful women everywhere, whether they be housewives or mothers, professionals or thinkers, artists or laborers (or any combination thereof), without whom all of us men would live much inferior lives. I am lucky to note that all of the women in my life have incredible strength of character and I look to them for my heroine, Bianca Savage. She's a woman who has difficulties all of us can relate to: love, sex, trust, integrity; while making them unique to the problems of being a succubus.

In memory of Gwen and Grace; Stella and Ruth; Clara and even Hallie. The strongest women in my family, all loved and missed.

And to the women who have shaped this work by sharing so much of their personal lives with me: Coreen, Miyuki, Rain, Roxanne, Cindy, Chrystal, Seona, Janice and Sue. And (for reminding me that I was missing a series featuring a powerful female lead) to Nicole.

Succubus for Hire:

The

Billionaire's

Heir

By

Michael Don Anderson

CHAPTER ONE

I was led to a table in the middle of the crowded restaurant by the *maître d'* personally. The dinner rush was always hectic in central Los Angeles. This was Long Beach. There should've been a few empty stations. There weren't.

Expensive suits. Dresses from high-end stores. Real jewels in their broaches and necklaces. Much bigger than the tiny emerald studs I wore. Clearly the rich and powerful liked the place.

It was called *The Meerkat*. Egyptian-flavors added to liven up high-end grub. Steaks. Lobster. The usual dishes twisted into the exotic. I loved Cairo street-food. Wasn't sure it would translate well into mainstream dishes. Overly complicated. Like this meeting.

The diners' energy tickled along my skin. Made wild with their sense of entitlement. Arrogance. My stomach grew cold with hunger at the presence of so much food gathered together in the busy restaurant. I pressed my hand against my belly. Reined in my power. Focusing on the table I was being steered toward.

My potential client, Henry Gibraltar sat with two young men. Hard to judge how tall he was sitting down. I'd guess about five-ten. He had silver hair. Fine lines marked his brow from frequent frowning. Narrow jaw. But sturdy. Narrow shoulders, too. Lean all over. Skin thinned with age. Still handsome at sixty-three except for a bitterness in his grey eyes.

I only recognized Gibraltar's face because it had been splashed on the news the day before. Presumably the reason he'd asked for this meeting. Although what a billionaire could need with a simple private eye was beyond me.

Gibraltar eyed the stiff-backed *maître d'*. The expressionless employee bowed and slipped away silently. Well trained to earn his position.

"Please have a seat, Miss Savage."

"I usually meet my clients at the office." I reluctantly pulled the chair out and sat down. None of the men stood. That was something in their favor. I knew it was probably an insult. Rather than an acknowledgement of my equality. But I was happy to give them the benefit of the doubt.

"Considering your nature, I felt a public meeting was safer." Gibraltar smiled but his eyes were empty. Hollow. Except for a smoldering impatience.

His gaze roamed from my woolen-knit beret to stare at my gloved hands. The dark crimson silk went all the way to my elbows. Snug and flexible so that my fingers weren't constrained. Only my shoulders were exposed. The beret was navy, like my skirt and blouse. The top was low cut, revealing enough décolletage to distract a man from staring into my eyes too long. Most women had the opposite problem. Of course the sunglasses helped.

"If you don't trust me, I doubt we have any business."

I stood. Annoyed that I'd wasted thirty minutes driving across Long Beach during heavy traffic for this meeting. Anger weakened my self-control. I felt my skin grow warm as the testosterone in the room prickled at my power. My stomach filled with icy needles of need. It wasn't just my stomach. Tendrils of ache stirred lower down. I'd learned long ago to ignore any potential sexual nature to my appetite.

If anyone had touched me just then, skin on skin, it would've been bad. My appetite spiked in the moment. Fortunately, no one was that foolish. Of course, I didn't have to touch someone to feed. But I'd had years of discipline to learn restraint. Breathing deeply, the sensation ebbed. I moved my fingers away from my belly.

My frown deepened as I glared at him. "You'll get a bill for wasting my time."

"Sit down," snapped the man on Gibraltar's left.

The youngest of the three, he was thin like his employer. His dark hair flawless combed into place. His pinstripe suit too fitted to be off-the-rack. Expensive, like most of the clothing in the restaurant. I knew a lawyer when I met one. He smelled of summonses and courtroom drama. Without the confidence.

"Hush, Mansfield. Miss Savage, I apologize for my attorney's zeal."

"More than an attorney, I'm guessing." I was good with faces. Matching details others might miss. I noticed genetic relationships no matter how slight. It came with being more than human. These men would have said 'less.'

"My grandson." Gibraltar eyed me speculatively.

"She Googled you," said Mansfield grimly. "Don't give her credit she hasn't earned."

"I said hush! Google doesn't know anything about you."

Gibraltar turned to his grandson. The empty expression in his grey eyes grew cold. Hateful. The old man didn't like being disobeyed. Good to know. I didn't like to be told what to do. We were off to a great start.

"Y—yes, Sir." Mansfield glanced down at the table. But not before shooting me a look of loathing.

"Please, Miss Savage. Sit back down."

Gibraltar tried to look humble. It wasn't a natural expression for him. Reluctantly, I took my seat again and waited.

"I expected your hair to be darker." Gibraltar spoke with compulsion. As if he had to get it off his chest. He didn't like surprises. "It should be black."

"Spawn of the Devil and all that?" I laughed. It was a good laugh. A sexy laugh. Men had been enthralled by that laugh, in combination with my gaze. Tonight I avoided Gibraltar's eyes. My sunglasses protected him. But I didn't want to see that sour expression for a moment. Judging me.

I surveyed the restaurant instead. Distracted from his fear by so much potential food. The two-legged kind. "Auburn goes better with my pale complexion. And I've never met the Devil."

The man grunted. "It's not as if there are people like you on every street-corner. Not even a handful on the world registry. Most of those dead by execution."

I appreciated that he considered me a person. Although from the look in his eyes, his words might've been more generous than his thoughts. The street-corner reference, though—sounded like he lumped me in with twenty-dollar hookers. I wasn't happy about that.

"There aren't many of my kind at all, as far as I know. Registered or otherwise." I held my temper. Better than I'd expected. He'd distracted me from being hungry. "I'll repeat, Mr. Gibraltar. If you don't trust me, I can't work for you."

I put my hands into my lap to keep him from staring at them. He'd ignored my breasts so far. Most men didn't have his restraint. Even gay men tended to admire them. Married men certainly. Curious about what sex with me would be like. How would it be different from ordinary women. From their wives or boyfriends. The thrill of danger and all that. Gibraltar was a cautious man. Distracted from any carnal needs by his unspoken desperation.

He struggled for the words. His composure wasn't the problem. He didn't know how to say it. "I need your help. The police have been useless. And this requires a more—more personal touch."

"I'm aware that your grandson Vincent was kidnapped. It's hard to live in Long Beach and not see it on the evening news."

Vincent Gibraltar was the heir to Henry Gibraltar's fortune. A billion dollar company with its headquarters right here along the waterfront. It wasn't common knowledge that the old man had two other grandchildren. One still living as evidenced by Mansfield's presence. I didn't know the name of the granddaughter. Or if she'd even survived into adulthood.

"Yes. Only—" Gibraltar stared at the third man. Mid-thirties. Well built. Handsome in that Tab Hunter, surfer kind of way.

Blonde and blue eyed. The Nazis would have approved except for one thing. He wasn't any more human than I was.

The man smiled, revealing two sharp canines. He shrugged harmlessly. I'd sensed the undeath on him before I'd reached the table. A metaphysical dead-spot. An absence of the energy that I could feed from. "I'm afraid Vincent may have been lured away voluntarily."

"And you are?"

I studied his hands. Neat. Well-manicured. Strong fingers. Most vampires were on the thin side. Came from having a strictly liquid diet. This man worked out. Even with his innate preternatural strength he'd developed an athletic physique. Not that I'd met many vampires.

"Joseph."

"Joseph? That's it? No last name?" I leaned back, crossing my legs at the ankle. It meant I couldn't move as quickly, but it was a crowded restaurant. No one had tried to kill me all year. I felt I could chance it. "I know it's L.A., but I didn't know vampires were divas."

"I'm Mr. Gibraltar's personal bodyguard."

"During the night," I countered. I glanced at the front of the restaurant. It explained why the meeting had been after eight p.m. This time of year, the sun didn't set until half-past seven. "Who guards your master during the daytime?"

"Such language, Miss Savage. What is this, the eighteen-hundreds?" Joseph watched me carefully. Relaxed. But behind his façade, he was assessing what kind of threat I'd be.

"I'm not that old. How old are you?" Some people thought it rude to ask. I didn't care. With vampires it was important to know. Assuming he'd tell me the truth.

"I was thirty-two when I crossed over."

"That's not what I meant."

He smiled, trying for harmless again. It probably worked with a lot of people. People like Gibraltar. To them, vampires should have black hair. Pale skin. The way Gibraltar had expected me to look. Anything preternatural should be dark and ethereal at the same time.

Not Joseph. In addition to being blonde, he had a rugged tan. One of the things the fairytales got wrong. Vampires kept some of their physical attributes at the time of undeath. Hair color and length. Amount of melatonin. Yellowing of teeth. They could lose and gain muscle but a lot of other things stayed fixed.

"I know." He didn't answer the question. I guess that was better than being lied to. "I have an associate who takes the day shift."

"Blood-linked?"

He blinked with surprise. I'd caught him off guard. It was a vampiric trade secret. "Since you are familiar with this term, yes."

"What's that mean?" demanded Mansfield.

Joseph ignored the grandson. Held my gaze without fear. Waiting for what I might say next. Wondering if I'd keep his secret.

"So he's human."

"Mostly." I saw a flicker of a smile.

"Not very discrete to admit." I looked at Gibraltar. "So you have a lycanthrope guarding you during the day. And a vampire at night. Now you're here with me. But money can't buy everything."

Henry Gibraltar grew angry. He focused it on me. Avoiding eye-contact with Joseph, who was the real source of his anger. Afraid to express his frustration directly.

I wouldn't hire someone I was afraid of. Of course, if the Gibraltars of the world didn't hire people they were afraid of, I wouldn't have a job.

The old man grunted. "It's illegal to discriminate."

I waited for him to elaborate. He just stared at the table as if he'd answered all my questions. Maybe he had. So I put a few more to him. "You still haven't explained why you need my help. To do what?"

Joseph answered again. "Vincent may have met some people who led him astray because of me."

That got my attention. "By people do you mean vampires?"

"We are people."

I smiled. All the way into my eyes. It probably didn't show through my glasses. "We're monsters, too."

"Can we get on with this?" asked Mansfield, struggling to sound professional. He wasn't very good at it. I doubted he'd be very good in the courtroom. Gibraltar probably only hired him out of nepotism. Not that I understood families. I'd never had one of my own. Not really.

"Time is of the essence," agreed Joseph.

Mansfield frowned. He didn't appreciate the support. Maybe he hated vampires. He definitely hated me.

"Your grandson isn't entirely wrong. I did research you, Mr. Gibraltar. Definitely beyond a quick Google. I understand that you had three grandchildren. But until Vincent was taken, none of them have appeared as public figures. No photos on the internet of the other two. Except for birth records, there isn't a paper-trail on them. Like they vanished."

He stiffened. "You know about what happened to my children? Their parents?"

I nodded. "Murdered in a failed kidnap-attempt more than thirteen years ago. Different from Vincent's abduction." I nodded politely at Joseph. "Vampires aside."

"The police never found the people responsible. My son and daughter dead. Killed by a forty-five caliber handgun taken from their bodyguard."

"Before Mr. Gibraltar upped his security to me." Joseph wanted it clear that it would never have happened on his watch.

Probably true. Except, Vincent had been taken during his watch. Because of him. If I took him at his word. Hard to say which was worse.

Joseph continued the story when Gibraltar stayed silent. "Their spouses were killed as well. The police were led to believe the children were dead. To protect Henry's bloodline. Instead, they were given different last names. Except for Vincent."

"Why not Vincent?"

"He's my chosen heir. The Gibraltar name will live on."

I glanced at Mansfield. His hands were clenched in fists. He wasn't happy about that. He and his sister hadn't been born with the Gibraltar name. Their mother had married an Everwright. Obviously they hadn't kept that name either.

"But you don't think he was kidnapped?" I watched Joseph's reaction. "He joined a coven of vampires voluntarily?"

The old man answered angrily. "Not voluntarily, Miss Savage. Vincent's only sixteen. He can't consent to be bitten until he's twenty-one."

"Or eighteen with court permission. I know the law, Mr. Gibraltar. I wouldn't make a very good P.I. if I didn't."

There was need in his angry grey eyes. "Can you help me?"

I stared at them all. "You still haven't told me anything. Why not go to the Feds? If he's sixteen, the vampires would have to give him back."

Gibraltar glanced at Joseph. The vampire sighed. An artifact. Vampires didn't breath. Any sighing was intentional. "We'd have to explain our association with these individuals. Prove that they took him. We'd rather not."

I stared hard at Mansfield. "How do you feel about your cousin's disappearance?"

He shook his head. "We aren't close. Grandfather thought we'd be safer if no one associated Maureen and I with Vincent. Or each other. Honestly, I don't know him well enough to wish him harm."

They were circling all the questions of motive. I couldn't decide whether to take the case if I didn't have the facts. I stopped being subtle. "But the money?"

Gibraltar put both palms flat on the table and shook his head. "The grandchildren all inherit a third of the estate by means of secret trusts, Miss Savage. Blake won't profit if Vincent dies.

Vincent will run my company, true. But under the guidance of a board of directors. There isn't extra money as a result."

I wasn't following the math. "Wouldn't he? It's divided in two then, isn't it?"

"No. I wanted to take away any internecine temptations. The shares of a deceased grandchild go to certain charitable trusts if they leave no issue." Gibraltar touched Mansfield's shoulder. The first sign of familial affection I'd seen. "Blake's life is better for not carrying the Gibraltar name. A reward for his sacrifice."

I wasn't an expert at corporate organization or business practices, but I knew Gibraltar was ignoring a lot of intangible benefits that came from being his heir. Whoever ran the company would have a driver. Extra bodyguards. An expense account. Hell, a whole high-profile celebrity lifestyle went along with it. It was more than enough for someone to kill over. Even a henpecked and cowed cousin like Mansfield appeared to be.

I decided to ignore the obvious for the moment. "Is your involvement with the coven illegal?"

I was a private detective. Covering up anything illegal on behalf of a client could cost me my license. I wasn't going to let that happen. Not even for a billionaire.

"No, Miss Savage. Morally ambiguous perhaps. I'll even admit to it being within the grey areas of business practices. A political détente if you will. But not illegal."

Gibraltar held my gaze. Peering through my sunglasses. They weren't as dark as my day-wear lenses. I wasn't completely masked. He'd forgotten I wasn't one of his usual flunkies. Someone to bully. He'd forgotten that touching me wasn't the only way to get hurt.

"Hank!"

Joseph grabbed Gibraltar's wrist. Squeezed it until pain filled the old man's eyes. Gibraltar blinked and tried to pull away. He slowly focused on the vampire. Like waking from a dream.

Joseph searched the old man's face. "You don't stare a succubus in the eyes. I told you that before this meeting!"

"Was I bewitched?" Gibraltar had trouble thinking. Slow to come back to himself. When he did, he grew anxious. Angrier than he'd been. "You used your power on me!?"

"No, Mr. Gibraltar. You did it to yourself." I didn't mention that I could've use his eye-contact as a gateway to my power. To control him. Make him answer my questions as part of an overwhelming desire to please me. But I'd spent decades learning to rein it in. I wasn't about to lose control in a room full of witnesses. The sunglasses were for everyone's benefit.

"You weren't mesmerized. Not yet." Joseph smiled at me. Not harmless. I saw the snake in his eyes. "Miss Savage's reputation is stellar. You don't use your power on clients. Even though you could influence a bump in fees that way."

"The laws against vampiric mind-control apply to me as well, Joseph." I started to stand again, glaring at the vampire before I faced Gibraltar. My appetite was returning. Fueled by his moment of forgetfulness. "No one would come to me if they couldn't trust me. And I won't work for someone who doesn't."

"Please." To my surprise, it was Blake Mansfield who reached out a hand. Sliding it toward me across the table. Stopping before touching me. Even with the gloves on. "My grandfather's just cautious. With as much money as he has, he has to be. Surely you can understand that."

Joseph nodded. No longer threatening me. Not harmless either. Something in-between. "A sixteen year old's life is on the line, Miss Savage."

"Blake's clearly older than Vincent. Why wasn't he given the Gibraltar name? Or named your heir as an Everwright?"

Mansfield turned to stare at his grandfather. Waiting for the answer. Even though he must've already heard it before.

Gibraltar frowned sternly. "My father passed this legacy to me as his surviving son. I would've passed it to my son, Charles."

"Vincent's his son." I looked at Mansfield. "You're not."

"In a nutshell." The young lawyer shrugged. Resentment in his eyes. Not hatred. Disappointment.

I stared at Gibraltar. "You trust Joseph? That he's not in cahoots with the coven?"

The old man looked up at me like electricity had run through his chair. "Joseph's been with me a long time, Miss Savage. I trust him."

The vampire clasped his hands together and smiled at me. "There's no profit in it for me."

"So will you do it?" Mansfield again. His eyes on my lips. He hated me. But he wanted my help. Curiouser and curiouser.

I took a second to consider them. "I'm not cheap."

Joseph shrugged. "But you're discreet."

I surveyed the patrons at the tables around us. It was loud. No one was listening. Despite the occasional stares our way. That didn't mean someone couldn't be eavesdropping electronically. Maybe Gibraltar's people had taken precautions against that. He was an incredibly rich man.

"That, yes."

"Then you're worth every penny." Gibraltar stood up. Mansfield joined him. "Enjoy your dinner. I've already told the *maître d'* to put it on my tab. A thank you for the inconvenience of meeting me in public. On top of your hourly rate."

He and Blake started to move away from the table. The vampire didn't join them. "Joseph?"

"You don't want the lady to dine alone do you?" He purred like a contented cat. Gazing into my eyes behind the sunglasses. Safe from my power, even if I'd wanted to use it.

"It's a moot point, Gentlemen. As you must know, I don't eat the kinds of foods humans do." I stood, annoyed that there was tempting food all around for the taking but all of it off limits. "I'm not in the mood for experiencing tastes for taste's sake."

I didn't mention that I'd be sick afterwards. Enjoying human spices and flavors had unpleasant consequences for me. A weakness they didn't need to know. Some cultures required that I dine with a client. Keeping my vulnerability a secret was part of my long life.

Joseph grinned without joining us on his feet. "You can drink alcohol. Ask me questions about Vincent's habits. His circumstances."

I didn't smile. Very few people knew I could drink booze without any ill-effects. Fewer than knew about a vampiric blood-link.

Had he met one of my kind sometime in the past? Was he old enough for that to be a strong possibility? I was curious about my people. But not enough to sit through a bottle of wine with Joseph on the off-chance.

"Have the information sent to my offices by tomorrow morning. I'll read it over. Then I'll have a reason to talk to you face to face."

"I like the idea of us being face to face."

Blake glanced at Joseph. It took him a moment to realize that the vampire was flirting with me. The young attorney stared at my cleavage as he spoke. "Can a succubus feed from the undead?"

Good boy. He'd learned from his grandfather's mistake. But I frowned at him anyway. It was a personal question. One that I'd never been asked before.

Joseph answered for me. "No. No they can't."

"How would you know?" I looked for any hint of deception in his eyes.

"You aren't the first woman like you I've met." He leaned toward me. "If you stay, I'll tell you all about it. You might even have a guess at how old I am."

"I'm not that desperate for a date," I said without anger.

He'd confirmed it. It was tempting. Even I hadn't ever met another succubus. Not in person. He might know things I hadn't learned, yet.

I stared into his eyes. His lips twitched into a smug smile. He thought he had me. Joseph was too confident. Too unafraid of my power. I wasn't used to being at a disadvantage. And there was one other problem.

"Just because I can't feed off of you, doesn't mean the reverse isn't true."

He ginned, pleased by my words. "Too bad. It would've been fun to try."

Joseph stood and the three men walked away. I stared at their backs until they were out the door. I touched the Glock at my hip for reassurance, hidden by my jacket. It was an ultra-compact model. Easy to hide when I went out in public, but completely Glock reliable.

Regular ammunition wouldn't help against the vampire. If he decided to try something for real. I'd have to start carrying wood-tipped shells. Usually, it was potential sex with me that was dangerous. In his case, I wasn't so sure.

CHAPTER TWO

I arrived at my East Village office the next morning an hour earlier than scheduled. My hair was tied up in a pony-tail. To keep it from distracting me while I worked. My daytime sunglasses were too dark to be seen through. I wore a navy-blue silk blouse that would allow easy movement if I had to fight. Or run. The frilled edges of a fashionable black sports bra peeked out of it. A silver cross nestled in the press of my breasts. My navy skirt was short. I could kick a man in the face with the heel of my running shoes without trouble. It would flash him my panties but not slow me down. A shiny black leather belt with silver clasp in the shape of a sitting-cat finished the outfit.

Janet Frisby, my receptionist, was arranging her desk as I walked through the door. She jumped a bit at seeing me.

"Bianca! You're never this early."

I smiled at the woman. Janet was fifty-four-years old. Thin but not frail. Her moplike, curly hair had started to grey. She left it natural. Wire-rimmed glasses sat on her small, no-nonsense nose. She wore a conservative one piece dress with a dark floral pattern that surprisingly didn't make her look like a granny. Her lipstick was a muted pink-brown. Just enough eye-shadow and base to keep from being washed out. She'd been unremarkable when I'd first hired her thirty-years earlier. Now she had character. No. Character was something a man had. She had a beauty which had been hidden behind her youth.

"A new client. Any files in the drop box?"

"I haven't checked. Give me a mo'." She trotted out into the hallway.

The office complex was on Broadway Court, between First and Ocean. From the third-story rooftop, I could see a sliver of the Pacific Ocean to the south. The individual office doors were kept locked and unlocked by the tenants. Depending on the hours each business kept. But the entrance into the main building hallway was almost always left open. Security cameras and a full-time guard kept it safe from burglars, homeless people and amorous teenagers.

Most of my tenants had mail slots in their doors. I had a drop box in the hall big enough to hold a dishwasher. The advantage of owning the place.

Janet came back in, carrying an armful of files. "I'm glad we're on the first floor. Someone has their reading cut out."

"I don't suppose you'd like to help?" I grinned at her.

"No, thank you. I remember the last time you conned me into taking files. I still have nightmares about the mutilated corpse."

"I really didn't think the police would include crime-scene photographs, Janet. I promise."

"I know. I'm not mad. Just—I'm just not willing to risk it again."

I smiled back at her grimly. "I was just kidding anyway. I think the less you know about this case, the better off you'll be."

"Dangerous?" She watched me. Worried. Looking for any trace of a lie.

"Probably. They don't come to me when it's not."

Janet made a noise of disapproval and walked the files into my office. Placing them carefully on the only clear corner. "Have you eaten?"

Her voice always tightened when she asked about my meals. She forced herself to say 'eat' instead of 'fed.' That would've been impolite. And Janet was anything but impolite. She'd gotten used to my rituals. The ones necessary for maintaining my celibacy. Neither of us wanted to think about the last time I'd slipped up.

"Not yet. I want to get a start on that." I pointed at the stack of files. "See what Kenny has today, would you?"

Kenny Lestrange was part homeless—part entrepreneur. Twenty-eight years old. Lanky. Filthy clothes because he liked them that way. Blue eyes that were haunted by memories no one else could see. He had connections on the streets that could provide me with questionable items. His business dealings were like Henry Gibraltar's. Grey area. Nothing illegal. Obtaining things that I could never ask Janet to track down for me.

She nodded. Even managed a weak smile. I hadn't seen the smile for several weeks after Kenny had provided three adorable puppies. Usually he had crates of rats. Animals suffering from terminal illnesses with no one to care for them. I'd had a little talk with Kenny after that. He promised no more puppies. Or kittens. Nothing cute and cuddly.

I plopped into my padded leather chair and got comfortable. Janet hadn't been joking. It was going to be a very long read. I pushed my sunglasses onto the top of my head and grabbed a file.

Flipping it open, a picture of Vincent Gibraltar was the first thing I saw. Cute. Doe-eyed. Innocent. I glanced at the back of the 8x10. Dated three months ago. He looked younger than sixteen.

Not that that meant anything. To me, everyone looked younger than they were. I'd lived almost seventy-some-odd-years among humans. Out in the open once they'd passed the Preternatural Tolerance Act in the 1960s. Before that, well, I'd spent my childhood in the forests of Canada. Alone at first. Hunters had killed my mother. Succubi didn't have fathers. Not living ones, I'd learned years later.

I rubbed my neck. I hadn't slept well. Something about Gibraltar's reaction to me at our meeting left me feeling dirty. Stirred memories about the past. Reminding me of eager and aggressive men who'd gazed too long into my pre-adolescent eyes. Men who'd tried to do more than just look once they'd been mesmerized.

I hadn't known what I was. Not until a half-blind Christian woman found me. Took me in without judgement.

Matilda Oglethorpe had been old enough to be a grandmother. Not that she'd had any kids of her own. Kindly. Lonely. She'd taken me in and saved my life without realizing it. Too many people had witnessed my first mistakes. Instincts for self-preservation that left the victims dead but my virtue intact.

Granny Oglethorpe had only seen me as a helpless young girl wandering alone in the woods. Dirty. Hungry. Always hungry because I didn't know how to feed properly. Only out of fear. Because men had tried to force themselves on me. Or kill me.

Even when Granny's weathered hands had first felt along my scalp, brushing my hair so long ago, she hadn't been afraid. She'd paused, touching the nubs of my horns. Took the time to feel them for several minutes. But she hadn't thrown me out. And my power hadn't reacted to her. Hadn't tried to feed from the first honest affection I'd ever known.

She was the one who'd told me what I was. Her. A devoutly religious human. A Christian who'd never met another creature like me. I asked if the horns made me evil. She'd laughed. She said she didn't believe anyone was inherently evil. Not even the Devil. She believed that he was a trickster. Put in our path to tempt us. But we all had free will. God would never be so cruel as to force someone into darkness. It was the first time someone had made me feel valued for more than lechery.

Granny taught me how to hide my needs. Suppress them. She even kept me from encountering any men who might come around. Men were the temptation of any girl she said. Human or otherwise. She hadn't known just how right she was. I'd never told her what they'd tried to do. It was too dark for a soul as pure as hers.

Women were safe for me. Mostly. I didn't have accidents with women. Feeding on them wasn't any more satisfying than draining a dying mongrel. I'd have settled for a dying animal just then. My arms trembled with need.

"Bianca?"

Janet stood in the open doorframe. Watching me reminisce. Her expression reminded me of Granny Oglethorpe's face. Kind.

Worried. Demanding. Each in their own ways. Hopefully Janet hadn't seen the hunger in my eyes.

"Yes?"

"Kenny says he's having an inventory problem."

I stared, brows furrowed. "What the Devil does that mean?"

"That's what I asked."

"And?" I tried not to lose my patience. Janet had a habit of forcing me to pry for the details. Dramatic presentation I supposed.

"He said no one's seen a rat in the city for three days."

"That's a first." I kicked off my shoes and placed my feet on the desk. It annoyed Janet but she'd learned to pick her battles. "The Mayor'll be happy about that. Good for tourism I suppose. Kenny knows I need a regular delivery!"

"He said things came up. Sends his apologies. He also said he doesn't know when he'll have anything in stock." Janet wasn't smiling. We both knew how serious this problem was. Maybe for Kenny. Definitely for me.

"What about the Rodriguez family?"

Janet blinked, confused by the segue. "The lawyers?"

"Really? Attorneys might help out my food problems?" I demanded.

"No need to get sarcastic."

I bit back another sardonic remark. "The Rodríguezes that make the tamales for us at Christmas. My old clients. Doesn't the son raise goats?"

Janet threw her hand to her mouth. "You're not bringing goats in here! And what would we do with the bodies after? No!"

"You know as well as I do that the longer I go without feeding the more I lose control." I stared at the ceiling. Water-stains plagued two of the corners. A defect my plumber couldn't resolve. Usually I could ignore them. I liked imperfections. It meant things were real. Today I wanted to paint over them.

I hadn't eaten in almost a week. Janet didn't know that. And I didn't have a good excuse. My appetite had been all over the place lately.

She shook her head. "You can go a day or two without any problems. Don't kid a kidder."

"You're a kidder?" I gave her my best innocent expression.

She scowled. "Get to your files. I'll call Kenny back and put a fire under that butt of his."

"Careful. Kenny might like it."

She disappeared around the corner in a huff, but raised her voice disapprovingly. "No homophobic remarks, Bianca. It's not becoming."

"Setting his ass on fire has nothing to do with sexual orientation!" I shouted back at her. "I know some straight men who are just as keen."

She stuck her head back through the doorway. "Implying a man might like anything done to his backside is most certainly inappropriate."

Janet's eldest grandson was gay and she was fiercely proud of him. Not because he was gay. Although she admired the role model he'd become for the rainbow community. He'd been valedictorian in high school. Graduating a year early. Handsome and athletic. The first member of her family to get into a serious school. Biology at U.C.L.A. Quarterback on their football team.

She supported everything about him. Unconditional love. Like Granny Oglethorpe.

"Are you crying?" she asked.

I blinked away the moisture and scowled. "Why would I be crying? I'm not that hungry."

I buried my face into the file. She wasn't fooled. "I'm sorry, Bee. I know you don't have a bigoted bone in your body."

Joseph sprang to my mind. I opened my mouth and then closed it. I didn't know very many vampires. Not well enough to say I didn't like them. I wanted her to be right. That didn't stop me from being cautious.

"Janet, could you call the gun-shop? Order wood-tipped ammo for the Glock 43. They should carry it. If not, I'll pay for same day delivery from their supplier."

She stared at me. "This case?"

I nodded. "You might want to start wearing a cross."

"But I'm not religious like you."

"The vampires won't know that." I stared at her to make my point.

"I'll order extras just to be safe." She paused and stared at my desk. "The same for your Sig in the drawer."

Shit. I had another thought. "Better add silver."

"Silver." She swallowed hard. I gave her credit for not asking if it was for something demonic or lycanthropic. "Might as well order an Uzi while we're at it."

It was meant to be a joke. She hadn't realized how close she was to the truth. "It's on special order."

She scurried off and I felt bad. I'd scared Janet for no good reason. I could've ordered the ammunition myself. Hell, I might not even need it.

I pictured Joseph's smile and shuddered. I wouldn't need it. Sure. And Santa Claus is real. Fear might just be the one thing that kept Janet safe.

CHAPTER THREE

I was just starting the fifth and next to last file when I heard a bleating from the hallway. I stood up. Walked to the opening connecting Janet's office to mine.

She was missing from her desk. I went out into the hallway. Found her shooing a small pygmy goat from eating her skirt. Juana Rodriguez held onto the black and white animal's leash. Letting it drag her along after Janet's clothes.

Juana was young. A teenager. Four-foot-eight. Her face still round with that last vestiges of baby-fat. She hadn't hit her final growth spurt. Black hair. Dark brown eyes. Wearing a knee-length skirt and baggy t-shirt with some musical artist I didn't recognize. Her feet were covered in pink tennies with white laces.

Andre Green, the security guard had an arm out in front of the girl, glancing toward us. "You send for this?"

Andre was a transplant from the Big Easy. Late twenties. Black and fit. Pleasant looking if not classically handsome. Hair cut in a short-cropped style. A soul-patch on his chin shaped like a perfect triangle. Andre was the breadwinner in the family. But he had a protective Baptist mother and insecure white girlfriend. Neither of which knew he worked for a succubus.

He was loyal and otherwise impeccably honest. I'd been lucky to find him. It was easy to pretend that Janet was the real owner of the building if it kept his personal life happy. I'd even gone as far as putting the deed in her name. He understood it was all a ruse for his benefit. That gesture on my part had cemented our friendship.

"It's all good, Andre, thank you." I smiled.

He nodded curtly and turned his back to me. He knew it was dangerous to meet my eyes. I wasn't wearing my sunglasses and he was too polite to stare at my breasts.

I turned to Janet. "I thought you said no goats? I take it Kenny's no longer our supplier?"

"Oh, Bee! It's even worse than I pictured. It's adorable." Janet was practically crying. "I thought it'd be one of those ugly gruff things with ragged hair. It's just a baby."

"You asked for something small enough to carry," replied Juana uncertainly. "Hello, Miss Bianca."

"It's just 'Bianca,' Juana. We've been friends since you were five."

"Mama would spank me if I didn't speak politely."

Juana still had an accent. Born in Mexico, she'd gotten her green card in Texas. Eventually the family had made their way to California. Hard working and honest. We'd met on a case about ten years earlier. The first and last time I took a case out of state. Texas was not a place for someone preternatural.

I only saw the Rodriguez family once a year. Juana wasn't wearing much make-up. Child innocent. "You're always polite, Juana. How old are you now?"

"Fourteen."

She smiled shyly, glancing up at my horns. Curious but not afraid. I wasn't wearing a hat. Not in my own office. And definitely not when I wasn't expecting any appointments. After Gibraltar's typically human fear the previous night, Juana's acceptance was refreshing.

"Tell your parents to invite me to your *quinceañera*. All these years in California and I've never been to one."

She ducked her head. "I'll remember, Miss Bianca."

Janet was still distracted by her horror at the baby goat. I ignored the bleating. Smiling instead at the girl. Encouraging her to step out of her shell. "How's the naturalization application going?"

"My papa, he no talk about it."

I stared at her, frowning. Nine years in the U.S. and her English sounded as broken as her parents. "Why are you talking like your parents, Juana?"

She refused to meet my gaze. "I no know what you mean."

"Yes. You do. You speak perfectly good English. I may only see your family at Christmas but your mother brags about how well you do in school."

Her smile wilted. Afraid. First Janet. Now Juana. I understood being scary to the Henry Gibraltars in the world. But not to my friends.

"Luis says that customers buy more goats if they think we're illegal. He makes me talk like that."

"I'm not a customer. Well, I am a customer. But I'm not just a customer. And the term's 'undocumented' not 'illegal.'"

"Sorry, Bianca." She rubbed one arm at the sleeve. There was bruising.

"Did Luis do that?"

She shook her head unhappily. "It's nothing."

I stiffened. Angry. "Does he do that often?"

She didn't answer. I stared at her round features. She resented her brother's bullying. So did I. "Should I have a talk with your mother?"

Juana tensed, shooting me a flash of dismay. The goat bleated as if on cue. "No. Oh, please. Not that!"

I nodded, slowly taking a breath. "Okay. How about I talk to Luis?"

She glanced at my horns. Thinking. Worried. "You wouldn't hurt him would you?"

I laughed. "No. Not the way you mean. I might just scare him a little."

"Bee, no! You can't." Janet wasn't happy that I'd offered to talk to the young man. I saw something else in her eyes. She wasn't worried that I'd scare him. She was afraid I'd lose control.

"I wouldn't feed off of him!" I couldn't hide my wounded expression.

"No. Of course not." She frowned. Sad and guilty that I'd said it aloud.

Great. What was wrong with me today? I sighed. "You think I might enamor him to make my point."

Janet nodded.

"It'd wear off after a few days."

"And in the meantime?" Her gaze hardened like a disappointed mother's.

"He'd obsess over me." I looked at Juana. "Have Luis come here. Janet will schedule a time. Tell him I want to talk to him about reoccurring business."

Janet mouthed a silent 'no,' staring at the baby goat. But she didn't argue. Too horrified to trust herself not to say something awful. I rolled my eyes.

Juana bit her lower lip. "If it's a lie, he'll take it out on me. Even if you scare him."

"Don't worry. I know how to protect you while making my point."

Janet finally found her voice. "Why here?"

"Because you'll be here to keep an eye on me."

I looked at the baby goat. My body thrummed with hunger. Icy pangs biting into my belly. I could feel the animal's life force crawl along my skin. It was male. I knew it. Something about my body chemistry reacted to anything with testosterone. The energy it would provide wasn't as good as sexual energy. But it'd take the edge off. The way a vampire could drink refrigerated blood. It wasn't great. But better than nothing.

"Take it away." I smiled at Juana but my eyes were tight. The thought of feeding made me focus on my hunger. The goat's warmth seeped past my shields. I shook my head, shivering as I blocked the sensation. My control wasn't as good as it usually was. Better not to meet with a young man at the cusp of his sexual peak under the circumstances. "But don't schedule Luis today. I've got work to do."

"Luis won't like me bringing the goat back."

I felt a wave of cold tighten my belly. Goosebumps trailed along my arms and legs. The equivalent of a human's stomach growling. I stared at the baby goat with longing.

"Bee?" Janet's tone was hard.

"Yes?" I forced myself to meet her eyes. She'd seen my expression. Disapproval in the tightness of her lips. I couldn't keep fasting. Then I had an idea. "Never mind. Tell him I want something older. Bigger. Have him bring it himself. Today."

"Will he do that?" asked Janet, still unsettled.

She stared at the goat tugging at Juana's leash. It had stopped bleating. Dazed by even that momentary draining of its lifeforce. Janet glanced at me suspiciously. Thankfully she didn't know just how long I'd been going without.

"I think a bigger payday will motivate him. Won't it?" I put a hand on the girl's shoulder. Even starved, her essence was safe from my touch. I wasn't sure I could drain a woman if I tried. Although, there had been a few cases of succubi left locked up too long draining everything living in range.

Juana nodded.

I smiled. That would kill two birds with one stone. "Then have him bring it today. Tell him we'll pay double."

The girl stared at me. Finally nodding before she scooped up the baby goat. She rushed through the hallway and out the door. Juana seemed like a good girl. And I hated bullies.

The Rodríguezes were almost friends. As close as I came outside of professional contacts. With a few exceptions. And I'd avoided Luis most of the nine years I'd known them. For obvious reasons. Young pubescent boys reacted strongly to me. Nothing I did stopped it.

He was older now. Time to remake his acquaintance. And find out just what sort of man he'd become. Find out why he would ever think it was okay to bully anyone. Much less a girl several years younger than him. And make it stop.

CHAPTER FOUR

I finished reading the files on Vincent Gibraltar and sat there. Reclined in my chair. Thinking. Feet propped on the desk. Worried.

There was far too little information on the vampire coven in the documents. Or even generally about vampires. They called themselves 'the Atlantic Street Revenants.' Monied from the looks of things. Not as rich as Gibraltar. No one was that rich. But they owned several apartment buildings along Atlantic Avenue. Decent income for their eternal lives. Of course, they occupied the largest one.

The coven's members were registered with the Federal authorities as required by law. Some of them. The numbers didn't match up. But they'd managed to stay off the government's radar somehow. Most of the filings had been done under a California Limited Liability Corporation. Meant to last as long as the coven did. Not tied to any particular individual or subgroup of members.

I called loudly through the opening between our offices. "Janet, phone Henry Gibraltar's people. Tell them I need to speak to Joseph at first dark."

"First dark?" I heard her noisily push her chair back. The sound of her heels on the wood floor. She appeared at the doorway with that look, again. The one she'd been giving me all day.

I never referred to meetings by position of the sun. "Yes, Janet. He's a vampire."

"But not the villain in the story?" She clutched at her chest without realizing it.

I fought a smile. "He might be. For that matter, so might the cousin, Blake Mansfield. You know the drill. Right now everyone's a suspect."

"Even Henry Gibraltar, the client?"

I started to nod. Then thought about it. "No. Probably not him."

"Only probably?"

"I can't be a hundred percent sure of anything yet." I frowned at her. "Please call and make the appointment."

"Will he be coming here?" She tugged at her waist to straighten her dress. Professionally cool. Her version of disapproval when she didn't know what to ask for in order to fix a problem.

"I think that's best. Don't you?"

I still wasn't wearing my sunglasses. She held my gaze the way a man couldn't. "You'll be alone."

"Also for the best. I don't want you in his crosshairs. In case he turns out to be part of the problem."

"The wooden ammo's not in yet." She was trying to talk me out of it.

I shrugged, unconcerned. "They said by dark."

"What if they don't make it by dark?"

I stared at her unpleasantly. "I'm not helpless, Janet. And Andre will be patrolling."

"But you're not immortal. A vampire can hurt you. Part of your DNA comes from a human."

"I don't think he'll risk anything. It took a lot for his kind to become mainstream. The courts frown on violent offenders. Reflects badly on the entire group. You know about the meeting. It'll be in your computer. Too many loose ends. Joseph isn't that stupid."

"So you'll be dead if you're wrong. But vampire rights will suffer. Great." She stomped off and I let her.

I'd made a point of avoiding association with other preternaturals over the years. Vampires. Lycanthropes. The most common kinds of non-humans. Unfortunately, that also meant I didn't know much about them. Now I was dealing with both types.

Janet was right. It was dangerous to be wrong. Thankfully, I knew people who could make sure I wasn't. If they'd answer the phone for me.

CHAPTER FIVE

It was almost closing time when I heard bleating again. I glanced at the clock. Luis Rodriguez had cut it close. Twenty minutes late without a courtesy call. Another mark against him.

"Send Luis in," I called through the open doorway.

"What else would I do?" shouted Janet snidely.

I couldn't think of a clever comeback, so I left it alone. She'd won that round. "I don't know, Janet. I don't know."

I loved the woman. We had a true friendship that allowed for a little rough banter. We could even get mad at each other. But it never lasted. Most importantly, she always told me the truth. Helped me feel human. Even when everyone else reminded that me I wasn't.

I heard his voice. Felt Luis through the walls. Vibrant masculine energy. Strong and trembling with adrenaline. Fear.

My stomach grew cool. Power broke out of my flesh, danced along my arms. Something mystical that I couldn't explain. I'd never seen it described in a textbook from the point of view of a succubus. What human scientists wrote about it was like a blind person describing colors.

The sensation of power gathered in my fingertips and face. It made my neck and palms itch with need. Luis's energy was ripe with delicious, untapped testosterone. It called to me. Broke through my shields in a surge of desperation.

I clenched my fists, digging my nails into my palm in panic. Forced the power back inside me. Blood rose in my cheeks. My flesh flush and sweaty. Not from the hunger. It was embarrassment at losing control. I was grateful that no one had seen.

"Just go in," I heard Janet repeat to the young man.

The goat's front-half appeared first. Its shaggy grey head stretched toward my workspace. Its tongue extended in an effort to ensnare papers at the edge of my desk. The beast was as large as a Labrador. But emaciated. Ribs and hip bone showing through mottled skin. Luis reluctantly followed the goat into my office.

"Luis." There was a pleasant expression on my face. My tone stern. Reproachful.

He jerked the goat back by the rope around its neck. "Miss Bianca."

I didn't tell him to drop the 'Miss,' as I had with Juana. I was trying to remind him to respect women. Including his sister. Especially his sister.

"Thank you for coming." I stared at the goat. "Please keep the animal from my desk."

He pulled harder on the leash. The goat made off with one sheet. I knew what it was. A copy of a paid invoice. The animal could have it. My grim indifference would make Luis more nervous.

"Is it warm in here?" He searched the room for a source of the heat.

It was me. I took a deep breath. Rubbing my arms. My belly was cold. My appetite growing.

I focused my power on the goat. Felt its complex mammalian lifeforce through the mystical process my body used to sustain itself. Learned more about it than that it was male. I was able to read the animal the way a fortune teller might read Tarot cards.

The goat was well past its prime. Sickly. There was something wrong with its stomach. Not cancer. Some illness that animals got that humans didn't. I sensed it. But couldn't name it. A vague knowledge that it would suffer but not die quickly.

I opened myself to the goat. Felt another wave of my power splash outward. It drew energy from the animal. And more. I tasted Luis' fear like an aphrodisiac. He stood next to the goat. More appealing to my hunger than livestock.

My focus shifted to him. His emotional bouquet even more complex. Enhanced by too many days of fasting. The way food smelled like ambrosia to a starving man. I took a step forward, lost in his flavor.

He whimpered. "Please don't kill me."

I slammed my shields down hard. Cutting off my power in a backlash of icy pain along the nerves of my skin. His youthful terror helped calm me. Shamed me. I was bullying him the way he'd bullied his sister. Worse. I'd almost lost control.

Fear smelled good. Not as good as sex. But it added spice to testosterone. Terror made it bitter.

"I'm not going to kill you."

He stared like he didn't believe me. At my face. Into my eyes. I'd forgotten my sunglasses.

"Stop looking at me!" I shouted.

He dropped his gaze to the floor. Another spike of fear. The bitterness prickled unpleasantly along my nerves. Luis wouldn't look at my breasts. Good boys didn't do that. Not intentionally. Bad boys who were terrified of me didn't either. I wasn't sure which he was yet.

"What do you know about me?" I softened my voice only enough to get him to respond. Not gentle. Just less threatening.

He kept his eyes focused on the wood floor, hard. "I don't wanna say."

"Tell me or I'll be very angry."

He swallowed. Loudly. Crossing his legs as he stood there. Trying not to piss himself. This was going much worse than I'd hoped. Hunger took away more than one type of self-control.

"Luis. Luis, don't look into my eyes. Listen to my voice. Hear the melody of my words. You want to tell me what you know about me. Prove that you know why you should be afraid."

"Y—you're *la hija del Diablo*." He didn't even seem to notice he'd switched to Spanish. Didn't matter. I spoke enough to understand.

"I'm not the daughter of the Devil." I moved slowly around the edge of my desk. Mustn't frighten the prey. "What I do to this goat I won't do to you." I paused, to make sure he was listening. "Unless, of course, you hurt your sister again."

His head jerked up but he stopped himself before his eyes reached mine. He focused on my lips. Licking his own. Not with sexual interest. Trying to wet them. He watched my ungloved hands move toward the goat. Tracked the way my fingers brushed the animal's scruffy hair.

I felt its pain even clearer the moment I made contact with its skin. Stronger than discomfort. It didn't fear me. Not like Luis did. I kept thinking of it as an 'it.' Impersonalized the process. It was dying. All I could sense was the pain of whatever was wrong with the goat's intestines. A long suffered agony that it had learned to ignore. What else could it do?

Luis couldn't see the waves of nurturing energy that flowed from the goat toward me. That travelled along my skin. Seeped into my flesh. Warming me as the goat's eyes rolled back into its head. Dying faster than the sickness would've caused. Still unafraid.

I didn't just take. I gave. Luis had started to feel a hint of arousal before fear had overwhelmed his body. The goat felt something less carnal. A sea of euphoria. It washed away the pain as I took the animal's life.

One final surge of energy and the goat collapsed at Luis' feet. Dead. No more pain. No cruel fear of the butcher's knife. I'd given it a kindness which made me feel slightly less monstrous for feeding from a living creature. But the goat's lifeforce had barely touched my hunger.

I was too close to Luis. His scent swirled at the edges of my power. My stomach grew cold with renewed hunger pangs. Crept lower into my loins. He was an adult male. Meant for sexual interaction. His need responded to me.

My power tried to spill out again. I'd waited too long to eat. The goat hadn't been nearly enough. Especially since the animal's age meant a reduction in testosterone. Only fierce restraint on my part kept Luis safe. The shock of pulling my power back into me actually hurt. I hissed in frustration.

"*Madre de Dios*!" He looked up at me despite himself. Then closed his eyes when he remembered not to meet my gaze. "Please, no, no, no. Do not kill me."

"What did I say, Luis? Listen to my voice and answer me. What did I say." The power of my words was almost nothing compared to staring into my eyes. But there was something mystical in my voice. Enough to override his fear. For him to hear me.

"You won't kill me like you killed the goat."

"As long as?"

He swallowed. "Don't hurt my sister."

"Don't bully your sister. Don't bully anyone." I sat on the edge of my desk to avoid stepping closer to the young man. "I'm not dangerous to people I respect, Luis."

"People you respect?" The young man's voice broke. Reminding me that the emphasis was on 'young.'

"I don't respect bullies."

He nodded, as if trying to shake something loose. Violent jerks of his chin while tears streamed down his eyes. Fighting a need to sob.

I felt Janet watching me from the open doorway. I glanced at her, somber. A flash of remorse in my eyes. I hated making Luis cry like a frightened child. But he was a man. Didn't matter that he was younger than some. I didn't stomach men bullying women. Much less bullying young girls. Family protects family. He was letting his family down.

"Are you going to be a bully, Luis?"

"N—no, Miss Bianca."

"Then we're still friends."

That confused him. I'd threatened him. Killed a goat in front of him with just a touch. He'd felt my power lick at his lifeforce in an accidental loss of control. He'd lusted after me all while being terrified. And I'd let him think it was intentional.

I was treating him like some of the bad men I'd experienced in the world. Scaring him more than I should have. Being a bully myself.

Damn it! It was my hunger. He was my food of choice. Since I was keeping my lust in check, that only left anger.

"Friends?" He swallowed again. His eyes stared down at the goat. He didn't trust himself to look at any part of me.

I counted to three. Taking a deep breath at the end of it. "I care about your family, Luis. Your parents are good people."

"Yes, Miss Bianca. They work very hard." His voice trembled.

"And you? Do you work hard?"

"Y—yes." He jerked his head upward but stopped himself. "Juana said you don't like us to sound Mexican."

I frowned. "That's not what I said. I said I don't like people lying to me. That I know perfectly well just how good her English is."

"Most people expect illegals to sell goats and chickens. Not college graduates."

"And most people don't expect college-educated brothers to bully their sisters. Or say 'illegal' instead of 'undocumented.'"

He shook his head, raising his eyes. His gaze lingered at my lips, fought against meeting my eyes. He struggled for a response. Afraid to argue with me. Afraid to admit what he'd done.

"As long as Juana doesn't come visit me with any new bruises or tears, we can be friends again, Luis. Do you want to be my friend?"

That jerking 'yes' motion again. I was afraid his neck would break. "Yes, please."

"Good." I ran my nails along the wood of the desk. His eyes followed their movement. Like a rabbit wanting to run. But knowing it had to remain frozen. "How many old male goats can you provide? Like this one."

"By when?"

I watched him, clutching at my stomach. Digging my fingertips into my ribs. Sometimes pain helped me fight the hunger. Sometimes it did the opposite. "Tomorrow?"

"F—five? I can ask around for more."

"Five will do. But don't be late like you were today. If I'm not here, leave them with Janet. She'll pay cash."

"I will?" asked Janet from the doorway, no longer trying to be surreptitious.

"You will."

"And I'll just lock the five goats up in your office, shall I?"

"There's the janitor's closet in the hallway. Just move everything toxic into your office so the goats don't die."

She frowned unhappily. "Fine. But you're going to explain to the cleaning crew why there's feces in the closet."

"Mary won't complain. We pay well enough." I stared down at the corpse. "The dead goats will be a bigger problem."

"Can I go now?" A rush of words as Luis edged away from me.

"Not yet."

He stiffened. Turning to Janet for help. A mere human woman. The only refuge when facing the daughter of the Devil, I supposed.

Janet was a soft-sell. She put a hand on the young man's shoulder. "Relax, Luis. You heard, Bee. She wants to be your friend."

"Then why can't I go?"

I laughed. "Because you haven't been paid for this goat. And you don't know how often I'll need more delivered."

"Oh." He took a few deep breaths. Nodding slower than before. "Okay."

"I want five tomorrow and after that, one a day. Two if you can manage."

"One a day?" He blinked and looked up. I turned away and it reminded him. He finally dropped his gaze to my breasts and then looked at Janet, horrified by his lapse.

"You can't manage that?"

"No. I mean, I can. I think I can. I'll have to get them from other farms. Most don't keep the old and sick ones."

"Old's only for moral benefit. Male and adult is a must. No little ones."

That seemed to reassure him. "I—I can do it. Probably two."

"Good. This will give you and I an opportunity to get to know each other better."

He swallowed hard and tugged at his belt-loop with two fingers nervously. "Juana usually delivers."

"Do we have a problem, Luis? Don't you want my business?"

Again that head bob. "No. I do."

"Did you drive it here?"

He motioned outside. "There was a parking spot two streets over."

"You walked that animal two blocks in downtown Long Beach?" Janet glared at me again, shaking her head. "How's he gonna manage five?"

"I'm sure Luis will think it's worthwhile. As I told Juana, we'll pay double his usual rates."

"Really?" Luis forgot to be afraid for a second. Money was almost as powerful as magic for some people.

"You may leave, Luis. Janet, pay him. I want all future deliveries before three in the afternoon."

"Can Juana help me bring the five? I can manage two but—?"

"Of course."

He bobbed a rushed 'thank you' without looking at me and followed Janet eagerly into her outer office. I stared down at the dead goat. "Luis? Can you take the body with you?"

"But you're paying for it," he protested.

"And now I'm done with it. Go on. It won't affect how much you get."

He came back in much more reluctantly than he'd left. He grabbed the front legs of the goat and dragged it into Janet's office. I doubted he'd drag it the entire way back to his truck but that wasn't my concern. I was starving and had a case to deal with. The only upside was that interviewing vampires wasn't a problem being hungry. Not on my end.

Maybe I couldn't sense undead energy, but Joseph could feed on me. That was a different problem. One that wood-tipped bullets would solve if they had to. If they arrived in time.

CHAPTER SIX

Janet had her sweater draped over one arm. Her purse slung over the opposite shoulder. She glanced at her watch. "Are you sure you don't want me to stay?"

"I don't know how this is going to go or how long it'll last. You've been a great help today."

"If you say so." She eyed my cross. "Won't that be a problem for him?"

I tucked it under the lacy bra. Only the chain was visible. "Better?"

"I suppose." She forced a smile. "I don't want to come in tomorrow morning and find blood all over the floor. Especially not yours."

I patted my shoulder holster. "Wood-tips locked and loaded. Now stop playing mama hen. You've got a family to get home to."

"And Bob'll have burnt the lasagna again. Men. Sometimes I think they turn off their brains when they marry a competent woman."

"I wouldn't know." I grinned at her. It didn't stop her from looking sad on my behalf. "Now scoot! Don't give Bob more reasons to make you retire."

"With what you pay me?" She barked with laughter and I joined her. "Good night, Bianca. Call if you need anything."

"Thanks, Janet. Give him my love."

"If he burns my lasagna again, I'll promise him just that." She disappeared, still smiling.

I heard the outer door close. She locked the latch. Habit. I heard her unlock it again. Then silence.

I glanced at the clock above the two client-chairs. Ten minutes to dark. Thirty minutes until Joseph was supposed to show. Gibraltar's secretary had insisted he'd need twenty minutes to get across town. I assumed by car. Vampires couldn't fly. Except in the movies.

Time enough for a phone call. To find out what I could before my meeting. I used my rolodex to find the number. Teresa Waldheim. Folklore specialist at U.C. Santa Barbara. And my version of a good friend.

It rang twice before she picked up. "Bianca?"

"Caller I.D. is a wonderful thing. Glad to know you'll still pick up for me."

She sounded hesitant. "I was just on my way out the door."

"Hot date?"

"Popcorn and cuddling with Snickerdoodle."

"What grown woman names her Airedale 'Snickerdoodle.'"

"A grown woman without a life. Without a man." She paused. Adjusting herself. I heard the squeak of plastic as she settled into her office chair. "Alright. Snickerdoodle can wait. What's up?"

"How do you know it's not a social call?"

"Because my caller I.D. says it's Bianca Savage. She doesn't do social."

I frowned at the phone. "Okay. I deserved that. When was the last time we went drinking?"

"Who's President?"

"Ha ha." I screwed up my face in thought. "It rained as we were leaving the bar. Spring?"

"Four months ago."

"Really?" I hadn't realized so much time had passed. "It doesn't feel that long."

"I missed you, too."

"Ter, I'm sorry. You know I'm not good with this end of things."

"This end of things? You mean friendship?"

"Yeah. Okay. Friendship. Work keeps me busier than you might imagine."

"Seriously. What can I do for you?" She didn't sound angry. But I felt like I'd just missed an opportunity to fix something then.

"I have some questions about vampires."

She perked up. "I'm listening."

I explained cryptically about the kidnapping. What little I knew about Joseph and the Atlantic Street Revenants, without naming names. She'd figure out it was Vincent Gibraltar because the case was all over the news. What else she guessed depended on how much she paid attention and put two and two together.

"What can you tell me about covens?"

"It's pretty straightforward. People like to think of vampires as solitary creatures. Hunting prey and hiding in some lonely basement. But they're social. Like bats. Like people who are bats."

"Vampires aren't bats. They don't even turn into bats."

"I know. But people see the fangs. They only come out at night. Movies make it worse. So they get lumped in with chiroptera. I'm just drawing on the folk references we study."

"You like saying chiroptera."

I heard the smile in her voice. "I do."

"Alright. Go on. Vampires are social. How does that apply to the coven?"

"There's a single dominant vampire in the group. Part of the coven. But above the rest in status. They feed socially. Sleep socially. All of them in the same room. Touching."

That seemed odd to me. I couldn't resist asking. "Why touching?"

"They're undead. It isn't about body warmth or safety. They have a lifeforce of sorts. Touching strengthens that connection. Balances it."

"I don't follow. Balances what?" I hadn't felt anything inside Joseph that I could've fed on. Nothing I could classify as a lifeforce. Not even a flicker.

"Energy levels. The undead energy they gain from feeding."

"Go on."

I could hear her grow frustrated. "Let me try it this way. Imagine that a coven is five vampires. Three of them are able to feed well. Two not well at all. Too new or too weak— metaphysically speaking. When they sleep during the day, their bodies metabolize the blood they've consumed. They store energy for when they wake. The ones who feed well, those three share some of their energy with the two who haven't. Touching allows this transference."

"What happens if a vampire doesn't eat enough? If the two were on their own, for example?"

"They wouldn't die if that's what you're thinking. They wake. Sluggish. Slower than if they'd eaten well. Groggy, the way someone who oversleeps gets. Less aware, too. And they wake hungry. It makes them more dangerous. To others and themselves."

"So just an evolutionary adaptation?" I asked.

"Exactly. They aren't doing it on purpose. They sleep together because they know they feel better when they wake." She sneezed. "Sorry. One of my students had a cold and I think he passed it along."

"Must be tough." I smiled. I hoped she did, too. "Alright, so tell me more about the dominant vampire?"

"He's called the Rake."

"A scoundrel. Sounds appropriate. And?"

"And what?"

"How is he dominant? Does he rule them like a master controlling slaves? Are they shared bloodlines? What?"

"We've been friends for how long and you know almost nothing about your own kind?"

I held my breath. Angry. Startled that her words felt like a slap. "I'm not a vampire."

"But you are preternatural."

"Not one of the undead."

"No. I know." I heard genuine remorse in her voice. "I didn't mean to be offensive. You aren't ordinary like me and Snickerdoodle. Your kind have abilities."

"I keep telling you, Teresa, I don't know anything about my kind. My mother was killed when I was little. A human raised me. An old Christian woman. I haven't ever even talked to one of my own kind. I'm not keeping deep, dark secrets from you."

"I know I'm in shit when you call me 'Teresa.'" She didn't elaborate.

"Is that supposed to give me time to calm down?"

"If we want to continue this conversation, yeah."

The distance grew between us. Almost palpable. I'd done it again. Made things worse. The goat hadn't been enough. I'd almost fed from Luis. Even my emotions were harder to control.

"I haven't fed in a while."

I heard the shock in her voice. "How long's a while?"

"A goat today. But about a week before that."

"Damn, Bee! Why would you do that?"

The question was a good one. "I don't know."

"You sound scared."

"Do I?" I shook my head. I realized that she was right. I felt out of control. Luis had proved that. I was scared. "Maybe I am."

"You are." Teresa softened. "It isn't natural to be celibate. Not for humans. Definitely not for you."

"I've been managing."

She wasn't buying it. "Doesn't sound like it."

"I just wasn't hungry. Now I am. Really hungry."

"Does this have anything to do with the vampire questions?"

"No. That's a client thing."

"He the client?"

She was trying to figure out if the police, F.B.I. or the family had called me in. My reputation for being discrete was well earned. Even friends didn't get any juicy tidbits. "No. Bodyguard. And as for the kidnapping, the client thinks that teenage-seduction's probably closer to the truth. I'm going to be investigating the vampire coven. I need to know what I need to know."

"That's a lot." She took a deep breath. Cleared her throat. I knew she was preparing for her lecture voice. "The Rake's a leader. They follow him because he—or she—is the strongest. Strongest personality. Strongest energy. Magics. Whatever you want to call what vampires can do."

"But they can disobey. Other members of the coven."

"Yes. Just like children can disobey parents and criminals can disobey the law. The threat of punishment and severity helps keep the others in line. Starvation usually. Confinement. That part's a little more opaque."

"What happens if someone in the coven challenges the Rake outright?"

"A battle for leadership occurs. A real battle. Fangs. Claws. Magical powers. The winner takes over. Anyone who refuses to pledge fealty is kicked out. It's hard to find a new coven. No one wants to be on their own. Most vampire executions result from individuals who don't have a social network."

"So if the coven seduced a sixteen-year-old into their group, it would've been done with the Rake's knowledge and permission."

"I don't see how it could be otherwise. Unless an individual did it and hasn't told the Rake. But Bee, that's dangerous for the individual. Some people think the Rake knows what the rest of the coven is thinking. It's not true. Mostly. Abilities vary."

"Can vampires tell if someone's lying? Generally?"

"Lycanthropes can. They smell changes in body chemistry. Hear the change in heartbeat. The quality of a person's tone. Vampires don't have any of that."

"So the group might not know about the actions of an individual."

"No. Only, members of a coven are rarely alone. They don't have any individual space. Territory if you will. They don't own a house or a cave somewhere away from the coven."

"But they could."

"Sure. Money and means aside. That's not the issue. A coven shares blood. Not just human blood. They drink from each other."

"I thought vampire blood doesn't nourish another vampire."

"It doesn't. But I've told you about blood-links." She sounded nervous. A very temperamental vampire had revealed this fact to her during an attempt to seduce her. Seduction without vampire tricks. A short fling that she'd only gotten involved with because she'd been young. And he'd been incredibly handsome. Charismatic. Up until the time he fled the police for a slew of crimes she'd never known about.

She'd trusted me with that secret over a long night of wine and Scrabble. If he learned that she'd shared the knowledge with anyone, he'd threatened to come back. I hadn't met him but she believed him. So I did, too.

"I thought that was only between a vampire and a human. Or non-undead person at any rate."

"I guess I left out a lot the last time we talked about this stuff. Wine'll do that." She took a deep breath. Digging into more secrets no one should know. "No. Drinking each other's blood creates a similar bond between the members of the coven. They know where each other is. Have a sense of what they're doing. If they're in danger. If they're feeding. Limited shared knowledge. More than they get from touching while they sleep."

"When it's a human, is it a two-way bond?"

"It's much stronger then. The vampire knows what the human knows. My understanding is that the human doesn't." She cleared her throat. Sniffled a bit. "I didn't work up the courage to try it before he fled. None of this is documented. It's not like vampires queue up to provide details about their existence. They certainly don't provide human servants to testify."

She wouldn't even say his name. That's how much she feared him. And she wasn't afraid of much.

"What would their motive be for seducing a young man into the coven? A high profile, potentially wealthy sixteen-year-old?"

Teresa didn't answer right away. The silence meant I'd startled her. "That kidnapping?" She'd finally figured out the victim. Not who she'd been expecting. Were there other kidnappings that I didn't know about?

"They wouldn't. Federal civil liberties are still very tenuous. It doesn't take much to get on the wrong side of the law."

"You sound scared."

"I am. Maybe a little. If a coven did this and word got out—other covens would respond. They'd destroy the offenders. Leave nothing behind." She went silent for a few heartbeats. "I thought this was something out of state. Missing street kids in Saint Louis and New Orleans. This—a prominent and wealthy kid taken close to home makes this dangerous."

"Are there that many covens in Los Angeles?"

"Wouldn't matter. They'd come from everywhere. California's pretty liberal. We believe in human rights for everyone. Everything sapient. Places like Oklahoma and Massachusetts barely keep vigilantes from taking out suspected vampire dens."

"Hence the Federal Vampire Privacy Reforms ten years ago."

"Exactly. Just because the law gave preternatural creatures legal rights doesn't mean that God-fearing zealots don't decide God's laws are above Man's laws."

"Don't blame it all on the Christians, Ter. I'm Christian. My church-friends don't go around trying to kill other people. Not even undead people."

Teresa laughed, a disgusted unpleasant sound. "You know, sadly, you have vampires to thank for your modern rights, too. The reforms ten years ago were built on the laws enacted in the sixties for all preternaturals."

I didn't answer right away. The call was taking longer than I'd expected and I was still angry. She was still angry. Better to stop talking or find common ground again.

"So in your opinion, the vampires wouldn't have taken the boy. Even if he'd wanted to join them."

"Unless they were suicidally stupid, no. They'd make him wait until he was eighteen and get court approval. Or twenty-one. He could do whatever he wanted then."

I glanced at the clock. "Thanks for the information, Ter. I've got to go, my next appointment's almost here."

"Be safe, Bianca."

Teresa hung up with such finality that I wondered if I'd ever see her again. A slow, creeping sadness mingled with my hunger. Pushed my need to feed deep down inside me.

Sorrow was the only emotion that could mask my appetite. It was also the one emotion I rarely gave in to. I had too much to be sad about if I paused to dwell on it. Too many friends who'd died while I kept living. Some of them had died protecting me. Something I felt bad about.

Guilt was fine. I had survivor's guilt up the wazoo. It turned into a nice, useful anger at times. Made me harder than I'd be otherwise. I was dealing with cases involving missing people, murderers and the supernatural. Hard was a good way to survive in my business.

I focused on the sadness of losing Teresa's friendship. I could feel my body settle down. My power muted. It didn't last long. My belly grew icy. My hunger once more in control.

Not that it mattered with Joseph. I couldn't accidentally hurt him. It was more about not losing my cool. I suspected the man was going to try to push my buttons tonight. I was determined not to give him the satisfaction.

CHAPTER SEVEN

Joseph showed up right on time. Freshly showered. Wearing a sexy, black button-up. Long-sleeves. White pearl buttons. Black leather belt. Black buckle. Expensive black trousers and Gucci loafers.

"You going to a funeral or just an AC/DC fan?"

His smile wilted just a fraction. He produced a bouquet of white roses. "I thought the black would frame the roses to better effect."

"Right." I accepted the flowers awkwardly.

There were no empty vases in my office. No vases at all. I didn't do flowers. I saw enough death without keeping reminders around me. I laid them respectfully on the desk. "Thanks."

"We're talking here, correct?" I nodded and he produced a bottle of Moscato. Condensation on the glass, suggesting it was chilled. "A gentleman never arrives unprepared."

I actually smiled. "*Barefoot*. One of my favorites."

He stared at the bottle as if he were disappointed to be holding it. "I wanted to bring something much more expensive. To show an earnest interest. But I was told that you preferred this. It's local to Central California and that matters to you?"

I ignored the implied criticism. "Do vampires drink alcohol?"

"We do a great many things." He smiled like it was date night.

"Do you get drunk?"

He shrugged, his smile lingering. "Sadly, no. We don't metabolize it any more than you do meat."

"But you enjoy the taste."

His smile turned lecherous. "I enjoy many things."

"Stop with the flirting already. This is a business meeting. Our time's limited. And on the books."

"Gibraltar's research said you were no nonsense. I thought perhaps the chance to enjoy sex without the danger of killing your partner might appeal to you."

"I'd like my choice of partner to appeal to me."

He clutched his heart theatrically. "Ouch. You wound me to the quick."

I didn't smile. Instead, I took the Moscato and grabbed two empty tumblers from behind my desk. They'd have to do as I didn't keep wine glasses handy. I opened the bottle and poured us each a drink. He took the glass I offered. I sipped mine.

The carbonation gave the wine a lightness that I liked. "Nice."

"A bit sweet."

I frowned. He was trying to be contrary since flirting was off the table. "Can we get to business?"

"Of course. Ask away."

I took another sip, considering the information Teresa had given me. I trusted her as a researcher. But it didn't hurt to ask the source directly. "Why would the Atlantic Revenants want

Vincent? Would they gain access to his money? Control of the company?"

Joseph sipped his wine in imitation of me. Taking his time. Playing games as a type of dominance. I held my tongue, watching him with a strained smile.

Finally he gave in. "No. It's not about money. Dead or undead, Vincent's share goes to a trust he can never touch. He'll no longer be the heir to the empire, so to speak."

"Why then?"

"The grandson of one of the richest men in California? Even if Vincent can't touch the money, his grandfather might be persuaded to help them. If it helped Vincent. A grandfather's love. Favors. Resources."

"You don't sound very convinced."

"I'm simply answering your questions."

"You and Gibraltar seem to think Vincent left voluntarily. The F.B.I. report shows the window was forced from the outside. That he was taken from his bed in the middle of the night. Sheets spilled on the floor. He didn't take any clothes or toiletries."

Joseph just watched me, waiting for me to say or do something to distract him from the v-line of my breasts. "That's what security says."

"Where were you when he was taken?"

"Watching over Hank at his office. A business deal with Chinese nationals. They were still on Beijing time."

"Who was watching Vincent?"

Joseph frowned, setting the tumbler on my desk. I picked it up and stuck a mostly decorative coaster under the glass. He bobbed his head in apology. "Supernatural bodyguards aren't particularly commonplace, Bianca. I can call you Bianca, can't I?"

"Go on."

"Henry keeps Anton and I on his personal rotation, 365 days a year. Vincent, however, is protected by a top-of-the-line human security team."

"Anton's the werewolf?"

He nodded.

"Why do you have to make every answer a winding road through the country?" I didn't mention to him that my secretary had a similar bad habit.

He leaned back. "I'm trying to paint a picture. I wasn't responsible. I'm not responsible for the team overseeing Vincent. Gibraltar insisted on that himself."

"Fine. You aren't to blame for his disappearance. Now continue."

"It's a standard five-man team watching inside the house. Two people assigned specifically to Vincent. All of that in addition to electronic surveillance."

"The F.B.I. report doesn't mention the two guards."

"We didn't mention them."

"Because?"

"They disappeared as well."

I stared at the vampire appalled. "You mean they could've taken Vincent themselves."

"No. The security company's too high-end. Their assets vetted. The team's probably dead."

"So why not tell the Feds? Any lead might help them find Vincent."

"The company tasked with protecting Vincent has a reputation to uphold. If word got out that they'd lost two men in addition to a valuable client? People might actually believe they took him. It could cost the company billions in revenue."

I held my glass frozen, inches from my lips. "Billions?"

"Over a period of ten years. Yes."

"And Gibraltar would rather protect this company than give the F.B.I. all the help he can in finding Vincent?"

Joseph picked up his wine and swallowed it in one quick swig. "The Company also provides the security assets who protect Maureen and Blake. If Henry throws them under the bus, he loses their protection."

"What am I missing?"

Joseph studied me. Playing with his glass, tilting it to cause the last lingering drop to dance around the bottom. Finally, he shrugged.

"The Atlantic Street Revenants have been pressuring me to get them hired on. Additional protection for the family. Without Henry's current security firm, he'd be forced to seriously consider them."

"They're blackmailing him into hiring them?"

"I think they persuaded Vincent to join them as leverage. Give us the contract and he comes home safe and sound. Don't and you have no one to protect your grandchildren."

"Why can't Gibraltar just hire other humans from another company?"

Joseph studied me. "This is where the discretion gets weighty."

"I've never betrayed a client's confidence unless it was confession of an impending criminal act. That was in the document your boss signed before I met with him."

"Just want to make sure you understand. The security company's more dangerous than any non-disclosure."

"Tell me who."

"Amperdyne Technologies."

I'd heard of them. Not much. New gadgets for the future. Government contracts. That sort of thing. "A tech company provides security?"

"What better security than hi-tech weaponry. Surveillance. Tracking."

"You have the F.B.I. on this. You have Amperdyne and all their gadgets looking for Vincent. Adding me into the mix is like hiring a sniper at a bar fight."

"All the technology in the world is useless if the person employing the tech is under the sway of another." Joseph held my gaze. If he was trying to use vampiric powers on me I couldn't feel a thing. The same way he didn't feel alive. But I was betting he was testing my ability to withstand his power all the same.

I smiled and took another sip. I really did love Moscato. One of the few vices I could enjoy without any serious repercussions. "I see. You have official channels covered. You have espionage covered. But you need someone on the preternatural side. To deal with the coven without being misled by them."

"Exactly."

"If Amperdyne's so good, how'd they take Vincent in the first place? Even if a vampire could—how did you put it? Sway them? Why would they let one get close enough?"

"That's why we think Vincent was involved himself. The bodyguards would've been smarter than that. The solar screens on the windows were disabled."

"Also not in the F.B.I. report." I raised my brows.

"Nor is the fact that all recording devices within thirty feet of Vincent were simultaneously deactivated."

"An E.M.P."

Joseph nodded. "Gibraltar thinks you get by on your abilities. On your seduction. I told him you're smart."

"Flattery won't help find Vincent."

"No. But I want you to know that I respect you. Trust you. The old man and his grandson treated you like they treat me. A monster. They underestimate you. And they fear you. I trust you. That's why I asked to be the one to deal with you."

"Gibraltar's safety had nothing to do with that?" A thought occurred to me. "Wait, if you're here with me, who's watching him?"

"Anton Thrace." My blank expression amused him. "The werewolf puts in overtime in situations like this."

"The files you gave me were thick. But they lacked almost any pertinent information. Such as the werewolf's name. Or his location at the time of the disappearance. Nothing about Amperdyne. Nothing useful at all."

"You'll never find anything in writing about Amperdyne. Other than corporate filings. Required minimal paperwork. Patents and payroll. Internet scrubbers see to it. And they respond rather—severely if their privacy is encroached upon by clients."

"Alright, let me get that part straight. Tell me if I heard you right. Gibraltar can't hire human replacements for Amperdyne because the Company will, what? Assassinate them?"

"Hardly. Every death will appear accidental. Mechanical or tech failure." Joseph reached for the glass but it was empty. "More please?"

"Lush."

He grinned. I fought a smile in return and refilled his glass. Then I stared at mine and did the same for me. "Amperdyne either continues to guard the grandkids or the Atlantic Revenants are Gibraltar's only choice. Vampires can survive any accidents the Company might throw their way."

"Now you're up to speed."

"That seems like a long game for the vampires to play. For what? What do they get by being the new bodyguards?"

"Besides an unprecedented legitimacy and a buttload of money? Don't underestimate the value of being placed in a position of trust and power for a group long forced to live in the shadows." He laughed. "All that aside, do you know how much a contract like that pays?"

I shook my head. "You said billions over ten years. I still find that hard to believe."

"Henry doesn't pay that much on his own. I was referring to the Company's client base disappearing overnight. But he does pay a pretty penny. Each grandkid's security is about a million a year. That doesn't include installation of tech. Servicing the tech. Updates even more."

"The vampires wouldn't be paid upgrade fees. Or for any tech. So they'd get the million for providing bodyguards."

"Per grandchild."

"Three grandchildren is only three million a year."

"Only?"

"Sorry. It may be a lot of money to some people, but wealth is low on my list of priorities. And even so, it isn't really that much money. Not for Gibraltar."

"No. But for vampires who have no legal means of income except passive businesses? Legitimacy is icing on the cake. It's definitely a motive."

Something nagged at me. I sipped my Moscato. Smiled as it tickled on the way down. Then I had it. "Vampires can't guard them in the daytime."

Joseph blinked at me. "Am I an idiot? Damn it. No. We can't. That's why Anton handles the day. The coven would need dayminders as well."

"Dayminders? Isn't that the term for people who guard vampire sleeping grounds?"

He nodded, still focused on the problem of who they'd hire. "Can't be anyone human. Amperdyne would take them out. The grandkids would suffer. Vulnerable during the day. They'd have to have a plan. It wouldn't work otherwise."

"If Amperdyne's so high tech, aren't they a threat to the coven? U.V. grenades, that sort of thing?"

"Sure. If they were going to assassinate the coven. But Amperdyne operates on a black ops level of secrecy. Accidental deaths are one thing. Outright assassination of several registered vampires brings them into the light. No pun intended."

"So if Amperdyne doesn't find Vincent, Gibraltar can't keep using them. They've failed him. He'll have to turn to the coven. So it's imperative to Amperdyne that they find the boy."

"That sums up that, too."

I drank some more. Wishing I could get a little bit intoxicated. I felt like I needed something to take the edge off. Or maybe it was my hunger returning. I hadn't really dealt with that.

"Is there any possible motive for Amperdyne to have taken Vincent themselves? Not just a couple of rogue bodyguards. But the Company?"

"No. I told you, they lose everything because of it."

"Is there someone I can talk to about the missing bodyguards? A way to figure out if they decided to go rogue?"

"No. That would be dangerous for everyone. Including Hank."

I studied him for a moment. Noting the handsome strength of his jaw. The way his blue eyes caught the light. Saw my own reflection in them. "Does Amperdyne at least know that you've hired me?"

"Yes. That much we had to tell them. I knew you'd need access to the villa. They still protect the grounds until the matter's settled one way or the other."

I glanced at the files. "What about Maureen. No reference to her or Blake in the files."

"Part of Hank's paranoia. Trusting you with the F.B.I. material was easy enough. Some of the specs on the layout of the house. A history of the family."

"Up to Gibraltar himself. Nothing on his kids or their kids."

"Exactly. As far as the public knows, two of the three grandchildren died when Gibraltar's children died."

"When in reality, they're under his watchful eye."

"Yes. As for Maureen? She's a year older than Blake. Works as a computer-tech for one of Gibraltar's subsidiaries."

"Is she a Mansfield?"

"No. Anyone suspecting they were alive would be looking for a brother and sister. She's an Edwards."

"Married? Single?"

"Single. None of the grandkids have been encouraged to foster relationships."

I stared at Joseph. That raised an interesting possibility. "Vincent's only sixteen. Was he even allowed to date?"

"No. That's why it was so easy for the coven to get their fangs into him."

I stared in horror. "They fed on him?"

"No, Bianca. It's just a turn of phrase." He took a drink. Slower now. Savoring the wine like I had. "He's still a virgin according to his security detail. Although he does rustle around under the sheets enough alone to know he's capable of more."

"That's an awful degree of intimacy invasion. I can see why Vincent might have wanted out." I swirled the wine in my glass. Watching it dance in the light. "How did Vincent get introduced to the coven. You said it was your fault. Details also not in the files."

"Hank needed the coven for a job. Don't ask what for. He refused to go to them for the first meeting. So they insisted on coming to the villa. I had to arrange for them to enter. The U.V. traps are only at the windows and extraneous external doors.

Otherwise I'd burn up just doing my job. But the bodyguards had to be prepped. Cameras disabled for the rooms they entered."

"So vampires do show up on film?"

"No. But our voices do. I don't understand the physics of it. Not that I really care."

"Alright. Good to know." I eyed him shrewdly. "Vincent wasn't supposed to be there."

"He insisted. I was the only vampire he'd ever met before that. The only excitement in his life. He wanted to watch from the second floor landing. I didn't see the harm."

"But he came downstairs?"

Joseph nodded. "His bodyguards were with him. The same two who went missing, in fact. The coven didn't hurt Vincent. They didn't even sway him in any unnatural way that first night. But he talked to a couple of them at great length."

"How many came?"

He frowned and stared at my fingers holding the glass. "The entire coven."

"You sound upset."

He raised his eyes to hold my gaze. "There was no reason for them all to come. It felt like—like an invasion. A show of force by sheer numbers. Psychological intimidation."

"But they left of their own accord. Nothing happened."

He grunted. "No. Other than that Chilton left his indelible imprint in the house."

"Chilton? The Rake?"

Joseph blinked. "Yeah. You've been reading up on us."

"A good P.I. does her due diligence."

"I bet."

I wasn't sure what he was implying, so I left it alone. "Your connection to the coven. You always say it like it's personal. Like you know them well."

"I should. I was the Rake until Chilton showed up."

I blinked. Ready to drop this case because they'd withheld too much information. There was more I didn't know than knew. "How long ago was that?"

"Still trying to glean my age?" He frowned. "Long. Chilton's European. Not as mainstream as some of us want to be."

"Meaning?"

Joseph shrugged. "Meaning I don't know what he would or wouldn't do. I left the coven and he took over. It's as simple as that."

"You and Mr. Gibraltar haven't been very forthcoming, Joseph. Is there anything else I should know that wasn't in the files that I haven't thought to ask yet?"

He stared at me again. Not gazing down at my breasts. Nothing lecherous. Suddenly tired. "Nothing I can think of. I know I said that they probably took Vincent for leverage. Promise to return him unharmed if they get the contract. But if you find that Chilton has Vincent, Gibraltar won't hire them. Even if Vincent was a willing accomplice. He won't concede. He doesn't like to be tricked or trapped. He'll cut off his own arm before he'll give in."

I watched him stare into space for a second. Lost to thoughts I couldn't guess. Finally I prompted him. "But?"

"But he wouldn't have to fire Amperdyne if Vincent assisted the coven. The Company's reputation remains intact. More or less. Hank believes that if he calls their bluff, they return Vincent undamaged rather than risk—the consequences."

"Retribution against the coven for violating federal law."

Joseph nodded. "We'd need proof that they'd turned Vincent. Otherwise, we'd have already tried that approach."

I frowned. He'd admitted to a willingness to kill potentially innocent vampires on the chance that they'd taken Vincent. Would've killed them if the other covens wouldn't require proof. I liked Joseph and Gibraltar less by the minute. But Vincent was an innocent. I didn't have to like my clients to do my job well.

"If they took him by force?"

"Then Amperdyne has to figure out how. Otherwise they lose their reputation. Which is everything. Like I said. If they failed in any way, Hank can't let them stay."

"So what happens then? No coven. No Amperdyne."

Joseph let worry show in his eyes for the first time. "Without some kind of specialized protection, the Gibraltar legacy dies with Hank's grandchildren."

CHAPTER EIGHT

Joseph left and I sat in the quiet of the darkened room. I needed to think about everything he'd said. I had a final glass of Moscato, which finished the bottle off. And still hadn't figured out whatever I was missing. My instincts were whirring. There was something staring me in the face that I hadn't put together. A pattern that left the motive just at the edges of my consciousness.

Sighing, I locked the outer door of my office and walked through the brightly lighted hall. No shadows for muggers to hide in. Refracted glass to prevent snipers from shooting true. Precautions the previous tenants had insisted on. I'd never inquired why because the same safeguards suited my needs.

Of course, it had been a few years since the last real assassination attempt. Angry husbands or wives aside. That time, Christian fundamentalists had found common ground with Islamic fundamentalists. Their shared God, my God, the one true God despite where the Koran and the Bible differed, wanted me dead. At least, according to their manifesto. Thankfully, God hadn't agreed. I was still alive. Some of them were, too. Serving a very long prison sentence. Hate crimes included targeting preternaturals.

I stepped into the night and felt an ocean breeze caress my skin. I thought about Vincent's sexual innocence. Being watched every waking moment. Never touched by another person. Not intimately. I could sympathize. It had been too long for me since I'd even kissed a man voluntarily. The Bible frowned on premarital sex. I was a good Christian. Not that good. I wasn't a virgin by choice. My chastity was the sacrifice I'd made to keep people safe.

"Bianca Savage?"

I turned toward the voice, my fingers slipping around the hilt of my gun. I hadn't sensed the man. He'd blended into the shadows between buildings. Not moving.

He stayed leaning against the cement wall, hands visible. "Easy. I'm not armed."

He was mid-thirties. Muscular. His stance masculine but relaxed. I should've tasted his lifeforce long before he'd gotten this close. But I'd felt nothing. Still couldn't feel anything. Not even undeath.

I gripped my 9mm tighter. "What are you?"

"Pardon?" He seemed startled by the question. "You mean, 'who am I?'"

"No. I mean 'what?'"

"A man." He pushed away from the wall and took a step toward me. Hands still raised. As if to insist, hey, I'm harmless. If I couldn't sense his lifeforce, he wasn't harmless.

"That's close enough." The Glock was in my hand. Drawn and aimed. A reflex. One that had saved my life more than once.

"No need to shoot me." He tried to smile but my expression was grim. His lips twitched into a frown. "Please."

"Then tell me—." I started to reveal the truth. That I couldn't sense him. But I didn't want to give that secret away. I opted for his question. "Who you are. Why are you here?"

"My name is Paul Chandler. We have a mutual acquaintance."

I waited.

"Do I have to spell it out?"

"I know a lot of people, Mr. Chandler. Not all of them on my Christmas list."

He scowled. "Blake Mansfield."

That surprised me. Chandler took another step forward. I raised the gun to aim squarely at his heart. "Lift the shirt please."

He jerked it up carefully. Revealing something that looked like an ornate back-brace. "You sensed it, huhn? I told him you would."

"Go on." Asking anything would tell him that I didn't understand. That I didn't have a clue what he was talking about. I liked to keep my ignorance to myself.

"Blake paid a pretty penny for it. Guaranteed to keep you from sucking me dry."

"I'm not a vampire."

"My lifeforce or whatever. But I knew you'd know it was there."

I tried not to get impatient. The fact that tech existed that could keep my powers at bay was news to me. "Why are you here?"

"He said he didn't trust the vampire to tell you what you needed to know. So he sent me."

"How are you acquainted with Mansfield?"

Chandler smiled and shrugged. "I do odd jobs for him. Stuff off the books. Even his bosses don't know about me."

He'd said 'bosses.' Not 'grandfather.' Was he being discreet or did he simply not know Mansfield's true identity?

"What did he tell you about the vampire?"

"That you're helping find the old man's heir. That the bodyguard was supposed to answer questions. Mansfield wants to make sure his employers aren't being two-timed."

"I see. And what can you provide that the vampire didn't?"

"I know stuff, see? I've been skulking around for Blake a long time. It's why I knew where to get this here charm." He patted his belly.

The shirt clumped around the edges of his pants. He looked like a hobo. Not quite homeless. But close. And his speech was affected. A bad hodgepodge of movie quotes from the forties. Fifties.

"And where's that?"

"Oh, no. Nice try. I promised I'd keep that bit on the down low. In case you wanted to put them out of business."

"Okay. Then tell me what you came here to tell me."

"The other vamps, they know about you. They know you've been hired to find the kid."

"Who told them?"

"Blake thinks it was Josh."

The way he said it sounded like he disagreed. "Who do you think it was?"

Chandler grinned. "I appreciate that I am duly appreciated, Miss Savage. Or can I call you Bianca?"

"I don't have a preference."

Formality was a means of creating class distinction. I didn't need a title to know who I was. Or how powerful. Miss. Mrs. Madam. President. Men had set up that system for their own purposes. As a woman, I didn't give it power. As something not human, I cared even less.

"Okay. Thanks, Bianca. So, I think it was the Company."

"Gibraltar's company?"

His eyes widened with frustration. "No. Don't be ridiculous. The Company. You know, the security people."

"You can say 'Amperdyne Technologies.'"

"Shsh. They got ears everywhere." He peered up at security cameras on various buildings. "I think they even read lips."

"They'd have to, to know I said their name."

Paul Chandler was paranoid. A drinker, given the alcohol on his breath. But I didn't see track marks. No signs of other addictions. If Mansfield trusted him, there must be more to him than I could see.

"Look, Bianca, I'm trying to help here. Can we just be safe and say 'the Company?'"

"Fine. Why would the Company tell the vampires about me?"

"That's just it, see? You're the competition. If they find the kid, they're golden. You find the kid, and it's all tits up and stuff."

"You aren't English."

"What?"

"Americans don't say 'tits up.'"

He squirmed. "Oh. I watch a lot of B.B.C. America. What's that have to do with anything?"

I stared at him. Intrigued by the mystical totem around his waist. Wondering how much more he was hiding from me. There wasn't any dirt under his nails. His shoelaces were new even though the shoes were haggard. The stubble on his face was shaped.

"Never mind." I'd have to look into him later. If Chandler was even his real name. I believed the bit about him working for Mansfield. They seemed like a natural fit. "Go on."

"Alright, then. Like I said, see, if the vamps know you're coming, they can take you out. Then it's just the Company and the F.B.I. again. And we know the F.B.I. ain't gonna solve this first."

"Mansfield could've told me all this over the phone. Why the melodramatic confrontation?"

"No way! Nobody talks about the Company over a telephone! They scan calls for their name. We're talking the highest of high techs."

He reached around behind him. I pulled the hammer back on the Glock. Just to make a point.

"Whoa, now! Just got something to give you." He slowly withdrew a manila envelope from the back of his pants.

I took it, keeping an eye on his hands. "What's this?"

"Open it when you're at home. Away from cameras and windows." He glanced up at the security cameras above us. "Don't underestimate the enemy this time, Bianca. Oh, and my number's in there. In case you need to call. My rates are reasonable."

"One last question. Why is Mansfield helping me now. When I first met him, he clearly didn't like me."

"It's not you he didn't like."

"What was it?"

He squirmed a bit before answering. "It's that Joseph suggested hiring you."

"He hates Joseph that much?"

"He hates vampires that much. Good luck." He smiled and trotted off down the street.

I had the gun still pointing at his back. A car came around the corner and I moved the gun to my side. Out of the car's line of sight. It drove past and was gone. So was Paul Chandler. I stared at the envelope but I didn't have x-ray vision.

Fine. I'd been planning on getting the lay of the apartments on Atlantic. See what kind of activity the vampires engaged in. The comings and goings of tenants. Lighting. Get a feel of the neighborhood before I visited them. A trip home to feed the cat was probably a good idea. And I could see whatever it was that Mansfield felt I needed. Needed so badly that he'd purchased an expensive totem and sent Chandler skulking around.

CHAPTER NINE

My one-bedroom condo was small. Only four hundred square feet. Set in a secured building. Brick and cement. Small windows. Security doors outside each unit. More defensible than a sprawling townhouse. And it had underground parking the led directly into the building. A building I owned.

I got out of my Honda Civic. Listening as much as 'tasting' for intruders in the garage. The alarm beeped as I activated it. No other sounds. I closed my eyes and reached out. No lifeforce bigger than an insect. Not even rodents.

That was probably my fault. They sensed my presence and avoided the complex. Like I was a snake slithering through the halls. Only there wasn't anything reptilian about me. Not even my tail. Furred, no scales. Almost feline except for the narrow tip.

My phone rang and I jumped. My hand near my gun hilt. Ready to draw. I shook my fingers loose and answered the phone. "Janet?"

"Just making sure you were okay."

I smirked. "Joseph didn't try anything untoward."

"Thank goodness for small favors." She sounded embarrassed. "Sorry for bothering you. Have a good night then. Unless you need anything?"

"Say, can you call Gibraltar before bed? Tell his people I want to talk to Anton Thrace."

"You want him in the office?"

"No. Not this time. Tell them I'll come to him. Find out what time in the morning and where I can interview him. The earlier the better."

"Daytime. So not a vampire." She sounded relived.

"Werewolf."

"Damn it, Bee!" Janet was still muttering to herself when she hung up.

I made it inside the building and to my door without incidence. I was being jumpy. Everything I'd learned about the coven and Amperdyne warned me that I was dealing with some very bad people. Getting rid of a pesky private detective would be child's play for them. Especially if they disappeared my body.

The only advantage I had was that there wasn't a lot of information out there on people like me. Succubi. I'd looked. I'd paid good people to look. Computer hackers. Experts in finding secrets. Very little had turned up. My enemies wouldn't know what my full abilities were. Or how hard I was to kill. For that matter, I didn't really know the answers either. That's why Chandler's little belt bothered me. Someone knew something. I'd worry about that after I'd found Vincent. Undead or alive.

The moment I opened my door, a small furry shape darted for me. It climbed up my skirt and blouse, perching on my shoulder. "Martini! Naughty kitty."

The heavy Bengal cat was my only pet. A fire-rescue from a previous case. She'd been a mewling kitten back then. Light fur with dark spots. The woman giving her away thought she was an albino tabby. Turned out Martini was a seal-lynx snow Bengal. I hadn't been sympathetic when the woman realized the high dollar value of her mistake and tried to get the kitten back. Obviously she wasn't successful.

I rubbed Martini's head, rewarding the Bengal despite her bad behavior climbing up my clothes. I needed to feel wanted. Loved. Not lusted after. A cat was better than an empty home. Or a man I couldn't touch. Especially since cats were special.

For whatever reason, I couldn't accidentally drain the lifeforce of a cat. Not even if I was starving and on death's door. A secret I hadn't shared with anyone because I didn't know what it meant. Maybe that's where the folklore about witches keeping cats as familiars came from. The idea made me smile.

"I'm not staying. Food for you and a change of clothes for me." I went to the kitchen. Martini dropped onto the countertop to watch me with her sky-blue eyes. "Bad kitty. You aren't allowed up here."

"You aren't very convincing."

I bit back a cry of fright. My gun was in my hand without thinking. Reflexes were a wonderful thing.

Two figures moved out of the shadows. Into the brightness of the kitchen's florescent bulbs. A man and a woman. Dressed in dark colors.

Martini leapt to the ground with a hiss and disappeared. They'd startled me and that pissed me off. More people I couldn't sense. I was glad I had the wood-tipped ammo.

"Breaking and entering's a crime. Especially for vampires."

"We weren't sure we could get inside," said the female.

"I know you don't have to be invited in. That's just an old wife's tale." I watched them as I reached for the phone.

The man spoke. His voice uncertain. Soft. "Please don't call the police. We're here because you're looking for us."

I hesitated. "Pardon?"

The woman laughed derisively. "Not us. Our coven. We're from the Atlantic Revenants."

"Even if I wanted to talk to you, I didn't give you permission to enter my home. Give me a better reason not to call the police. Or better still, a reason not to shoot you?"

The man glanced at the window. "How about the fact that there's a sniper on the roof of the building across from your window?"

"Is that a threat?"

"No." The female vampire put her hands on her hips, annoyed. "Do we look like we could shoot our way out of a paper bag?"

"Not really." They were young. In both senses of the word. Early twenties and new vamps. Couldn't be more than a year old as undead. They lacked the stillness of older vampires. That patience that Joseph had periodically displayed. Sparring with his words, his body had been completely relaxed. These two practically fidgeted by comparison.

"We were coming to see you at home since it was after-hours. Naturally we did a little surveillance first. Spotted him before we came inside."

"Why should I believe you?"

The man glanced at the woman. She sighed. "It's gonna hurt."

"Chilton won't be happy if we just leave."

"What are you going on about?"

The woman went to the window. The curtains were drawn. I never left them opened. Not just for security. I liked to walk around my apartment naked. Even without someone knowing what I was, I had a nice figure. Open curtains would make for a peeping tom's wet dreams.

She turned on the lamp and stretched. Leisurely. I heard a tinkling and soft plunk. The sound of a bullet hitting flesh. The woman spun and fell. She dragged the light down with her. I started to rush to her but the man held me back.

"No. We want you to be dead."

I pressed my Glock into his chest. Heart-high. "Excuse me?"

"Her you. Not you you." He frowned at me. "My friend took a bullet for you."

A cellphone went off. He answered it. "Yeah? Great." He hung up and smiled. "You can get up, Rhoda. The sniper took off."

The woman didn't move. "Rhoda?"

He rushed over to her. Knelt down and rolled her onto her back. She opened her eyes and laughed. "Gotcha."

"That wasn't funny!"

I stared at her blouse. There was a hole where her heart was. No blood trickled out. Vampires didn't bleed. Good to know.

"It was. Really, Dusty. It was." She sprang to her feet with preternatural strength. Vampires weren't superfast. But they were strong. She eyed me. "What?"

"If he'd been using wood you'd be dead."

Her jaw dropped. Horrified. She wasn't that good an actor. Neither of them had thought that through. Still, I had to question the staging of it all.

"How do I know you didn't have one of your friends shoot you to convince me?"

She threw her head back exasperated. "Oh my freakin' God! I took a bullet for the bitch and she doesn't even care."

"She's got a point. We didn't think about that."

Rhoda sulked. "Maybe they should've used wood then, huhn? Would she have believed us then?"

"My sofa." I was ignoring the two vampires. Part of me believed them. They were too pathetic to be lying. But there was a hole in my the cushion where the bullet had gone through her. "It took months to find one in this color!"

"White?" asked the male vampire. Men didn't understand color. Neither did a lot of women.

"Cream," countered Rhoda. Guessing. She sounded uncertain.

"Biscuit, actually."

I found my tweezers in a basket on my reading table and poked around the stuffing. The vampire's body had slowed the bullet enough that it hadn't passed all the way through the stuffing. It took a couple of tries but the tweezers gripped it.

I pulled it out. "Silver."

I stared at the drawn curtain. At the hole in the fabric.

"For werewolves?" asked Rhoda, confused.

"Succubi," said Dusty. "Legend says that demons are susceptible to silver."

"I'm not a demon." I didn't say anything about the silver. They didn't need to know that it bothered me. Not like it hurt a lycanthrope. Or the way wood hurt a vampire. It interfered with my powers. Short-circuited them. I'd been shot with silver once before. Same reasoning then as now. Succubus equals demon to most humans.

Silver could be very bad even if it didn't kill me. The previous shooter hadn't been far enough away. Neither had his hostages. All of them dead at my hands. Janet and I never mentioned it. Too painful.

"So you believe us?"

"Yeah. I believe you. Why come to me? I have an answering service for after-hours. They forward important calls."

Dusty looked sheepish. "We didn't know. It said nine to six online."

I sighed. Clearly I needed to update my website. Or make sure my residence was scrubbed from the internet. Unfortunately, that would involve moving. I hated moving. I'd done it too many times over the decades.

I eyed them. "Now what?"

"Now we take you to Chilton."

"I was on my way to your apartments after I fed the cat."

Rhoda folded her arms over her boyish chest. "He's not at the complex."

"Oh? And where am I supposed to be going?"

"You like to dance?" asked Dusty, hopefully.

I stared at him. Hoping I was wrong. "A nightclub."

"Yep."

I shook my head. Crowded bars tended to have an excess of testosterone. Drunken men with fumbling hands. It wasn't a good combination for a hungry succubus. But I needed to talk to the coven tonight. It took three nights to make a vampire. That's why there weren't more of them. This was night number three. Assuming that they'd already started.

"Let me change. There's no way I'm going in public dressed like this."

I didn't wait for permission. I shut the bedroom door behind me and went to my closet. Not much to choose from. I didn't date. I worked long hours every day. I had one nice dress. Something Janet had gotten me for her grandson's graduation.

I pulled it out and frowned. A little formal, but Janet had said that a black dress worked for most occasions. Meeting a master vampire would be added to that list.

CHAPTER TEN

The vampires took me to *Bubbles,* a relatively new club on Ocean Boulevard across from beach. It was loud and packed for a Wednesday evening. Strobing lights changed angles as they flashed along the ceiling and down onto the floor. Men danced without shirts. Danced with other men.

I smiled. I didn't like clubbing. But when I did go out, gay bars were my preference. Better music. Stronger drinks. And I didn't have to fight off constant sexual advances. Not as many anyway.

My need to feed had subsided before we arrived. Without rhyme or reason. The goat hadn't been enough. But I felt sated. Otherwise being around this much testosterone would've been dangerous. For them of course. Lust was lust.

"Don't worry, they won't hit on you," shouted Rhoda as Dusty led us to a section of private tables at the back of the bar.

"The men or the women?" I shouted back, laughing. "I've been here before."

She eyed me oddly then. Glancing at my breasts. The curve of my hips. Not lustfully. No lechery at all. She was thinking I looked too feminine to be a lesbian. Clearly she hadn't been to many gay bars.

"Chilton likes the music. Says it's the closest thing we have to London."

"He's right. Unless you're willing to drive to WeHo."

"What's that?" she asked.

I stared at her, frowning. New and from out of the area. A runaway? No. She had to be in her early twenties. Not pretty enough to be an aspiring actress. That left writer or singer.

"What kind of music?" I asked.

"Pardon?"

"What kind of music do you sing?"

She flashed surprise. "Can you read minds?"

I grinned and she frowned. "Sorry. No. I can't. Lucky guess is all."

"Right." She didn't believe me. Fair enough. I hadn't believed her at first. She pointed at a tall, slender man in his mid-forties. "That's Chilton."

I studied him for a moment. Silver hair, without the lines of old age. Not quite handsome. Quirky. Mouth a little wide. Droopy lids that made him look perpetually bored. Slightly large straight nose. Popular features maybe a couple of hundred years ago. If I was remembering my history right. I wasn't quite old enough to know it for a fact. But I'd studied the past a lot in an attempt to understand what I was.

"Miss Savage." He spoke loudly, to be heard above the noise. Standing so that he could take my hand. I had a clutch purse in my left hand for the gun. Couldn't figure out how to strap a holster underneath the dress. Too tight. Too short. And I wasn't going to have it rubbing against my inner thigh.

"Chilton. Don't you use last names among vampires?" It was a trick question. Inspired by my conversation with Joseph. Chilton had referred to me by my last name. I only knew his first. I was curious whether he'd become Rake by being more powerful or smarter than Joseph.

"Fledglings like Dusty and Rhoda use last names. A powerful vampire commands attention. There aren't so many that when one says 'Chilton,' I might be mistaken for any other, lesser vampire."

He sounded as bored as he looked. His tone polite. Pleasant even. But it had that tired quality. That I'd disappointed him.

Psychological games. The way pick-up-artists had been taught to insult women to make them become more interested. By acting as if I were disappointing, he hoped that I'd try to please him. Show him that I was more than I seemed. I'd majored in psychology before switching to criminology in college. And really, who fell for that nonsense, anyway, in this day and age?

"You might, however, be mistaken for a guide on motor repair." My smile didn't change and I managed to keep the sparkle out of my eyes. Not that he could see through my sunglasses. Not in this lighting.

On impulse, I pushed my glasses onto the top of my head. They nestled at the front of my beret, secure. The dancing men were at my back. Safe from my eyes. I wanted to make sure the vampires could see my full expressions. It was a rare opportunity to be unguarded so I took it.

He frowned. I saw just a slight twitch of his eyes toward a woman at the table with him. A redhead with a short pixie cut, feathered bangs and sides. He didn't understand the reference. Apparently he hadn't learned to work on his own vehicles growing up. I let it sit out there without explanation.

"Please, join us," said the redhead. To ease Chilton's discomfort.

I shrugged. I'd won the round. We both knew it.

"Unless you'd rather dance?" asked Dusty hopefully.

He moved away from the gyrating men on the dance floor. They'd bumped him with their backsides as they danced near us. He wasn't any more comfortable around gay men than Rhoda was. Straight and insecure. Or maybe closeted. People tended to run from the things they desired when it frightened them.

"I think sitting's better. Hard to ask questions while focusing on the music."

"My apologies for the unorthodox location. I had an engagement scheduled here already." Chilton stared at Rhoda's chest. "You were careless?"

"N—no." Rhoda actually grew frightened.

I didn't like her reaction to the man. Men had picked on and bullied women most of human history. I tried to remedy that whenever possible. Like Luis with his sister. Vampires were no different.

"She was incredibly brave to take a bullet meant for me. So that I wouldn't miss this meeting." I didn't look at Rhoda. I held Chilton's gaze.

His frown deepened. "I didn't ask her to play bodyguard. Our lives are just as valuable as any bleeder."

"She didn't jump in front of a bullet if that's what you mean. She made the shooter think she was me. Took a bullet so that he'd leave and we'd be free to come here. Or didn't you instruct her to make sure I made it tonight?"

He opened his mouth and shut it. Not happy but unable to express his annoyance without seeming petty. He'd find other ways to punish Rhoda for doing what he'd asked. I could see it in his eyes. I definitely didn't like Chilton. And it had nothing to do with him being a vampire.

"Xian is watching her apartment, like you asked," said Dusty. He glanced at me hopefully. "We'll make sure you make it back in one piece."

"Thanks." I couldn't help but sound droll. Better than derisive I guess. He wasn't sure whether to smile or not. "I'm a big girl, Dusty. I can defend myself."

"From a long range sniper rifle?" asked the redhead, flashing her eyes at me innocently.

"Never know." I smiled at her. The kind of smile women give to their enemies. I didn't even know her but I knew her type. "I've survived a lot of attacks in my life."

"Enough." Chilton raised a hand to silence his people. "I know you think we have Vincent Gibraltar hidden away. That we lured him using vampire charms."

Chilton watched me as he spoke. Holding my gaze. It was the one thing we had in common. Humans should never look either of us in the eyes. For different reasons.

I felt the press of Chilton's will. A dull ache at the edges of my temples. I relaxed my shoulders. Let my power spill out along my skin. Not toward him. The lust in the room was powerful. I let it soak into me. A controlled taste. Hunger flared in me unexpectedly. My control wavered but Chilton's power was brushed aside by my own. He and his vampires were dead spots in a room full of sexual energy.

"Shit," murmured the redhead.

I looked around. The nearest men on the floor hung onto each other. As if suddenly too drunk to stand. I gnashed my teeth together, digging my nails into my palms harder. The pain wasn't enough. I needed something to numb me. Something—something undead!

"Dusty."

"Wh—what?"

I grabbed him. Pulled him against me. "Kiss me."

The young vampire stared at me. Then glanced at Chilton. The Rake must've nodded because Dusty suddenly pressed his lips against mine. It was an inexperienced kiss. Chaste at first. Strange because the energy I tasted didn't include his. Like kissing a cool, flexible plastic doll. Then I stuck my tongue in his mouth. Pricked it against his vampire teeth unintentionally. I wasn't entirely inexperienced in kissing humans. But this was my first vampire.

I tasted my own blood in that kiss. Ran my hands along his skin. Just as cold as his mouth. Unnatural. Something about him being undead soothed my hunger. Cut me off from the rest of the room.

I felt other hands. Another vampire pressed against me. Rhoda. Reluctantly wrapping her arms around us both. Several other vampires encircled me in a group hug. They'd figured out what I was trying to do. At least, that's what it seemed like.

My power crept back inside me. The hunger ebbed. I glared at the Rake silently.

"I did not mean to cause that," said Chilton apologetically. "Merely testing to see if you were immune."

He thought he'd caused me to lose control. Even though he was wrong, he was smart. He'd understood what I was trying to do. I was grateful. I should never have agreed to come inside.

I was glad he couldn't read my mind. "I'm alright now. You can step back."

The vampires moved away from me. All but Dusty. He kept his hands on my arms. His chest against my breasts. Staring into my eyes like he was trying to see into my soul.

"You heard her, Dusty. Back off." Rhoda grabbed him and yanked. Territorially. She liked him. Romantically.

"So beautiful." He smiled at me. Smitten.

My power didn't work on the undead. Joseph had said so. I believed him. The undead had nothing to feed me. Dead spots in a sea of living energy.

"What's happening to him?" Chilton looked at the redhead.

She stared at Dusty for a hard moment then looked at me angrily. "She did something."

"I didn't."

Dusty seemed to come back to himself. Waking from a dream. If he'd actually been enamored, he wouldn't have shaken it off that easily. "She didn't do anything. She's just that good a kisser."

"As if you'd know what a good kiss was," said the redhead snidely.

"Leave him alone, Bonnie." Rhoda stood between Dusty and the other vampire.

"Enough!" Chilton's tone was threatening. The vampires flinched. Dusty and Rhoda clustered closer together. Even Bonnie kept quiet. "You can search our properties. Talk to our members. But I assure you, we don't have Vincent."

"You have motive," I said.

"Motive?" He studied me puzzled. Then the light went on. He hadn't expected Joseph to tell me everything. He didn't smile but he nodded with understanding. "Yes. We want Henry Gibraltar to hire us. To give us a legitimacy we lack in human society. But taking his grandson buys us nothing."

"How did you know you're a suspect?"

"Joseph may not be one of our members anymore, but he forgets sometimes. Tries to interfere. He demanded I return the boy unharmed. I laughed in his face."

"You have any idea who did take Vincent?"

Chilton shrugged. "No ransom has been demanded. It makes the security people look incompetent. I don't know. I've offered to help. Joseph says we aren't welcome."

"But you're going to look anyway."

I made a note that he knew things that only law enforcement and the family should know. Maybe Joseph did more than demand Vincent's return. He might've given away all the crucial details of the kidnapping. It would give Chilton an out, if the police learned that the Rake happened to know something only the kidnapper should.

He smiled. "Of course. If we find the boy and return him unharmed, it'll make Henry indebted to us. Sugar over vinegar, Miss Savage."

"No other suspects so far?" I began to feel the press of the living men again. Their grinding and arousal pricked at my hunger. I should never have taken that small taste of them.

Chilton started to seem bored again. "A list of Henry's enemies is as good a place as any."

I'd already checked that out. So had the F.B.I. "That's a pretty long list. Not particularly helpful."

"Family members wanting a larger share?" He watched my reaction. Looking for leads into his own search. Not just for Vincent. But for the other two grandchildren, if I was right. Which meant they weren't convinced by the paper-trail saying that the siblings had died with the parents.

I smiled. Making my face into a pleasant mask of inscrutability. "Another dead end."

He frowned. Chewing on his lower lip. "You've talked to the other grandchildren?"

It was my turn to stare. Puzzled for effect. He seemed sure that the answer was 'no.' If it wasn't, he was intrigued.

Had they been following me since the restaurant? How else would they know what I'd done or who I'd talked to. And if they'd been at the restaurant, was that because they'd followed Gibraltar there? Or me?

"No. Considering the papers reported them killed with their parents, I know enough to discount them as probable suspects."

"No need to be misleading, Miss Savage. I know the two survived. Reading between the lines is one of my specialized skills."

"Even if they were alive, as I said, I know enough to discount inheritance as a motive."

He nodded as if that answer made more sense. He didn't know that Blake Mansfield was one of the grandchildren. But he wanted to know who they were. Why?

"Are the other grandchildren of particular interest to you? If they're actually alive?"

Chilton laughed softly to himself. "Ah, Miss Savage. Who do you think we'd be hired to protect if we find Vincent. The boy, certainly. But not him alone. I was merely curious if the siblings were both still alive."

"How do you know about them at all?"

"Being vampires doesn't make us computer illiterate," sniped Bonnie. "And genealogy websites have a wealth of information these days."

I nodded. "Easier than going down to City Hall." I'd have to remember that next time. It would've saved me a research trip. And by me, I meant Janet. "If Vincent turns up having been turned—or killed by vampire bite—it'll mean a federal warrant for your extermination."

"We don't have him, Miss Savage." Chilton's energy flared but it felt cool against my skin. It forced back my hunger. Better than an unwanted press of undead corpses.

I smiled to show him I wasn't bothered by his efforts. "One last question for now. Do you have any enemies that might want to frame you?"

Chilton's brows furrowed. He glanced at Bonnie with a flash of distress. They hadn't considered that possibility. "A human, no matter how motivated, can't imitate a vampire bite."

"Can't they? Obtain vampire enzymes. Create artificial fangs. Inject the enzyme into the dying body. Drain the blood through the puncture holes. A high-tech company could do it easy."

"No, Miss Savage. Vampire 'enzymes' as you call them, do not survive outside our bodies. They only transfer if the bite is 'live,' if you will."

"But if a vampire were to do it. Say the money was good enough. Your lot could be framed?"

That shook Chilton. He hadn't considered the possibility that a random vampire would try to incriminate them for cash. People always forgot just how powerful the almighty dollar could be.

"So, any enemies I should look into?" I repeated.

"Other than Amperdyne?" Chilton considered for a moment. "No one in Los Angeles County. No one recently."

"If anyone springs to mind, can you have your people call my office?" I glared at Rhoda and Dusty. "And no more night visits to my home. Not without calling first."

Rhoda stared at me as if to say, 'I took a bullet for you, Bitch.' But something in Chilton's expression made her swallow it. She'd already forgotten that I'd tried to defend her against the Rake. Some women just didn't like other women. No matter how hard we tried.

"We'll call first," agreed Chilton.

"Fine. I'll see myself out." I stood and moved quickly to the front of the club. Weaving and dodging the sexy, well-built men. Avoiding contact with their naked chests and bulging arms.

I didn't run, but the energy was like a weight against me. My stomach grew icy cold, the spiking need stabbing even lower. I clutched my belly, digging my fingertips into the hard muscles there.

My ability to feed on lifeforce was weird from a biological perspective. I fed through my skin. Through touch or waves of hunger that flowed out of my entire body. But all the energy I consumed wound up in my stomach. My gut processed that lifeforce like it was a burger with all the trimmings. Instead of it soaking into my body directly. Guess that had something to do with having a fair amount of human DNA.

I made it outside. Sweating. Palms bleeding from digging my nails into my flesh. I leaned against the brick exterior of the club. Swallowing hard before I strode down the street. Away from the cluster of gay men smoking out front. Laughing. Making out before heading home for more intimate acts.

I used the Uber app on my phone and a driver responded almost instantly. Less than a minute away. Probably expecting a drunken pickup at the club. Still, I didn't trust that kind of readiness.

When the car pulled up, I peeked inside first. He seemed harmless enough. Alone in the four-door S.U.V. I got in the backseat and strapped on my seatbelt. Once I was safely on the way home, I reached into my clutch and gripped the handle of my Glock. I stared out the windows at anyone on the street. Ready for anything.

Some people had comfort-food. Me, I had a Glock that would kill a person with one well-placed shot. With my new ammo, even a vampire.

CHAPTER ELEVEN

The answering machine was flashing when I walked in the door. The caller I.D. displayed Janet's home number. I pressed play as I scanned the condo for Martini. Still hiding. She didn't like strangers. Vampires were no exception, apparently.

"Anton Thrace can talk to you at five-fifteen at the Gibraltar home. He starts work thirty minutes before dawn so he'll be able to answer your questions without distractions." There was a rustling before I heard her annoyed sigh. "I was told not to leave any messages on your cellphone. Apparently the security company can access your mobile calls. But the landline is fine. Something about your answering machine being as old as I am. Call me on your way out the door so that I don't worry."

There was a click. The whirr of it rewinding. The next message would automatically record over it since I hadn't pressed 'save.' I dialed Janet from the landline.

"You're home." Her voice was breathy. "You got my message."

"Yes and yes. But if they can intercept my calls, can't they just listen into my condo with a directional mic?"

"I don't know. Can they?" Janet sounded flustered. "Go back to sleep, Bob. It's just Bee."

"Tell Bob, 'hi.'" I stared at the curtain and its single bullet-hole. By now, Amperdyne would probably suspect that they hadn't killed me. No police presence. No gunshot victim in any of the nearby hospitals. I had no doubt they were tracking emergency services.

Janet ignored my message to her husband. She knew as well as I did it would just be a barb in his side. She did, however, respond to my question about directional mics. "Does that mean I shouldn't call you? They can hack your email, too. Gibraltar's people sounded paranoid. Made me feel the same."

"I'll turn the volume down to zero on the machine. They shouldn't be able to pick up your end of any conversation. I'll just be careful in my replies."

"For how long?" She sounded worried. It warmed my heart that she cared. I usually pretended it didn't matter. But tonight I wasn't feeling so cold.

"I don't know. I've never been vulnerable like this before. People interested in me in the past were curious about me as a succubus. Even the hate-groups never needed to spy on me. Not that I'm hard to find. But until now, I've never been the target of a long-range sniper attack."

The fundamentalists from two years ago attacked with handguns, baseball bats and torches. Janet had been on vacation with Bob. My attackers had planned it that way. Killing the daughter of the Devil was one thing. Murdering a fellow human being was more than they could stomach. Small favors.

"This case scares me. When the good guys try to kill you, I don't know what to do, Bee."

"I'll figure that out soon. For now, be careful and I'll talk to you tomorrow."

"Hang up!" Bob's voice was muffled but annoyed. Groggy.

"Fine." Janet forgot to say 'goodbye.'

I placed the receiver in the cradle and looked at the clock. I'd get four hours sleep. If I was lucky. I checked the deadbolt. Kept the lights off as I made sure all the windows were secure. I found Martini and brought her into the bedroom along with the food dish and water. The interior door had a deadbolt just like the front door. I braced the window with a security rod. It wouldn't hold someone super-strong, but they'd have to wake me to get inside.

"Be a good kitty." I put Martini on the bed and set the alarm-clock.

I slipped under the covers and closed my eyes. But I wasn't sleepy. I could feel the city around me like an irritating buzz. Not that there was anything new about that. I was just wired with the excitement of a new case. A puzzle to solve that actually challenged me. More than cheating spouses and headhunted employees.

I shifted on the silky sheets, unable to find a relaxing pose. The energy of my neighbors crept in on me. The other condos were occupied by ordinary people. Some of them having sex. Men whose loneliness echoed at the edges of my power. I didn't latch onto any of them. I was in control again. But it was like listening to music just loud enough to disturb my sleep. My nerves tingled with awareness.

I tossed and turned for a long time before I nearly dozed off. Nearly. Martini curled around my face and roused me. My focus went beyond the cat. Something had changed. I listened with my ears. No sounds except cars down on the street. Maybe a dog barking far away.

I switched to my other senses. The metaphysical ones that included tracking prey. My neighbors had finally all fallen into a heavy slumber. Except for one elderly couple who never seemed to sleep. They were faint impressions of life. Not the source of my sudden apprehension.

Then I felt it. A flare of power that I could touch. Taste. Not lust. No emotion I could put a label to. Powerful. More than human in the same way that I was more than human. Not one of the undead. Nothing I recognized.

I touched Martini's head gently. Ignored her purring to pinpoint the source of that power even as I grew suddenly tired. The strange energy came from someone on the streets nearby. Looking for something. Or someone. And it had found me.

The energy surged along my preternatural hunger. It ate my anxiety. Spilled warm comfort along my nerves and I fell asleep. All my recent worries wiped from my mind. The way a human dream fades upon waking. My thoughts faded away into the cradle of darkness and I was out.

CHAPTER TWELVE

My alarm-clock woke me up with just enough time to shower and get dressed. I felt rested for the first time in weeks. My muscles were knotted, but I couldn't enjoy the hot water long. Just enough to rinse off the soap. I put on a dark, professional outfit. A little cleavage showing, but otherwise uninviting.

It was still dark outside. There was hardly any traffic at this time of morning. My car's engine sounded unnaturally loud in the quiet. No one was awake to hear it. The drive prolonged my sense of feeling at peace. Except for a niggling of excitement at meeting my first werewolf face to face.

Being preternatural was a two-sided coin. I stayed clear of other non-humans to avoid their complicated existences. But I was definitely curious about what their lives were like. Was it harder or easier than being a man-eating succubus? Would they know things about my people?

I rolled my window down to enjoy the ocean breeze. Glancing at my phone occasionally. I followed the G.P.S. directions, even though I knew the city well. Without other cars to slow me down, I made it in good time.

The Gibraltar villa was off of East Ocean Boulevard and 64th Place. Well-lighted in the pre-dawn. Every wall glowed with subtle blue hues. Mood lighting that served multiple purposes. No shadows for bad guys to hide in. None of it glaringly bright to disturb the occupants. Or Gibraltar's neighbors.

I parked along the street beside the villa. Getting out quietly in the pre-dawn silence. My car lights flashed as I activated the alarm.

The building was considerably smaller than I'd expected for a man of Henry Gibraltar's wealth. But it looked expensive. Mediterranean architecture with the Pacific Ocean bordering the southern property line. Palms of various types and heights decorated the yard. The elegant stonework would've looked more at home in a European village than in Southern California but I approved. Not that I'd been to Europe. Long flights in isolated cabins full of irritable humans wasn't the safest choice of travel for someone like me.

The villa was heavily fortified. Security cameras everywhere. Covering every square inch of the property. Even the nearby street access was under surveillance. Probably to record the comings and goings. Just in case. A deterrent for common thieves and anyone else who might be tempted to trespass.

I couldn't see the ultraviolet barriers framing the narrow windows that Joseph had mentioned. But I believed they were there. Probably inset inside the jambs. Motion detectors were placed near doorways. Black clad security guards patrolled the narrow strip between the villa and its neighbor to the north. I assumed the same was true on the western side.

Joseph had said that Amperdyne employed a five man team when Vincent had been taken. Now, however, I estimated a minimum of seven. Four outside. At least one watching security cameras that I couldn't see. And at least two patrolling inside, visible as they passed the windows of the dimly lighted interior.

Not all of Gibraltar's protection was in the villa. A black sedan with tinted glass sat parked across the street. I couldn't see inside the vehicle but I felt them. Two men. Watching. Waiting patiently. Not visiting the neighbors whose house they'd parked in front of. They were watching Gibraltar's place. Definitely new security. Or Feds. Either was likely.

I heard a buzzing as I walked up to the gate. I glanced upwards. Saw two small drones approaching. Each had red blinking eyes. Cameras. They circled before disappearing again. Aerial surveillance. Made me realize the uselessness of technology in this instance. Vampires wouldn't have shown up on camera.

"Miss Savage?"

I spun, angry that I'd been surprised. Surrounded by all of Gibraltar's protections, I'd fallen into a false sense of security. A man stood there. Loose-fitting jeans. An oversized polo shirt. Worn running shoes. All of it dark-grey. Harder to see in the dark. It didn't hide the fact that he was athletic. Lean. Wiry but powerful. His hair was medium brown. His eyes even darker. I thought I saw a spark of gold in them before he smiled.

"I'm Anton Thrace. You were expecting me?"

"Not in the middle of the street."

"Sorry about that. We're not allowed onto the property early. Mr. Gibraltar's very insistent about that."

He studied me. Curious. No sexual interest, despite a quick glance at my breasts. His nostrils flared as he discreetly sniffed the air. Most people wouldn't have noticed. I wasn't most people.

I think he was more concerned about the weapons I wore, hidden out of sight. Gun oil was a distinctive smell. And I cleaned my firearms regularly. This morning I carried the Glock. Cross-holstered at my side, under my burgundy leather jacket. The Sig was tucked inside a special holster built into my thigh-high leather boots. They matched the jacket and if necessary, dropping to one knee would put it right within easy reach. People usually figured after they took one weapon off of you, they had them all. Especially a woman.

I glanced up and down the quiet street. Not happy. I scanned for anyone hiding in the shadows. Ignoring the men in the car. "So we're stuck standing outside while we talk?"

He raised a brow and smiled. "I thought a nice walk along the beach would work? I've already got my run in."

I stared at him. Even if there were only federal agents in that car, Amperdyne knew I was here. Gibraltar's cameras had spotted me driving up. Confirmation that they'd failed. A walk on the beach out in the open was the last thing I wanted.

"Option two?"

He frowned. Clearly he didn't have an option two. "It really is a lovely night. I don't get the opportunity very often to just stroll when I'm here."

"We go inside the house. Gibraltar said I get full access to it. And I want access to you."

He glanced at the villa. His hands pressed together in a nervous dance. "Joseph?"

It was my turn to frown. He hadn't raised his voice. But he spoke as if Joseph was listening. As if he knew that the vampire would respond. Not just cameras lined the place. There must've been microphones, too.

I recognized Joseph's voice from the gate speaker. "Come in. Use the library."

A click was followed by a buzz. Anton stepped around me and held the gate open. He bowed slightly but his eyes remained alert. His gaze never stopped moving. Checking the street behind us. The rooftop of the next-door neighbor's residence. Even the shadows of the alleyway to the far side of the villa.

I smiled at him. "Thank you."

Walking onto the property, I felt the hum of electricity. I wasn't sure anyone fully human would've sensed it. I was surprised that I could. Maybe it was because I fed on energy. Living energy. Sometimes that allowed me to perceive other kinds of power. Even if I couldn't do more than feel its presence. And this place was wired to the hilt.

Anton closed the gate behind us and trotted up to the closest door. He put his palm on a flat screen next to the entrance. A soft click and the door opened. He stepped inside and I followed. Then he closed the door behind me with a final glance outside.

"You aren't even on duty and you take your job seriously."

He shrugged, unhappily. "Doesn't matter who's on duty. Being here makes me responsible."

That made sense, so I didn't comment. He motioned toward an opening to the right. It faced away from the ocean. I felt ahead of me with a splash of sudden hunger. Cold spikes gnawed at my belly. A slight loss of control as I felt the testosterone of someone on the floor above me. Nothing from Thrace.

Oh, I sensed him there. He was a living man. But it wasn't only his wolf trapped inside his body. His lifeforce was restrained. Subdued. That intrigued me. But this wasn't the time for playing preternatural biologist.

I let my power spill out in front of me. I was willing to risk feeding briefly from someone over being caught in a trap. I took a deep breath. Nothing living waited on the other side of the doorframe. I stepped into the room. Pulling my metaphysical surge back inside me. Thrace hadn't seemed to notice.

It was a small library. Twelve feet tall but less than a hundred square feet of floorspace. Every bit of wall was filled with books. Some old and ratty. Others new. Paperbacks. Hardbacks. Handbound manuscripts. Glancing at the titles, it appeared to be mostly non-fiction.

"I take it people in this family don't read for pleasure?"

Anton laughed, surprised by my observation. "I'm not sure they do much of anything for pleasure."

He didn't bother to shut the door behind us as he took a seat in one of the two oversized leather-chairs. He watched me. Like a wolf watching a rabbit. No. Like a wolf watching a new predator entering its territory.

"Microphones?"

Anton nodded. I didn't look around. There would be cameras, too. The man shrugged. "Mr. Gibraltar will want to know what we talked about."

I saw something else in his eyes. It said, 'see, if we'd walked along the beach we could've had privacy.' That made me wonder what he might've wanted to say that I wouldn't hear now. Still, I'd take safety over privacy. Besides, I didn't care who knew what I asked or what the answers were. Well, anyone except the person who'd taken Vincent. If Thrace had anything urgent to tell me that he didn't want his boss to know, he'd find a way later.

"Tell me about Vincent?"

The werewolf swallowed and frowned. He began to sweat, nervously. His energy changed. I could feel it prickling at my senses. Tried to wake the part of me that fed from men. He smelled of wonderfully appealing testosterone. No longer subdued. Wild in its rush.

Feeding from him would be different. Not because he was gay. I'd fed from more than one gay man in the past. Accidentally. Never taking too much. Topping off at a nightclub to keep my self-control in check.

It was just, I'd never met a lycanthrope before. There weren't that many in Los Angeles County. For a reason. I wasn't the only one who had to restrain myself. Losing control on a full moon made werewolves less trustworthy than vampires. Fewer survived the transition into legal protections. Given a choice, most people would rather become a well-groomed vampire than a savage beast. I'm not sure I agreed, but statistics supported the trend.

"What about Vincent?"

"Why does thinking about him make you nervous, for one?"

He made a face. Schooled his expression back to indifference. But I could still feel the tug of his testosterone. He wasn't nearly as good a liar as Joseph. It made sense. Werewolves could smell the truth on people. Each other included. Lying would be a bad thing.

I tried again with something less confrontational. "How well did you know him?"

He grew still. Forcing himself into that preternatural stillness. He slowed his heart. Nearly stopped his breathing before answering. His energy stopped rubbing along my skin. Reminding me of Martini. I stared at him hard. How was that possible?

"I've been watching over Mr. Gibraltar for six years. Sometimes that included keeping Vincent safe. He's a good kid. I wasn't responsible for his security."

Not really an answer. He knew Vincent better than he was letting on. A fact he didn't want anyone to know about. I shook off my surprise at his ability to block my hunger. Focused on the real questions. Had the boy confided in Thrace about a plan to run away with the Revenants? The werewolf was definitely sympathetic enough.

"Who do you think took him?"

"The vampires." He said it too quickly. Too eagerly. He wanted to blame them. So that I didn't think Vincent went along willingly? Or to cover for someone else? Or—could Vincent have simply planned an elaborate escape from the life of Gibraltar's heir? Billions of dollars were hard to hide from.

"No other suspects?"

Anton shifted in his seat. He couldn't get comfortable even though he'd calmed his body. No energy trickled out. He just couldn't slow down his thoughts. "It's not the Company, if that's who you're thinking."

"Amperdyne Technologies?" I wanted to be sure that that's who he meant by the 'Company.' The same way everyone else called them the 'Company.' Mostly, though, I wanted them to hear me say their name aloud. Considering that they'd tried to kill me.

"Yes. Them."

"The same Company that tried to assassinate me earlier last night?"

Anton flashed with genuine surprise. He hadn't known. So he wasn't in league with Gibraltar's human security. Didn't mean he wasn't helping Chilton. Preternaturals tended to stick together. Humans didn't give us much of a choice. And vampires weren't nearly as homophobic as lycanthropes.

"They didn't! They wouldn't." He didn't sound sure, his gaze flickering up at a wall. One of the hidden cameras. Not the only one surely.

"Yes. They did."

"You aren't going to the police with that are you?" He was more nervous than before. Terrified was the word for it.

"They get one free pass. If they make it up to me. Another attempt of any kind and things are going to get incredibly messy. For them I mean."

"And if they manage to kill you?"

I smiled. "Won't matter. I have multiple redundancies in play to get the word out. Mr. Gibraltar will be forced to fire them. Faking accidents to get rid of people is one thing. A shooting? Even something passing as a mugging? No. My police contacts will know exactly who to look into. My journalist friends will see that proof or none, everything about this case will leak. My discretion only lasts as long as I'm alive."

"Why are you telling me?"

"I'm not." I finally took a seat. It was more comfortable than I thought. "I don't care if Amperdyne finds Vincent before me. I get paid for my time. I'm always happy when a victim is returned safely. Men are competitive because they're insecure. Smart people—and I do mean women—are competitive within themselves. Bettering themselves without regard for besting others. Unless the men in their lives have screwed up their priorities. Sadly, that happens far too often."

"So you know you're being watched. Now you're doing a public service announcement for women's lib." I'd confused him. Distracted him with something political. Something he had little investment in as a gay man. It gave me a baseline for his relaxed, honest expressions.

"I'm just emphasizing to the Company that I'm not a threat. Even if they mistakenly thought so. That I'll share my information if it means that Vincent's safely found. Unless I believe they're involved. Which, considering that they stand to lose everything, I don't think they are."

I flinched at hearing myself parrot Chandler's words. But I believed him. I couldn't figure out any way in which Amperdyne benefited from Vincent's abduction. The papers he'd given me weren't much though. Just a longer list of vampire names. Addresses. Hardly worth the face to face.

"In other words, answer your questions as if we aren't being recorded?" He didn't seem happy with dropping the pretense. Why pretend when everyone knew that's what we were doing?

"Please. Now. How well did you know Vincent."

"I told you. I've known the kid for six years. I like him. Feel sorry for him in fact."

"Because he's cooped up without any freedom?"

"That. And he can't be who he is." Anton twitched as if he didn't like what he was saying. "Mr. Gibraltar has his whole future planned out. Destination C.E.O. of the Gibraltar Global Empire. Ivy league college before that. No chance to become anything else."

"A lot of families make plans for their children. It's unfortunate that those children don't get to find their own ways in life. But inheriting a billion dollar company isn't the worst thing I've seen."

"Maybe."

"So Vincent had motive for wanting to leave?"

He blinked and swallowed. "The vampires were getting pretty chummy with him. I saw the way his eyes lit up talking to them. Sheltered, he could easily mistake their interest for exciting new friendships."

"And that's the main reason you think it was the vampires that took him?"

He nodded. "Did he go with them willingly? I don't know. The law's puritanical about that stuff. As if a sixteen-year-old doesn't know his own mind. There's a reason the age of recognized adulthood was thirteen for centuries."

"Puberty means sexual maturity among lycanthropes. I'm not sure any age is suitable for adulthood." I took out my notepad. "I know more than a few forty-year-olds who aren't grown up. Now. Let's get down to details."

"Details?"

"Where were you at the time of Vincent's abduction?"

Anton seemed to smile with relief. "I have an alibi."

"Not at home alone? Sleeping?" It was most people's alibi at the time of night in question.

"There was an afterhours party at *Bubbles*. The Company's already verified that I showed up on the surveillance footage."

"So you're gay?" I already knew the answer. Always good to get verification from the source. Watch their reactions when they told the truth. Or see them lie.

Anton squirmed again but finally nodded. "It's not popular among my kind."

"Most people are stupid. Why should werewolves be any different?" I smiled softly, mostly with my eyes. The sunglasses made it harder for him to see. Not impossible. I'd opted for my nightwear lenses.

He blinked, confused. "Are you making fun?"

"Of people who are homophobic. Yes. Any kind of bigotry offends me, Mr. Thrace. I'm the poster girl for bigotry."

His expression grew sympathetic. "Spawn of the Devil you mean?"

I nodded. "Only, my daddy was human. Not Lucifer." I crossed my legs at the ankles. "So, you have an alibi. Great. What about ideas on the abduction. Even if Vincent helped, how'd it go down?"

"Why ask me?"

"You handle Mr. Gibraltar's personal daytime security. You have to know the ins and the outs of the villa better than almost anyone."

"Oh." He pulled his knees up against his chest. It made him look younger. Uncertain. "From all accounts, Vincent managed to bring a small E.M.P. device into the house. Activated it and went out the window."

That was the first concrete evidence I'd heard suggesting he'd been complicit. "Where would he have gotten his hands on such a device? Secretly I mean. Money being no object. Or doesn't he have access to a fair amount of cash?"

"He does. Did. But I don't have a clue. I mean, his bodyguards watched his every move. And I mean every, single one." He eyed me meaningfully.

It took me a second to process what he was hinting at. I'd already guessed that the boy couldn't masturbate without being watched. Not in his bedroom. Then I realized a more likely place. "Isn't it unusual for a security company to monitor bathroom use?"

He shrugged. "Mr. Gibraltar wasn't taking any chances. The trusts set up by his old man are pretty strict."

"I thought he set up the trusts? Are we talking for the grandkids? Or rather, the great-grandkids in this case?"

Anton nodded. "I ain't seen the docs, mind you. But yeah, I heard that much."

"Thrace, Joseph wants you." A new voice came through a speaker hidden in the room.

The werewolf's eyes widened with fear. He stood, hugging himself as he glanced at me. "They said to answer all your questions."

"Gibraltar assured me that I'd have complete cooperation. I'll join you."

The unknown voice spoke again. "No, Miss Savage. Joseph instructs that you remain."

"The hell I will." Did I mention I hated being told what to do? "Unless I'm being fired from this case? Shall I inform Mr. Gibraltar that Joseph terminated me?"

There was silence. Anton waited, watching me. Hope in his eyes. Finally the voice replied. "Never mind. There's only minutes before the day-shift begins. There won't be any extensions for the interview."

Not much time to ask all the questions I had percolating in my mind. "Chilton and the other vampires spend time at *Bubbles*. Do you know them socially?"

"I've met them. We don't hang out if that's what you're asking. None of his vampires are gay."

That certainly tracked with the degree of homophobic discomfort I'd seen in Dusty and Rhoda. "If the vampires took Vincent, you have any idea where they'd be keeping him?"

"No. The Company scanned their apartments. No warm bodies anywhere."

"What about dayminders?"

"Their human followers? Not allowed inside. They watch from outside the complex."

"Has Amperdyne run a financial check on the properties owned by them?"

"You'll have to ask the Company."

"That's next on my list." I tapped my pen against the paper. Something was nagging me. I couldn't figure out just yet. "Did Vincent have any crushes? In school? Among the vampires? A staff member?"

"He's home-schooled. All the staff is male and our contact with Vincent was limited, not just recorded. I don't know about the vampires. He seemed infatuated with them all."

"What did you smell after the abduction?"

"Pardon?" Anton hadn't been expecting that question. He seemed surprised by the very idea. It would've been one of the first things I'd have asked a werewolf on my payroll. Check for scents. Familiar or otherwise.

"You didn't personally investigate the crime scene?"

He stammered. "I—I wasn't allowed in."

"Was that the Company's call? Or Gibraltar's?"

"That I can't answer. I don't know."

A voice came through the speakers again. "Time's up. Anton report to Mr. Gibraltar. Miss Savage?"

I watched the werewolf scurry away like a nervous rabbit. "Yes?"

"Yuri Kamaguchi, head of household security, will see you in his office."

I smiled. Now we were getting somewhere.

CHAPTER THIRTEEN

Yuri Kamaguchi looked like his name. Mixed-race. Japanese and Russian. His hair and eyes were the darkest brown I'd ever seen. The bridge of his nose more pronounced than a pure Asian. The shape of his face masculine. Somehow pretty at the same time. Full lips. Epicanthic folds. The best of both peoples.

He had an athletic build. Hard muscles on a delicate frame. His shoulders weren't quite wide enough. Made his body look slightly overdone in that department.

"I felt we should sweep the past behind us." He smiled as he spoke, his eyes cautious. Watching me like I was a dangerous animal. I felt weapons aimed at me from somewhere. Even though I couldn't see them. Call it P.I.'s intuition.

"Then perhaps your men would be willing to put their weapons away."

Kamaguchi stared at my breasts, using peripheral vision to scan my expression. He avoided my eyes despite the sunglasses. Smart and cautious. A respectable combination.

He made a gesture and the sense of foreboding was gone.

"Thank you." I bobbed my head at the neck. Taking the seat opposite him without being asked.

Once I was comfortable, I studied him. "Shall we catch up on what we do and don't know about Vincent's abduction?"

"It seems unfair that we will be providing the bulk of the information."

"You did try to kill me." I smiled as I said it.

"Fair enough. A bit overzealous on my part. As long as there are no hard feelings?"

"You heard me. I just want to find Vincent one way or another."

"What happened at the faggot bar?"

"Excuse me?" I frowned. My skin warmed and my stomach grew cold as my power surged unexpectedly. I hated that word. It was an indication of ignorance and laziness.

He stiffened. My power licked at him. He used anger to hide his fear. "You attack me after I show good faith?"

"You're the one who used derogatory language in my presence. I tend to lose control when I'm pissed off."

He thought about what he'd said. I saw him mouth the word again as if he was surprised I'd reacted so strongly. "I'd heard you frequent such clubs. But since the word doesn't apply to women, I didn't think you'd care."

"I'm not black either, but I get even more pissed at the n-word."

He started to say that word and I intentionally let my power spill outward. His wasn't the only muffled cry. I reined my energy back in just as quickly. It was enough to taste them. Six men of varying ages hid just outside the room. Different locations. There must be secret access points in and out of this area.

"Am I not making myself clear?" I asked without any smile at all.

He didn't hide his smoldering anger. "Yes, Miss Savage. You are making yourself clear."

I studied him. Confused by his open use of such inappropriate language. Then I nodded. "I see. I was mistaken."

"How so?"

"I assumed you were American because of the mixed-race thing. You were raised in Russia."

He cocked his head to one side. Puzzled. "How can you know this? I don't have an accent."

"You do. Not much of one."

I didn't know if he had an accent. But the fact that he'd cursed softly in Russian when I'd scared him with my power suggested the truth. I wasn't exactly lying. Call it a bluff.

I leaned toward him, as somber as I could be. "But it explains your casual and comfortable use of such outdated and unwelcome language. Words are less biting in another language than your own."

"I see. Then you have a very good ear." He signaled again. Reassuring his men. I looked for an earpiece. It was small. Well-crafted. It even matched his skin tone.

I changed the subject. Otherwise I suspected we'd get into a real argument. It wouldn't end well for one of us. "Nothing about the Atlantic Revenants was in the F.B.I. files. Nothing on Thrace for that matter."

Kamaguchi reached into a drawer and handed me two files. One very thick. The other not so much. "This is what we have so far. The F.B.I. doesn't need to know about Mr. Gibraltar's involvement with preternaturals. Even you." He seemed to make a decision and reached into the drawer for a third file. This one was thinner still. Maybe empty it was that flat. He tossed it to me.

The thickest one was on the vampire coven. The thinner one on Anton Thrace. I paused at the skinny one. My name was on the tab. I stared at him. "Not a lot of material."

"Didn't think including police documents on your work as a detective would help anyone. This case isn't related to any of your earlier ones."

"So if this isn't a professional file, what is it?"

I was afraid to look inside. To get my hopes up. Over the years, I'd hired some pretty talented people try to find out about my past. None of them very successfully.

"Take a look for yourself. But my time is limited. What do you have to share with me?"

"How'd you know about the bar? You have people following the vampires?"

"Something like that. What happened there? The Rake apologized for something. It was never clear about what."

"You've got them bugged somehow. Let me guess. Tracking devices? On their clothing? Something they wear all the time?"

"You aren't going to spoil things by telling them are you?"

"No. As long as you aren't tracking me."

He smiled. It didn't reach his eyes. "Perhaps check your shoes when you get home."

I wasn't happy. At least he'd told me the bugs existed. Not that I was taking his word for it. Chances were, my shoes weren't the only place they'd placed transmitters.

"Fine. In the spirit of cooperation, the Rake tried to mess with my mind. Eye to eye stuff."

"And it worked?"

"No. But it made me angry." I'd let him draw his own conclusions. I'd already shown him what happened when I got angry. No need to tell him that I'd actually lost control at the bar.

"You asked one of them to kiss you. Succubi cannot feed on the undead. Why the kiss then? I know you don't date."

"I wasn't sure they knew that about me. Thought maybe I'd scare them in return for trying to screw with me."

Yuri nodded. I wasn't sure he believed me. I could lie easily enough. But I didn't do it often enough to come up with really good ones. Bluffing was easier.

"What else?" he asked.

"What else do I want? I want to watch the footage from the day of Vincent's disappearance. The day before as well."

Kamaguchi frowned. "We've been over it multiple times with a fine-toothed comb."

"I haven't."

He grunted. "Fine. But you'll have to watch it on your own. My people don't have time to babysit." He called to someone out of sight. "Hoshi, set Miss Savage up at the safe screen."

A panel in the wall opened where there hadn't been a door. A Japanese man without a trace of Caucasian motioned for me to follow him.

"What's a safe screen?"

"It's where we allow law enforcement and visitors to view confidential material. No one can transmit or record or duplicate anything. Show her how it works and then get back to work."

I went to the panel. "Thank you for cooperating."

"You didn't really give me a choice."

Hoshi moved into the dark hallway behind the panel. I joined him and the panel closed. Soft floor lighting came on. Like in airplanes. It directed us toward a door. The sign said 'media room.' Clearly not the only one. Maybe the police would've questioned the phrasing of a 'safe screen.' As if all the incriminating material was hidden somewhere else. It probably was.

I opened the door. Walked into the tiny room. One chair. A single oversized widescreen monitor. Hoshi waited until I sat down and then showed me the controls. Basic time selection. Fast forward. Rewind. How to switch between cameras. And a button to summon help when I was done.

"Thank you."

He bowed silently and left. I stared at the screen. Left frozen on Vincent's bedroom three minutes after his abduction. I glanced at the paper files. Unable to keep my focus on the monitor. Wondering what they'd found out about me. If anything new could possibly be in such a skinny file.

Finally, I gave in to temptation. Growling, I tossed aside the thicker two. Breathing deeply before I opened the one they'd composed on me.

Only a few sheets of paper. A lot of the material was familiar. Granny Oglethorpe had been born 'Matilda June Oglethorpe' in a small mining town in central Canada. A frayed copy of an ancient birth certificate had been photocopied alongside her death certificate. The one I'd turned over to the county when they'd asked for identification of the body. It listed me as the informant on the death certificate. There had been no one else. I was the only person alive who'd been close to her.

No official birth certificate on me. Just the phony one Granny Oglethorpe had registered with the local Canadian jurisdiction. I hadn't expected a legitimate one since succubi didn't usually give birth in hospitals. Granny had guessed at my date of birth. A mostly arbitrary guess, based on her favorite month and a rough approximation of the year. The name of my mother was fake, too. Lana Savage.

I wasn't exactly sure how old I was. Now or when my mother had died. Definitely not when Granny Oglethorpe had found me. They were details that hadn't really seemed important until I realized I'd never know the answers.

I flipped past the death and birth certificates and stopped breathing. My heart pounded in my ears. There was a DNA test. Labeled '*anonymous subject.*' My name was handwritten in ink at the very bottom. I'd seen my DNA enough times to recognize it. That's not what made my heart race.

On the flip side, a paternal match. Perry Davidson. Dead of unknown causes. Another handwritten notation. '*Lifeforce drained. DNA on file corresponds.*'

A name for my father. Someone had found what I never could. I'd already known he was dead. That's just how it worked for my kind. But his identity? That was more than I'd ever hoped to learn.

I did the math. I'd have been born just about nine months after my father was killed by my mother. At least, if succubi and humans shared that much in common. It seemed logical. That meant I was seventy-nine years old. Not an exact birthdate. But it was more than I'd known.

Granny had been off by two years. If my mother had gone the full nine-month term, my birthday was soon. Sometime in the next twenty days, probably. I was going to be eighty years old. Not that I looked a day over twenty-five. It'd be years before I could look in a mirror and track any new changes to my features.

That was one of the very few things I'd been able to learn about succubi biology. That anyone had documented anyway. The older I got, the slower I'd age. My childhood had been almost human rapid. When puberty kicked in, Granny Oglethorpe had noted a change in my development. I wasn't outgrowing my clothes like I'd been. I didn't develop breasts as quickly as other girls my age. And my menstrual periods weren't monthly. It was the only physical test of how slowly I aged. I'd bled once every three months. Then every six months. Then once a year. A methodical progression as time slowed down for me.

Like human women, I grew hungrier during the time I was fertile. Unfortunately, that made me very dangerous, too. This recent fluctuation in appetite worried me. That was something new. Not related to my menstruating at all.

I scanned the rest of the file but there was nothing as interesting as my father's identity. Half of my DNA had come from him. Converted into a new lifeform by my mother's metabolism. There wasn't a picture of Perry Davidson. Just his date of birth and disappearance.

And a hand-scrawled line along the edge of the paper: *American feral-game hunter.*

It was an odd notation. Not 'big-game' or 'wild-game' hunter. 'Feral-game.' I'd have to look into it later.

I frowned. Puzzled. American. Was that North American? Or did it mean then what it meant for most people now? A U.S. citizen? Granny Oglethorpe and I'd always assumed my father was Canadian since that's where I'd been born. Maybe not.

I perused the only other page in the file. It listed a few other facts about succubi. Question marks next to them. Some I'd read before or learned through experience. We often kept cats as familiars. Not witches. Witches didn't use familiars. Especially not cats. They weren't entirely cooperative. Someone had mixed up the two bits of folklore way back when.

There was a notation that we could fly. That we turned into bats. I didn't have wings. Horns and a tail, sure. But I couldn't change shape any more than a vampire could. That really was a witch thing. It required ritual magic. And it wasn't anything close to instantaneous.

The question marks were bigger next to the word 'fly.' Whoever had dug up this information wasn't an idiot. The handwriting looked feminine. So far, all of Amperdyne's employees I'd met were male. Maybe they'd acquired the file from a secondary source.

The last thing the page noted about succubi made me re-read it twice. *'Eggs must remain cold to hatch.'* Eggs? It had never occurred to me that I wouldn't give birth to a living baby if I ever got knocked up. Not that I was planning on it happening. Maybe never. I didn't want to be executed for murder. That was one more thing about succubi. We drained the life of a human sex partner. No ifs, ands or buts.

Whatever source they'd gotten this last tidbit from had to have been making it up. How would anyone know that except a succubus? The egg-business was too specific. A notation confirmed a nine-month hatching period. Ambient energy provides amniotic nutrition. No additional details. But what there was felt more than anecdotal.

Could the notes have been made by someone like me? Another succubus living in the mainstream? Unregistered if they were. I shook my head. It was a funny idea. But not helpful for me or this case.

I tossed the file away from me and pulled out the one on Anton Thrace. A lot of vital statistics. Birth certificate. Family-tree going back five generations. All of his people born and raised in America for the first four generations. German-Italian ancestry before that. Parents still alive. Human.

There were the usual law enforcement dossiers. Police and F.B.I. No criminal record. Not even speeding tickets. I suspected that was only because he didn't drive. There was a California State I.D. No driver's license.

I flipped through the official background dossier. Home-schooled in rural Virginia. Odd until I saw the date of an animal attack reported to the local sheriff. Thrace had been six, playing in the woods with a sister. A wolf attacked. Killing the girl. Leaving him changed.

The parents kept his secret until puberty. He'd broken free of his monthly restraints and killed most of the family livestock. His folks still hadn't turned him in. He'd done it himself. After that, he was sent to the Federal Lycanthropy Assessment compound in Nevada.

Eventually deemed in control of his beast and released at eighteen. Hired by Gibraltar almost immediately after.

Interesting but not relevant. I scanned his personal biography until I came across a sheet of associations. Nothing official. A couple of suspected romantic entanglements. Men, as I'd expected. Camera shots of stolen kisses in out-of-the-way spots. Clearly Gibraltar had had his security man followed on his off-duty hours. I wondered if that had only been in the beginning of their relationship. Or if it was ongoing. I'd have to remember to ask.

The next page jumped out at me. The word 'werewolves' was typed in all caps and underlined. Eight names were listed under it. People Thrace had met at the Federal Assessment facility. All men. I didn't know if the place was co-ed or if they just kept the sexes apart for obvious reasons. But I assumed it wasn't coincidence.

Two had the word 'born' next to their names. Since everyone was born—except succubi apparently—I assumed it meant they'd been born lycanthropes. If so, it surprised me that they'd been placed in the assessment facility. Being born into a werewolf family meant being raised in a pack. People who would help teach them to maintain control over their beast. They shouldn't need to be placed in federal care.

There were dates of Thrace's contact with the eight. None of them more recent than five years earlier. I wondered if that was the time that Thrace had come out. When they'd cut their ties with him. Most of the eight resided in Nevada. If the sheet was current. Outside of Las Vegas in the less populated foothills. A four-hour drive if I needed to ask them about their former friend at some future date.

Nothing in Thrace's file suggested he was involved with the vampires. Or that he needed money. I found a financial page at the back of the paperwork. He was worth a lot in both cash and real property. No gambling debt. Hell, no debt of any kind. In this economy, that was impressive. Or would've been if I hadn't known how much he made a year working for Gibraltar. He spent some of it, but that still left a tidy sum in his savings.

I stood and stretched before picking up the file on the Atlantic Street Revenants. It looked like several hours' worth of work. I needed some coffee. Or a soft-drink. Anything with caffeine. Male lifeforce might replace food to sustain me, but even a succubus could benefit from a little pick-me-up.

I pressed the button and someone appeared almost instantly. Not Hoshi. Another Asian. Japanese or Korean, I wasn't that good at distinguishing them apart. Maybe the racial overlap from all the invasions in the historical record had something to do with that.

"I'm not done, but I need some caffeine. Coffee preferably."

The man stared at me, inscrutable. Not because he was Asian. He had an effective cop face. Finally he nodded and disappeared without asking if I wanted milk or sugar.

I went back to the last file and flipped it open. I skimmed everything because a lot of the material was inconsequential. I wanted a feel of the organization before I worried about the finer details. The coffee arrived without a knock. A woman dressed as kitchen help set it down on a tray, away from the video equipment. She slipped away before I could thank her.

Smart of them to protect their gear. Not smart to relegate a woman to the job of serving tea. It made me question Thrace's comment that all the staff was male. Or didn't the kitchen staff count?.

I took a sip, ignoring the packets of artificial sweetener. It was black. I preferred just a dollop of cream but that hadn't been provided. Didn't matter, I had a lot to do and too little time to find Vincent.

After a third swallow of coffee, I skipped to the back of the file. Sure enough, the financial records and supporting documents were there. Copies of deeds. Articles of incorporation. The coven was set up independent of its members. But specific members served as the operating board. Not all. There were probably documents hidden away that anticipated the loss of all current leadership at once due to disaster. But they weren't in the Amperdyne security file.

Money wasn't an issue for them, either. True. Maybe they didn't have the tens of millions that Thrace had tucked away. But the assets of individual vampires had been deeded over to the coven when they'd joined. The Revenants had nearly three million in cash and the properties were worth another five.

That was unusual. The Feds frowned on monetary incentive to recruit vampires. Something else to look into when I had the time. Sloppy of Amperdyne not to have provided information on that. Or on anything deeper than public legal recordings.

There were police reports. A few stop and frisks by cops who'd failed to realize they weren't completely human. No drugs or alcohol. No murders laid at their feet. But there were a couple of battery charges. Filed by separate individuals. With the same supporting witness. Also unusual but immaterial.

I recorded all the seemingly pertinent facts in my notebook, skipping more than I bothered to read. I didn't care where the individual vampires came from. Or their family backgrounds. The list wasn't as comprehensive as what Chandler had given me. If there was a clue there, I was pretty sure Amperdyne would figure it out. I was looking for more tenuous connections. Logical motives. That sort of thing. The stuff missing from the file. Again. For a security company, Amperdyne seemed to focus on raw data. Overlooking the patterns behind the obvious.

Finally, tired of reading, I pushed the thick file away and adjusted the chair to face the screen. I stretched and finished my coffee. Then started examining the footage.

I played with the controls a bit to get the feel of them. Rewinding to the moment Vincent was taken. The E.M.P. left a hazy blank spot on the recording for several seconds around the abduction. That didn't matter. I wanted to see who'd come and gone. What Vincent, himself, was doing just before the E.M.P. blast.

The first image that came into focus as I scrolled slowly back from the blank spot was Vincent draping himself with a quilt. It was summertime and he was dressed. His expression grim. I zoomed in.

I couldn't tell if he was being surly or determined. Definitely not happy. The detail of his expression was amazing and I had to appreciate the image resolution of the expensive security equipment.

The image continued to scroll slowly in reverse. The quilt came off his shoulders and he bounced upwards. Off of the bed. Away from the stuffed hippo next to his pillows. I paused the recording. Studying his expression again. He glanced at something in his hands. A piece of paper. Maybe writing on his palm. The angle was wrong to see. I tried another dial. Changed the camera. Zoomed in on his hand.

Not a note. An origami wolf made of lavender rice paper. I resumed scrolling slowly back to see where it had come from. He set it down on the windowsill and walked backwards toward the door to his bathroom. I zoomed in on the wolf from all angles. No writing I could detect.

I sped backwards. Vincent came out of his bathroom. Left his room. The origami wolf just sitting there. Probably not a message then. A souvenir or gift from someone. Time passed and I stayed with the room. I'd track Vincent's movements outside the room later. The teenager came back in. Or rather, went out, walking backwards into the room.

This time he wasn't alone. A young woman sat on the edge of the bed. Mid-twenties. Hazel eyes. Shoulder-length hair the color of freshly cut wheat.

Vincent joined her, laughing. Picking up the hippo, he handed it to her with surprise. She took it. Which meant she'd given it to him.

I zoomed in on the woman's face. She looked enough like Vincent, Blake and Henry Gibraltar that I knew she was the third grandchild. Maureen Edwards. I stopped the video. Played it forward to re-watch the scene. She wished him a happy birthday. He took the hippo. Squeezed it before setting it next to his pillows in a place of pride.

I scrolled backwards again. The cousins danced around the room talking and laughing. Suddenly the origami wolf was gone. I slowed the recording but their bodies blocked my view of the window. I switched cameras until I found one pointing directly down from the top of the window-frame.

Vincent's cousin plucked the paper wolf from the sill. Placed it in her purse while the boy wasn't looking. Another birthday gift? If so, then why had Vincent seemed troubled by it?

Maureen left the room. A few moments later, a male servant came in. Vincent picked up a package from underneath his bed and gave it to the man. Dressed in a uniform of sorts. Gardner or janitor. Definitely not part of the Amperdyne security team. I had to keep replaying what I saw backwards in my mind. The servant had brought in the package. Vincent stared at it only a moment before sliding it under his bed.

Was this the source of the E.M.P.? The file hadn't mentioned the package. Or the cousin's visit. Which meant the documents were incomplete rather than simply inadequate. They still weren't cooperating fully with me. Even after my warning.

"That's it!" I stood up, annoyed. I pressed the button and the same man as last time opened the door.

"Finished?"

"No. Not with the video feed. But I am finished having my hands tied. Take me to Gibraltar. Now!"

"Mr. Gibraltar's in a meeting." He stared at me, allowing his own frustration to show. He didn't understand why I was angry. "You've been given access to everything."

"Where's the report that references the visit from Maureen Edwards? The gifts Vincent received the day he disappeared? Especially the mysterious package he shoved under his bed?

"There's no report. We were told you understood. No written reference to any of the grandchildren." He glanced at the screen. "If

Vincent hadn't disappeared, that footage would've been erased by now. No trail leading to the identity of the non-heirs."

I opened my mouth then clamped it shut. He was right. They'd mentioned something to that effect. I hadn't assumed it would include surveillance details.

"Who do I ask about those things then?"

"Joseph has the relevant information. Didn't he share it?"

"Apparently I didn't ask the right questions." I left out the part where he'd flirted with me enough that I'd kicked him out as soon as I could. I'd anticipated having all the information I needed in the files he provided. "Has any other information besides the grandchildren been excluded from the files?"

"Meetings with the vampire coven." He didn't try to play coy or pretend that I didn't know about it. Was Henry Gibraltar, himself, bugged? Or had he told Amperdyne details of our first meeting?

"You're assuming that what they did for Gibraltar and Vincent's disappearance are unrelated."

The man nodded silently.

"What if you're wrong? I need to know."

"No."

I waited but he didn't expand upon that limited response. "Then it's your fault—and his—if I fail to find Vincent in time. If you're wrong."

"If we're wrong, we must accept the consequences."

I nodded. Billions of potential earnings was a lot to risk. I'd have to trust that they were too paranoid about losing that kind of money to make a mistake. But they hadn't provided deep background on the legal-work done for the coven. Was that because it would reveal their deal with Gibraltar? Or sloppy research?

It pissed me off but I took a deep breath. Politeness never hurt anyone. "Any other deliveries or visitors before the cousin?"

He shook his head. "Most deliveries are done at the corporate offices where things can be fully vetted. And only special people visit the home."

"Why wasn't this package sent to the offices?"

The man's gaze flickered toward the screen. Not quite as surreptitiously as he might have liked. "We aren't sure where it came from."

I stared at him. "Who brought it in?"

The man shook his head. "It doesn't match any of the items brought in by the staff. And while this is a serious concern, the package wasn't the source of the E.M.P."

"Are you sure?"

He frowned. "It shares the epicenter of the blast. But we couldn't find any electronic components in the box."

"What about magic?"

His eyes narrowed, lips pursed tightly together. "Magic?"

"Surely a spell could short out electronics as much as an electromagnetic pulse."

He cursed in either Japanese or Korean, neither of which I spoke, before disappearing out the door. I opted to follow. He went through several narrow passages until he entered the main surveillance room again.

Yuri looked up at us and scowled. "What's going on?"

They spoke in what I finally decided must be Japanese, without regard for my presence. I watched as Yuri's expression changed from questioning to astonished and then finally, furious. He faced me, finger pointing. "You're sure?"

"I only asked if you'd checked the possibility."

He paced, agitated. "We protect against a good many things, Miss Savage. But magic isn't one of them. Attacks by magic, certainly. We have cornerstones on the property which prevent death spells and such. But nothing which would keep out something—how would you call it? Inimical?"

"I think you mean inactive. Passive."

"Yes, passive." He studied my lips as if I wasn't being completely honest. He mouthed 'inimical' to himself a couple more times. Trying to feel the meaning of the word. I didn't want to tell him he'd gotten it reversed.

I tapped my fingers along the wrist of the opposite hand, thinking. "Where are the items from the box?"

"Returned under the bed. The room has been left intact for the purposes of law enforcement."

"One way to find out. Bring in a witch."

"No! Mr. Gibraltar will not allow anyone like that in this house. Allowing you here is stretching his tolerances."

"Why?" I glared at Yuri. "He's guarded by two other preternatural beings."

"They are not the children of a devil."

"I guess that's a demotion."

He didn't understand my joke. "What do you mean?"

"A devil instead of the Devil?"

He blinked, puzzled. His English was good. But not native good. Idiomatic expressions were always harder to master. He pressed his finger to an ear, his gaze losing focus. Someone was speaking into his earpiece.

When he was done I made an alternative suggestion. "Fine. Then let me take the box to a witch myself."

"Not acceptable."

I waited. He folded his arms across his powerful chest and just looked at me. Unpleasantly. I counted to three. Took another deep breath. Not because of my hunger this time. I didn't want to wind up punching him in the face.

"Why not?"

"You might lie. Pretend it is or isn't the source."

I snarled with surprise. "And why the blazes would I do that?"

"To thwart our investigation. Make us look bad."

His attitude had changed since that moment with the earpiece. "Why don't you trust me all of a sudden?"

"Because of your relationship with the bloodsuckers."

"My relationship?" I was too confused to remain properly pissed off.

"Mr. Gibraltar will pay you for your time. But you are no longer welcomed here."

I didn't move. "What's going on?"

The man whose name I didn't know started to touch my bare arm. He wasn't wearing gloves and an angry part of myself almost let him. But I didn't want his death on my conscience. Even a brief contact could create a spike of power that would kill him. Not always. But if it did, the connection would remain for lingering seconds after he released me.

A scientist friend was working on ways of testing how my metaphysical powers worked. Why physical contact was so potent. So far he hadn't had much luck. Either way, understanding it or not, the results would be the same.

No matter how upset I was with Yuri and Gibraltar's little games. I jerked away and headed toward the entrance. Doors opened in front of me as I remembered my way out. I saw no one except for the man scurrying in my trail, making sure that I left.

When I finally stepped outside, the sun was already well above the Santa Ana Mountains. It must've been around ten or so. I'd been reading and watching video footage a lot longer than I'd realized.

The patrolling security guards held their weapons loosely in their grips. Ready to shoot me if I put up a fight. I trotted down the sidewalk, stomping loudly in my leather boots. Angry enough that was I seeing red. Thankfully, the gate buzzed open as I reached for it. I was prepared to give it a good, solid preternatural kick if it hadn't.

I hesitated. Turning toward the hidden microphone. I wanted to ask Joseph what had gone wrong. But I noticed the car still parked across the street. Probably recording me. I pivoted and kept walking until I reached my car. I jerked the door open almost too hard. Slipping angrily behind the wheel, I pummeled the plastic circle hard enough to make it creak with protest.

I turned the key, cursing and staring at the villa. The car started without any difficulty but the roar of the engine startled me. Shit. I hadn't checked for bombs. It had never occurred to me that I might need to. Not before this moment. Flashbacks to a variety of spy movies came to mind. Hopefully my threat to Amperdyne was still enough to keep me safe.

On the drive home, I made a few calls. The first to a friend with the C.I.A. I'd helped her solve a particularly career-wrecking case and gotten rid of an abusive supervisor all at the same time. To call her a friend might be stretching it. But she felt she owed me. I hadn't played on that debt very often before. Today seemed like the day for it.

She sounded excited to hear from me. "Bee! It's been too long." A slight pause and her tone turned suspicious. "Which means you need something."

"Why do all my female friends say that?"

"You mean it's not true?" Beverly Link's sense of humor was dry and facetious. I laughed despite that it stung.

"Okay. Maybe it is. There's name I'd like you to run. Part of a case I'm working. Whatever you can legally find out."

"We're the C.I.A. We'd never do anything illegal." I heard the same humor in her voice. "What's the name."

"Paul Chandler. Works with or for a Blake Mansfield. Attorney for Gibraltar Global Empire."

"Hmm. Sounds familiar for some reason. Can't remember why off the top of my head." She spoke to someone on her end of the call. Then she was back. "Anything else I can do for you?"

I started to say 'no.' Then I thought about it. "How about drinks tonight? You still in Long Beach?"

"Norwalk. But it's not a bad drive. Are we drinking? Or *drinking*?"

"If you get too wasted, you can sleep at my place. I have a very comfortable couch." I thought about it, annoyed. "If you don't mind the bullet-hole."

"Excuse me?"

"A story for drinks. What time are you free?"

There was a momentary silence. Then she responded cheerfully. "I can be there at six."

"A little early for me. Gives you time to grab a bite beforehand."

I may not call my friends very often, but I remembered things like common courtesy. Just because I didn't need to eat real food, didn't mean I expected them to go hungry.

"Then drinking. And talking. But of course, most importantly, drinking."

I smiled despite myself. "I know just the place."

She went silent a moment. "No gay bars this time, Bee. Please? If I only see you once every couple of years, can't it at least offer a chance at getting laid?"

I heard her get all weird in the silence. She knew I couldn't just have sex. The C.I.A. had been one of the sources I'd turned to for information on my past. Without any success. But they'd tried. Just because I was stuck being celibate didn't mean she should be.

"Like I said, I know just the place." I put a smile in my voice and she relaxed. Or pretended that she hadn't stuck her foot in it.

"Great. I'll be at your office as close to six as traffic will allow."

She hung up. One of my friends who definitely wasn't in the habit of saying 'goodbye.' I wrinkled my nose as I reached my condo complex. I told myself that she wasn't a friend. Just someone who owed me. But I kept calling her a 'friend' in my mind despite my internal protests.

Maybe I didn't want to admit we were friends. I treated her like I treated Teresa. I never called for social stuff. Hell, I usually turned down invitations to parties and drinks. Not the best quality in a friend.

I had time for one more quick call. Janet picked up on the first ring.

"Savage Investigations."

"I love how that sounds." I laughed to myself. It never felt silly reading it on letterhead or referring people to my office. But Janet's professional yet maternal phone-voice made it giggle-worthy.

"I thought you weren't going to use the cellphone!"

"I'm not using my cellphone. One of the burners. Or hadn't you noticed that the caller I.D. didn't give me away?"

"Oh. Oh!" She seemed relieved. "How'd it go this morning?"

"I got fired."

"Record time, even for you. What happened?"

"I'm not sure. I'm just pulling in at the condo. Won't be in until after lunch. But I need a few things before I get there."

"Such as?"

I gave her the names and numbers of the people I wanted to arrange meetings with and left her to it. I parked the car and sat in the silence once the engine was off. I stared at myself in the rearview mirror. My glasses looked good. Hid just how angry I was.

"Get a grip, Bianca." I muttered a few choice curse words and then checked the parking-garage for skulkers. For anyone who shouldn't have been there. Not that Amperdyne had had time to put new surveillance into play. Not the human kind anyway.

There were people gathered near one of the cars. All familiar faces. Mr. Huong and Mrs. Chavez hauling groceries from Mrs. Welby's powder-blue S.U.V. The old lady could drive, but she couldn't carry and walk with her cane.

I had lovely neighbors. The thought of moving troubled me. But that bullet-hole in my couch was proof that I needed a very discrete residence. Or at least one with no street-facing windows.

I opened the door and stood up. My shoulders ached. Stiff from sitting too long.

"Morning, Bianca!" called Mrs. Welby.

She hobbled along after the beaming Mr. Huong. He couldn't wave properly and his effort almost spilled the grocery bags in his hands. Instead he shook a foot my direction.

I laughed. "Good morning to you. Can I lend a hand?"

"Two would be better," teased Mr. Huong.

He was a local elementary school teacher. Laid off during the recent Los Angeles County school consolidations. His wife was a doctor at Long Beach Memorial. From what I understood, they didn't need his additional income. But he loved teaching. His hopes were high that he'd be rehired soon. As it was, some of the children wrote him letters saying that they missed him. That said something about how good he was.

I wasn't the sort that did positive-thinking rituals, but he was like a beam of sunshine that I didn't mind. "Be right there."

"I left your package on your doorstep, Bee."

Mrs. Chavez was a plump, middle-aged Hispanic woman. Her father was Mexican. The mother Cuban. Somewhere in her background was someone much darker than either race. She was short. And quite pretty, despite the roundness of her face.

We went to the same church, which was odd because she was Catholic. I wasn't. I'd asked her once why that was. She said she didn't like the services as much at her old church as she did at Universal Gospels, two blocks over. And the food was better at mine.

I didn't question it after that. She insisted she was still a devout Catholic. I had horns and a tail and believed in God. Who was I to judge?

"Package? Who from?"

"A handsome young man delivered it. But you were already out." She giggled. "What does a beautiful young girl like you do at five in the morning? Surf?"

"Not what you're thinking, Mrs. Chavez." I smiled and locked my car before I took a handful of groceries and joined the parade. "Meeting a witness who works the early shift."

"Now what else would I be thinking, *Chica*?"

"I don't know. Meeting a mystery man?"

"At five in the morning? Before the sun comes up?" Mr. Huong eyed me with laughter in his eyes. It was contagious.

"I couldn't be meeting a mystery man that early? It's just as valid as at five at night."

"She's right. Especially if he's married." Mrs. Welby giggled like she'd been naughty.

I smiled back at the elderly black woman. She was thin, but still managed to have a shapely figure. Raised in Alabama until her father, a military man, had been relocated to California forty years ago. She'd met the love of her life in Long Beach and they'd lived here happy and content. Until the day he died of cancer a few years ago.

Mr. Huong was like living sunshine. Mrs. Welby was the soul of our complex. Kind and maternal. Made me wonder what I was.

Before Mrs. Welby's husband died, he'd fixed things around the place free of charge. Things a handyman wouldn't even try to repair. Coffeemakers. Garbage disposals. Even the odd engine trouble-shooting for his neighbors. Now the complex looked after her in repayment.

Mr. Huong and Mrs. Chavez laughed at Mrs. Welby's remark. This was their idea of risqué talk. Their naïve innocence was absolutely refreshing. I did not want to leave these people!

My smile wilted when I realized what she'd said about the delivery. A man personally delivered a package during the tail end of night. That meant it wasn't an official service like UPS or FedEx. Amperdyne knew where I lived. A bomb could take out the whole building. But I'd threatened to expose them if anything happened to me. So probably not the Company.

Vampires also knew where I lived. I hadn't threatened to expose them if I died. Not that I knew anything I could hold over their heads in any event.

I quickly set Mrs. Welby's groceries beside her door. "I've got to dash. Sorry I wasn't more help."

"I know all about unexpected dashes for the door," called out Mrs. Welby.

I heard giggling again from all three as I raced up the stairs. I turned the corner on my landing and saw the package on the doormat. Large. But not too large. If it was a bomb, opening the box might be the wrong thing to do. If it wasn't, it might be something pertaining to the case. I risked it.

I carefully scooped up the cardboard container and took it inside my condo. Nothing went bang so I walked it into the bathroom. Set it down in the tub. Martini tried to follow me but I closed the door on her. She wasn't happy. But I'd rather not blow her up if possible.

I crawled into the tub with the box and tore the paper carefully. A shoe box. Nothing ominous about a shoe box. Except that I knew it wasn't shoes. I carefully pried the lid open, holding the box low in the tub so that the iron edges would absorb as much of the blast as possible. Tissue covered the contents and I set the box on my lap. I'd die if it blew up in this position, no question about it. I peeled the tissue away from the center and found another, smaller jewelry box. Beneath it was a white envelope. No bomb then. Or a tiny one. I read the card.

'*Thinking about you. Dusty.*'

Simple. Handwritten. Cryptic in a way. What did the vampire mean? Was it a threat? Would there be a heart in the smaller box? From an animal? A human? I realized just how little I knew about the vampires.

It was a viable threat. Loss of my heart would kill me. I opened it slowly. Anxious.

I was right. There was a heart. Not from an animal. Or human. A silver chain and tiny heart-shaped pendant.

I sat in the tub feeling foolish and confused. Jewelry from a vampire. I hadn't even considered the possibility. Then I had another thought. Yuri's earlier reaction to me. Collusion with the vampires, he'd implied. Amperdyne had known about the delivery. Maybe even about the contents. As high tech as their gadgets were, they could've easily scanned the box with a portable x-ray. No mistaking the jewelry for anything else. Which meant they still had my place under surveillance. That was less surprising than the gift.

One kiss and I'd turned the vampire's head. Great. Dating a vampire wasn't exactly a problem. I couldn't kill him. He wasn't even alive. But that was just it. I wasn't into necrophilia.

More than that, Dusty was too young. Too inexperienced. Not that I was much more experienced. Not with regards to sex. But everything else. I was ancient by comparison.

CHAPTER FOURTEEN

I showered again before heading into the office. Being cooped up in Gibraltar's video room left me feeling stale. Not to mention my exertion over the potential shoebox 'bomb.' I didn't smell bad. Even after a five mile run, I never needed deodorant. A benefit of being a succubus. My sweat was sweet to people. Almost pheromonal. No magic in it. Just natural, sexual biology.

I wore dressier clothes for my meeting with Beverly later. Not too sexy. Finding the tracking device took some time, but I left the burgundy trench-coat and matching knee-high boots at home anyway. Janet would be pleased. She called it part of my steampunk look. I liked them, but being in a bar without getting the wrong kind of attention was hard enough dressing normally. Or maybe it was the guns that people noticed.

The downside to getting rid of the heavy jacket meant I had to switch out my holsters. The custom clutch-purse would work for a slow draw. But sometimes the difference between life and death was a few seconds. So I opted for a black, mid-thigh silk skirt. Just enough boning to flare at the hips and hide a gun. I wore a thigh holster on each leg. The Glock 9mm closer to my right hand. I could shoot with the left, but my accuracy dropped a bit. That's why I kept the 45 on the left. It packed a bigger wallop when I missed the bullseye.

The skirt would hide the guns as long as I didn't fall on my ass or flash the room. Neither of which I expected to do. There were special slits in the fabric near the hilts. Open pockets that I could slip my hands into and draw without much effort. The slits were designed not to flare no matter how I moved. Not a perfect replacement for a side holster's fast draw. But we were going to be in public. I hopefully wouldn't need the weapons at all.

I was tempted to unload the wood-tipped ammo. There were five or six hours of daylight left. Vampires couldn't come out until dark. But I knew we'd probably go drinking directly from the office. And the way Beverly drank, it would definitely be dark by the time we called it a night.

I had a dark-red beret clipped to my hair. My horns could hold it in place on their own. As long as I didn't exert myself. But a careless waiter had once brushed against it with the edge of a tray. Knocking it onto the ground. People had screamed in horror. The restaurant had even banned me. Once was enough.

I stared in the mirror, checking the woolen hat from every angle. No hint of a pointy tip anywhere. And it looked good on me.

I adjusted my décolletage, framed nicely in a blood-red blouse. It matched the beret without being the same shade. Men would stare at my bosom before bothering to look up at my eyes. Still, I put on my Maui Jim sunglasses to be safe.

They cost a bit more than I liked to spend on eyewear, but the red tones in the arms worked with the outfit. They also framed my face nicely. It was their Sandy Beach model. Scratch resistance and made for playing in the sand. They'd survive a fight better than some of my day-to-day sunglasses. Dark enough to keep anyone from seeing into my eyes.

I laughed at myself. Some women had closets full of high heels or sandals. Men had collections of fine watches or expensive sneakers for every occasion. I had about sixty pairs of sunglasses in a special display built into my condo closet. I'd have to have a new one built if I moved. Another reason not to want to change residences. Not a great one. But I was hanging on to any excuses that I could.

The landline rang and I picked it up. "Hello?"

"Bee, your first appointment's here." Janet sounded annoyed.

I glanced at the clock. "They're five minutes early. I'm on my way."

"Hurry." She didn't sound afraid. Unhappy, definitely. But not under duress. It wasn't like her to rush me, so I grew anxious when she hung up.

I slipped on dark-grey dress shoes. No heels in case I had to run. But otherwise they looked like they belonged in a nice restaurant. I didn't like to be too matchy matchy when it came to clothing. Even so, I tended toward reds and blacks. These at least didn't have any bugs hidden in them.

I walked down to my car. The parking lot was empty. I wasn't attacked by ninjas or vampires as I got into the driver's seat. So far so good. I still hadn't checked for bombs. But, honestly! I wouldn't know what to look for anyway. The key turned without an explosion. Luck was still with me.

I got to the office in less than five minutes. Parking took almost as long. When I walked inside, I heard the bleating of goats from the supply closet. Jackson Grant, one of my tenants came out of an adjacent office and glared at me.

"This is certainly not acceptable for a professional building!"

Jackson was a thickly built man. Tall, almost six-three, with as much muscle as fat. He used to be a professional linebacker before a car accident tore up his legs. He could walk without a cane or crutches, but it wasn't very graceful. He operated an accounting service. Not all football jocks were mindless brutes.

"My apologies, Mr. Grant. I hadn't considered the effect of this particular delivery on my tenants."

"Well do something about it! I had a meeting with a new client today and she walked out after five minutes of that bleating!"

He disappeared back into his office. I couldn't fault him. It was terribly unprofessional. Sickly dogs and rats didn't make enough noise to bother anyone. Especially since they were usually kept in my soundproofed office, away from the hall. I'd have to consider a different strategy for the goats.

Janet popped her head out. She'd heard Jackson's complaint. Probably not the first time today. "Finally!" She eyed me, worriedly. I thought I looked nice. Maybe I didn't. Not from her expression. "Eat. I'll stall."

"Thanks."

I didn't bother opening the supply closet door. Proximity was all my power needed. Not line of sight or anything like that. Spells required line of sight. Ones that targeted people. Vampire seduction required eye contact. My power didn't recognize wood or steel or plaster. I put a hand to the surface of the door, more to focus than because it was necessary.

I felt my belly grow cool before the rush of power spilled outward. The goats stopped bleating. They sensed my power without understanding what it was. It enveloped them. Soothed them. An emotional paralytic. Like certain arachnids.

Then, predictably, their gamy animal testosterone opened the floodgate to my hunger. I felt the pit of my stomach fill with icy butterflies. Almost painful.

The goats' lifeforce flowed into me with a rush. Warm. Full of physiological information about my prey. Two of the males were younger. Not kids. But not at the end of their lives. Three were older. One sickly. Close to death. Closer than I liked because I could taste its impending demise with the rest of the energy I absorbed.

Their lifeforce ran along my skin, warming my flesh. Filling my cold stomach with the equivalent of nourishment. Easing the pain of having fasted so long.

I felt rather than heard them drop to their knees. Captured by my power. No screams of protest. Acceptance of a sweet, dreamlike oblivion. They laid down and died. All five drained. Not enough to sate me. But I felt better. More in control. That's what feeding was for me. A way to control my own body.

I might as well have been a model for the fact that I was always on the edge of starving. Never able to eat enough to satisfy my body's needs. But no one died as a result of my caution. That was what mattered.

I went to the office door and found Janet's chair empty. Voices came from my room so I walked straight inside.

"I'm a very important man and my time is valuable!" complained Henry Gibraltar. He wasn't sitting in either of the client-chairs. Instead he stood in front of Janet, berating her.

I spoke loudly enough to assure his attention. "So is mine, Mr. Gibraltar. You're not on my appointment list."

He spun, angry. "You tried to meet Blake without my knowledge! You were fired!"

I was grateful for the sunglasses because he stared right into my eyes. "You might want to read our contract again, Mr. Gibraltar. You can only fire me for cause or once the case is settled."

It was a point I hadn't tried to argue with Yuri. He was just the hired muscle. So to speak. So was Joseph for that matter. The fine points of my contracts were saved for lawyers and the clients themselves.

I glanced around the room. There were just the three of us there. I hadn't passed Anton Thrace in the hallway either. "Where's your security detail?"

"Why's that any of your business?" He was too furious to understand the question. What it implied. I'd pissed him off more by telling him he couldn't fire me.

"Janet, did he come here alone?"

Janet nodded. Afraid to speak. Not afraid of Gibraltar. Afraid he'd turn his rant back on her and she'd say something she'd regret. Janet had much more self-control than I did. But she wasn't weak.

"Where's Anton Thrace?" I repeated.

"He's—he's!" Gibraltar hesitated. I saw a wildness in his eyes. He stared around my office. As if he didn't know where he was or how he'd got here. "He was with me."

Janet shook her head again. I took a step toward Gibraltar. "He didn't come inside with you. When did you last actually see him?"

The man trembled with rage and confusion. Worse, I saw his paranoia shift toward me. "You arranged this! You devious whore of the Devil!"

"That's enough!" Janet grabbed Gibraltar by the lapel and jerked him around to slap him in the face.

He staggered more from shock than the force of the blow. "You—you hit me."

"You were being hysterical." Janet turned red with shame. Her anger bled away as she realized what she'd done. She didn't condone violence. Except maybe in self-defense. "It was for your own good."

"I haven't been hit in fifty years or more." He spoke calmly. Anger still present in his voice. But rational. Once more in control of his emotions. Like me. "I could have you arrested. Sued."

"You could. But then we'd have to sue you for assault, trespass and slander."

I smiled but my eyes were hard. He turned to me, unable to see my complete expression. It ruined the effect.

"Why are you smiling? What have you done with Thrace?"

"I've done nothing with him. When did you last see him?"

He thought about it. Eyes glancing toward the doorway. Wondering if someone would rush in and kidnap him. Or if I was going to drain his lifeforce away like I had with the goats.

Reluctantly, he answered my question. Hating me for it. "My driver let us out in front of your building. Thrace opened the door for me and I came inside."

"You were alone by the time you reached my desk," said Janet.

I motioned to her urgently. "Check the security footage for the front. See what happened."

Janet nodded and went to her computer.

My client was about to resume his raging tirade and I politely indicated a chair. "Please, Mr. Gibraltar. Have a seat. We need to talk."

He stared. Confused by my politeness. There wasn't any submissiveness in it. That's what confused him the most. "This isn't some elaborate plot to get your job back?"

I took my seat. Started to put my feet up onto the desk, then remembered the dress. No need to flash him my panties. Even if they did match the blouse and bra perfectly.

"I told you, Mr. Gibraltar. I don't need to do anything to get my job back. Our contract specifies that you can't fire me without cause."

"I had cause!"

I kept my tone even despite his shouting. "No. You didn't."

Spittle flew from his lips. "You're in league with the vampires!"

"Nope. Not even close."

He grinned hatefully at me. "I know about your little love token."

"You knew about it before I did. Shocked the hell out of me when I opened it." I leaned forward and frowned. "I don't date, Mr. Gibraltar. Especially not corpses."

"Really. Then why did the coven send you that gift?"

The question troubled me. I didn't like men who abused women. But I hated women who manipulated men just as much. I never meant to be one of them.

"I may have given one of them the wrong impression. A kiss to threaten them with my power may have been misconstrued."

"You admit to the kiss?"

"Yuri already knows about it. It has nothing to do with me working with the vampires. Why shouldn't I mention it?"

"You—you can drain the power from a vampire?"

"No. But I wasn't sure Chilton and his lot knew that."

"Bee!" Janet called from the other room. I turned on my monitor. She had remote control of my screen and displayed the footage.

"Got it." I turned the screen so that Gibraltar could see, too.

Thrace held the door open for his employer. The driver pulled Gibraltar's black four-door away from the curb. Immediately behind it, an older-model van without side or rear windows pulled up. The werewolf glanced at it over his shoulder. Hesitated. Time enough for someone to shoot him with something from the sliding side door. Two men in ski masks grabbed Thrace and dragged him into the van. The vehicle pulled out of camera range.

"What—what happened?" Gibraltar began panicking again. "He's a werewolf. How did they take him?"

"Why's a better question." I picked up the phone and he grabbed my wrist.

I hadn't put on my elbow length gloves yet. It was one of the things I did when I arrived at the office. They were a safety precaution for others. But I hated wearing them. I was tactile. I liked to feel the natural grains of my desk. The cool ceramic finish of my coffee cup. The fibers of quality paper. Martini's silky fur.

My power flared in involuntary response and I jerked away before I could do more than make him sick. But it wasn't over. I had to concentrate. Fight my body like trying to stop an orgasm's residual shudders.

I stabbed myself with a letter opener from the desk. Drew on my own power to keep from killing him. The effort used up the energy I'd gotten from the goats. But I was able to cut the residual link left by physical contact. If I hadn't eaten, Henry Gibraltar would have fallen dead on my office floor. Despite my best intentions.

My stomach grew cold with hunger. Blades of icy pain spiked through my intestines. Down into my female parts. Damn it! The goats might as well have never died for what his touch cost me.

I hissed at him through the agony. "Don't ever touch me again!"

"I—I forgot. But you can't call the police."

I stared at him. Not moving until I was sure I could control my appetite. Until the pain ebbed enough that my expression wasn't twisted into agony. I took deep breaths. Didn't count. The pain kept track of how many I needed.

Finally I could speak naturally again. "He was abducted. Possibly by your own security company. It's a federal offense. The F.B.I. needs to be brought in."

He watched me. Warily. Leaning back. Away from any impulse to touch me again. "Someone's trying to take everything from me. If the F.B.I. gets involved in this, the investigation will slow down even more! They're already interfering with Amperdyne looking into my grandson's disappearance. Tying my hands."

"Only if you're doing something illegal to find him. Are you, Mr. Gibraltar?"

He glanced away. "They're vampires. They shouldn't have any rights!"

I didn't try to keep resentment out of my voice. People were too afraid to speak to him honestly. Billions of dollars meant nothing to me. Not compared to my self-respect. "And I'm a succubus. I shouldn't have any rights either."

He didn't answer. I hadn't expected him to. Didn't matter. I was really pissed off.

"You get once chance here, Henry." I used his first name. Not professional. But I knew it would get his attention. Piss him off more. He was too powerful for most people to be casual with him. Courtesy wasn't buying me any leverage. "I can either help you find Vincent and Thrace. Or you can pay me my early termination fee and I'll walk away."

"No F.B.I.!"

I stared at him. His grey eyes wide with uncontrolled rage and fear. "It's illegal not to report a crime in my line of work. Either way I'm going to make the call."

He glared at me. Trying to burn me to ash with his look. "I didn't know they tried to kill you."

I smiled. His denial was acknowledgement that he had. Not that it mattered. Vincent mattered. Now Thrace.

"I'm not a vengeful bitch, Gibraltar. But my reputation matters to me. When you live this long, no matter what else people take away from you, reputation is all that's sacred."

He nodded. Something about that appealed to his own vanity. Weakened his resolve. "I'll tell my people to cooperate. Fully this time. Nothing held back. And call the Feds if you have to."

He stood, shoulders drooping. Then he looked at my face again. Trying to see my eyes past the sunglasses. A habit with people in power. Wanting to judge my reaction. Or the truth of my words. Cow me with their perceived self-importance. "Why did you want to speak with Blake, again?"

"To see if he could reason with you about letting me find Vincent. Without all these barriers you keep putting in my way through Amperdyne. To ask questions that would help me continue even if you didn't come around."

Suspicions clouded his mildly handsome features. "As I recall, your termination fee is more than you'd get doing the job."

"It's not always about money, Mr. Gibraltar."

He grunted and took out his phone. Pressed a single button. Autodial presumably. "I need backup security at Miss Savage's office. Send the armored car this time. Thrace was kidnapped. No, I'm fine. And Miss Savage is back on board. Full cooperation."

He glanced at me. A light had gone out of his eyes. He'd started to believe that Vincent was dead. That Thrace's abduction was just the next step in destroying his world. His spirit had been crushed. So much defeat in a short time after a lifetime of brutal success.

Suddenly the spark returned as he shouted. "Full! How full? Treat her like she's my god-damned self."

CHAPTER FIFTEEN

Within ten minutes, Gibraltar's team of Amperdyne ninjas arrived. Dressed in black clothes. Black body armor. Even black woolen masks. Similar to what the men who'd kidnapped Thrace had worn. But not the same.

They didn't say a word to me. Neither did the old man as they shuffled him off into another black sedan. This one had cars in front and behind as they sped off.

"You meet the nicest people," said Janet snidely.

I nodded, smiling from the building entrance. Another sedan pulled up. Squealing to a stop in front of me. Parking despite the posted signs.

F.B.I. Four agents spilled out. Two men. Two women. Sunglasses and suits on them all. Right out of a TV show. Professionalism was professionalism.

A blonde waved her credentials in the air. "Where's Henry Gibraltar?"

I pointed at the disappearing cavalcade. "You just missed him."

"You let a witness leave?" demanded the woman. I gathered from her attitude that she was in charge.

I read the name on her badge as she flashed it. Olivia Wisniewski. Late-twenties. Eastern European features. Polish, considering her name. And the shape of her prominent nose. She was five-eight with green eyes. Fit. And she wore her suit well.

She might've been attractive once. But scars covered the right side of her face. From the temple down to the bottom of her ear. They were from an old injury. Probably before she'd joined the F.B.I. Maybe the reason she'd joined in fact.

"I'm not law enforcement. No kidnapping charges for me, thank you." I stared her down through my own sunglasses.

"You have security cameras?" asked another woman.

Her partner's badge said Abigail Hardwicke. I assumed partner because the two men held back. She joined Wisniewski without hesitation. Mid-thirties. Black. Probably mixed-race because she had mocha skin and Asian features. I knew some gorgeous Kenyan women who had Asian-like eyes. But they were much darker skinned.

Hardwicke's afro was natural but neatly shaped. The woman was shorter than Wisniewski and more delicately boned. Her full lips were covered in a dark red-brown lipstick and there was just a touch of rose eye-shadow that looked almost natural. She was the prettier of the two. No, not pretty. She was beautiful in an unassuming, subdued way.

"Janet, show her the footage."

The female agents followed Janet into our offices. The two men took positions out front. Looking for signs of being watched. They seemed harmless enough. My tenants might not be happy but they'd get over it.

I joined the women at Janet's desk. Hardwicke was scrolling through the relevant thirty-second clip for the third or fourth time. Even annoyed, she was lovely.

"No license plate. No faces captured on reflective surfaces. We can have the tech guys go over it, but I don't think it'll give us anything useful."

"Make and model on the van narrows it down." Wisniewski didn't look at her partner. She continued to try to intimidate me. "Any idea on their motives, Ms. Savage?"

"It's Miss," I countered.

I only corrected her to be disagreeable. Hardwicke had been polite and respectful. Professional courtesy, if I could call it that. Wisniewski lacked any kind of courtesy. Made me not want to cooperate. If it weren't for the legal obligation to cooperate with law enforcement attached to my private investigator license, I'd have told her just where to get off.

She glared at me even harder. "Any ideas about their motives, *Miss* Savage?"

"No. Not really."

"How about a guess?"

I shrugged. "They might be trying to undermine his employer's sense of security. This would be the second person close to Henry Gibraltar that had been kidnapped in the past three days. Obviously Thrace wasn't kidnapped for ransom."

"I'm aware of the pending search for the boy."

She glanced around Janet's office. Nothing much to see. James Gurney *Dinotopia* limited-edition prints on the walls. Janet liked a happy, whimsical environment. With all the crap she had to put up with from me, it was the least I could do. A copy of my P.I. license was behind her desk next to a signed poster from the Gurney promotional 1992 anniversary of the coining of the word 'dinosaur.'

I decided to press Wisniewski back. "What would someone gain by kidnapping a bodyguard?"

"Agent Wisniewski!" A skinny man with a blonde ponytail and glasses as dark as mine rushed into the room. "Got a call from the home office. Anton Thrace's a werewolf."

Wisniewski turned from the blonde man to glare at me suspiciously. Even Hardwicke studied my expression. I could almost read their minds. Had I known Thrace was a lycanthrope? Was the information relevant or incidental? Preternatural conspiracy? All the probable questions forming in their skeptical, law enforcement trained brains.

I fought a smile at the very idea. Preternaturals were more likely to kill each other than team up. If there hadn't been laws against it. The killing. Not the teaming up. The only time we did work together was when humans were the common enemy.

Hardwicke finally chimed in. "Two preternaturals involved in a billionaire's business?"

I laughed which startled them all. The blonde man hadn't gone back outside. Watching the door was a boring business. But he'd left his partner alone. Not smart. Or protocol.

"Three preternaturals. Anton Thrace is Gibraltar's daytime protection. Joseph—no last name—is his night-time security. A vampire."

Wisniewski wasn't happy at that news at all. "I thought he employed Amperdyne for security."

I shrugged. Clearly they'd limited the files they'd shared with the F.B.I. just like they'd done me. It sort of made me feel less singled out as a succubus.

"There's household security and then there's personal bodyguards. Humans are easy to kill. Preternaturals not so much."

"How are you involved with Gibraltar?" demanded Wisniewski.

"Can't say. Client confidentiality." It was hard to stare her down through my sunglasses. But the rest of my expression was equally stony. "I'm investigating something for him. The details are only his to disclose."

"Olivia, look at this." Hardwicke used her first name. Wisniewski glared, but the black agent didn't notice. She was too busy pointing at the monitor. Then Hardwicke looked up at me. "There's a woman in the background. She was there before the black Cadillac dropped off our rich guy. Hard to make her out though. Sunglasses and a hoody pulled over her hair."

I walked around the desk to peer at the footage. I hadn't noticed the woman. It was a busy street. People walked to and from the beachfront businesses all day. A lot of them with sunglasses because it was sunny Southern California.

Hardwicke was right. The woman wasn't dressed in the same styles I liked to wear. But she was hiding the same parts of her body. Head and arms covered by the hoody. Hands covered in gloves. Eyes hidden from sight. Too much similarity to be coincidence.

"Know her?" asked Hardwicke.

No hard edge. No accusation. Just curiosity. Good cop to her partner's bad cop. Hopefully not an act.

"No. I didn't even notice her when we reviewed the footage." I reached past her arm, careful not to come in contact with her skin and rewound the image. The mysterious woman didn't disappear until I'd scrolled back nearly an hour. "Looks like I have a stalker. Unless she's law enforcement."

Hardwicke shook her head. "Could've been personal surveillance. You have someone interested in who you meet with? Or your comings and goings?"

"Not that I know of."

I kept my face expressionless. We were both thinking it. The woman in the hoodie was a succubus. Just like me. I'd never met another one of my kind. Seen one, sure. Years ago. Not that they'd let me talk to her. I'd born silent witness to her execution in Texas with mixed emotions. She'd murdered five men before they caught her. Five that they could prove. I suspected there were a lot more they hadn't found. If my appetite was any measure.

"She didn't leave the scene until she heard the sirens. Probably not part of the kidnapping." Hardwicke looked at Wisniewski. "But you never know."

Wisniewski nodded. She apparently hadn't come to the same conclusion. Her response was indifferent. "We'll have undercover cars patrol the neighborhood. See if we can find our mystery woman."

"Let me know if you find her. I'm kind of curious now."

I didn't look at Wisniewski for confirmation. Hardwicke was the more cooperative. The black agent nodded. But I'd provoked her suspicious nature. Hard to be a cop of any flavor and not be suspicious of most things.

Wisniewski stood away from the monitor to stare at me. "We'll pull Thrace's file. Does he have a pack that might know something about his enemies?"

I shook my head. "No. My understanding's that he isn't affiliated with anyone these days because he's gay."

They'd find that out on their own. By volunteering the information, it would look like I was cooperating. Which I was. Just not as much as I could've.

Hardwicke didn't miss a beat. "He got a boyfriend? Husband?"

Gay werewolves didn't appear to be a big thing to the agent. Or maybe she was just that professional. Either way, it was another tic in her favor. I'd help her in the future if I could.

I shook my head. "I know nothing about his love life. We'd just met this morning."

"Here?"

"At Gibraltar's villa. Part of my confidential business." I smiled. Wisniewski didn't smile back.

"If we get Mr. Gibraltar to okay it, you'll talk to us? Tell us everything you know?"

Hardwicke stood up as a Hispanic man came into the room. The last of the four agents. Guess he didn't like being left on his own any more than I thought he should.

He was shorter than the women. Dressed in a similar nondescript suit. If the F.B.I. had a height requirement, he had to be at the very low end of the threshold.

"Hey there, Ybarra." Hardwicke tapped Janet's screen. "Transfer this video to our server."

The man sat down with just a cursory glance at Janet and me. I saw the wedding ring. It didn't keep him from glancing at my breasts more than once as he settled into the chair.

I wasn't bothered. I framed them for that purpose. Looking wasn't offensive. And it kept people from accidentally being enthralled by my eyes. It bothered Hardwicke, however. She moved in between his eyes and my bosom.

"Miss Savage? If he consents?"

"Sure, Agent Hardwicke. If Gibraltar gives me permission in writing, I'll tell you everything."

"In writing." Wisniewski soured up again. "Why in writing?"

"So that he can't sue me or accuse me of violating his trust. People have to have faith in me in order for me to help them." I folded my arms beneath my breasts. Ybarra had leaned back and the movement distracted him. Hardwicke didn't notice so I kept their attention on me. "Until then, ladies, I can't tell you anything more."

I turned to walk into my office. Wisniewski grabbed my shoulder. She was wearing gloves, but she was sill careful to only touch the fabric of my blouse. "I'm not done with you."

"Then follow me into my office so that I can sit down and get comfortable." I didn't wait for a reply and pulled out of her grip. I could feel her bristling anger at my back like a summer storm.

Once I'd settled into my chair, my ankles on the desk, legs crossed at the knees to hide my panties, I stared up at her. I knew she wouldn't sit down. Law enforcement officers and C.E.O.s were trained in power posturing. Standing over someone as a form of intimidation. I simply smiled.

"Tell me about the dead goats." I blinked, my smile wilting. She saw my reaction. It was her turn to grow smug. "Didn't think we'd notice? Satanic ritual?"

"It's not that. I was just surprised that you'd waste time on something as irrelevant to the case as dead livestock." I grabbed my office phone and started dialing.

"Who're you calling?"

"My A.C.L.U. attorney. Reporting you for harassment and bigotry due to my preternatural status." I held the receiver to my ear.

Her expression turned puzzled. Nervous. "How is asking about dead goats harassment?"

"It's about me. Not your case. Obviously. What other reason could you have for asking? Hello, Grant?" I stared at her as I spoke into the phone. "I'd like to file a complaint against an agent of the F.B.I."

"Alright! You freakin' win!" Wisniewski's eyes widened a little too much in panic. I was betting it wouldn't have been the first complaint she'd received. Maybe mine would've been the one that got her fired. Her reaction suggested as much.

I stared at her, silent for a few seconds. "Never mind, Grant. I look forward to lunch next week." I hung up, absently removing my beret and tossing it onto the receiver like a rack. I echoed my warning to Gibraltar. "You get one chance, Wisniewski."

She glared at me. Sweating. Eyes wild like a crazed horse. Like I was provoking a physical reaction in her. It wasn't the phone-call that had unnerved her. It was me. Her eyes kept going to my horns.

"What's your problem, Wisniewski? Why do you loathe me so much? Is it preternaturals in general? Or did I do something to you personally?"

She tried to close down her expression. But I could see something in her eyes. Resentment. No. Religious fervor. I'd seen it often enough in my life. Not so much in my actual church. My congregation was much more reasonable. Part of its appeal.

Her gaze dropped to the cross nestled in my cleavage and she touched the scars on her face as if remembering something. "You've already threatened to file a report for asking personal questions. I'm not going to give you reasons by telling you how I feel."

"I'm asking. You get a pass. Whatever you tell me is because I asked. That's different than you just jumping all over my ass for no reason. I won't file a grievance for answering my question." I raised my brows. "Well?"

She finally blurted out her resentment. "You make a mockery out of Christianity."

I'd been right. I played with my cross, not looking at it. Keeping an eye on her. She seemed to realize she was touching her face. Forced her hand down with a grimace.

"You think someone like me can't believe in God?"

Her gaze flickered to my horns. "You don't. You wear the cross like the rest of your clothes. Hiding beneath the skin of good and decent people. While in truth? You're a monster."

I sighed. Returned the beret to my head. Normally I didn't respond to or interact with people who felt like she did. Life was too short. And too many people used God as a reason to hate. They hated interracial marriages. Gays. Islam. The members of my church agreed with me. Those kind of people weren't really Christians. That didn't make them any less repugnant.

In Wisniewski's case, I couldn't just walk away. My private eye license wouldn't allow it. I was going to be working with her on Thrace's kidnapping whether I liked it or not. Better to get our conflict out in the open than letting it fester unsaid.

"I take my faith seriously, Wisniewski. I attend Sunday meetings. Say my prayers like a good little girl." I smiled, sardonically, trying to reach her through humor. "Although, admittedly my pastor says I don't go to services often enough."

"Why, because you're that evil?" She stared at my beret as if she could still see the horns through the heavy woolen fabric.

I laughed with outrage. "No, because I'm in his congregation. He says that to anyone who doesn't go at least three times a week. Honestly, with a busy life, that's a bit excessive for most people."

She stared at me. Fingers twitching as if wanting to reach for her gun to avoid touching her scars. "You hide the horns and your tail. And God knows what else. That doesn't hide what you are."

"I understand that you find this hard to believe, but I'm not the spawn of the Devil. I'm not evil. Yes, I'm not quite human. And yes, I feed off the energy of living things." I paused, trying for common ground. "You eat meat, Wisniewski?"

Her eyes narrowed as if trying to figure out why I wanted to know. "Steak and potatoes, kind of girl. Why? Does that improve the flavor of the people you drain?"

I held my breath and counted to three before I could speak without sounding angry. "Animals die to feed you. Animals die to feed me. Neither one of us can help that fact. It doesn't make you evil. Doesn't make me evil, either."

"The way you look, how can you say you believe in God?"

Her question was irrational. I threw it back at her. "How can you believe that I don't? What, am I too pretty?"

She touched her scars again. Brushed her gloved fingers along the ridges like a relief map. She didn't answer but there was pain in her eyes. Pain behind the anger. I'd struck a nerve.

"What happened to your face?"

I asked it gently. No heat in my voice. Trying not to be cruel. I expected her to tell me to go to Hell. Instead, she just bowed her head in shame and stormed out.

Hardwicke stepped into the room. She'd been leaning against the doorway. Listening. "You have a reputation for being trustworthy."

I stared at her without responding. Waiting for her to make a point.

"So I'm going to trust you with something I shouldn't." She glanced over her shoulder. Took another step into my office. "Her *baba* was a hardcore religious zealot. Over the top fanatic. Fire-and-brimstone the-world-is-full-of-nothing-but-sin kind of witch."

"*Baba*? She's Ukrainian?"

Hardwicke nodded, impressed that I was familiar with the term. "Parents came here as political refugees. Brought her *baba*—as if anyone that cruel should be a grandmother."

"What does that have to do with her scars?"

"Her *baba* told bedtime stories that would give adults nightmares. About horned demons that take the virtue of anyone they can. About how good girls could grow those horns if they do bad things. That evil creatures were always evil. No matter how they behaved, once God turns his back on them."

I tried not to get impatient as I repeated my question. "The scars?"

Hardwicke looked over her shoulder again before continuing. Her voice softer. "Olivia was a pretty girl. They lived in a tightknit Eastern European community in Pennsylvania. North of Philadelphia. Overcrowded apartments. People practically sleeping on top of each other. Multiple families in the same units. Her *baba* caught an older boy showing too much interest one night. He'd crawled into her bed. Held her down and tried to touch her. She was eleven."

I stiffened, swinging my legs off the desk. "He raped her?"

"Tried. The old woman woke up on the other side of the room. Saw what was happening. Beat the boy with her cane until his family rescued him. From what Olivia said, he screamed so loudly, they thought he was being tortured. Olivia's sheets were splattered with blood from the injuries to his back."

I shrugged. Slightly pleased by the grandmother's brutal reaction. "That's pretty rough. Sounds like he deserved it."

"Maybe. Olivia would've probably been okay if it had ended there." Her face grew pale with grim dismay. "It didn't."

"The grandmother left those scars?" I could hardly speak. My delight at the boy's beating turned into a sickening weight in my gut. I'd been involved in several missing children cases. Discovering that someone in a position of trust had done unspeakable things to them. Too many times. That didn't make it any less horrific.

"She poured boiling water on Olivia's face. To, quote unquote, keep the sin away. If she wasn't pretty, she wouldn't tempt boys to do these things."

"The grandmother blamed her." I grew angry and felt my skin warm. Ice trickled inside my gut. A warning sign. I pulled my power back.

"What the fuck was that?" asked the man at Janet's desk.

"We get drafts," I heard Janet say, although I knew she'd felt it, too. Covering for me like a good personal assistant.

I focused on Hardwicke's grim expression. "I'm sorry. But I understand now. She sees me as a personal affront to the evil her grandmother spoke of. She was a good girl punished simply for being pretty. And here I have horns and people respect me for my work ethic. That sort of thing?"

Hardwicke nodded, offering a smile of gratitude. "That's the only reason I'm betraying a confidence. I'm trusting you to make this less painful for her. Your reputation says you protect women. Not just that you keep your word."

"I earned that reputation because it's true." I sighed. "Fine. I can't stop looking like I do. But I'll try not to rub anything in."

"Whatever you can."

Hardwicke looked into the other room again. Then trotted out without another word as Wisniewski came back in. She'd been walking the hall from the length of her strides. Oblivious to the conversation I'd been having with her partner.

Her eyes were red. She tugged on her jacket as if it were misaligned. Recomposing herself before speaking. "I let my personal views get the better of me, Miss Savage. My apologies."

I heard Hardwicke speak from the other room. "And?"

Wisniewski frowned, annoyed. "And I appreciate you not reporting the incident."

I smiled, leaning forward. "It happens to the best of us. So, what else can I answer for you? Outside the limits of client-investigator confidentiality?"

She studied me suspiciously. Her voice was thick with emotion. "Why are you suddenly being cooperative?"

"I clearly upset you because of my faith. That wasn't my intention. It's also none of my business to ask about whatever sadistic person scarred you. My apologies."

I took a deep breath. Angry just thinking about what her grandmother had done. I wanted to hurt the old lady. That's how pissed off it made me. I counted to three again. Something I'd been doing a lot lately. Took another deep breath.

I was able to produce a genuine smile. "I want to find out who took Anton Thrace. And Vincent Gibraltar. We should be allies. Work together. Not adversaries."

Wisniewski wasn't happy with my friendliness. She suspected something else had changed. But she didn't know what. I could tell she was the sort of person who didn't like not knowing. I could relate.

Her eyes were hostile again. "Trying to use psychology against me? Be the bigger person? Turn the other cheek? The Devil's been known to hide behind the image of Christ."

I laughed again. "Never met Old Nick. Not even sure I believe he's evil incarnate. Granny used to say that she thought he was a trickster. Meant to tempt us. Not destroy the goodness inside us. Anything bad we do is already inside us. Sometimes put there by horrible experiences we encounter." I fought a moment of sad nostalgia. I missed the loving, nearly-blind old woman who'd raised me, even after all these decades. "I tend to agree with her interpretation of things in the Bible. Regardless, I'm not a minion of evil. I've never killed anyone to feed."

I kept smiling but my heart grew heavy. I had killed. More than once. Especially as a young girl. When men had tried to enslave me. To use for darker things than I was willing to share with Wisniewski. No matter that she'd been in a similar situation at least once.

It wasn't a lie. Yes, I'd killed them. But not to feed. Self-defense.

"That's what your file says. The government keeps pretty close tabs on its P.I.s and preternaturals both."

"She's not reporting you. Try harder," called Hardwicke firmly, with a touch of kindness.

Wisniewski's mouth twisted, lips pursed together as if trying to keep the words in. "Alright. I'll give you the benefit of the doubt. I'm sorry I prejudged you."

"It isn't the first time I've experienced that. Won't be the last." I adjusted the cross on my chest so that the chain wasn't twisted and left it alone. "They were lunch."

"Pardon?"

"The goats."

She glanced at my beret. Trying to use imaginary x-ray vision to see my horns again. A little pale at my confession. "That's a pretty dangerous appetite."

"I don't usually consume so much. My regular supplier has been having problems coming up with livestock. I was trying to make up for a short and unintentional fast."

It was as much as I was willing to admit to the woman. There had been a case in the early 1900s of a succubus being jailed for killing her fiancé. Somewhere in one of the Canadian territories that had tolerated preternaturals back then. She'd claimed it was accidental. That she'd tried to stop feeding to prove she wasn't a danger.

I understood just how stupid that had been. Didn't know if it was the truth or a lie. But the idiots who jailed her had extended her fast. Unintentionally. They'd given her regular food. Like the other prisoners, while awaiting arraignment. On the sixth day, they found the entire jail complex filled with corpses. Even the female employees. No one ever made that mistake again.

That succubus had been executed by beheading. They'd burned the body just to be safe. Thankfully, laws weren't so barbaric any more. But if Wisniewski thought that I was fasting on purpose, she'd take action. It wasn't legal for anything preternatural to fast. That was the difference between involuntary manslaughter and first degree murder with the intent to do great bodily harm. There was talk in the legislation to give it its own special name. Intentional carnage. Willful frenzy. Something like that.

"Five goats do the trick?" She watched me cautiously. I saw a strange defocusing of her eyes. She was trying to see if she could feel my power getting away from me.

"Yep. And don't worry, I found a new supplier for regular feedings. Mankind's still safe from the evil, succubus private-eye." I spoke in a mocking tone. Not mean. Playful. She didn't take it that way.

"Wisniewski!" Hardwicke called from Janet's office. Stopped her partner from whatever scathing retort had been on her lips with news. "Gibraltar won't give Miss Savage permission to talk to us. But he'll answer our questions personally. Said we could meet him at his offices in twenty minutes. Otherwise he's got appointments scheduled the rest of the day."

"Fine." Wisniewski glared at me one last time. "Keep yourself available. We'll have more questions. I can promise you that."

"Schedule an appointment with Janet. I'll certainly do my best." I smiled, glad my glasses hid my eyes. They were hard. Angry. I may have sympathy for the woman, but I definitely didn't like her attitude.

When the Feds were gone, Janet came into the room. "I heard most of that."

"Eavesdropping?" I frowned. "Or have you bugged my office again?"

She didn't answer, which was answer enough. "Damn it, Janet!"

"Oh, please! No *Rocky Horror* references! This is serious Bee!"

"Accidental reference." I smirked and covered my mouth. "Doesn't make it less funny."

Janet ignored me. "That poor woman."

"She's a hardass. Scars or no. Be careful of her. Just because we had a little talk doesn't mean she won't jump on any chance to lock me away."

"But you've done nothing wrong."

"Janet, you're a dear. But even an agnostic like you should understand the danger of religious zeal. I may go to church every week, but Wisniewski still sees the Devil in me. A demon. Guilty until proven innocent. And even then, the standard of proof is much higher."

"So she might frame you?"

I didn't answer right away. It was a good question. Finally, I shook my head. "No. I think she's an honest cop. But I think she'll take the littlest scrap of evidence and run with it." I sighed. "Enough about her. We have a case to solve. And a kidnapping to thwart."

"What about her, though?"

I was confused. "Wisniewski's out of our hair for now. Just be careful."

"No. I mean the woman watching the building."

I ran my nails along the wooden surface of my desk. "Could be anyone. Preternatural groupie. Hate monger. Law enforcement keeping an eye on me, no matter Hardwicke's denials. As long as no one threatens you or the office, I'm not interested. At least, not until Vincent Gibraltar's found one way or another."

"If you say so." Her expression said she didn't agree. "What do we do about the dead goats?"

"They'll take them tomorrow when they bring the replacement."

Janet was horrified. "But the smell!"

"Buy a fridge. One of those top-opening kind. Big enough to hold the bodies. We'll keep the meat refrigerated. That way it won't smell or spoil."

"People are going to eat that?" She shivered.

"Honestly, I don't know. I've never talked to anyone that's eaten an animal I've drained. Actually, I haven't fed from livestock since I was a child. People get less angry when all the rats and mice in an area die instead of a cow."

"What's the budget on the fridge."

I looked at her long and hard. "Have we ever met?"

"What's that supposed to mean?"

"Why are you asking me about things you usually handle? You know I don't care about that stuff. Not where your good judgment is concerned."

"I—I don't know. I'm suddenly afraid to make any decisions on my own."

I stared at her. She hadn't been acting normal since the agents left. "You've dealt with the Feds before. Where's my wildcat who backs down anything with two legs?"

"I—I?" She took a step sideways and sagged. She hit her head against the doorjamb. Blood trickled into her hair.

"Janet!" I rushed to her side. Felt a wave of power flow into me. Nothing I'd ever experienced before. Then memories flooded back. That sensation from the previous night. Definitely the same soothing power. The way I made the goats feel even as I drained the life out of them.

I dropped onto my knees. Unable to call upon my panic to fight it. Then I collapsed onto Janet, face first. Out before I finished falling.

CHAPTER SIXTEEN

I woke slowly. Weighed down by a tangible blackness. Like climbing up from a deep, dark cave. Thoughts didn't come together in my head. Not in any logical fashion. All I knew was I needed to get higher. Toward a sense of light at the top of the darkness. I moaned and my lids fluttered. My senses kicking in as I tore through the last layers of shadows.

"About time you woke." Janet's voice.

I opened my eyes. My leather jacket was folded. Placed under my head like a pillow. Janet peered down at me. Sitting on one of the client-chairs. She hadn't moved my body other than placing the jacket beneath me.

"What happened?" I saw the dab of blood on her temple. "Are you alright?"

"Superficial." She frowned unhappily. "I didn't know who to call. You're never sick. You don't have a G.P."

"This isn't an illness. Someone did this to me. To us."

Janet glanced at my desk. Her eyes wide. Her lips pressed tightly together fretting. "They left a note."

I tried to lift my head. To sit up. There wasn't any pain and the last of the darkness bled away. My muscles worked without effort, so I stood. "Who?"

I asked the question as if Janet should know. She wouldn't have a clue. I knew, though. More than just a guess. Some preternatural instinct or connection with the power that knocked us out. It had been the woman watching from across the street. The same person who'd hid her head and eyes like I did.

My heart pounded. My first thought wasn't that it was just another succubus. A stranger. Wishful thinking or something else, I thought it must be a closer connection. Personal.

The possibility of family overwhelmed me. A sister or aunt. Cousin. Anything. Why else seek me out? Why else leave a note?

Janet pointed at a white pastry box. To the piece of paper folded in two resting on the box. "I already read it. I don't understand."

I reached for the note, ignoring the box. Unfolded it slowly. Almost reverently. Afraid of what I would discover. Hope was a powerful thing. Not always good.

I scanned the strange writing. Done by a female hand. Not in any language I understood. Not even one I'd seen before. Pictographs. Unfamiliar shapes. It had the feel of great age. Unrefined in the way that modern languages had become.

"Did the security cameras catch our visitor?"

Janet shook her head. "They were off, remember? The F.B.I. needed to see that earlier footage. It meant cancelling the live recording. It's automatic. I never thought we'd need to do both at the same time. I'm sorry, Bee. I didn't get an overlapping system."

"Stop fretting. Not your fault. We really shouldn't have needed a camera in the middle of the day. Not along a crowded street." I stared at the box. "Can you please step out of the room. Just in case."

She stared at me, sheepishly pushing her eyeglasses up her nose. "It's not a bomb. I peeked inside already."

"Janet! That was very dangerous."

"I wasn't going to leave you alone. And it's not like I had anything else to do the last twenty minutes."

"Twenty?" I was unhappy with that news. I glanced at the clock. Three-fifteen. Still plenty of time before I met with Beverly for drinks. But that was a long time to be knocked unconscious. "So what's inside then?"

"See for yourself."

"Why the blazes doesn't anyone ever answer my questions?" I laughed bitterly. Unamused by my question. Less happy with Janet's flash of self-reproach.

I was frustrated but I didn't want to get angry at my friend. She'd been frightened by the attack. Hell, so was I, for that matter. I'd never met anyone who could whammy me like that.

Maybe it had been a spell. No. That was unlikely. Witches usually left me alone. After all, I advocated for women's rights.

I thought about the attack. My assumptions. It was definitely the same energy that had put me to sleep the night before. I could remember the previous attack now. No harm done in either case. If the intent had been to kill me, they'd had two opportunities.

Hope warred with my objective analysis of the two incidents. I wanted it to be someone like me. Someone related to me. Found after years of searching. But why not reveal themselves to me directly? Why a note in this strange language?

And there was one more thing. Her power. I couldn't do what she'd done to me. Not without draining the person's life. Killing them.

Or could I? I blinked in annoyance. I didn't know. It's not like I'd gotten a manual. Orphaned before I could learn anything about my abilities.

Reluctantly, I slid the box-top upward. Off the base. No explosion. No smell of blood. Or bodily functions. Just a cluster of tiny flowers. Some type of Jasmine. Fragrant. Small and white. Shaped like delicate stars.

"Flowers aren't usually threatening." I glanced at Janet. "There wasn't anything else inside?"

"I didn't touch the contents. Just peeked. And no, nothing flew out if that's what you mean." Janet's eyes were haunted, gaze flickering toward the entrance to our offices. "Why knock us out to deliver a peace offering?"

"Scan the note. Send it to anyone discrete we know that deals in archaic languages." I secured the lid back over the flowers, just in case. "Include details about the Jasmine. In case it has ritual significance. Oh, and send it to Teresa Waldheim. Tell her it's a hush hush case."

"That professor at U.C.L.A. with the cheating husband? I dunno, Bee. You may have helped her, but I think she still blames the bearer of that particular bad news."

"No. You're right." I thought about our conversation about vampires. I hadn't helped us get closer. "She's angry enough not to be professional. How about the gay couple in Santa Barbara?"

"They were grad students."

"Wasn't the dad of one a retired linguist? Had a lot of books on dead languages. He might know who to ask."

"Could post it on reddit," suggested Janet.

"And have everyone and their kitten know what it says once it's translated?" I stared at her. The suggestion wasn't all bad. "On the other hand—don't scan the whole thing. Maybe pick a sequence of the writing that looks like a word and send that."

"But I don't understand, Bee! Why would someone send something in a language you don't know?"

"Maybe I'm supposed to know it." I didn't want to scare Janet. Maybe if my mother had lived, I'd have been taught how to read the note. Maybe it was my family's native tongue. Why shouldn't an ancient preternatural race like succubi have their own writing system?

"What are you going to be doing in the meanwhile? Shouldn't we report this to the F.B.I.?"

"Hell, no!" I laughed at the very thought. "This is personal. Until I know otherwise. She could've hurt us. Kidnapped us. Killed us for that matter. I don't think we're dealing with an enemy."

She eyeballed me like I was out of my mind. "I don't like how they're stacking up as a friend."

"Just do it, Janet."

"Bossy, bossy, bossy," she muttered and went back to her desk.

I glanced at the clock again. Habit. I couldn't track the sun like vampires or werewolves. The day was slipping away. And I still had no idea who'd taken Anton Thrace. No time for hope. Not for me anyway. Better to save it all for Vincent.

CHAPTER SEVENTEEN

Blake's office was on the fourth floor. Dark woods. Polished chrome. A view of the ocean. It looked expensive. But felt soulless.

He looked up as I barged past his secretary. "I'm busy." My expression got his attention. Even with the sunglasses hiding my eyes. He dropped his pen. "What happened?"

"Anton Thrace was kidnapped."

"From Mr. Gibraltar's office? Not possible." He glanced past me to his secretary, fuming at my back. "It's all right, Dana. This is important."

I waited for the door to close before I spoke. "From my office. When your grandfather showed up instead of you."

"He said he'd handle it. Why didn't he call me?" A troubled expression crossed his face. "How'd you get past my security?"

"I've been given full access by the old man. I guess that means leaving me alone with you."

"Fine. What do you want? Why was the werewolf taken?"

I studied Blake's expression. He wasn't a very good liar. Unless he was so good he could pretend to be bad. "I was hoping you might have an idea."

"Grandfather would never pay ransom for him. It's part of the contract. Professional risk."

"So it's either about screwing the search for Vincent or someone's trying to scare your grandfather." I paced back and forth. Trying not to gaze out at the ocean-blue horizon. Better to ignore the sun slowly dropping towards it. Time running out. "Was Vincent's kidnapping about money? Or has this whole thing been about power? Your gut."

"Power? No one gains any power if Vincent is killed." I saw the look in his eyes. The loathing.

"Or if something worse happens to him? If he's made into something preternatural?"

"Something undead. I have no problem with you, Miss Savage. You're a living, breathing woman. Maybe not completely human. But you're more human than those bloodsuckers."

"Your grandfather spends a lot of money on security. I've been told that a bad job could cost Amperdyne billions." An idea flashed into my head. "What if this isn't really about Vincent at all? Are you sure this isn't about hurting Amperdyne? That your family's only incidental?"

"If they'd killed Vincent, dropped his body someplace public, that'd hurt the Company more than his disappearance. Even Grandfather thinks Vinnie went along willingly."

"Maybe taking an innocent life's too much for whoever took him. Maybe they only want to hurt Amperdyne. Not any one else. Not permanently at least."

"Only the Company would know the answer to that question."

"And they aren't going to share that with me."

"Besides, Miss Savage, motive isn't the real problem. Knowing why someone took Vinnie won't get him back."

"Vinnie? That's twice you've slipped into a nickname. You said you hardly know your cousin."

"Maureen's called me several times. Worried sick about him. She's tried to find ways to spend time with him over the past few years. Says family's too important. She calls him 'Vinnie' when we're alone."

"I suppose she's the one family member, besides Vincent, I haven't gotten to talk to."

I only had two more hours before I was supposed to meet Beverly. For some reason, keeping my word to her and showing up on time was more important than this case. Teresa had already made me feel like a jerk for not calling her in months. I needed to prove to myself that I could be a good friend to someone. That there was more to my life than just work.

My mind drifted back to the mysterious note and the Jasmine. Maybe I did have something more. Or would. The possibility that I had family watching me. Reaching out. It excited and terrified me both.

"You can't be seen meeting with Grandfather, then me and then going to see Maureen. If you're being tracked. Watched. They'll put us all together."

"I'm not stupid. You met with me once already. It would be odd if I weren't consulting you about the case from a legal standpoint. In fact, I should be dealing with you more than Gibraltar himself. Arrange it. Schedule a meeting for me with your sister for tomorrow. Not too early. I've a feeling I'm going to have a late night."

"Vampires?"

Not who I had in mind. But I suspected it wasn't going to be all pleasure before the night was done. "Yeah, them, too."

CHAPTER EIGHTEEN

I made it back to my office with thirty minutes to spare. I'd walked around the block a couple of times first. Looking for the cowled woman. I reached out for her with my other senses. Felt nothing.

She'd either given up waiting or expected me to read the note and respond accordingly. I doubted I'd find her casually watching the place again. Especially after knocking me out with her power.

I entered the hallway. Smelled the musky scent of animal before I remembered the closet. Five dead goats. Being dead didn't lessen their pungency.

Janet saw my expression as I entered the office and she stuck up a hand. "I know. The fridge is on its way. No sense in deodorizing things until they're safely tucked away, now is there?"

"No, I suppose not. Any more complaints from the tenants?"

"I pointed out the eviction-without-cause clause in their contracts if they opened their mouths again. Didn't even need to remind them of the phenomenal savings in rent they were enjoying."

"Hard to get the right kind of people willing to occupy offices belonging to the daughter of the Devil." I grinned as I said it. But it felt hollow.

I was the daughter of a living man. I knew his name now. Perry Davidson. More than I ever expected to know about him. The woman watching me—if she was a succubus—wouldn't be related to me through him.

If she was related at all. I'd jumped on that notion too fast. I'd probably get my heart broken. Most succubi didn't register with the federal government as required by law. They didn't make themselves public. I'd wanted the legal protections. More than that. I was tired of hiding. Worrying that someone would find me and cut off my head. Or burn me alive. Whatever misguided way they'd try to make sure I stayed dead.

I thought about my motives for registering the moment the law had gone into effect. I hadn't even hesitated. The answer was easy. I'd wanted to be accepted. Not in the warm and fuzzy sense. I didn't make friends easily. But I wanted to belong somewhere. The way any new immigrant wanted to fit in.

Canadian born, I hadn't technically been an American when I first snuck across the borders into Washington. The Registration Act allowed me to petition for citizenship. My past swept aside.

I felt giddy. I was an American at birth after all. Because my father had been. That made me American through parental citizenship. Not that it would change anything. I'd become a naturalized citizen decades ago.

Still, even believing that I'd come to America as an immigrant, I'd lived here for a very long time. Paid my taxes. A lot of taxes. Contributed to society. I felt American. I loved America. Especially California.

"What're you thinking, Bee?"

Janet was leaning against the doorframe. Watching me. Her eyes full of compassion. A sad smile on her lips.

"Just thinking how lucky I am to live in the greatest country in the world."

She frowned and laughed in surprise. "What brought that on?"

"Perry Davidson. Turns out my father's American. I was naturalized in the sixties when regulations were a little looser. When the first registration draft went into effect. Just realizing I would've been a citizen by birth if I could prove that I was his daughter."

"Do you even have a birth certificate? I mean, I've never thought to ask. It's never come up on a case."

"A dodgy one. Granny Oglethorpe guessed at everything. Father was unknown. That much was true. Made up my mother's name." I laughed, bitterly. "I just realized now that the reverse is closer to home. I know my father's name and have no clue who my mother was."

Loneliness welled up in me. I glanced at my computer screen as if I could see my long dead mother through the screen-saver. Even a real name would be more than I had. It wouldn't be enough. But something.

"You want me to see what our researcher can find out on him?"

I blinked as if I couldn't focus. My skin had grown warm and pinpricks of ice bit into my belly. My hunger rose on its own. Even after consuming five adult male goats. It should've been enough to tide me over but Gibraltar had messed that up by touching me.

"Bee?"

"I'm listening. Thinking." It wasn't the complete truth. I didn't want Janet to worry. She worried too much as it was. "Amperdyne supposedly dug out everything there was." I thought about what I'd just said, focusing on my father to ignore the flash of hunger. "Only, they didn't provide original sources. Just notes on the DNA test."

"A DNA test? Bee, there wasn't any DNA testing back in the 1930s."

I shook off the hunger. Astonished that I'd ignored something so important. "I know that! Blast it. I should've asked about that when I saw the notation. How could anyone know that I was related to Perry Davidson?"

"I'll get Mack on it."

"No. Use Deshawn. He's expensive, but the best."

"He's also a criminal."

"Hackers aren't all criminals. Doing illegal things doesn't make someone a criminal."

"Um, by definition I think it does."

"Um, no." I gave her the look she hated. It reminded her I was much older than she was. That she was the child by comparison. "Speeding is against the law. Murder is against the law but excused in self-defense. People who commit certain crimes aren't criminals."

"I understand what you're saying. But I think the dictionary will prove you wrong." She turned and went to contact Deshawn Brown as I'd requested.

Deshawn and I had crossed paths twice. Once because he'd been curious about meeting a succubus. Not in any kinky perverse obsessive way. Just intrigued by preternaturals. The second time had been because he'd needed help with a non-hacking criminal charge. I'd proven that he was innocent. He owed me for that. But I paid him for his services anyway.

Janet didn't understand that dynamic. I couldn't fully explain. Someday I might need him to do something important. More important than looking for information about my father. Someday, someone's life might depend on calling in a favor that money couldn't buy.

I looked at the clock again. Time was running out. And I was letting my personal life interfere with finding Vincent. I choked down laugher. What personal life? The name of my father. Impossible DNA. And a woman who had the power to make me fall asleep from a distance. I was more of a mess than I realized if that was my idea of a personal life. Shaking my head, I returned my focus to Vincent until it was time to meet Beverly.

CHAPTER NINETEEN

Beverly called to say she was off work even earlier than expected. I told her not to bother meeting me at the office. I still had a few calls to make. She didn't object to meeting me at *Dalton's Speakeasy.* As long as I didn't stand her up.

I managed to arrive only five minutes late. That was a record for me and social obligations. Business meetings I arrived early. Maybe that said something about my priorities.

I scanned the room for the best place to sit when I recognized Beverly's rigid but well-dressed back. Former military, she never relaxed her ramrod posture.

She was at the bar instead of one the few empty tables. I preferred to be a little more isolated for conversations. Jimmy was the greeter. Curly brown hair and pierced ears distracted from his angular features. He was only five-five and thin. His slight build made his large hands and feet look awkwardly disproportionate.

He knew me well enough to check the seating chart before glancing toward the back where I usually sat. "Let me move the suits to a window."

He smiled and dashed off without waiting for confirmation. Polite but determined, he approached a group of businessmen at my table. I watched apprehensively. I didn't want to cause a scene. Or bring any grief to the energetic young man.

One of Jimmy's many decorative pins, which the employees were required to wear on their shirts, was a pink triangle. He didn't cater to me out of sexual interest. Or because I tipped well. Although I'm sure that didn't hurt. No, he was loyal because one night, I'd scared away a bunch of drunken, out of state frat boys. They'd seen the pin and decided to show Jimmy what Denver 'thought of fags,' as they put it.

The suits, three men and a woman, all beamed at whatever he told them. Picking up their drinks, happy to move. Maybe they preferred a window view to being near the kitchen door. Not me. I was happy with the clank and noise that kept people away.

I glanced back toward Beverly. She'd seen me and raised her drink, pointing at the barstool next to her. I shook my head. Pointing to the table abandoned by the suits. She glanced forlornly at the hunky bartender for a few seconds before turning back to me. Her shrug was eloquent.

I gave the bartender a better look. It was Bryce. Jimmy's on-again off-again boyfriend. He was incredibly handsome. Muscular and athletic. Smart. Kind. Funny. Early thirties. I wasn't surprised by Beverly's interest in him.

I met her at the table as Jimmy rushed back to wipe it down. Beverly didn't catch the look in my eye as she touched Jimmy's wrist politely. "The bartender. Is he single?"

Jimmy glanced at me and I laughed. "I'll fill her in. The usual, Jim."

"Coming up, Bee the Beautiful!"

"Fill me in on what?" She glanced at Jimmy, saw the slight swish to his gait. "Oh. They a couple?"

"Sometimes. He just can't seem to stay faithful."

"With a body like that, I can imagine." She sighed, wistfully. I laughed again and she glared at me as if I were mocking her. "What?"

"Not Bryce. He's head over heels for Jimmy. Jimmy's the one with intimacy issues."

"He's the tramp?"

"A sexy little tramp," I replied, quoting Bryce on a rare moment of mutual intoxication. Well, maybe not mutual. But I'd matched him drink for drink.

"If you say so." She eyed me sternly. Her gaze eventually flickering down to a file she'd placed in front of her. "Two drinks before we talk shop."

"Okay. Why?"

"Because once we start, it'll be nothing but." She slammed the rest of her drink. Unlike me, Beverly didn't have a 'usual.' The glass had a green residue at the bottom. Something Midori probably.

"Fine. How are things on your end?" I asked with a smile.

"About two pounds heavier than the last time I saw you. When are we going to start working out together again?"

"I take it Mario didn't work out?"

She glowered at me. Then beamed when Jimmy dropped off a Malibu and Coke. "Bring me another Midori Sour. Oh, and a shot of tequila."

"Are you driving?" I watched her for any hint of a lie.

"Not tonight. I'm going to make sure I can barely stand when I leave here. Don't worry, I'm not imposing. I'll take a taxi home."

I frowned. "What's the occasion?"

"How often do I get to go drinking with my girl, Bee?"

"So you and Mario are done." It wasn't a question this time.

"What makes you think that?"

"He's the reason we stopped working out together."

"Fuck him. On to new and better things."

"What happened?" I didn't need to ask. Mario had been controlling and jealous from the beginning. Beverly had believed that because she was with the C.I.A., she was stronger than him. That she only made the choices she did because she wanted to. Not because he forced her to.

A lot of strong women did stupid things when they were in love. Hell, so did a lot of strong men. I wasn't one to judge, though.

"He decided to trade down for a newer model."

I raised one brow. "How much newer?"

"Twenty-four."

"Half his age."

She studied me suspiciously. "You said age doesn't matter."

"It doesn't. Except that I was thinking someone half his age might be more his level of emotional maturity."

"I don't think it's her maturity he's interested in. Top heavy is an understatement."

I glanced at her breasts. They were full. Firm. Round. More than a few guys in the bar had been trying to decide if hers or mine were more appealing. I couldn't help noticing. Being a P.I. wasn't something I could just turn off.

"He's stupid if he left you for bigger boobs."

"Fuck him." She looked around the room and then met my gaze again. "I'm sorry."

"For what?"

"For being that friend. The one who dumps her friends because the guy wants more time. Because he suddenly becomes the center of her universe."

Jimmy came back with her drinks. She practically tore them from his grip before he could set them down. "Thanks."

She slammed the tequila and stared at Jimmy who seemed startled by her behavior. "Do you need something?"

"No, Ma'am." Jimmy disappeared on queue. One of his best qualities as a waiter. Not so good in a boyfriend.

"It happens, Bev."

"I can't believe I became that woman! Strong women don't let men do that to them."

"Now you're being stupid. Love makes fools of us all. As the saying goes. It's time tested and well-proven."

"Fuck love." She took a sip of her Midori Sour.

I smiled, relieved when she didn't slam it. I followed suit, sipping my Malibu and Coke. "Mario was never good enough for you."

"Tell me something I don't know."

"He tried coming onto me."

She put down her drink and blinked at me. "Come again?"

"I didn't tell you because you were smitten. All the signs were there. I'd be the one you hated. Not him."

"That's not fair. Or true. I'd have never hated you for his actions."

I eyed her sternly through my sunglasses. "I recognize this place. Pyramids. Desert dunes. And that massive river!"

"I'm not in denial!"

I laughed and she scowled. "Okay. So maybe I am. I thought he'd be the one. My biological clock's ticking. I wanted kids with the bastard. I wanted the ring and the white picket-fence. The works."

"At least he didn't propose before this all happened."

"Enough about my miserable love life. What about you? Still celibate?"

"Yep. Still celibate."

"It's just not natural, Bee." I laughed and she looked sheepish. "I'm sorry, that came out wrong."

"I know. And you're right. Celibacy is the most unnatural thing for an adult of any flavor. It's not like I have a choice."

"True. Nothing I could do for you if you were up on murder charges." She sighed and took another sip. "I just wish there was someone for you. You've helped so many people. I'd put you up for a sainthood but I'm not Catholic."

"Neither am. And I don't meet at least one of the most important criteria."

She eyed me sadly. "Being human?"

"Being dead."

We laughed. Her shoulders loosened. Her eyes stopped narrowing with anger. "I'd be very sad if you were dead."

"Me, too."

She smiled but her eyes were serious. "Do you realize that you're my only remaining girlfriend? Everyone else couldn't compete with the job, long before Mario came along. He knocked you and the last couple of die-hards out of my life. You're the only one to accept an invitation back in."

"Give it time. Or make new friends."

"One good one's better than a dozen maybes."

"I'll take that as a compliment."

"It was."

I took a bigger gulp of my drink. "Now, if we're done with the foreplay, can I see the file?"

"I said two drinks!"

"You've had two. Working on your third."

"You know perfectly well what I meant."

"I know. But if we talk about men all night we'll both be frustrated and more than a little lonely."

"A regular Pollyanna you are." She slid the folder over to me. "What are you into, Bee? And I don't mean kink."

"What do you mean?"

"This guy's MI-6. Deep cover. I got asked by some pretty important people why I was looking into this identity."

"What kind of important people?"

"Stop answering my questions with questions. You wanted info, I got it. No questions asked."

"But now you're asking."

"I need to know if this is gonna come and bite me on the ass. There's a lot of it to take a chunk out of."

"What'd you tell the people asking why?"

"I told them it was a background check on an anonymous tip." She looked worried. "I don't think it flew too well."

"It's closer than you think. Paul Chandler stopped me outside my office last night. Gave me information on the Victor Gibraltar kidnapping. Not much, but it was his persona that raised my flags."

"That's F.B.I. business. Not C.I.A. We aren't allowed to operate inside the U.S."

"That's not entirely true. Preternaturals fall under C.I.A. jurisdiction, don't we?"

Beverly nodded and tried to take another sip. She stared at the empty glass annoyed. "You investigating Gibraltar doesn't make that C.I.A. interest."

"How about the fact that the kid might've been seduced by a local vampire coven?"

Beverly's eyes perked up. The booze hadn't hit her yet. She could hold liquor better than a lot of men I knew. Not as well as I could. But that's only because it was nearly impossible for me to get drunk.

I touched her arm with a gloved hand. "To top it off, Gibraltar's daytime security's a werewolf named Anton Thrace. He was kidnapped earlier today."

"F.B.I. reported that one to us. The director passed on it." She pushed back in her chair to sit ramrod stiff again. "Might've been different if we'd known about the coven. So what's Chandler's involvement in this?"

"He claimed to be working for Blake Mansfield. One of Gibraltar's attorneys. Wanted to give me insight into some of the things his employer did and didn't say. But my Spidey-sense went off. MI-6 makes perfect sense. Only, why are they involved?"

Beverly pulled out her cellphone. I reached out a hand to make her stop. She shook her head and I pulled my hand back. Leaning back I watched her patiently. Hoping she wasn't breaking my confidence.

"Thompson. Link here. We get a call from the F.B.I. about the Gibraltar kidnapping three days ago?" She listened patiently. Probably to silence. Then she started nodding. "The Director passed on that, too? No. No, I know. The Director can damned well do whatever he wants. Alright. Thanks."

"So it was reported."

Beverly nodded. "I knew Henry Gibraltar had pull. I just didn't realize how much."

"He wouldn't have mentioned the vampires to the F.B.I. I was thinking though, unless they're idiots, they'd have realized the possibility from the video footage of the abduction."

"The F.B.I. did suspect preternatural involvement. The Director has the latitude to pass on domestic stuff relating to preternaturals if the F.B.I. is already investigating. I don't get it. Normally, especially kidnappings, we'd jump on it."

I waited. There wasn't much else to add on my end.

"How much of your code-of-silence have you broken?" She watched me. Curious. No criticism. It was as if I'd let her into my inner sanctum by sharing anything at all. She knew I didn't betray client confidences.

"Technically, nothing. Confirming a suspicion that vampires might have been involved is probably stretching things. But I trust you. And by law, I'm required to divulge certain facts. My clients always sign contracts acknowledging that."

"But you didn't tell the F.B.I.?"

"No. I'm not required to tell them."

"Tricky. So you accept my offer for drinks and get yourself off the hook at the same time." She started to frown.

"No! I don't have anything concrete yet. I'm not required to tell anyone anything until I do. But we're friends. So I told you even before confirmation. Just so it doesn't bite you on the ass."

That seemed to reassure her. She smiled and waved down Jimmy. "Another round please."

"The shot as well?"

"Make it two."

Jimmy glanced at me and I shrugged. He trotted off, placing the order with Bryce. I watched as the handsome bartender smiled and flirted with the smaller man. They were in an on-again phase. I was glad. I liked them both. Together they were sweet and almost innocent. I could use some innocence.

Beverly and I sat in silence, then. Thinking about things until Jimmy brought the drinks. He set them down, eyeing the second shot with disapproval. When I didn't touch it, he strolled off to another table.

"You know I don't drink tequila. Ever."

"Who said it was for you?" Beverly slammed the shot closest to her. Then she picked up the second one and downed it. Taking a deep breath of satisfaction, she put both elbows on the table to lean in. "Alright. I can't help you with Chandler. Asking around's not gonna be possible." She eyed the file meaningfully. "What you have there is it. Why he's in the States or dealing with Gibraltar could be any one of a dozen things. International threats. International terrorism. International espionage."

"I get it. Anything Gibraltar's company might be doing that could affect the U.K." I finished off my first Malibu and Coke and began working on the second. A thought popped into my head. A long shot, considering how much time had passed. "Could MI-6 be keeping tabs on an English vampire?"

Beverly put her Midori Sour down. "The Rake of the Atlantic Street Revenants?"

I watched her reaction keenly. She knew something. "That's the one."

"We keep tabs on them. We know he supplanted the previous Rake." Her eyes widened. "Who now works for Gibraltar as personal security." She played with her glass, watching my lips. "He wasn't involved with keeping the kid safe was he?"

"No. Just the old man." I felt silly referring to Henry Gibraltar as the old man when I was about ten years his elder.

"MI-6 deals with preternaturals the way we do. Tracks their movements. But the Rake—what's his name again?"

"Chilton."

"Right. Chilton's been here a long-ass time for MI-6 to still be on him."

"Vampires play the long game. They live a long time." I didn't have a point. Only reminding Beverly that keeping an eye on Chilton this long might be relatively nothing to the vampire.

"That actually may be reassuring."

"How so?"

"Director Goldberg might not have passed on these cases for Gibraltar. He might've done it for MI-6. They'd have informed us of any long-term operations in the States. Not for just anyone to see. Top level eyes-only kind of clearance."

"Which you don't have."

"Not yet. One promotion away." She raised her glass as if to toast. "Which is why I needed to know if asking about Chandler was going to bite me in the ass. Guess I can honestly say more about the anonymous call when I write up the report tomorrow."

"You complained that I'd only talk about work once we started. But I have a sort of personal question."

Beverly frowned and took a swig of Midori. "Now why don't I believe you?"

"That I have a question?"

"That it's personal." She chuckled wryly. "Does Bianca Savage have a personal life?"

"It is. And maybe I don't. But—are there any new succubi registered in Los Angeles County?"

"I'm on the to-be-notified list. Don't you think I'd have said?"

"Just checking." It was my turn to frown and take a sip.

"Why?"

I shrugged. No sense in keeping anything from her. She'd know about it eventually. And we were friends apparently. Better ones that I'd thought before tonight. That made me happy. I wanted to keep at least one person in that category. "Someone was watching my office from across the street. We caught her on surveillance. Hoodie and sunglasses. Too warm for the hoodie. Great way to keep skin from touching or being touched."

Beverly sat up, alert despite the hint of glaze in her eyes. "Checking out the competition?"

"I dunno. Thought maybe it was someone with some answers."

She shook her head. "You're one of three registered succubi in the entire United States. Living ones."

My voice came out unexpectedly bitter. "How many have you executed again?"

"I didn't execute any." She looked unhappy.

"Sorry. I'm not trying to be an ass. Eight of us have registered since the law went into effect. And five have been killed not long after. Wasn't sure if the numbers had changed."

She eyed me uncertainly. My apology hadn't been enough. "Two weren't killed by law enforcement."

"Doesn't make it better. Okay. Maybe a little better. And yeah, I know. The three executed had all killed people." I touched Beverly's hand with my gloved fingers. "I understand why they were killed. Raised without mothers the way I was. I had Granny Oglethorpe to thank for being a good girl."

"That's not true. Marcy Mason as she called herself was a spree killer. Raised by a mother we still haven't caught. Marcy only registered just to learn how the system worked."

"I read the reports. Only no one understood why she went off the deep-end after bothering to register. She could've slipped away. Moved to another state. Another country. But instead she chose to kill everyone at the Georgia Preternatural Confines. Other preternaturals as well."

"It was a suicide-by-cop kind of deal." She didn't look certain.

"No. No, she killed everyone within a quarter mile of her. I think she expected to get away. The fact that she didn't doesn't explain her motive."

I smiled and shook my head. Beverly and I both liked solving mysteries. We also liked to argue cases. As much as she'd implied that our disagreement was all my fault, I knew better.

"Homegrown preternatural terrorist, Bee. If the boy next door can turn to evil like that, why not someone already on the fringes?"

"I don't like it. Doesn't make sense to me."

She laughed, no longer sad or hurt at my earlier snipe "That's because you're clever. And you don't think like a terrorist."

"Why doesn't that sound entirely like a compliment?"

"Because you're looking to be contrary. You have eaten recently haven't you?"

"Of course." But she was right. I'd been on edge the entire time we'd been in the bar. Usually I could repress my hunger without too much effort. I'd spent more than seventy years practicing. On the other hand, I'd never fasted this long before.

"How's Janet?" Beverly kept her gaze focused on my sunglasses. Possibly considering her reflection in their dark surfaces.

She'd changed the subject so drastically that I blinked. "Did she call you by any chance?"

"No. Should she have?"

"No. Just curious."

We watched each other in comfortable silence. I enjoyed my drink, catching Jimmy taking a phone number from a muscular man in a button-up shirt while the man's female companion had gone to the bathroom. He must've felt someone watching because he glanced at Bryce. The bartender was busy waiting on a trio of coeds. I looked away before he knew it was me.

"Say, Bev, you have any idea what a feral-game hunter is?"

She eyed me, like she thought I was joking. Took another swig of her drink.

I set my glass down. "What? Why are you looking at me like that?"

"You get your hands on some outdated C.I.A. files or something?" She continued to watch me carefully. Wearing a mask. The question had triggered something. She was in law-enforcement suspicion mode.

I shrugged. "No. The phrase came up in research."

"Don't make me pull teeth, Bee. What kind of research?"

I took a breath. Held it before speaking. "On my father."

She seemed surprised and chugged down the last of her drink. Sucking in air afterwards. She reminded me of some men I'd known. Occupational hazard when doing a job traditionally filled by alpha-type males.

"Bee, a feral-game hunter hunts preternaturals. Werewolves mostly. Before they had any legal protections. Specially trained operatives."

"Trained by who?"

"Us." She did a little circle of her hand, index finger pointing upward.

"America?"

"MI-8."

I frowned. "England? I'm confused."

"No. MI-8 was ours. U.S. Military Intelligence. Part of the army established around 1917, if memory serves."

I leaned back, astonished. "My father was in the army? Trained to kill werewolves?"

"If he was a feral-game hunter. Which, like I said, was code for the division that went after preternaturals. Yeah."

"Did they hunt succubi, too?"

Beverly frowned. "They did. Still do."

"So my mother could've raped my father and killed him to conceive me because he was hunting her."

"Bee! You're only guessing." She searched my expression. Worried. All the women in my life worried about me. That's why they were my friends. Even if I wasn't a good one in return. "You were born in Canada. There were werewolf troubles in the late 1930s. He was probably one of the operatives sent there to track them down. Maybe he met your mother and fell in love."

"Fell in love on a werewolf hunt? I know I can be a romantic at times, but I'm not a fool." My stomach felt cold. But not from hunger. An emptiness that was pure self-loathing tried to take hold.

Beverly's tone grew urgent with sympathy. "Let me look into it for you. What's his name?"

"According to the information I have, he's Perry Davidson. Only, it makes no sense. How could anyone have done a blood DNA comparison on him? He was dead before DNA was a thing."

"DNA testing wasn't around. But blood tests were. For lycanthropy. Vampirism."

"What are you saying? There was a stash of his blood somewhere?"

"Since meeting you, I've taken time to read into all the old stuff about preternaturals. More than the job requires. Feral-game hunters had blood drawn each time they went out in the field. Retested when they came back. It's not impossible that some blood survived."

I stared at her, mistrusting my emotions at the moment. "Can you find out for sure? Not having family was bad. But believing the wrong man's my dad would be worse. That he was seduced, raped and drained by my mother is something I came to terms with a long time ago."

"I'll make it a priority first thing tomorrow."

I smiled at her, appreciatively. "I think I need another drink."

"If only to make me feel better." Beverly laughed ruefully. "I'd be happier if you could get drunk."

I glanced around at all the men in the bar. Many on dates or with friends. Full of energy. A wall of testosterone always held at bay by sheer discipline. Discipline that would go out the window if I was intoxicated.

I shook my head. "No. No, you really wouldn't."

CHAPTER TWENTY

I saw Beverly safely off in an Uber an hour and four drinks later. It wasn't as late as I'd expected. Only because she'd been drinking especially hard. A rare night of cutting loose. Or so she kept saying. It was an excuse when she didn't need one. Not with me. I knew she didn't drink alone or at home. Not the way an alcoholic did.

I was one of the few friends she had that wasn't work-related. Which meant she hadn't been drunk in months. I was someone safe to lose control with. And something was bothering her. Something big. But she was too professional to share. The kind of work we both did took its toll. Hers more than mine. I'd call her tomorrow when she was sober and remind her of that.

Tonight, I still had work to do. I scrolled through my phone and called the Atlantic Street Revenants hotline.

"Atlantic Street Revenants. How many I assist you?" The woman who answered was pleasant. Good phone voice.

"Bianca Savage. I need to see Chilton tonight."

She grew cool. Aloof. Angry. "I'm not sure our Rake has time for you, Miss Savage. What's the nature of your business?"

"If I don't see him tonight, I'll make sure that the C.I.A. hauls the entire coven in for failing to cooperate with law enforcement representatives." It was an exaggeration. Beverly might be willing to stretch the law for me. But technically I was only a private eye. Emphasis on 'private.'

"Very well. Let me check his calendar." She was even more pissed at me for threatening the coven. Not too angry to schedule a meeting with Chilton. Apparently I'd done something wrong since I'd met them. I didn't ask what. That would come from higher up.

She came back, her voice clipped. "Shoreline Village in twenty. He'll find you." The phone went dead. I sighed. How to make friends and influence people. Even sober I wasn't very good at it.

Twenty minutes later I stood facing the ocean in Shoreline Village. Just south of Parkers' Lighthouse. Waiting for Chilton as instructed.

"Miss Savage."

I turned. The English Rake approached with a small entourage. At his right was a handsome black man in his thirties. Behind and to his left, Bonnie, the flat-chested read-head from the nightclub. Dressed more casually, she looked like she was twelve. Shorter than I realized. Freckles. Probably turned when she was barely legal. Before a final growth spurt.

No sign of Dusty. But Rhoda was there, pushing past the redhead. And pissed as hell. "What did you do to him!"

Chilton turned to Rhoda and she flinched, taking a step back. Her lips pressed together in silence. Against her will. Not vampire magics. Just ordinary fear.

"Where's Dusty?" I was disappointed the young vampire wasn't there. We needed to have a talk. Cut off any budding infatuation before it got started.

Chilton's expression tightened. He was better at suppressing his anger than Rhoda. But not completely. Good to know, in case I ever needed to see if he was telling the truth.

"We'll talk in a moment, Miss Savage." He put a finger up to his lips. Motioned the black man forward.

The dark man's hair was covered by a cowboy hat. He wore snug fitting Wrangler jeans tucked into burgundy cowboy boots and a white button-up dress shirt. His features were model pretty, except for the masculine set of his jaw. His full lips were soft and the lower one caught on his vampire teeth.

The intelligence in his eyes was hard. Like he would do whatever was necessary in any given situation. Not dangerous. Just practical. I'd seen the same look in my own eyes.

I let him approach and he withdrew a small wand-like device. "Evening, Ma'am."

"Evening, Sir." I matched his level of politeness word for word. Not giving away to any potential eavesdroppers that he was checking me for bugs.

When the wand reached my beret it lighted up. No auditory signal. That made sense. Why let the listeners know they've been found out.

He turned back to Chilton. The Rake gave a curt nod and the man took out another device. I thought it was a garage remote-control. I felt the charge of magnetic particles brush across my succubus senses.

How had Amperdyne gotten their hands on my beret? The same way they'd bugged my boots. Probably after the sniper attack. It was the one article of clothing I hadn't checked.

My heart began racing as I recalled the evening. What had I said in the privacy of my office that I wouldn't want anyone to know? Or in my conversation with Beverly? Personal stuff about my father. Public details on succubi and my suspicions about Vincent's kidnapping. The business with the goats. That was all, right?

I'd have to think about it. I needed to know how much leverage I'd given Amperdyne before I confronted them again.

"It's done." He smiled then, his eyes still wary. "The name's Maverick."

"As in James Garner?"

He bobbed his head. "I was an extra on a couple of episodes. Ol' Jimmy caught me doing an impersonation of him. Liked it so much he started calling me 'Maverick' instead of my real name. Kept it ever since."

"Bianca Savage. A pleasure to meet you, Maverick."

He smiled that I'd bothered to introduce myself. They all knew who I was. But Granny Oglethorpe had stressed manners. She'd been right about most things. This was definitely one of them.

"We figured the Company would be keeping an eye on you. This place is too loud for a directional microphone and too public for any shenanigans."

I raised a brow at Maverick playfully. "Do people still say shenanigans?"

"I do."

He stepped aside as Chilton approached me. The Rake leaned against the rail facing the water. Avoiding my gaze. "I'm aware that Dusty sent you a gift."

"Is that a problem?"

"Before that kiss, Dusty was courting Rhoda. Slowly, perhaps. Awkwardly. He'd been turned as a virgin. Inexperienced with women even at his less tender age. A rarity in the twenty-first century, don't you think?"

"Not really. You'd be surprised at how divided the current population is between being promiscuous little tramps and shy innocents."

I used Jimmy's phrase because he was the person I pictured representing the group who engaged in casual sex. He wasn't ashamed, so there was no offense in it. Bryce wasn't shy or innocent. Just monogamous. Vincent Gibraltar, whom I'd never met except in the video footage I'd seen of him, represented the innocent.

Chilton's voice was unhappy. "What did you do to him?"

"Nothing."

"Lies." He stood up angrily. "If you refuse to communicate openly and honestly with me, there's no point in this meeting."

"I'm not lying. I kissed him. He shielded my power. All of your people did." I looked at him and swallowed my pride. "I forgot to thank you for that. It was appreciated."

He refused to meet my gaze. Before, it had been a challenge he knew he could win. Now, after Dusty's reaction to me, he was afraid. "You did something. He's changed."

"Everyone there got a dose of my hunger. Anyone else feel different about me?"

He frowned and stared at the waves catching light from the street. "No. But none of us kissed you, either."

"I admit that I've never kissed a vampire before. But trust me, my kiss has no special power that any skin on skin touching doesn't have."

It hadn't been just skin on skin, though, had it? I suddenly had an inkling about what might've happened. Dusty had tasted a few drops of my blood. I didn't understand how that would've made him susceptible to my charms. But there wasn't any other answer. Not something I was going to share with the Rake.

Chilton wasn't buying it. "While you're a beautiful woman, I truly doubt Dusty was swayed by ordinary means."

"Such a charmer." I frowned and he finally glanced at me. "If I'd kissed a human, used my powers on him, the effect would've either killed him or worn off after a few hours. Obsession only kicks in with prolonged and repeated exposure to my eyes. Dusty's admiration doesn't fit any of that criteria."

"I've read the literature. But it also says vampires are immune to your hunger. Your seduction. Dusty wasn't. Isn't."

I shrugged. Dusty had paused after my kiss. After swallowing my blood. It was possible he was more than infatuated. "Give it a couple of days. If it hasn't gone away, I'll see what I can find out about this."

"I do not like my people being manipulated. He and Rhoda put themselves at risk to get you to our first meeting safely."

"I don't manipulate people, Chilton. I certainly didn't intend to affect Dusty, if I did." I glanced over at Rhoda. "Are you sure he wasn't just impressed by the unexpectedness of the kiss?"

"No!" Rhoda heard. She couldn't keep quiet. "He loves me!"

"Calm down, Child. It was only a question." I looked back at Chilton. "We'll figure it out. I give my word, I don't know what happened. And whatever it was, if anything, was accidental."

He looked up at the sky. Still plenty of hours of dark left. "For now that will have to suffice. I need you to find Vincent and vindicate my people. What do you want from me?"

"Did you hear about what happened today?"

"Today?" He turned but avoided my eyes. "Has the boy been found?"

"No. Anton Thrace was kidnapped in broad daylight."

He laughed bitterly. "Then you know we had nothing to do with it."

"I only know that your coven didn't do it personally. What can you tell me about it?"

"Nothing! This is the first I've heard of the matter." He glared bitterly at my lips. "And who would tell us? Not Gibraltar. Not Joseph. Definitely not the Company."

Plausible. The vampires were suspects. No one in law enforcement would share that news with them unless they were being interrogated. "Can you think of a motive for taking Vincent and Thrace?"

"Anton was friendly and polite. Not what I'd call an alpha. But maybe that was just because he likes men. The only enemy that I know of was his pack. That's why he left them. Started working for Gibraltar."

"You seem to know a lot more than I expected."

Chilton continued to frown. "I learn as much as possible about my associations."

"What did you do for Gibraltar? He said it wasn't illegal. But if it wasn't, then what?"

"No, no, Miss Savage. If Henry won't tell you, I certainly won't."

"You still hope to get the security contract."

The Rake let a grim smile touch his lips and he bowed his head in acknowledgment. "Which is why we wouldn't risk touching the boy. Henry Gibraltar might be forced to give up Amperdyne for failing to keep his family safe. But he'd never trust us if we had any involvement. We could never force him to take us in their place."

I stared out at the ocean. The English vampire was making too much sense. From what I'd seen, a single whiff of their complicity in the kidnapping and Gibraltar would do anything to keep from rewarding them. Amperdyne didn't benefit either. The kidnapping made them look weak. Incompetent. Who the blazes did that leave?

I turned to look at Chilton but the Rake was gone. All of the vampires had vanished. Not preternaturally fast. Just silent. Lost in the crowd. Amid unsuspecting humans enjoying the seaside before drifting off to bars or home.

I decided home was my choice. I'd done all I could tonight. I'd managed to logically eliminate all the suspects I had. Tomorrow, I got to start all over. Happy happy, joy joy.

CHAPTER TWENTY-ONE

My meeting with Maureen Edwards was masked as a general interview of Gibraltar employees. The cover-story was that I'd come to clear disgruntled workers as suspects. Anyone who might have wanted to hurt the old man. It was a waste of time but Amperdyne was calling the shots on discretion.

"Thank you for speaking with me, Mr. Carrasco. Please send in the next person."

I glanced at the clock. Blake had insisted on setting the order of the employees and I'd already been at it for three hours. So far, no Maureen.

A tall, blonde woman entered and I sat up, alert. "And you are?"

"Donna Doyle. Should I stand or—?"

"No. Please, sit." I leaned back again, disappointed. One more charade to make my way through. "I'm asking all the heads of departments about any potentially disgruntled employees."

"Oh, I knew there had to be a mistake!" She seemed relieved. "I'm the assistant department head. You want Maureen Edwards."

"I see. Easy mistake to make. Is she available?"

"She was down in the servers trying to find a faulty drive. I can try to find her."

"Please do. Send in the next person in the meantime?"

I wanted to tell her that I'd wait. But that would be odd. Why wait on one woman when there were still several others to interview. I didn't even have the list in writing. Gibraltar was taking no chances.

"That'd be Pauly Jackson" She dashed out of the room relieved.

There was an explosion that shattered the door inward. I was knocked backwards. Splinters struck my left side. Blood trickled down my arm. Along my cheek. I crawled close to the back of the desk. Drew my 9mm and held it against my leg. Waiting to see who came through the opening left by the bomb.

There were screams and moaning. Someone called out a name. "Donna!"

I peered over the desk. Struggled to see through the quickly dissipating smoke. Amperdyne security agents appeared with weapons drawn.

A tall, lanky man in black called into the office. "Miss Savage?"

"Yes."

"Stay where you! We're clearing the room for additional explosives."

I didn't argue. I could survive a lot. A bomb wasn't one of them. Someone had tried to kill me. "What happened to Donna? Donna Doyle?"

"Epicenter. Cameras caught the whole thing before the blast shorted them."

I frowned. Donna had been carrying the bomb. But she'd left the office as quickly as possible. Guilt or fear. Most department heads only got called in when they'd done something wrong. If she knew she was carrying the bomb, she'd have left it. Probably at her feet when she sat down. Before rushing out.

She'd taken it out with her. Which meant she hadn't known. Someone else had used her to try to kill me. Another innocent victim.

"Clear!" called the tall man. "We've swept for additional devices."

I stood cautiously. "How many dead?"

"Six." He sounded grim. "Another mark against the Company. Someone wants to end our relationship with Gibraltar Global badly."

"I'm not sure which of us is more important."

"Pardon?" he blinked at me, confused.

"I think the bomb was meant for me. Any problems it creates for you are just secondary."

He frowned, shaking his head. He didn't agree. I didn't think he would. But he kept silent. Most people didn't consider me that much of a threat. They were wrong. And apparently, someone else knew it.

I heard sirens through the ringing in my ears. Emergency service crews on their way. I sat on the edge of the desk. Unwilling to look at the mess that had been Donna Doyle. Waiting while Amperdyne agents stood guard over the crime scene. Making me feel like a prisoner. I suspected that I was. After a fashion.

E.M.T.s arrived in record time. Already in the area, probably. Pure luck. Several of them took care of the Gibraltar employees. One of the Amperdyne ninjas ushered in a female E.M.T. who immediately began fussing over me. Blake Mansfield rushed into the room. Pale. Hand to his mouth. Not happy to have seen the carnage outside. Glad I'd passed on it.

Mansfield stayed silent. Maybe he thought speaking would cause him to vomit. Watching the E.M.T. pull out tweezers and go to work on my pale skin was more relaxing. A distraction he needed.

A few minutes later, the E.M.T. finished wriggling the last splinter out of my face. She carefully wiped away my blood with a disposable cloth. I studied her. Annoyed at her caution.

She was mid-forties. Square but not stocky. Round face framed by curly black hair. A surgical mask protected her mouth. Wide safety glasses kept particles out of her pale brown eyes. Latex gloves kept her from accidentally make skin on skin contact.

Her name tag just had one name. Yvette. Not standard. Should've been a first initial and last name. But after Chilton and Joseph, a single name was becoming commonplace to me.

I started to tell her my blood was safe. But then I thought about Dusty. She couldn't catch any diseases from me. If I'd had any. Now I wasn't so sure about the impact of my blood on her mental state.

"Do you heal normally?"

I stared at her, confused. "Oh, you mean like a human. Yes. No hyper-fast metabolism like a werewolf."

"I could put tiny bandages on every wound but—?"

"I'd look like a patchwork doll. No, just the ones that are likely to keep bleeding. Please."

She resumed working on me. I bothered to glare at Mansfield. I needed a distraction from being tended to. Perceived as weak. I felt self-conscious. I hated that. "Stop staring."

"Security said you think the bomb was for you. Why? Do you know who took Vincent?"

I glanced at the E.M.T. "We should probably wait to have this discussion."

He paced, unable to keep himself still. "Amperdyne said the explosive was untraceable."

"I heard him fire four people on the way up here. Am I gonna be in trouble he didn't listen?" The E.M.T. glanced up from her bag. She focused on my glasses even though she couldn't see my eyes. Her expression was amused. Worried. Amused that Mansfield couldn't wait. Worried that she'd be burned just for being present.

"That'll be public info once the police finish their investigation. You're safe." I smiled at her and she nodded, placing another tiny surgical band-aid into place with deft, gloved fingers. "What I'm curious about is how the explosive made it inside the building. I was scanned when I entered. Is there anyone who isn't?"

He shook his head, staring at the dark-haired E.M.T. As if suddenly realizing she was there. "How much longer, Nurse?"

I answered before she could. "She's an E.M.T., not a nurse."

"What's the difference?" he demanded.

"A huge student loan debt which I'm glad not to have." Yvette stared at me, challenging me to say something else on her behalf.

I shrugged and nodded. She was right. It was her right to speak out. There was a fine line between protecting someone and treating them as weak. I must've been more shaken up than I realized. I didn't usually make that mistake.

She stood. "I'm done."

"Thank you, Yvette." I took the red stained cloth she offered. to pat at the remaining dots of blood on my skin. "Mr. Mansfield, shall we find a less damaged office to continue our conversation?"

He grunted and moved toward out into the hall. I started to follow when my phone rang. I raised a finger to him.

"Janet?"

"Bee, you need to get down to the office. I think we have a problem?"

I gave Mansfield a look. "I'm in the middle of something. How urgent is it?"

"The Rodríguezes are here."

I couldn't hide my confusion. "Why?"

"I don't know. But they seem terrified. Definitely upset."

Shit. "Fine. I'll wrap up here and head back."

I walked briskly to where Blake stood. He held another door open for me. I didn't fret about equal rights over courtesy. Men held doors open for each other half the time. It was about power. He had the power to decide where we talked. I understood the psychology of it all too well.

We were barely inside when he repeated his question. "Why you, Miss Savage?"

"Because I must be getting close."

His expression grew intense. "You know how the vampires did it?"

I frowned. Last night I'd eliminated all my current suspects. Definitely not getting closer. "No. In fact, I don't think they had anything to do with this."

"It had to be them! There isn't anyone else."

"You mean because there's been no ransom."

Mansfield played with his lapel unhappily. "The F.B.I. said no ransom demands means he's probably dead."

"That makes no sense. If whoever took him just wanted him dead, they could've bombed his room. An E.M.P. and an explosive device are about the same size."

He stared at me. Confused. Anxious. "Then, again I ask. Why bomb you?"

"Maybe someone saw me talking to the C.I.A."

I also considered Rhoda. She'd threatened me. But this attack had happened in the daytime. Not to mention that vampires weren't known for using technology to kill people.

"You spoke to the C.I.A.!?" Mansfield's eyes went so wide that he reminded me of a frenzied stallion. A shared characteristic between grandfather and grandson.

"She was a friend. I didn't divulge information. I only asked about some personal things. Ask Amperdyne. They had me bugged at the time."

He calmed down but his eyes were still wide. Afraid. He lacked any confidence. "How do you know they bugged you?"

"I found it." They'd told me about my shoes. They hadn't bothered to mention the beret. I didn't blame them. I'd want to know what my competition was up to if I weren't so scrupulous.

"I'll look into it. What about Maureen? I don't think it's a good idea to talk to her today. Not after this."

"No. You're probably right. And I have another matter to deal with. Although why—never mind. But I should be going." I avoided looking at the splattered body parts as I moved down the hall. Mansfield followed. "Set up another reason for me to be in the building. I'll wander around and find Maureen myself. Don't tell anyone why I'm coming. Someone knew I was here. Knew I was asking questions."

"What are you suggesting?"

"An inside man. Or woman. Get Amperdyne to figure out how they brought the explosive in. We're working together."

He frowned again. "If it's not too late."

"It's not vampires. At least, not Chilton's people. They don't have the motive. Not a smart one. We're missing something. And that's probably because I let everyone direct me toward the undead."

"It has to be them? They have a great motive!"

"No, Blake. They don't. Think about it. Your grandfather's a hardass. Would he hire anyone he even suspected had interfered with his family? Tried to force him to hire them?"

"No." Mansfield suddenly seemed to understand. I could practically see the lightbulb over his head. "He'd look for ways to destroy them."

I nodded. A bit more extreme than I was thinking. But good to know. "We've got to have faith that Vincent's still alive and well. Today isn't over. Not yet. Now, schedule me for tomorrow. Early. I'll keep following up on my leads."

"Paul said I should trust you. That you're that good." The attorney seemed impressed by that fact.

The non-sequitur took me a moment to process. Paul? Oh. Chandler. "He say anything else?"

"Yeah, but I don't think you'll like it."

I paused to stare at him. "Let's have it."

"He said you might be more woman than he can handle."

I cocked my head to the side. "Can or could?"

"What?"

"Did he say 'can handle' or 'could handle?'"

Mansfield searched his memory. "Oh. 'Could,' I guess."

"High praise indeed." I smiled and strode to the end of the hall. He didn't follow. I'd confused him too much.

Blake finally called to me as I reached the elevator doors "Wait, what's the difference?"

"One suggests he already thinks he owns me."

"The other?"

"That he might like to get to know me better."

The elevator arrived. I stepped inside, turning to face Mansfield as I pressed the lobby button. I smiled at the man as the door closed. More delighted by his confusion than the fact that an MI-6 operative might fancy me.

Even with that protective totem, dating a human could only lead to trouble. Dating someone in an intelligence agency, that was worse.

CHAPTER TWENTY-TWO

Janet was fretting, waiting in front of my office building when I arrived. My hand went for my Glock automatically. "What's wrong, Janet?"

"Mrs. Rodriguez broke down into tears twice rambling in Spanish. They're terrified. I couldn't sit there listening anymore." She took a moment to see all the bandages on my face. Along my exposed arm. "What happened to you?"

"Nothing." I didn't want to add to her anxiety. "And that's got you all up in a tizzy?"

She stared at the injuries for several hard seconds before finally deciding that they weren't the priority. "Did you do something to the boy?"

I blinked. Then laughed. "What's wrong with you? You were here the whole time. I was on my best behavior."

"Then why do they act like you've done something awful?"

I frowned. The Rodríguezes weren't technically friends. More like close acquaintances. I thought they liked me. Trusted me. Despite the horns.

They were waiting for me in my office when I entered. The wife was sitting. The husband paced back and forth. They moved closer together like a choreographed dance at seeing me.

Seraphina practically sobbed as she pleaded with me. "Please, Miss Bianca, don't take my boy."

I froze, glancing back through the office door. Janet watched me. Disapprovingly. Like I'd lied. I was hurt and not in the mood.

"What is wrong with everyone today? Why would you think I'd hurt Luis, Seraphina?"

"He's still just a boy. Not a man. Please, no take him!"

Pablo hugged his wife to his side. He wasn't crying. Only trembling with fear. Anger lurked under that fear. "I punish him. Whatever he done! Don't kill him."

I opened my mouth to say something scathing. Then closed it again. I took a breath and counted to three before responding. No sense in letting a near death experience make me nasty towards them. "I'm not planning on killing, Luis. Or hurting him. Why would you think such a thing?"

Seraphina's arms reached out to me from a distance, clutching at the air as if beseeching me to stop. "He say you ask him to come. He ascared at dinner last night. Juana say he in trouble with you."

"I made a business deal with him. That's all. I need goats. He's going to provide them."

Pablo nodded violently. Refusing to look higher than my waist. "I bring you goats. Many many goats! As many as you like!"

"You're not hearing me." I spoke slowly, like Chris Tucker in *Rush Hour*. Maybe it was a little derisive, but better than yelling at them. "I'm not angry at Luis. I'm not going to hurt him."

Seraphina half-stood, then dropped back down. Dragged into Pablo's embrace even tighter by his strong arms. "But Juana say he do something bad. I know you punish people who are bad. My boy, he no bad."

"I had a talk with Luis, yes. But listen to me!" I practically shouted and Seraphina whimpered in response. I gentled my voice. "Sorry. But please. Listen. I would never hurt your children."

"You no threaten Luis?" asked Pablo with a hard swallow. A father wanting to protect his child.

"Well, I might've threatened him a little. But I didn't threaten to kill him."

They stared at me like lost sheep. I sighed, avoiding another glance at Janet. I could already feel her mood across the room.

"Look, I just asked him to treat women with respect. Is that any different from what you teach him?"

"N—no," stammered the mother.

"And honestly, I'm not mad at him. I don't plan on hurting him. I just wanted him to take me seriously."

Pablo glanced from Seraphina to my lips with hope. "You no kill our boy? You swear?"

"I don't swear. But I give my word." I sat in my chair hard. Sagged with an emptiness I hadn't felt in a long time. "I only wanted him to be respectful to his family."

"He is! He very respectful!" Pablo nodded his head so hard I worried he might have an aneurism.

"Then he's safe. We're all friends here. I've watched your children grow up for years. Why would you think I'd suddenly want to hurt them?"

Pablo didn't respond. Seraphina was taking huge gulps of air. Trying to regain her composure. Finally she answered with trepidation. "Because he no more a child. I think he not a man. He my baby always. But he a man."

I frowned. Uncertain what she meant. "So?"

"In Mexico, we hear of a Devil-woman like you. She take the eldest *hijo* of each family and—it is the death sex."

"Why did people let her do this?" I ignored the Devil-woman comment. They were scared. Maybe that's even how they really thought of me, deep down. But they'd treated me like it wasn't. I was willing to forgive the moment.

Pablo answered. Squeezing his wife's shoulders as she clung to his wrist. "She protect them from *banditos*. Drug runners. The government."

"All in exchange for their young men?" I grew angry. Not at them. Maybe a little. For being weak. Letting any creature prey on their children. It was offensive to me. "I'd have killed her and dealt with the other problems as they came up."

"You kill your own kind?" Seraphina made the sign of the cross.

"I'd want anyone evil punished. Taking your young men is evil. I would never take Luis from you."

"You hear her. She give her word." Seraphina was pleading to someone in the doorframe. I glanced over, expecting it to be Janet. It was F.B.I. agent Olivia Wisniewski. Badge visible in one hand.

"I did." Wisniewski eyed me suspiciously.

"And I keep my word. So, Pablo, Seraphina, please. Go home. Relax. This was all just a misunderstanding."

With a witness in the room, Pablo gained courage to press me. "We tell Luis he safe?"

I wanted to state a condition. That as long as he treated women, including his sister and mother with respect, he was safe. But it would only confirm that I'd threatened him. Not to kill him. Just enough to scare. In front of the F.B.I. Not a good idea.

"Tell him I'm pleased with his help. That should reassure him."

The Rodríguezes clung to each other as they left. Another relationship with me broken. Janet's I-told-you-so expression wasn't even necessary this time.

"Agent Wisniewski, what can I do for you?"

"Should I know something?" She eyed the fleeing couple meaningfully.

"I was trying to help their son stay on the straight and narrow. I might've overplayed my hand."

She took a seat opposite me and smiled. "It's rare that I meet someone capable of admitting their mistakes. At least, without evidence to shake in their face."

"I believe in the truth. Besides, if I own my mistakes, I can own learning from them."

"Whatever. I wanted to follow-up on our conversation with Mr. Gibraltar. Did you overplay your hand with him, too?"

I stared at the woman. "What do you mean?"

"He seemed pretty scared of you. Kept repeating how you had his complete cooperation."

I laughed. Bitterly. I'd been tired when I'd come into the office. I was exhausted after that emotional confrontation with Pablo and Seraphina. I'd honestly liked them. My request for an invitation to

Juana's *quinceañera* had been sincere. Guess I wasn't going to scratch that off my bucket list.

"Look, Wisniewski, I don't know why he'd be afraid. I told him that I didn't stand much chance of finding Vincent without his cooperation. Hardly an intimidation."

She considered my answer. "Maybe it was his way of saying talk to you?"

"Nice try. But anything he wanted you to know, he'd have said."

She nodded and took a moment to look at the minimal decorations in my office. Finally she came across the picture of Martini I had framed on the desk.

"Snow Bengal?"

I nodded. Surprised. "Seal lynx. You know your cats."

"I'm allergic as hell. But I can't resist 'em." Her focus shifted back to me. "I know you think that if you work with me, I'll take all the credit and leave you in the dark. But a boy's life is at stake."

"Absolutely. I'd never leave out anything or do anything that might keep us from bringing him home alive."

She tapped a finger on her badge. Thinking. "What am I missing here? Why the preternatural diversity fest?"

"I don't follow."

She settled into the comfortable chair. Smiling despite herself. "Fine. Let's make it simple. Start at the beginning and work forwards. Why hire you to help find Vincent?"

I pursed my lips together. "You're in confidentiality territory."

"Nothing at all?"

I leaned forward. "Fine. I'm a good P.I. I admit, I wondered why the overkill. F.B.I. Police. Amperdyne security doing their own investigation."

"And?"

She was law enforcement. Withholding information on the case could cost me my license. Even though I'd discounted the Atlantic Street Revenants from my list of suspects, nothing was certain. I'd been forbidden from mentioning them unless I had proof. I didn't.

"As a succubus, I have certain abilities. Immunities. Things that might be useful."

"You mean the werewolf couldn't hurt you?"

"Of all the preternaturals I've encountered, I suspect a werewolf is one of the most dangerous. Maybe I can't be infected, but I can be torn apart by claws and fangs. They can definitely hurt me."

"You're trying to be helpful. Okay, I can play the game. If not a werewolf, something else preternatural? Another succubus?" I sighed and she laughed. "I was kidding. I know you met with the Atlantic Street Revenants last night."

"How?"

"A tail. Two plainclothes agents."

I didn't smile. "You have a warrant for that?"

"Preternatural Act doesn't require a warrant for public surveillance. Why, you have something to hide?"

"Like most Americans, I value my privacy." I felt a tingle of pride as I said 'American.' Earning citizenship had been hard. Knowing I belonged by birth felt empowering.

Wisniewski took my silence as confirmation. "So the vampires are involved somehow."

"That much I can respond to. No. At least, I don't think so. They don't have a motive."

"I wouldn't think so. If they have the boy, automatic daylight savings for the whole coven."

"Daylight savings?"

"Daylight saves us the work of staking them." She smiled. I didn't. "Take the stick out of your ass, Savage. It was funny."

"If you say so."

"I'm trying here. Don't have to be a bitch about everything."

I bobbed my head, staring at the desk. Ran my fingers along the wood. Counting to three. Someday I'd have to count higher than I ever had. Not today.

"I'm preternatural, Olivia. When you suggest that killing preternaturals somehow serves society, just because they're preternatural? That doesn't take me to my happy place."

"Fine. You're right. Maybe we're both being bitches. Truce?"

"I thought we were on a truce."

"Okay. A better truce then?"

"I can try if you will."

We sat in silence again. I wished I had another bottle of that Moscato. I wanted the bubbles to tickle my palate. Give me a moment's respite from a really crappy day.

"How sure are you that the vampires aren't involved?"

"They've tried to cooperate. Amperdyne has checked them out and found nothing. And like I said, their motive doesn't exist. Just the opposite. They'd like a chance for legitimacy. Kidnapping isn't the way to start that."

"But they're why Gibraltar hired you at first?"

I shrugged but my eyes sparkled with the answer. I changed the subject. "What about Thrace? Any idea why he was taken?"

"There wasn't a ransom demand for the boy. Now the bodyguard? Amperdyne sucks as security so far. We'll probably find them both dead and dumped in the next few days. Someone wanting to intimidate Gibraltar. Or maybe hurt him."

I shrugged, a slight shake of my head revealing my opinion. "In fairness to Amperdyne, they weren't protecting Thrace. He was supposed to be protecting Gibraltar"

"Fair point. So let's keep going forwards. Gibraltar hires you because he thinks vampires might be involved. Don't worry. You didn't tell me. Confidentiality protected. But that makes total sense." She winked and I rolled my eyes. "What?"

"I'm maintaining my confidentiality. You discovered the vampire connection on your own. A wink sort of implies I broke my word to tell you something."

"Oh. Right. But you hinted that you were brought in because of preternaturals."

"That's a pretty generic fact."

Her expression soured as she realized the implication. "So you were only meant to keep which preternaturals a secret. If I hadn't had you followed, you wouldn't have mentioned them."

"Unless I found evidence pointing in their direction. Conjecture doesn't rise to the standard of reporting. I know the law, Wisniewski."

"Alright, alright. Back to the simplification. Why Anton Thrace? Why hire a dangerous monster?"

I glared at her. Ineffectual because of my glasses. I could've taken them off but I wasn't in the mood. Eventually she got the idea and waved her hands in the air. "Sorry. I've seen some brutal werewolf murders."

"Someone was murdering werewolves?" I asked blandly.

She opened her mouth to correct me then smirked. "Okay. I had that coming. You're smart and funny for a broad that never smiles."

"Broad?"

"Caught an old Mae West film last night before I fell asleep. Love her sass."

"Her what?"

Wisniewski frowned. "You heard what I said."

"I did. I love her sass as well. Admittedly, 'broad' implies strength and substance. Women have been called much worse."

"Back to the case?"

I gave her a look. "You brought up Mae West."

"For pity's sake, stop!"

I grinned. "Now I feel better. Back on point. He hired Thrace because he wanted someone who could survive an attack. Someone who'd be loyal to Gibraltar. Because Hank had been loyal to him."

"I read the report on Thrace. Gay. Kicked out of his pack. Dates casually. Never anything serious. And never near the full moon."

"All good monsters try to know their own weak points."

She glared at me. She thought I was fucking with her. "You just got mad when I said monster."

"I didn't mean it pejoratively. Besides, it's an ingroup thing."

She considered my words a moment. Finally shrugging without defensiveness. "You mean like gays can call each other 'fags' because they're gay."

"Aren't you enlightened. It's still derogatory. But the hate aspect is mitigated."

"That's right. You majored in psychology in college, didn't you." She eyed me shrewdly. "Wanted to better understand the humans you live beside?"

"I'll try not to take offense to that question." I glanced at the clock. "Can we speed this up? While I'm hopeful that Vincent's still alive, every day that passes without finding him lowers the odds."

"Any real suspects? Do you know anything that might help us help you find them?"

I hesitated. "You know someone tried to blow me up earlier."

She looked startled. "You were involved in that Gibraltar explosion?"

"I'm confident I was the target. It almost got me, too."

"Why?"

The same question Blake Mansfield had asked. I still didn't have an answer. I wasn't going to throw Rhoda under the bus no matter how much she hated me. Not without proof.

"I think someone knows I talked to the C.I.A. I mean, it's a guess. A stretch even. But it's the only thing I can think of."

"We got the report and I glanced it over. Amperdyne techs confirmed what our own people found. Generic gunpowder residue. Basically a homemade pipe bomb. Nothing to help us figure out who planted it."

I nodded. "And these days, anyone can find a video online on how to make a bomb."

"Exactly." Wisniewski frowned suspiciously. "Why'd you reach out to the C.I.A.?"

"It was a friend. Met her for drinks. Nothing about the case exactly."

"Exactly?"

"I wanted to make sure the Amperdyne information meshed up with what the C.I.A. had."

"Clever."

"Thanks. Look, your people have seen the same video footage I saw. An E.M.P. went off in the room and the boy disappeared with two Amperdyne guards. The E.M.P. package just appeared in the house. No one knows how it got in. The bomb at Gibraltar's building also got in without anyone knowing how."

"You're saying it was an inside job. The same people who kidnapped the kid and took the werewolf probably did the bombing."

"It'd be really strange if they weren't connected."

"One of Amperdyne's employees straying from the straight and narrow?"

"Maybe. Only, the motives are thin there, too. No ransom, so no financial benefit. Amperdyne pays their people incredibly well. They're gonna lose money if they have to cut ties and run. And Amperdyne will lose their contract with Gibraltar if the boy isn't found. More in the trickle down loss of confidence among other clients."

"So they suck as suspects. Unless it's not about money. What if the Company screwed over one of their people? And this is just old fashioned revenge."

"Maybe. Whoever it is, they don't have the guts to kill the boy. But the longer he's gone, the more damage to Amperdyne's reputation. Yeah, I could see it. It's weak, but it's possible."

"If you're such a great P.I., how is it that you've eliminated two groups of suspects without finding any new leads?" She eyed me, serious but playful, too. My professional ego could handle the hazing.

"Because I made the mistake of letting other people lead my investigation at the start. I was steered toward the vampires. I was steered toward Amperdyne employees."

"Who else could it be? A disgruntled Gibraltar Global employee? Would they have insider access?"

"To the building, sure. To his home? No. And yes, I'm still sure we have an insider doing this. That or as you said, Amperdyne security sucks. Which I doubt. Not as much tech as they employ."

"Or as much money as they make. Alright. We always consider an inside man. This time, we'll do more than consider. It should be easy to put together a list of all the people at the house and the offices. The overlap is our suspect."

"That assumes one suspect."

"It's a start. Thanks for the help."

"What, no information for me that I haven't already gathered on my own?"

She threw a piece of paper down on my desk. "I think someone wanted to know if Thrace's old pack might've been in town. This is where they live. A recent change out of Nevada. Three hours by car. A shorter hop by plane."

"You want me to go."

"Can't enter their territory without a warrant. You're a civilian."

I stared at her shrewdly. "You planned this from the start."

"What? Little old enlightened me?" She grinned and walked out the door.

I fought a smile. Annoyed that I was starting to like her. Not that I'd tell her that. The paper had a scribbled address. San Bernardino County. Joshua Tree, California. Hadn't been there before, but I'd always wanted to visit. Guess now was the time.

CHAPTER TWENTY-THREE

"Does Joshua Tree even have an airport?" I dropped the slip of paper Wisniewski had left me onto Janet's desk, exasperated.

Janet gave me the stink-eye as she checked into flights out of L.A.X. "As a matter of fact, no. United only has one flight this evening going anywhere near. Returning tomorrow morning. You'd have to fly into Palm Springs and then drive to Joshua Tree. You're only saving two hours by flying."

She showed me the online roundtrip cost and I winced. Between the airfare and car rental, it'd cost more than my entire spring wardrobe. Sure, I'd be reimbursed for my expenses. But I hated spending that much. I tended to conserve my client's costs as if they were my own.

"Two hours isn't worth giving up my guns. I'll drive it."

"You shouldn't be going alone."

I gave her a mocking smile. "What, you wanna come?"

"No I don't want to come. Who in their right mind would want to go to meet a bunch of werewolves?"

"I believe the correct term is a 'pack.'" I grinned and she swatted my sleeve. "Who'd you have in mind then, Janet?"

She rolled her eyes in frustration. "I don't know. Just someone."

"Don't worry, Mom, I'll be fine."

She wasn't smiling. "I'm not driving through the desert looking for your body if you don't come back."

"If I don't come back, take the petty cash and go have a few drinks in my honor. Invite Bob. He'll be thrilled."

"Bee! That's not funny."

"Apparently, I'm not nice to my friends. And I don't have a sense of humor. Anything else everyone has decided about me, before I leave?"

She grew sad. "Yes. You're wonderful and I'd be heartbroken if you died."

"Thanks, Janet. I'll try not to die." I used humor to avoid my own feelings.

Janet was more than a friend. She was family. Maybe not the blood kind. But I hadn't met any of those, so I had nothing better. And truthfully, Janet was like Granny Oglethorpe. More than I deserved. More than I ever dreamed I'd have. Better than blood.

"Do more than try."

I left the office and drove home. I didn't need to pack because I wouldn't be spending the night in Joshua Tree. But I had to make sure Martini had plenty of food. No. That was a lie. She had enough food to last three days. Perpetual water-dispenser and food-bowl. I just wanted to see her before I left. And maybe change clothes.

Meeting a pack of werewolves wasn't as simple as I'd made it sound to Janet. I was a preternatural. They'd treat me like one of their own invading. Probably. I was only guessing.

Each pack was different. Some tried to modernize. Some went rustic. End-of-days feral. I knew very little about Anton Thrace's former people. A location. No numbers. No names beyond those few connections from the facility he'd grow up in.

It was foolish not to wait until I had more. But Vincent really was running out of time. I'd wasted too much already being led around by the nose.

I did my usual surveillance of the condo complex as I approached. Drove around the block once to see if any cowled women were watching. No-one stood out. Nothing amiss. No tell-tale reflections from the building across the street. Not that Amperdyne snipers would use reflective surfaces. Still, it made me feel better checking.

I pulled slowly into the garage. Parked and carefully opened the door. Empty. My heels echoed on the cement loudly in my ears. I was definitely on edge. The bombing had come close to ending my life. It was the closest I'd ever come to being killed. Things like that tended to unnerve people.

When I reached the landing of my floor, I felt him before I saw his silhouette down the hall. Or rather, I felt the blankness of him. His back against the wall at my unit. One foot propped up against the sienna painted plaster.

"If you leave a mark, you're cleaning it." I walked past Paul Chandler and put the key in the lock as if he weren't there.

"And hello to you, Bianca."

The door opened and I hesitated in the hallway. Finally, I looked him in the eyes. "Is this business or personal?"

"Would you like it to be personal?"

I frowned and went inside. Shutting the door behind me. I tossed my keys on the counter and braced for Martini's rush at my leg. She climbed to my waist before I grabbed her in my arms and began petting her.

"I am a very, very bad cat person! Even if you are my very first cat."

Paul rapped gently at the door. I answered with Martini held against my bosom. "Yes? May I help you?"

He blinked at me. "*League of Gentlemen*? Is this a local shop?"

"Yes." I tried to imitate Tubbs' voice from the British TV show but I wasn't really into acting. "I thought it might make you feel more at home, being MI-6 and all."

"Not out here!" He glanced over his shoulder and pushed his way inside. "Shut the door if you're going to blab my business to the world."

"You have something that'll block receivers and directional mics?"

"Of course." He patted the cellphone at his belt. I looked at it more closely. Whatever it was, it didn't receive telephone calls. A façade to mask it's true function.

"Impressive."

"How low are you looking there?" He smiled at me innocently.

I straightened my back and glared at him. He could see the twist of my lips. Even if he couldn't see my angry eyes.

I smiled then and that startled him. When I removed my sunglasses, he could see that the glint in my eyes was threatening.

He swallowed uncertainly. "Are you sure you should be doing that?"

"Just testing your little magic totem there." Martin rubbed her face under my chin and I resumed stroking her. "Someone's a lonely kitty."

"I thought cats liked to be independent."

"They do. But they're still social creatures." I nuzzled her face with my nose. Then set her on the ground. She wasn't happy. But it was the one thing she understood. "What do you want, Paul?"

"Thought maybe you'd like some company to the desert."

I cocked my head to study him. "You have my office bugged?"

"You had it swept. Twice. How'd I manage something like that?"

"I also had my clothing checked. Wait. Was the beret your bug?"

"Who else? Amperdyne? Please! You called them on that early in the game. They'd be stupid to do more."

He seemed overly confident. Pleased with himself. It only pissed me off.

"What the fuck gives you the right to bug a private citizen?"

"Easy now, Doll. It's a bit different in the spy-game. I figured you'd be ticked if I bugged you. But I had to risk it."

"Why?"

"For your safety, of course. You're always running off without backup. You nearly got yourself killed at Gibraltar's offices because of it." He seemed genuinely angry.

"Am I screwing up your own investigation?"

His gaze softened and he took a step closer. "No. I just don't like the idea of you being dead."

I didn't back down, but I didn't let him brush against me either. "We met once, Paul. And talked on the phone once. Hardly time for an attachment."

"I don't often meet women I'd like to attach to."

I couldn't keep from laughing. "Talking that way, I'm not surprised. Who'd like to be on the receiving end of sexual impropriety?"

"You'd be surprised." He spoke gently. Invitingly. But I saw his eyes shift. "Sorry. It's part of my cover. Been doing it so long I don't know when to stop."

"How long you been tracking Chilton?"

It was his turn to look surprised. "I thought you didn't learn anything from your C.I.A. contact."

"I didn't. Not more than that you were MI-6." I studied him. "If you actually care what happens, make sure she doesn't suffer any negative consequences for poking around."

He nodded. "I can do that. Happily. If you'll let me go with you."

"No."

"Fine. Then 'no.'"

"Pardon?" I studied his expression. He was being serious. "You'd blackmail your way into going with me?"

"Absolutely. I'm a spy. We do that sort of thing."

"I thought your interest was personal?"

He grinned. "Reprehensible, aren't I?"

I fumed for a few seconds. The idea of having professional backup might actually be really nice. His constant flirtation not so much. Still, with the mystic belt keeping him safe from my hunger, it might be good practice.

"Deplorable. You can go on one condition."

He beamed at me, flirtatiously. "I already said 'yes.' She's off the hook."

"Okay, two conditions."

He frowned, as if I'd disappointed him. "Sorry, no sex on the first date."

I clenched a fist but didn't lash out. I didn't believe in unnecessary violence. Although, he brought me damned close. "Forget it! I'm sorry I even considered it."

"Wait, wait! Sorry, sorry. Go ahead. What's the second thing."

I counted to five. Three didn't cut it this time. Hunger. Sleep deprivation. Being whammied and bombed. I was in a seriously pissed off mood all of a sudden. "No more cover. No more games. Be yourself and only yourself the entire trip."

He scrunched up his face as if it was a painful thought. Contorted into a child's expression. Then he nodded, letting out a long breath. "You can't keep calling me 'Paul,' then. It's sort of a trigger. Long term programming."

"What should I call you?"

"Oliver."

"As in Twist?"

"Only it's my birth name. But yeah."

"Fine, Oliver, give me five minutes to get ready."

"I'm just going as back up. It's your dime."

I started toward the bedroom. Martini put herself in my way, nearly causing me to tumble. I knelt down and petted her a moment. "I know, I've been gone longer on this case than normal. I'm sorry."

"Why not bring her along?"

"You've never owned a cat, have you?"

"Dog person myself."

"Cats aren't dogs."

He smiled. Playful but not lecherous for a change. "No one's perfect."

CHAPTER TWENTY-FOUR

We made decent time out of Los Angeles, but I was beginning to regret not accepting Paul's offer to take his car. A convertible. The air-conditioning worked well enough in my car. But the idea of letting the wind blow through my hair instead of keeping it bound under the beret sounded better and better once we'd left L.A. traffic behind.

I was also having trouble thinking of him as 'Oliver.' In my mind, he was still 'Paul.' He was only 'Oliver' if I called him by name aloud.

He broke the silence, glancing at my hands firmly on the wheel. Ungloved. "What do you know about Killian's pack?"

"Who's Killian?"

Paul stared at me, horrified. "You know nothing about the werewolves you're off to meet?"

"I didn't have time to put my resources on it." I gripped the wheel firmly. "I'm beginning to worry that we're running out of time. Vincent's been gone four days now. If he turns up dead because I delayed anything, I'll—."

I couldn't finish. I wouldn't kill myself. The guilt would eat at me. Praying wouldn't make it go away. Believing in God didn't mean that every death should be met with joy and peace of mind. It should've.

But that much Zen meant that there was something wrong with you. No one was that detached. No one sane.

"You care about the kid. Why?" I could feel his stare pressing against my nerves.

"He's a kid." I refused to look at him. I knew he was frowning. "He's an innocent. Trapped in a world not of his own making. Not being allowed to grow up the way other kids in the world are."

"So he's basically you."

I did turn. Startled. Annoyed that he thought I was talking about myself. Then I realized maybe he was right. I wasn't consciously defending the innocent because they were me. I was doing it because I understood how hard the world could be to people like them. But yeah. People like me.

"Just because I was born a succubus doesn't mean I'm some worldly-wise woman who manipulates people to get what she wants."

"Some people think that?"

I nodded. I didn't like talking about myself. Especially not with a practical stranger. Even a handsome and flirtatious stranger.

"I don't."

I listened for mockery in his tone. All I heard was kindness. Sincerity. I took a deep breath. Didn't need to count. I just wasn't used to men offering me compassion. Lust took over long before they could.

"Thanks. Historically, my kind have done just that. Whether by choice or simply because that's how our power works, I don't know."

"You work so hard not be like them. Like that."

"Yeah, I do. You think I like hiding my eyes all the time? Covering my skin? Never knowing a touch of someone else?"

"You could date a vampire."

I frowned. He wasn't teasing. "You really want to know why I wouldn't consider dating someone not alive?"

"I guess that pretty much covers it. Yeah."

I laughed. Bitter. Self-depreciatingly. "As if I'm one to talk. Being with a man—a living man—would kill him."

He patted his belly but it was the totem underneath he was signifying. "Unless they used protection."

I laughed for real then. A knee-jerk giggle that made me feel better. "I don't even know if I can get pregnant the old fashioned way."

"Old fashioned? You mean sex?"

I studied his handsome profile. "I know you've done your homework. Don't play stupid. It's not a good look on you."

"I figured sex was involved. Pregnancy sort of requires it doesn't it? I'm just not sure what you mean by 'old fashioned?'"

"Draining the lifeforce of a man is, what—how do I say it? It generates fertility. A condom would be nothing more than another bit of clothing with anyone undead."

"So a fertile vampire—."

"Is there such a thing?"

"Hold the interruptions. I'm hypothecating." He grinned at me. Kindness in his eyes.

I wanted to trust that it was real. But he was a spy. Hard not to believe that despite his promise, everything he did was a lie.

"Fine. Go on. Hypothecate."

"A fertile vampire could never impregnate you."

I shook my head. "Nope." Then I had an odd thought. "Unless there was some major kink."

"Pardon?" It was Paul's turn to be startled.

"Having sex with the vampire—assuming a fertile vampire existed—could lead to a child if another man were there. Human. Alive at least. Donating his lifeforce."

"You make it sound like he's giving away an old set of golf-clubs."

"I was trying to be delicate."

"Better than sucking him dry at the same time as you're doing a vampire?"

I glared at him. No smile on my lips. He didn't even squirm.

"I couldn't resist. You said 'kink.'"

I sighed. "I did. So, Oliver, tell me about Killian?"

"He's smart. Less brutal than some. Punishes rebellion harshly, but doesn't bully for the sake of bullying. Incredibly homophobic. Been in charge since Thrace's time." He shook his head. "I don't see him giving a toss about Anton Thrace otherwise. Out of sight, out of mind."

"How do they support themselves?"

"Government funds the land. Allocates territories in out-of-the-way places. The pack hunts for wild game to supplement their federal food subsidies."

"They're living on welfare?"

"No one's gonna hire a werewolf. Gibraltar aside. Only the strongest don't lose control on the full moon. Not many at all that can stop the change. And they're pack animals. They need a family. It's almost pheromonal."

"Thrace is that strong? He stays human on the moon?"

Paul nodded. "He's gay but the man's got preternatural game. I don't know how he does it. He's not an alpha. Too submissive for that. If he wasn't, he could probably take on Killian."

"Would the pack tolerate a gay alpha?"

He laughed. "I haven't a clue. Maybe as long as he didn't try to bugger the rest of the males, they'd live and let live. It's all one-on-one challenge. If he could kick Killian's ass, he could beat them all."

"All of this is interesting. But not especially useful. What happens when we enter their land uninvited?"

Paul's smile grew serious as he studied my expression. "Depends on how you do it."

"Suggestions?"

"Stop at the gate to their place. Outside the line. Wait to be invited in."

"They'd just walk up to me and say, hey, since you're stalking us, why not come in for a cup of tea?"

"I would. If a beautiful preternatural woman like you showed up, I'd be damned curious."

"Did you just sneak in another compliment?"

"I didn't think I was being sneaky. Outright brazen that was." He smiled. No lechery in it.

I realized that I felt uncharacteristically relaxed around him. Too comfortable for my own good. It made me nervous. Yeah, I know. Oxymoronic to say the least.

"Can I carry my guns onto their land if they invite me in?"

"You can. They won't consider them dangerous."

"Even with silver-tipped ammo?"

He twisted in his seat, restricted by the seatbelt. "Why in the bollocks are you loaded with silver ammo?"

"Same reason I'm loaded with wood-tipped bullets. A girl can never be too careful." I smiled sweetly.

He scowled and faced away. Staring through the passenger window. "Don't take the silver inside. They'll smell it. Treat you like a threat instead of something more pleasant."

I gave him a look. "Like dessert?"

"Maybe." He didn't smile. I think he might've been serious.

"What'll they do to you?"

"As long as I act submissive to you, they'll discount me."

"You have it in you to act submissive at all?"

"Depends on what you have in mind!" He caught himself and raised his hands in surrender. "Sorry! That wasn't me being 'Paul.' Not exactly."

"What, a spy who likes to be dominated? Now isn't that a hoot."

"You Americans and your funny words. What does it mean to be a 'hoot?'"

"Funny. Hilarious. I guess 'hoot' is a type of unexpected bark of laughter. Instead of a chirp or guffaw."

"You're making that up."

"No. I'm guessing. There's a difference."

We drove a while in silence before Chandler spoke softly, staring out the window. "Would you consider going out with me?"

I turned to him, certain I'd misunderstood. "Pardon?"

"You heard me. Don't make me ask again unless the answer's 'yes.'"

I stared straight ahead at the road. The thought of touching a man. Kissing his lips. My hunger rose like some biological imperative. Just at the thought of something that could lead to sex.

Thankfully he was a blank spot. A void my power spilled around, finding nothing to feed from. I didn't call it back. I let it fill the car with need. Testing the totem's potency.

"Can you feel that?"

He turned to me. Vulnerability in his eyes. No mask. Unless he was that good. I didn't think he was. No one was that good. Not after as many decades of deceit I'd learned to survive through.

"Feel what? Cool indifference?"

I laughed. Surprised. "No, Secret Agent Man."

"What then?"

"You plan on wearing that totem forever?"

He frowned. His eyes narrowing with thought. He hadn't considered that. The problems of an actual future with me. My spark of tentative interest in the handsome man died. He'd thought about sex with me. Not about anything beyond. Typical man.

"No." He seemed to come to the same conclusion as I had. "Sorry. I didn't think."

"Nope. I guess not." An anger kindled where hope had flared. He worked with preternaturals. He should've known better. No. Maybe not. Maybe he knew vampires. Very few people knew anything about succubi. Other than that they could kill us if we broke the law. And that we sucked the life out of men when we had sex.

The rest of the drive was quiet. He didn't even try to teach me anything more about werewolves. The first man I'd ever met who knew when to shut the hell up and stay that way.

CHAPTER TWENTY-FIVE

I pulled onto a dirt road that looked like every other dirt road since we'd left the Twentynine Palms Highway. We were just north of Joshua Tree. A sprawling desert community. A lot of roads weren't paved beyond the three-mile mark. Some of the scraped paths could've been driveways on private parcels. Street signs weren't an indicator. People had put up their own. Corrals were visible everywhere. Often times no houses went along with them.

"How do we know this is the right way, Chandler?" He was no longer 'Oliver.' I'd lowered my guard for Oliver. Not anymore.

"G.P.S. says so."

He looked at his phone. The real phone. A G.P.S. app indicated our location. Indicated a lot more information than should've been available. Probably not legal. Spy stuff.

I frowned. "I see Joshua Trees. Small shrubs. And lots of open space. Nothing that would suit werewolves."

"There's a buffer of unoccupied land around the pack's territory. Helps keep people from living too close to unsettling sounds and sights."

"So keep going?"

"Another, what, hundred meters."

I drove, straining to see a change in scenery. The road sloped so slightly that I almost didn't notice. Then it curved and a rocky outcropping rose from the desert like a secret art-installation twenty feet tall.

"Stop just there. The rocks mark the official boundary. Park next to that stick in the ground."

I eyed the stick dubiously. "Not much of a warning that you're about to trespass on carnivorous lycanthropes."

"There aren't any herbivorous lycanthropes. Vegans don't stay vegan as werewolves."

"I've always wondered about that. Guess it takes a bite or blood on blood to pass it along."

He took a breath to say something then paused. Finally he continued. "My interest in you wasn't casual. That mind of yours impresses the hell out of me."

I didn't look at him. I could see him staring in earnest at me from the corner of my eye. Didn't matter. I wrapped anger around my heart like a shield.

"Water under the bridge. This is business."

He was silent for a few seconds. Then opened the car door. "If you say so."

I got out of the car a little more slowly. I'd automatically let my hunger spill out away from us. Toward the rocks. Finding lizards. Rodents indigenous to the region. And one human watcher. Young. Female. My power brushed over her but found nothing it wanted.

She sensed it. Me. I felt her rush away. Out of range.

I could've tracked her with a surge of need. Followed a good distance, in fact. I wasn't sure how far. I'd never fully tested it. Not since I was a child. Back then, I'd been running through the woods. From men who'd wanted to rape me. Wanted to keep me like some pre-pubescent sex-slave. Back then my power, meager as it was, had reached out to find them. Keep track of them as the one being hunted. Now I was the hunter.

"They know we're here."

He stared at me. "How'd you know? Secret preternatural handshake?"

"Yeah, that's it." I finally returned his gaze. His attempt to be funny unsuccessful. I asked a hard question. Wanted to see if he'd be honest with me about something impersonal. "Why the interest in an English vampire who's been here for years? Unless he's planning on going back home, he's not your problem anymore."

"Can't say. MI-6, remember? Official Secrets Acts and all."

"But it has nothing to do with Vincent's abduction?" Just because Chandler had been watching Chilton for some time didn't exclude the possibility of something more subtle. A long-game machination to hurt Henry Gibraltar. The vampires could've even been involved in the killing of his children for all I knew. That's how devious and patient the undead were.

"No. That was a surprise. The vampires weren't in on it."

"How can you be sure?"

He opened his mouth to answer when I felt the prickling of energy along my skin. I raised a finger and he closed his mouth. Waiting. Not even asking what. Maybe he would make a good submissive. Not that I was looking for one. I wasn't looking for anything. I don't even know what kind of man I'd want if I could safely date.

"Our friends are coming to investigate. Not a bad response time."

He tapped the device at his belt warningly. "You know they can probably hear you."

Werewolves had superstrength, super-hearing and an incredible sense of smell. That's really all I knew about their powers. But I'd chosen my words for their benefit. "Of course. You didn't think I was talking to a beta little boy-toy like you, did you?"

His face twisted up in a mixture of delight, annoyance and confusion. I'd hit a nerve. He hadn't been lying. Chandler liked to be dominated. How did that make for a good secret agent?

"Sorry." He looked down at the ground. But I saw intent in his eyes. This wasn't a real reaction. He was playing it up for the werewolves.

A man strode around a huge rock. Overly muscled. Broad and powerful. He wore jeans that were cut off just below the knees. They hung onto his lean, narrow waist with the help of a frayed belt. He was barefoot and shirtless. A diamond-shaped patch of chest-hair and dark line of it down his belly into his jeans.

"You should be," growled the man, threateningly.

"I assume I'm speaking to Killian? Alpha of this pack?" I stood up, off the hood of my car. "I'm not wasting my time with anyone insignificant."

I smiled. Hoping it was unnerving to him that my tone didn't match the smile. I'd seen a lot of powerful men confused by the dichotomy. And werewolf or not, he was still a man.

His frown deepened. He glanced at Chandler. The Englishman kept his eyes averted. His energy anxious. Hunger bubbled under my skin at the presence of the werewolves. Fighting to escape. I let it loose, just enough that I could sense them all. Even those out of sight.

Two men and a woman waited behind various boulders. Close enough to close the distance between us before I could stop them. Even silver ammo wouldn't be enough.

I could discern their emotions. Tasted it along with their lifeforce. Excitement. Intrigue. No anger. Nothing that suggested my presence was a threat to them. Or that they knew what I was.

"I'm Killian. Who the hell are you?"

I bobbed my head, removing my beret. I tossed it into the cab of the car through the open window. "Bianca Savage."

Displaying my tail would've involved getting practically naked. Not the only reason I didn't show it off. But the main one. The horns and my name were all he was getting. The name might mean nothing. If he hadn't spoken to Thrace the past few days it shouldn't. The horns, however, that should be a conversation starter.

"I heard of you." His grey eyes flickered to my hair. A subtle nod as if it had confirmed what he'd been expecting. No surprise at all.

"What did Anton say exactly?" I watched him closely.

His mouth twitched but his eyes stayed disinterested. I was right! He'd spoken to the gay man. But why? According to the Amperdyne files, Thrace had cut off ties with his pack years earlier. Killian had no tolerance for homosexuals. Typical of lycanthropes.

"Don't know what'cha mean."

"Did you know that Anton was kidnapped yesterday?"

He nodded. No pretense. "The Feds called. Asked if we knew who might've done it."

"Or why?"

A noncommittal grunt. "That, too."

"What'd you tell them?"

"Same thing I'm telling you. I ain't seen or talked to that faggot since we threw him out of the pack. Now get off our land and get the hell away."

"Technically I'm not on your land. And no one tells me what to do." I chose those words to play up my dominance. But it was also true. Granny Oglethorpe had said I got my stubbornness from my real parents. She was wrong of course. I'd learned it from her. I just usually kept that part to myself.

"You want us to hurt you, Girlie?"

I tilted my head for effect. "Girlie? Really? You get satellite up here? Binge-watching fifties black and white movies?"

"What?" He shook his head, trying to understand what I'd said. He'd expected fear. I'd practically laughed. He hadn't really been listening to my words.

"I'm not with the government, Killian. I'm just a fellow preternatural trying to do a job. Find a missing boy. Figure out what happened to Anton. He may not be your favorite person, but he's still one of us."

Chandler glanced up at me, despite himself. Surprised. Calculating. Was I being intentional with my language? Or did I consider myself more like werewolves than humans?

He was smart. Those questions would raise others. How much could he trust me? Worse, had he made a mistake coming here with me alone? I could practically hear his mind at work. But no time to allay his fears. Or even acknowledge them.

Killian grunted again. "Not like us."

"You don't think the people that took him wouldn't do the same to you? Or anyone else in your pack?"

"Depends on why he disappeared."

Disappeared. He hadn't said 'taken.' Or 'kidnapped.' I smiled pleasantly, lifting my glasses. I let him get a peek of my eyes. "Good point. Why do you think he disappeared?"

He stared at my face. Several long seconds and I dropped the glasses back onto my nose. Pushed them slowly back into place. His hands trembled and he shook himself off. Like a wet dog. Trying to shake off my power now that my eyes were hidden again.

"What'd you do to me?"

"Nothing. I showed you why I keep my eyes covered." I took a step toward him, hands at my sides. Open palmed. "A sign of good faith."

"What for?"

"I just drove four hours to meet you. The least you could do is invite me in for a more relaxed conversation."

Killian motioned toward Chandler. "What about him?"

"Just someone to kill time with in the car. He doesn't need to come."

I didn't look at Paul. Didn't care if he wanted to protest or object. He didn't matter. I was dominant. That was the performance. If he screwed it up, I'd be more than just angry at him.

"Fine. I suppose a cup of coffee and thirty minutes to shoot the breeze ain't unreasonable." He stared at my breasts. Then down to my hips and legs. Not interest. Attraction, sure. He'd have sex with me if I let him. But he already knew I was dangerous. He didn't want to die. Or even gamble that his werewolf strength was enough to survive my hunger. But he was tempted. Just a little.

I turned to Chandler then. "Stay with the car. And don't change my fucking radio station, again."

He ducked his head in obedience. Frowning as I walked away. "Call if you need me."

I smiled without looking at him. Killian didn't see but the watchers would. "I won't."

Killian led me around the cluster of boulders, through narrow passages formed between them. One of the men slipped out of hiding. Following. I could feel his eyes on my ass. I paused and turned abruptly. He actually jumped back.

"You keep staring at my ass like that and I'll show you why people don't survive sex with a succubus."

He paled. I resumed walking and could feel him hesitate. He didn't follow quite so closely after that. Killian paused to glance back, but he only laughed. Disgusted. Not at me. At the man I'd cowed.

"Won't ever be alpha if you let a little girl scare the pants off you."

I started to call him out. To point out that he hadn't been willing to risk it either. But I stopped myself.

The man behind me was thick with muscles. Not oversized like Killian. But definitely not weak. Killian probably didn't understand that being smart wasn't the same as being weak.

"It takes a certain kind of man to lead." My words were ambiguous. He took them as a compliment. I figured he would.

"Damned straight it does. I'm not a bastard, mind you. I only beat 'em when they get out of line. But they know better than to cross the line more than once."

"Did Anton cross the line?"

"He's a fucking fairy."

I didn't hide my contempt. "That's all he did? That was crossing the line in his case?"

Killian snarled but his eyes held secrets. "It was enough."

"Wasn't there anything he could've done to make amends? If he'd wanted to stay?"

He kept his back to me. But I sensed something change. A straightening of the shoulders. He was happy. Not in a light and fluffy kind of way.

Had he gotten revenge on Thrace? Punished him? Whatever it was, he felt self-satisfied.

"Did the Feds say when they're coming out here to search the property?"

Killian turned to me at the neck. Smiling. He was too relaxed. His eyes shrewd. "They didn't. But they can come anytime they want. They won't find nothing."

I understood his meaning. Thrace wasn't at the Joshua Tree property. But he was somewhere. I was more and more certain that the pack had kidnapped him. They wanted something from him. Money? It was a decent motive. Thrace was richer than these feral people would ever be. Forced to live in rustic isolation.

I shrugged for the benefit of other unseen eyes. "Hopefully they won't find it necessary."

We crossed a rise. Beyond it was a shallow valley with mobile homes set up in an 'H' pattern. A garden was fenced off on one side. A chicken coop and some goats tethered on the other.

Women were hand-doing laundry. No electrical lines connected the mobile homes to the rest of the world. The women looked up at me. Frazzled hair. Worn clothing. Suntanned skin over strong arms and legs. Children stopped running after each other to stare at us.

"I hadn't thought there'd be children." I'd never pictured werewolves as children. As babies. Not even as teenagers.

"What, you think we eat our kids?" Killian wasn't happy.

I'd fallen into the same stereotypes that ordinary humans had about all manner of preternaturals. "No. I just think of werewolves as very sexual beings. Children aren't that."

"No. They ain't. Anyone touches one of our young-uns and they'd wish they were dead. Literally wish it."

"I wouldn't even blame you."

I think that surprised him. When a werewolf threatened to torture and terrorize someone, most people were probably scared away. My enthusiasm wasn't typical. In fact, I was pretty sure my desire to protect the innocent was on the extreme edge of socially acceptable behavior.

"Alice! Mabel. Coffee and some bread for our guest. At the meeting table." He glanced at my horns. "Any of you wanna see a real live Devil-girl, come join us."

It was like he'd opened a set of cages. People swarmed out of the mobile homes. Women dropped their laundry into buckets. Teenagers slipped out from the pile of boulders overlooking the encampment.

I tried to count the werewolves quickly in my head. At least twenty-five people. Definitely more. That was a lot of lycanthropes. It looked more like a cult dwelling. Maybe they had a lot in common with cults. Isolation. Beliefs almost no one else shared. Living in a way that normal people wouldn't accept or tolerate.

"Sit here." A young woman, mid-twenties used a rag to wipe off the bench closest to me. "I'm Iris."

"Bianca."

She stared at my horns. Unafraid. Intrigued. Wistful. I'd seen children look at my horns like that. As if having them were special instead of a burden. It was refreshing to see an adult so intrigued.

I smiled. "You can touch them."

One of the teenaged boys was standing near me. Dark hair. Green eyes and full, pouty lips. Lean. Still growing. He reached out. I jerked away, startled. "Not you! Not bare-skinned."

He pulled back, pride wounded. "I weren't going to hurt them."

"I believe you. But they might've hurt you."

He walked around the far side of the table, confused. Hurt by my reaction. Killian slapped him hard on the back and he flinched.

"She's a succubus, Boy! And you got something dangling between your legs. They don't go together! Ain't we told you about their kind?"

"No, Sir."

Killian grunted with begrudging delight. "Then I'm glad she's here. Education for everybody."

I sat next to Iris. She'd withdrawn her extended fingers. I'd made it clear that the warning was for the boy. All the boys. Killian had reinforced the idea that it was because he was male. Iris apparently decided it wasn't a good idea for her, either.

I sighed. Maybe she'd miss out on telling her kids about touching a succubus horn someday. But the males would be safer if everyone was afraid.

"A succubus is a demon-girl. Mother sucks the life out of a man when they make a baby."

"Um, Killian?" I raised a hand respectfully. "May I tell the story? With a little less panache? As your guest?"

"Of course. I reckon you know more about the demonic powers of your own kind."

I counted to five. Not three. Five. Taking two deep breaths. Ignorance wasn't the same as hatred. No need to ruin the moment.

"Let me start with my own story. Payment for the coffee and bread."

I accepted a cup and took a quick sip. Some cultures required small gestures to feel respected. It was habit more than anything conscious. The coffee was bitter, but I smiled and nodded to the woman serving. Then I scanned the eyes of the eagerly waiting werewolves.

"Imagine one of you being born without a pack. Your mother and father dead. Alone in the woods. How much would you know about yourself? Learning everything firsthand."

"That happened to you?" The teenage boy eyed me warily as he asked the question. I'd betrayed his trust by the public rebuke. Some part of me wanted to win it back. It wasn't his fault he was raised in ignorance.

"It did. I didn't know what I was. What a touch of their skin on any part of my body could do to a young man." I held his gaze, even through my sunglasses. "If I'd only made you sick, nothing worse, well, that would've meant getting off lightly. I don't want to ever kill anyone again. Not on accident."

His eyes flashed wide as he stared down at his hands. When he looked up again, he nodded. Appreciation instead of resentment in his eyes.

"So you have killed." Killian smiled. "Guess that means you won't rain down judgment on us."

"I didn't come here to judge anyone." I glanced at a young girl with curly golden hair peering from behind a man who looked enough like her to be her father. "I admit, you're my first pack. The way I'm your first succubus. I'm here to learn your truths as much as anything."

The girl's blue eyes were full of innocence. Not fear. "Why do you have horns?"

She wasn't growing up in a scary world where her own safety was at risk. Killian wasn't a bad alpha if the children were brave enough to ask questions. Made it harder to hate the man.

"That's a very good question—?"

"Hettie." The father gave me her name with pride. "Five years old and ain't another one smarter."

"I see that. Well, Hettie, I have horns the same way you have fangs and claws and fur on the full moon."

She giggled and covered her mouth. "I ain't turned yet. You gotta hit pubity."

"Puberty," corrected Iris gently.

No familial similarity. She wasn't the girl's mother. I looked around. To test my skills. Watching for a mother's reaction to the girl's candor. I scanned all the faces, smiling so that they didn't misinterpret. The woman wasn't there.

"Did you really not know that puberty was the start?" asked Killian.

"I didn't do research before I came if that's what you mean. I was coming to meet fellow preternaturals. Fellow people. Help me keep other preternaturals from going missing."

"I had my first change two months ago," said the teenaged boy shyly. As if admitting to his first sexual experience. He blushed deeply.

I frowned. "I don't mean to be disrespectful, but you look older than that."

He beamed. "Thank you! That's what everyone says. Bigger an' my pa was at this age."

I turned to Killian. "From the accents, your pack has quite a collection of states represented. How's that?"

He shrugged. "The government sends us to whichever facility has the most openings. Don't care about uprooting families. Some states won't let us return from where they plucked us. So we look for homes elsewhere."

"You were gonna tell us about yourself!" reminded Hettie impatiently.

"So I was. Let's see, I should elaborate on what I said earlier about touch. In case any of you meet another of my kind, you should understand the dangers."

"We're wolves! We can handle anything!" boasted a ruddy boy younger than Hettie. He looked fierce and patted his skinny chest defiantly. His hair was long and tangled. Brown eyes tracking my every movement. No more afraid to speak than Hettie.

I grinned. "Wolves can handle quite a lot, Young Man. But even the strongest person has to be careful. I've never tested it, I'll be honest. But I suspect my ability to drain a man's lifeforce could do just as much to a werewolf."

"Prove it!" taunted the boy. He grinned, eager for me to try.

"I—I can't promise that if I started, I could pull my power back."

"Killian ain't afraid!" called the boy.

"Hush, Pete!" said Iris, gently but firmly. "You know silver can make us sick. You've seen it."

The boy nodded, biting his lower lip. "She's like silver?"

"Might be, Boy." Killian stood up. "But he's got the right of it. We should see what happens for our own benefit."

"Killian, no!" A handsome older woman, lines around her eyes and mouth, jumped up. Touched his arm intimately. "Don't risk it."

He turned to her. Kissed her tenderly on the lips. A long, slow kiss. Not his mother or an auntie. It was his woman. Ten, maybe twenty years his elder.

I'd come here wanting to dislike Killian for throwing Thrace out of the pack. I'd even been sure that I would hate him from the way he'd spoken to me at the car. Full of homophobic rage. Sexist point of view. But he kept doing amazingly decent things that made it hard to stick to my plan.

"I'll do it," said the teenaged boy.

"Absolutely not," I replied. "You may have had your first change but you're too young for this."

"Stop looking for trouble, Chase. It'll find you soon enough." Iris touched my arm. "You got a soft spot for children."

"I'm not a child!" Chase puffed up like Pete had. I could see the little boy in his face then. Hidden behind a spurt of maturing features. He was angry but I also saw fear. He believed that I could hurt him.

Unfortunately, he was at that age. Boys fighting to be men. If Killian could endure my power, he wanted to prove that he was just as strong.

"Not a child, Chase. But not a seasoned man." I eyed the others. They watched me apprehensively. I was treading on some well-set rules that I didn't understand. "How many women have you had? How many babies have you made?"

He had the decency to looked embarrassed again. Kicking the ground nervously. "None."

"Exactly. My power would ruin your whole future because of that."

"Oh." He smiled, relieved. I'd given him a way off the hook. He swam for the safety of that excuse faster than I could have hoped. "I reckon you know more about your power than I do."

"I do."

"It's to be me. Let's do this." Killian strode around the roughhewn table and the pack moved aside.

The woman who'd begged him to stop didn't repeat her protest. Her eyes were on me. Her expression plain. Woman to woman. Beseeching me not to kill her man. To turn him down.

"Your people need you. What if I can't control myself?" I didn't tell them I'd been unintentionally fasting. That I had sporadic flashes of power that I couldn't control. An appetite that came and went of its own volition.

He smiled wickedly. "I'm stronger than you think."

I swallowed hard. "Then we'd better move over to that clearing. Next to the rocks."

I didn't wait for him to follow. I put my back to the mountain of boulders. Sitting on the lowest stone in the outcropping.

I spoke to Iris and the women gathered near her. "If he collapses, drag him away. Keep dragging him until I tell you."

"They're my people. You don't give them orders."

"She's trying to keep you alive!" said his woman. Angry at him. "She knows you won't take 'no' for an answer. Smarter than I was when I first let you court me."

"You don't regret it." He eyed her playfully. Love in his gaze.

"No. Not a single day." She fought a bashful smile.

God, don't let me kill this man! I repeated my prayer several times before I took a deep breath. "Everyone male please stay as far away as the table. Just to avoid spillage."

"Get on with it, Woman. I'm ready."

Killian pulled his shoulders back, bracing for it. I sighed and gave up. Lowering my shields. My power seeped out toward him. Slowly at first.

It tasted his testosterone. Wild, like Anton's. Stronger. Savage. Full of life experiences. Or maybe that's just how much more powerful an alpha felt by his very nature.

My hunger reacted instantly. An icy pit formed in my stomach. My skin grew warm. Crawled with goosebumps as my power surged into him.

The first returning wave of energy was like a heady rush. I'd forgotten what it was like to drink from a human. Warmth spread through my arms and legs. Along the nerves into my cheeks. My fingertips. All my extremities alive. My strength growing proportionately.

He yelped with surprise. His fists clenching as I drew more of his lifeforce. I savored the heat as it began to melt the cold at the center of my belly. Driving away my hunger in a way I hadn't experienced since my first accidental kill. Even that hadn't been as satisfying.

"Stop!" I heard a woman cry out. His woman.

I'd closed my eyes. They flashed open. Killian was on his knees. Fighting to stay upright. I tried to shut down my power. Call it back. But I'd been right to be afraid. Like someone who'd been dieting for a long time, giving in to dessert, I wanted more. I couldn't stop myself.

"I can't!" Speech was difficult. Killian's lifeforce filled me like a drug. The world swam as I soaked it all in. His spark grew faint. He collapsed on the ground. I didn't see it. I felt it. "Get him away!"

Someone grabbed him. A woman. My hunger slipped past her. She began carrying him away as I'd instructed. But my power moved just as quickly.

"He's dying!" I heard her wail. She was right. I could feel his spark start to flutter.

Then someone else was there. Between me and him. Male. Less wild. Less powerful. I flashed my eyes open as I soaked up the first taste of his life.

"No!" It was my turn to scream.

Chase had placed himself in my power's path. He collapsed almost instantly. But it helped break my connection to Killian. Helped me fight myself. His youthful energy was too innocent. A child despite his protestations. My horror and revulsion broke the spell. I was in control again.

I reeled in my power so hard that the world swirled. Darkness tried to take me. I closed my eyes. Blinking away vertigo. Fighting to stay awake. It took longer to open my eyes between each flutter. Then blackness won and I collapsed into it. At the mercy of some very pissed off werewolves.

CHAPTER TWENTY-SIX

I felt the rumble of the motor before I opened my eyes. I was relaxed. My body sated for the first time in decades.

"Glad to see you're back among the living."

Chandler's voice. I gazed at him. Blinking away confusion. He was driving my car. I looked for road signs. We were on the Ten. That meant at least an hour away from Joshua Tree.

"What happened?"

"You blacked out."

"To the boy!" I hissed angrily.

"He's fine. You scared the shit out of him though."

"Back to sounding American?"

He frowned. "No sense in pretending that being myself is a good thing, is there?"

I sat up, wiping drool from my lips. Not much but enough to be mortified. "No, I guess not."

"Did you get what you needed?"

"Yeah. Sort of. Killian knows something." I glanced at him. "Killian survive?"

"Yeah. Out cold but breathing." He faced me. "What kind of something?"

"He's been in touch with Thrace. Might even have him. But if so, Anton's not at the commune. And keep your eyes on the road!"

He faced forward. "I don't think it's called a commune."

"Trust me, whatever it's called, it's a commune."

"If not there, then where? Why'd they take him?"

"I'm guessing money."

He shook his head. "Gibraltar would never pay a ransom."

"Not his money. Anton's."

That surprised him. "Oh. Kidnap him. Force him to hand over the funds. Then what? Release him? Kill him?"

"I don't know." I wriggled again to get comfortable in the seat. "You know, even though it's my suggestion that they might've done it for money, I don't like the timing. They could've done it much sooner. Or later, after he'd earned more. Why now, when Vincent's been taken." I jerked fully upright. "Wait! Does Vincent have access to his own personal bank accounts?"

"Some. Maybe a few hundred-thousand. A real kidnapping would've netted them millions."

"A real kidnapping. You know, people keep saying stuff as if they're being sloppy with their words. But they aren't. Subconsciously they're telling me important things."

He looked over at me and shook his head. "I don't know that it's not a real kidnapping. It's just, there should be a ransom."

"Exactly. No matter what the motive for taking the boy, there should've been a ransom. What's the difference between a kidnapping with a ransom and without? Procedurally?"

"The Feds don't put a full team into place until there's been a money demand."

I frowned, rubbing my face to simulate the blood. "That's not right."

"Let me rephrase it. When a ransom-demand's made, the F.B.I. begins a full scale effort to track the incoming phone calls. They identify the voices of the callers. They run a hundred checks and double-checks they don't do if no money's requested. Because no phone call's come in."

"And what would the benefit of that be?"

"I don't follow?"

"If there's no money to be had and the F.B.I. doesn't try to identify the ransomers—what does it buy the kidnappers?"

"Time. Only time." Chandler whistled softly. "Time to do what?"

"Can Vincent get them access to his grandfather's assets? Safe deposit boxes? A hidden vault? Real estate titles?"

Chandler shook his head. "The old man's too savvy for that. Vincent can't help them in anyway. Not financially. Other than his personal accounts."

"So then time for what? What else? What are we missing!"

"To get him out of the country?" suggested the man.

"Again, why? To ask for money later, once he's overseas? Seems unnecessarily complicated."

"Fine, smarty pants. You tell me why then."

"I don't know. I'd have better guesses if the two missing security guards turned up. Running away is definitely different than being taken."

He was quiet a minute. "Anyone check recent John Does at the morgue?"

I stared at him. "Wouldn't the F.B.I. do that? Or even Amperdyne itself?"

"Depends."

"On what?"

He frowned at me. "You won't like it. I'm a bit of a pessimist."

"Wow me."

He shook his head. "Better still, let's check it out personally."

He refused to tell me his suspicions. I couldn't take him entirely serious. Surely two powerful security-conscious groups like the Feds and Amperdyne would check everything even remotely plausible.

I actually dozed off. Content. A smile playing on my lips when I woke. No dreams. Succubi don't dream. At least, I never did. Never reached REM state. Not the way humans did.

The car slowed. We were in underground parking. "Where are we?"

"L.A. County Morgue. Just pulling into the garage now."

"They just let us in?"

He grinned. "I have my ways, Missy."

"Whatever. Now you gonna tell me what we're looking for?"

"What part of 'see for ourselves' don't you understand?" His expression was playfully mocking. But I saw a hint of pain in his eyes. How many men's or boy's egos could I crush in one day?

"Fine. Forget I ever thought you were a great communicator."

His eyes widened. "You did?"

"I said forget it."

I wasn't dizzy getting out of the car. The blackout had been the result of a biofeedback loop. It had happened once before. I'd done it to myself when I'd shut down my power that hard and fast. Now I was fine. No. Better than fine. I was well fed.

I realized there'd been a goat waiting for me at the office most of the day. The bleating would've driven my renters mad. Oh well, nothing to be done about it now.

We took the elevator down to the basement. It housed the morgue and an annex to the morgue that the county used during heavy casualties. Today that section was closed.

Chandler brushed through the swinging double-doors ahead of me. I entered in time to hear a doctor with a facemask challenge him.

"Who are you?"

She was blonde. Hair in a bun. Hands covered by latex gloves. Held up like before surgery. A habit to avoid touching something unintentionally.

Chandler gave her his best scoundrel smile. "Me? I'm nobody. My friend, she's definitely somebody. But we don't use names in our organization. We're here to help you out."

"Help me out?" The doctor reached for a button that I was sure called security.

"I wouldn't touch that if I was you. The police might find an extra body in one of them drawers."

I stared at Chandler but he didn't bat an eye.

"What do you want?" she demanded. Afraid. The beret was still in my car. She stared at my horns.

"I told you! To help you out. Where are your John Does?"

Her brows knit together in annoyance. "We don't have any."

"None? Is that even possible?" Chandler looked doubtful. Whether he doubted the morgue attendant or himself I couldn't tell. "I'm thinking maybe incomplete remains? Charred? Amputated?"

"Oh. Those." She nodded, and motioned with her upheld hand.

We walked to a far set of metal tables. They were pushed together to form a bigger station to work from. She eyed him anxiously. Something about him more frightening than my horns. He hadn't drawn his weapon, but if she dealt with enough law enforcement, she'd have seen the weight of the guns under his jacket.

"We're associated with law enforcement. Ignore his earlier threat. Please."

I smiled. She didn't return it. But she seemed to believe me. Her fear turned to begrudging cooperation.

"Well, we weren't sure just how many bodies there were so we haven't categorized them yet. All we can tell so far is that they're human." She glanced at my horns and jerked her gaze away.

"What state are they in?"

She walked to the far side of the tables, putting them between her and us. Her attention stayed on Chandler, not on the body parts clustered together. I looked down. The smell alone warned me what we'd see.

"Burned. Down to the bones. Arms and legs cut into individual servings."

I glanced up at her. "They were eaten?"

The doctor had the grace to look embarrassed. "No. Just a poor turn of phrase."

"Cut how?" asked Chandler. He nudged me with a sleeved shoulder. "See why I didn't want to say anything?"

"A warning might've been nice. I don't like it when my victims smell like barbeque."

The doctor eyed us with interest. Our banter reassured her further. Refreshingly, she wasn't preternatural-phobic. "Limbs were cut by a chainsaw. Nothing unique about the make or model. One of thousands sold yearly in the city."

"Damn."

I touched him. Forcing him to look up at me. "You were hoping torn off? Bitten?"

"Either would've told us more than a chainsaw."

"Fair enough. You think it's the two security guards."

Chandler nodded and glanced at the doctor. "Any DNA available?"

"Cooked through and through. Faces smashed in, too. No dental records until we figure out how to put the teeth together. If even then." She paused, hopeful. "You know how many bodies we should be looking at?"

I looked back down at the pile. "You can't tell?"

"Some of the pieces are fused together. Really intense heat. Hotter than a furnace. Maybe something industrial. Dunno. I admit, we've been slow to get to these. Gangland killings have been rampant this week. Weird though."

"Weird how?" I was beginning to suspect that anything that occurred around the time of the kidnapping was related. At least, enough to question the possibility.

"No gunshots. Broken necks. Strangulation. Gangs don't operate that way. But the victims were definitely bangers. Possibly a serial killer, I suppose. Don't usually get many of those. And never ones who target gang-bangers in L.A."

"The whys have it."

She blinked and then glared. "The whys have what?"

Chandler eyed me. "Who's on first?"

I frowned disapprovingly as I answered her question. "Why is a serial killer attacking now? Why would it make a difference? What would happen as a result?"

"That's technically a what," gibed Chandler.

"Oh grow up!" I hissed at him.

The doctor shook her head, ignoring the man. "We'd focus all our forensic resources on those bodies. We'd put available officers on tracking down the killer and his next victim. Serial killers are always L.A.P.D. top priority. Rare though they may be. And preventing retaliation from the gangs themselves against likely enemies."

"Which means these charred remains go to the bottom of the queue." Chandler was getting it. No longer playing the rogue. "Which buys more time, as you keep suggesting."

"Time for what?" asked the morgue attendant.

"That's exactly the right question, Doctor." I smiled but there was only frustration in my eyes. Not that she could see them through my sunglasses.

"Amperdyne could probably process the remains faster than the F.B.I. Definitely faster than L.A.P.D.," suggested Chandler.

I scowled. "Have them run forensics on their own people? No. Conflict of interest. It matters if they colluded or not."

"Then we wait for the F.B.I. to get around to it."

I pulled out my phone and called Olivia Wisniewski. She'd given me the address of the werewolves. My turn to return the favor.

Although, looking at the burned mess in front of me, Wisniewski might not see it that way.

CHAPTER TWENTY-SEVEN

Chandler was gone before the F.B.I. arrived. I watched over the charred remains as if they might disappear now that we'd discovered them. They didn't. No one came into the morgue except for the doctor who turned out to be the head coroner. I'd bothered to learn that her name was Helen Llewellyn. She'd graduated from U.C.L.A. medical school with the realization that she didn't like dealing with living patients. Human ones, at any rate. Hence, the morgue.

"Your friends are here." Helen wasn't happy at the intrusion. Or maybe she was and couldn't show it. The charred remains would no longer be on her plate. That should've excited her.

"Thanks."

Olivia Wisniewski strode in. Her partner, Abigail Hardwicke, close behind. Wisniewski didn't even say 'hello.' "How do you know who the remains are for sure?"

"I told you on the phone. I don't. Odds are just good that these are our missing security guards. They're the only John Does in the morgue. The only lead as to what happened to them."

"When'd they appear?" asked Hardwicke. She watched the coroner with professional impatience.

Doctor Llewellyn glanced at a chart rather than stating anything from memory. "Not my shift. Two days ago."

"Right after Vincent was kidnapped." I eyed Wisniewski. "Burned to make identification hard, if not impossible."

"Faces smashed," noted Hardwicke.

"Exactly."

Hardwicke turned all of her focus to me. I suspected part of her motivation was to avoid the unpleasantly pleasant smell of the remains. B.B.Q. human and B.B.Q. pork had a lot in common.

"You act like you know something. That how they were disposed of's relevant."

"I have a vague theory that everything's about buying time."

"Time for what?" asked both women simultaneously.

Dr. Llewellyn barked with derisive laughter. "That's apparently the question." She eyed the remains and looked at me unpleasantly. Not my horns. Me. The agents. Our intrusion into her morgue had left a bad taste in her mouth. "Time isn't something I have in excess. If you're done with me, I've got bodies to process."

"Don't mind us," replied Wisniewski with a questioning glance at me.

I watched the coroner disappear into another room before speaking. "Is forensics on its way?"

Hardwicke nodded. "We were close when you called. They're not too far behind. You wanna have the conversation you know we're gonna have someplace more private?"

"I was thinking maybe back at my office?"

The black agent shook her head. "That's halfway across town."

"Fine. I just have an annoying goat that I know is pushing my tenants' limits."

"You need to eat?" Wisniewski expression was full of implied warning.

"No. The werewolves took care of that for me."

"Werewolves?" Hardwicke looked from me to her partner. Wisniewski didn't react. Gave herself away. "What've werewolves got to do with this?"

"I went to check in with Killian's pack."

"That conversation we're going to have just got a lot longer." Hardwicke poked Wisniewski in the shoulder. "And you should've told me what was going on before it got to this point."

"A judgment call. We've been busy."

The pretty black agent put her hands on her hips and glared. "Busy my ass. Don't start that Lone Ranger shit again."

"I just gave her an address."

I nodded reassuringly. "Really, that's all she did."

Men and women in F.B.I. tech uniforms came into the morgue carrying what looked like hi-tech tackle boxes of tools and equipment. One of them waved at us when he saw the remains. "We've got it, Wisniewski. Looking good, Hardwicke."

"Keep in your pants, Cruz." Hardwicke gave me a very serious look. Less glare than Wisniewski had earned. "Then we can go have that talk, now. Again, someplace much closer than your office."

I shrugged. "Where do you suggest then?"

Wisniewski smiled. "I know just the place."

CHAPTER TWENTY-EIGHT

I left my car in the morgue parking-lot after retrieving my beret. They'd insisted. Hardwicke drove us in the black F.B.I. sedan which surprised me. Wisniewski seemed to have control-issues. I figured she'd make her partner take the passenger seat. I'd been wrong. It happened. Not often. But still.

The interior smelled good. New with a trace of two different perfumes. Faint enough that most people wouldn't have noticed. "Where we going?"

Neither of the women spoke. I thought at first that we'd talk while driving around in the privacy of the car. We didn't. Hardwicke made a few turns and parked in front of a shabby looking Polish café. Signs in English and Cyrillic indicated homestyle, old country cooking. At least, I assumed the Cyrillic said the same thing as the English next to it. I spoke some Russian but couldn't read a word of anything in that foreign script.

Hardwicke didn't strike me as the type to eat at any place so casual. She was classy. Dressed well even for a Fed. No, this had to be Wisniewski's hang-out. Clearly Hardwicke had adapted.

"The food good?" I asked the black woman.

She nodded wryly. "Surprisingly. Lots of carbs though."

"Just get out of the car," grumbled Wisniewski, opening her door.

I followed the women inside. It was smaller than it appeared from the outside. A reverse *Doctor Who* experience. The men and women occupying the round tables sat close together. Chatting loudly in what was probably Polish. Some Russian thrown in for measure.

My nose was keener than usual for some reason. Scents hit me before visual images. The people smelled of hard work, soap and cigarette smoke. Even though it was illegal to smoke indoors in California.

"No place to sit."

I eyed Wisniewski. She went straight for a door marked 'Private' in English. Hardwicke followed without any hesitation. I figured this was part of the ritual.

Through the door, we passed a busy kitchen. A woman shouted orders. A man shouted back. He slapped some of the dishwashers on the backs of their heads. Sons, given the resemblance. A family business.

There was a bathroom on the right that smelled clean. But it was desperately in need of repairs. Broken tiles. Chipped mirror. A plastic bucket with water that served in lieu of a handle for flushing.

At the end of the hallway, there was another door. The sign in Cyrillic. No English translation to help out.

"Is this some kind of mob hit?" I teased.

Wisniewski didn't smile. She pushed the door open and waited for us to follow. There was a large, elongated table. Some miscellaneous furniture. A buffet. China cabinet. Portraits of stoic figures from

Eastern Europe. It felt like a family typically clustered around the table for meals. I was betting the family in the kitchen.

"You don't eat, right?" asked Wisniewski. She didn't wait for me to answer. "Hardwicke, the usual?"

The black agent nodded. "Get Miss Savage a sweet wine."

"Been reading up on me?"

Hardwicke shrugged. "Professional hazard."

"And it's Bianca."

Wisniewski went back out the door. Presumable to place an order. I fought the urge to rest my fingers on the hilt of my Glock just under my jacket. In case this was a trap. Like Hardwicke had said. Professional hazard.

"Fine. Bianca. But we call each other Wisniewski and Hardwicke. Part of the job. Keeps everything feeling businesslike. Real. Please do the same."

"I understand." She was making sure that I knew her earlier lapse had been just that. A mistake. Don't take liberties. Keep it impersonal. Message understood.

Wisniewski returned and sat down across from where I stood. She motioned impatiently to the chair beside me. I sat, still surveying the room. No sign of cameras. Nothing to suggest the place was more than it seemed.

"So what about werewolves?" asked Hardwicke. "We'll start there."

I leaned back in the heavy wooden chair. It felt solid. Like the people in the café. No pretense. No need for fancy decorations. Good food. Good company. That was the old saying. Granny Oglethorpe had said it about me. That I was good company. A lot of people would say she'd been wrong. Not that she had much to compare it to.

I placed my hands face-down on the table. Watching the F.B.I. agents as I tried to figure out how much to tell them. "I think they know something. About Thrace's disappearance."

"Why?"

"Intuition. Years of honed skills at observing people. Picking up signs of truth and lies. He knew stuff he wouldn't have if Thrace hadn't been in contact. And he wasn't surprised that the bodyguard was missing. Yeah, I know you called him but even still, he knew something."

Wisniewski frowned, annoyed. "He?"

"Sorry. Killian. The alpha."

Hardwicke nodded. "Go on."

"I have no leads on Thrace's disappearance. It happened in broad daylight and they were prepared for a werewolf. Tranq dart obviously dosed for a preternatural. No mistaking who the intended victim was. No ransom demand for him since. Just like Vincent. Made me wonder if the two kidnappings were related. If so, why."

Hardwicke's eyes narrowed shrewdly. "What'd you come up with?"

"I'm pretty sure the Atlantic Street Revenants aren't involved in the boy's disappearance. And Amperdyne's gonna get screwed no matter how this falls, unless they recover the boy personally."

"Old territory," complained the pretty agent.

"I'm just catching up with my thinking. So who else has motive? For the boy, could be anyone wanting cash. Only no ransom. For

Thrace, I thought the pack might still harbor a grudge. Or might know who did."

Hardwicke nodded. "You're finally making sense. Keep going."

"I always make sense, even if you don't follow my logic." I paused a moment to let my criticism sink in. "Killian wasn't surprised by Thrace's disappearance. But he was confident that a search warrant would prove that the missing werewolf wasn't there."

"What possible motive could they have?"

"I keep trying to make it about money. The way everyone else has been. But that's where events aren't making sense. Vincent has access to his personal accounts. Only a few hundred thousand at best."

"Untouched. We've been watching," interjected Wisniewski.

"And Thrace has most of his earnings from Gibraltar unspent in a savings accounts. Some real estate investments. All of it totaling more than Vincent can access."

Hardwicke shrugged. "Also untouched."

I grunted. "So money doesn't seem to be a motive."

Hardwicke tapped the table with a well-manicured nail. "The alternate theory is that someone's trying to hit Gibraltar hard. Payback for something personal instead of business."

"Does Henry Gibraltar look like he does personal?" I laughed bitterly.

A young man came in with a tray. Blue eyes. Light brown hair. One of the sons. He set a coffee-mug in front of Wisniewski, water next to Hardwicke and a glass of white wine in front of me. The coffee smelled strong. Turkish style. I couldn't get of whiff of anything but that.

The young man put a bowl of some kind of stew inbetween the two agents. Shredded cabbage and ground beef from the looks of it. There were sausages. And two empty plates.

"Thank you." I was the only one to acknowledge him before he rushed off. He avoided eye contact. Even with my sunglasses on.

"We'll eat. You talk," insisted Hardwicke.

I was confused. Wisniewski had taken second seat to this interrogation. In fact, she'd hardly spoken at all since being accused of Lone Ranger tactics. How serious was the problem between them?

"Fine. As I was saying, money doesn't seem to be a motive. Neither does a personal attack on Gibraltar. This isn't about anything that straightforward. If either were the real motive, the boy would've turned up dead already. Not just the security guards."

"How are you so certain that the remains are them?"

"I told you, Hardwicke. They're the only John Does in the morgue." I left Chandler out of it. He wasn't crucial to the facts. And I wasn't sure I'd get any more cooperation if I outted him as MI-6. "In fact, I was thinking that whoever took Vincent couldn't risk keeping the men around. Or alive."

"Unless they were co-conspirators."

"Highly unlikely. Too much risk for the reward. Especially if money's not the objective."

Hardwicke looked as frustrated as I felt. "Not money. Not revenge. Let's pretend you're right. What then?"

"I keep bumping into the question, why do what they did? Why take the boy but demand no ransom? Why kill the Amperdyne men but make them impossible to identify? Why take Thrace at all?"

"And?"

"And each of these things buys them time."

Hardwicke stopped eating. "I get what the coroner meant now. Back to that question. Time for what? I'm also starting to see how your brain works. It feels plausible. And you're right. Nothing else is making sense."

"I don't see why we'd give up revenge so quickly." Wisniewski spoke with less forcefulness than normal. Hardwicke glared at her and she went back to eating in silence. Watching us over her stew.

"I've already asked the obvious question. What happens with Gibraltar Global Industries if Vincent is gone longer than not? As far as I can tell, nothing."

Hardwicke played with her spoon, nodding. "The boy's just the heir. He's not intrinsic to anything day to day. His absence is only a distraction for the grandfather."

"Not as much of one as his murder would be. Which hasn't happened." I sipped my wine. Not chilled. But sweet enough. "So again, what or who benefits from keeping Vincent away from his grandfather for a longer period of time?"

"You don't have any clue, do you?" Hardwicke stared at me disappointed.

"Not yet. But I've just learned that the werewolves know something. And that those two charred bodies are likely the security team. Vincent's still alive. Probably. Unless he's literally mixed in with that barbeque."

"Do you have to?" complained Wisniewski.

Hardwicke brushed past her objection. "But?"

"My gut says he's not. That he is alive. And the key to this whole thing."

"We considered an inside man. But Thrace was protecting Gibraltar when Vincent went missing."

"What if the boy wanted out?"

Wisniewski held her spoon mid-bite. Staring at me. "Out of billions of dollars?"

"Out of being a prisoner." I shook my head at her lack of imagination. "But what if you're right. What if there was an inside man? And it's Thrace?"

"Inside as in, he got his pack to help?" Hardwicke shook her head. "They're incredibly homophobic. They wouldn't do it out of the kindness of their hearts."

"Anton's got money. Maybe he hasn't drawn it out yet because it'd lead right back to Killian. Take the boy. Later, take Thrace. Once the boy is safely away, Thrace escapes from his abductors and siphons the money to his pack over time."

"That's a lot of supposition. I'd need more than your gut to get a federal warrant to watch Killian or his people on their own lands."

"My gut's all I have right now."

"We can get her their financials. It's part of their Federal registration agreement." Wisniewski waited for Hardwicke to consider it. "If you think that's a good idea."

"Alright, already. Stop playing the meek and mild. It's disconcerting." Hardwicke scowled. "Just tell me when you do crazy shit like sending a civilian into a werewolf pack's territory."

"Deal." Wisniewski smiled. "And I'll have those financials for you before the end of the day. If they own or rent anyplace that they could hold the boy, with or without a warrant, you can check it out."

"Thank you. I was running out of leads."

"Hopefully the charred remains will shed some light."

"I don't think they will. Killing the bodyguards was inevitable. They were too well trained. Taking them with the boy was just a distraction. A delaying tactic. Killing them hides any details of who took them. And why. If we hadn't found the remains—figured out who they might be—we'd still think they were in on it. Wasting more time."

"We already have a watch order for all public transportation. If Vincent runs, someone will spot him."

I stared at Hardwicke and raised my brow. "Why use public transportation?"

"Shit."

"Oh yeah. Shit is right."

CHAPTER TWENTY-NINE

The agents dropped me off at my car. There was no sign of Chandler lurking in the shadows, so I drove back to my office. Lost in thought. I was so distracted that I didn't even drive around the block once before parking. I'd forgotten about my mystery stalker. And the bomb.

I kept replaying the questions in my head as I walked from the garage. It made me oblivious to the people I passed. And the cars that went about their business. Even the ones blaring music, cruising the boulevard.

It was out of character and dangerous. A side-effect of being full. Or maybe just my singlemindedness in solving this case. Something woke me from my thoughts just inside the building entrance. I looked up from the industrial carpet that lined the hallway. Something was wrong.

A sound. No. The lack of sound. I didn't hear the bleating of a goat. One of the tenants had his outer office door opened because it was a nice day. I felt a gentle breeze brush past me from outside. He'd never have left his door open if an animal had been raising a ruckus.

I paused at the open door to our offices. Janet was sitting at her desk going through emails. Unperturbed. She looked up and smiled. "Bee. You're back!"

"Safe and sound." I frowned at her. Her smile wilted with uncertainty. I waved toward the hallway. "Where's the goat?"

"Oh!" She burst out with laughter. "The same place they were yesterday."

"Did it die?" I'd asked for sick or dying goats. Wouldn't be unexpected to lose a few if they were sick enough.

She shook her head. "You reminded me to use my initiative. Not just a fridge. Soundproofed the room and installed a small ventilation system."

"Wow. How much did that set me back?"

"Ten grand."

My mouth dropped open to protest when she chuckled wickedly. "Don't be ridiculous, Bee. I did pay extra for the same-day rush. But it's a small room. Four hundred and sixty-three dollars."

"Good job." I went into my office and plopped into my chair. I tossed my sunglasses into a bowl specifically for them and leaned back. A faint bleating startled me and I stood up. Tracking the noise. Aware of a musky scent in the room.

"Janet!"

She rushed in, a grin already plastered on her face. "You found the venting system."

"My office? Of all places?"

"It was either your office or a tenant's. Since you're the one— eating them, I figured fair is fair."

"I suppose you couldn't've run it through the existing air ducts?"

"The bleating travels. As you can hear." Her face relaxed and she sat on the edge of my desk. "What happened with the werewolves?"

"Later. I've had to go over those details twice already today. What've you got for me?"

"Bad news I'm afraid. The linguists we hit up all replied that they'd never seen the script before. It vaguely resembles Sumerian writing according to one of them. But only in the sense that it doesn't resemble anything else even remotely."

"Whoever left it expected me to be able to read it. A secret preternatural language. Great."

"So you're sure it's one of your people?"

"Who else?"

Janet pursed her lips together. "I can check federal law enforcement to see if any succubi are incarcerated pending execution. We might find out what it says that way."

"I doubt it. The last time we tried to reach out to a succubus in prison, neither she nor the Feds would let her talk to me."

"Can't hurt to ask."

"Fine. Check. But usually someone notifies me as a professional courtesy. Or preternatural courtesy. Some kind of guilt ridden motivation. Hey, we're killing another one of your kind. We know you're rare and all. Sorry but just thought you should know. In case you know them."

Janet glared at me. "Someone's in a mood. Did it go that badly with the werewolves?"

"Quit asking. But no. I'm not grumpy because of werewolves. Or the goat bleating into my office through the vent you kindly had installed."

"Then what?"

"Someone's reaching out to me. Expecting me to respond to whatever's in that note. And I can't do anything about it because I don't know a damned thing about the language. I'm not usually so helpless."

"There are still people looking into it. The ones you specifically asked me to email came up empty. But they forwarded the request to likely scholars. Someone will know something."

"What if the sender's just passing through town? What if they leave never to be found again because I didn't respond?"

She studied me with maternal concern. "I'm sorry, Bee."

"I know, Janet. And I'm sorry. Feeling sorry for myself when a sheltered, teenaged boy is out there somewhere! Dealing with the real world on his own for the first time. In the worst possible ways."

"No leads on the kidnappings?"

"Something. Not enough. Even if Vincent participated in his own escape from his grandfather, there are a lot of bad people out there. Someone who might take advantage of his innocence."

"He's not you, Bee. He's not a little girl who never knew her family."

"Shut up, Janet."

"Bee!"

I growled low and feral. "I know. I should shut up instead. I'm not getting overly involved. His situation's nothing like mine."

"But you protect the innocent. And the young."

"That's where I'm being hypocritical. Historically, Vincent would be considered a man. He's old enough to be one. But I keep thinking of him as a child. Because of how he was raised."

"Would it matter if you thought about him as a grown man?"

I stared at Janet. Blinking. "It might. It just might. I'm a bloody fool. What age was your first crush?"

"Kindergarten. A boy with big ears and buck teeth. The nicest, smartest five-year-old I'd ever met."

I gave her a look. "Your first sexual crush?"

"How are you defining sexual? You mean romantic? I was pretty much smitten in kindergarten."

"Someone after you'd hit puberty!"

"Mr. Jesep. Fourth grade substitute teacher while Mrs. Paddock had her first baby. He was only twenty-two or something at the time. All the girls thought he was dreamy. Why?"

"Because Vincent might've found a reason to run away. A romantic relationship that hadn't existed before. A crush on someone who was accessible in a world where he was trapped."

"Surveillance would've covered that."

"Not if we weren't looking for it."

"A teacher?"

"He's homeschooled. It's possible. Only—only the staff is almost exclusively male. That might narrow down the search really fast."

"Oh, Bee. Sometimes you are so human."

I felt a flash of annoyance. "Pardon?"

"You're making the same assumption about Vincent that fathers and mothers have been making about their sons since time began."

I frowned, my brows narrowing. Then it hit me. "That Vincent likes girls."

"What, you think only the werewolf might be gay?"

"Thanks, Janet. I needed a kick in the skirt." I stood up, feeling liberated. "Finally something to do."

I grabbed my sunglasses and slipped them on. Checked my beret to make sure it was pinned firmly in place as I marched toward the door.

"Where are you going?"

"Call Gibraltar's people. Tell them I'm coming to review footage again. And Janet, tell them. This isn't a request."

CHAPTER THIRTY

At Gibraltar's villa, I was immediately led to the same video room without any fuss or bother. The word was out. Cooperate with me or else. I didn't even get an acknowledgement of my arrival from Yuri Kamaguchi. With Thrace gone, they'd be responsible for all security until the matter was resolved.

I waved my escort away and began to scroll backwards in time. I paused and viewed any contact between Vincent and the staff. Most of the employers were in their late twenties to mid-thirties. That didn't matter. Young love was blind to a lot of things. Including an age gap that might offend modern sensibilities.

I didn't waste a lot of time on listening to conversations. Or worrying about what anyone constructively did. All I focused on was Vincent's face. When I saw his expression change the first time, I could've slapped myself. It was that obvious.

Janet had guessed right. Vincent didn't like girls. He wasn't enthralled with the vampires. But when he gazed at one particular member of staff, it showed. Anton Thrace. Vincent had a crush on the gay werewolf.

But was it reciprocated? I didn't see adoration on the man's eyes. For the most part, Thrace didn't seem to notice the boy at all. Was it misdirection? Make everyone think he didn't like Vincent to protect their relationship?

If Thrace felt the same, it would explain why he might've helped the boy escape. A better reason than sympathy for a trapped animal. A chance for them to be together.

Would that make Thrace desperate enough to reach out to his old pack? Pay them for helping the two lovebirds be united? Freed from the tyranny of a domineering and probably homophobic grandfather?

And there was no question. The werewolves were involved. If they were helping Thrace instead of being involved in kidnapping him, there was only one motive. Money. A lot of money to overlook the fact that the Thrace and the boy were gay. Money was a less convincing motive if they were on the other side. There'd have been a ransom. And I had to believe that both kidnappings were for the same reason.

The possibility changed some events in my mind. If Thrace and Vincent wanted to be together for the long haul, he'd disappear with the boy. And they'd need all of Thrace's money to survive on the run. They could never stop running. Leaving it in his bank account argued against it.

Thrace had struck me as more sensible than that. Definitely not cold-blooded enough to kill the two Amperdyne men. So who then? Killian? On his own? To protect his pack's involvement? Then hide the truth from Vincent and Anton both?

Another thing nagged at me. Less than two more years and it wouldn't have mattered. They could've been together no matter what Gibraltar wanted. Vincent would've been at the legal age of consent for sex. Not running from the law. So why would they run now? What would make them desperate enough? Unless the old man had begun to suspect the relationship. Planned to get rid of the werewolf. As in permanently.

More questions. New questions. No answers but definitely new possibilities. Things that made sense. Some of it. Not enough without proof.

I called Wisniewski. "It's Bianca. You freeze Thrace's assets? I mean, like completely?"

"He couldn't even get a dollar from an ATM. Why? You find something?"

I told her my new idea.

"Holy shit, Savage! No one at the bureau thought to look for signs of a love-struck boy in that footage. We'll follow up. Double-check as part of our failed due diligence. Once we confirm what you found, we can move on it."

"What more can you do besides keeping his money tied up to prevent them running away on it. I take it Vincent's money is still untouched?"

"Not even a balance inquiry."

"I'm going to talk to Gibraltar's attorney. See if he has any ideas on this new line of investigation."

"Would the werewolves be helping Anton though? Without money to pay them, a gay werewolf's more likely to have his ass kicked than be united with young love."

"That's why I want to make sure the money's going to stay frozen. I think if we passed that bit of information along to the pack, someone might just lead me to our lovebirds."

"Or might kill them. That's a big risk. I can't authorize it. Not without clearing it through chain of command."

"There's no proof. You aren't going to get permission."

She was quiet for a few moments. "Sorry, Bianca. I want to help. I like a good sting operation. But not if it means endangering the boy."

"I understand. I wouldn't even ask if I thought he'd get hurt. But you're right. He might. Fine. I'll come up with another plan. But at least you can follow up by presenting the new hypothesis."

"Can't you say theory like all the rest of us ignorant folk?"

"Nope." I grinned and hung up.

But my joy was just a flash. Burned up and gone like that.

I wound up muttering to myself. "If Vincent left on his own and I don't turn him in when I find them, I'm breaking the law. But if I do, I'm doing something much worse. Keeping him a prisoner. Sentencing Thrace to prison, too. Shakespeare had something to say about situations like this. Everyone winds up dead. Well, fuck him."

CHAPTER THIRTY-ONE

I decided to stop by the condo to check on Martini. And to shower. I showered twice a day on most cases. Lengthy stakeouts. Skulking in alleys. Chasing suspects. It wasn't a tidy job.

This time I didn't need to shower because I was dirty. I just felt unclean. Doing my job might mean destroying a young man's life. Might mean sending Anton Thrace to prison as a sex offender. Ridiculous as that was!

It wasn't my call to make. So then why was I so determined to find a way around it? Find a happily-ever-after where murder had been involved? Maybe it was because I'd never have a happily-ever-after of my own.

The garage was full of cars. No people. All my tenants safely tucked away in their condos. It was dark out. Another day shot to hell. But the night was just starting.

Hardwicke and Wisniewski had dropped off the financials on Killian's group with Janet. She'd left them on my desk before she'd gone home for the day. The sooner I went through that material, the better. And I had a meeting with Blake Mansfield in an hour. Also at my office. I was hoping he knew his cousin better than he'd let on. Knew about the boy's attraction to Thrace.

I got out of the car. Debating the problems of biology and the arbitrary nature of human legal systems. Remembering firsthand when thirteen was an adult. Girls were old-maids by fourteen. Times were different on the frontier. People needed to have kids. To work the fields. Build a homestead. Protect each other.

I didn't scan the building with my power. I wasn't looking for danger. Stupid of me. Ask anyone. That's usually when danger found them.

Someone struck me from behind. Knocked me onto my face against the chill cement. My Sig slipped out of the thigh holster. Skidded across the garage floor. Out of reach.

I rolled onto my back. Tried to grab the Glock in my shoulder holster while seeing who'd struck me. I couldn't look away from my attacker and the gun wouldn't come loose.

A blonde man loomed over me. Cast in shadows. Big. Heavily muscled. He lunged forward, arms reaching for my throat. He was fast. But I bent my knees. Kicked with all my strength as he dropped toward me.

I was stronger than a human. A lot stronger, especially after feeding on Killian. This guy didn't budge as my feet connected. I pushed myself backwards along the floor instead. Sliding away from him. He barely noticed.

Fear rose in me. Someone stronger than me. Something not human. My power unfurled instinctively then. Lashed out like a scream. Struck the blonde and lapped at his lifeforce. I tasted the feral nature of his energy. Lycanthrope. Someone I'd never seen before. There were other shadows behind him. At least two more. Big men. Just as powerful.

"Who are you?" I demanded, cursing silently that the fall had dislodged the straps binding the holster. Leather meant to keep the Glock safely pressed against my body was now tangled in the weapon.

"Your death," replied the lycanthrope. I wasn't certain which kind. He tasted like wolf. My interaction with Killian's group made it the best guess. Not that I'd ever met any other kind. The two with him hung back. One on one I stood a fighting chance.

He lunged at me again and I gave up on the gun. I rolled quickly to one side as his companions decided to join the attack. I didn't call for help. I didn't want one of my conscientious neighbors to come downstairs. They'd try to interfere. Even old Mrs. Welby. I couldn't let them. They'd died faster than I would. Without serving any purpose.

I felt icy shards form in my stomach as my power sucked at his lifeforce. I concentrated. Pouring it into him. Pulling it out hard, like I had with Killian. Only this time I didn't hold back.

The blonde dropped to his knees but the other two kept coming. I'd worked so hard at controlling my power that I didn't know how to unleash it fully. Not against a group. My panic at the initial attack had settled. My adrenaline under control. Worse, I wasn't hungry like I'd been before. Feeding on Killian had sated me more than I'd have hoped.

Taking down one of them was doable. The other two—I tried switching targets. A grey-haired older man. I felt another surge of heady energy. A rush of euphoria that slowed down my reaction-time like a drug.

My power made the man stagger. Woozy. But hitting them one at a time wasn't going work. The blonde was already getting back to his feet.

"God damn you all!" I glanced at the Sig on the smooth cement floor. I'd rolled away from it. Not towards. I cursed again silently.

The third werewolf leapt forward. A lean Asian man with smoldering brown eyes. Nails like claws. A hint of transformation. Must be close to the full moon. I hadn't checked the exact date it would hit. Dealing with werewolves, I should've.

I raised my arms to block the attack, unable to move out of the way fast enough. But the weight of him never struck me. No claws dug into my flesh.

I lowered my arms carefully. Saw the Asian wriggling with feet in the air, clawing at his back. Someone had the werewolf in a chokehold from behind.

Movement distracted me. The blonde rushed forward. Past me. Toward the struggling Asian.

I tried to see who held the Asian. They had to be preternaturally strong. A momentary flash of hope burned in my chest. The mysterious woman. But I saw the arms. Masculine. A man.

I rolled onto my belly, a less vulnerable position. Desperate to see who'd saved me. I recognized the vampire in time to shout a warning. "Dusty!"

The blonde werewolf lashed out, aiming for the vampire's kidney. Dusty spun, dragging the clawing Asian in front of him like a shield. The blonde drove his preternatural fist into the wrong target and his friend screamed in agony.

The older werewolf stood. He'd recovered. Circled Dusty and the other two werewolves. No way the vampire could stand against them all.

I scrabbled to my hands and feet and dove for the Sig. Apparently the grey-haired werewolf decided to ignore Dusty. He'd continued around the fighting men until he was almost behind me. Close enough to grab my ankle. He threw me away from my weapon, into Mrs. Chavez's white Ford Malibu. The alarm began sounding.

I heard doors open in the complex above me. Damn it! Innocent lives were about to be at risk.

"The police'll be coming!" I shouted. Pouring my hunger into the grey-haired werewolf. Drinking deeply enough that the room swooned. I'd never overeaten before. It was almost as bad as being hungry. Painful. Overwhelming my control. Keeping me from soaking up more energy.

"He's a freakin' vampire!" shouted one of the werewolves. "One undead was dangerous. Two's too much with the police on the way!"

"Grab Tony and go!"

My vision cleared and I saw Dusty knocked across the room. He smashed into a cement support column. The blonde and older man had the Asian's arms. Dragging him out.

I tried to stand. Wanted to give chase. It was a stupid idea. But it didn't matter. My legs gave out and I collapsed onto all fours. I stayed there. Breathing heavily. Waiting for my muscles to stop trembling.

Cool gentle hands touched my shoulder. Helped me to stand. "Lucky that I decided to stop by."

I stared at Dusty. Grateful that he'd been there. Then pissed off, too. "Why the hell are you stalking me, Dusty? I don't date vampires."

He pulled away but I sagged and he braced me again. "I don't mean to bother you. I just can't stop thinking about you. About our kiss."

"Yeah, well what about Rhoda? Isn't she your intended or whatever?"

"We flirted. She wanted more. I felt something. But nothing like this. She's like a shadow on a foggy evening. You're like fire in the middle of a thunderstorm. Warm. Exciting. Undeniable."

"I'm sorry, Dusty. This isn't you. My power must've affected you."

"Why does everyone say that? I felt your power when we kissed. I knew it briefly sparked something inside me. Something that made me want to grab you. Press you against me." He laughed nervously. "Hell, even tear your clothes off. I'm never that way with a woman. Never have been. But your power left me. I felt it go. I knew when I was thinking on my own."

I shook my head, staring into his earnest, steel-grey eyes. "I doubt it. No offense, Kid, but even once the charm is past its bloom, there are echoes of desire. Not usually with one whammy. But still."

"You're wrong." He folded his arms across his broad chest. More petulant than masculine. "An' I want a better reason than I'm a vampire not to want to get to know me."

"You're a kid?" I tried not to smile. Let's just say I wasn't too successful.

He grew angry. "I saved your life just now. How much of a kid am I?"

"Fine." I tested standing on my own. Nodded when my legs held. I gave him a better answer. "You're a virgin."

"And you aren't so that makes you better? That's a double standard."

I hesitated. "Actually, I am. I plan on keeping it that way."

I'd piqued his interest. His frown grew wistful. "Because you're religious?"

I opened my mouth to give him a flippant retort. Then stopped. I didn't believe sex outside of marriage was a sin. Not the way it was portrayed in the Bible. One of my regular and frequent arguments with my pastor. We each knew the other would never concede. Didn't stop us from trying.

Historically, it made sense. There'd been all sorts of social complexities about men not abandoning their duties to a woman and her unborn child. Men were warriors. Fighters. Killers. Women were submissive and meek. Stayed home and built a family. Because that was what was expected of them.

Those were the old rules. Women didn't need men to have or raise children. Well, they needed sperm. Just not the men themselves. Men didn't need women either to be a decent parent. A two parent family was only stronger than a single parent some of the time. When it was built out of love and mutual respect. Otherwise, I'd seen it in the past and in the present. A couple that fought all the time was worse than a mediocre single parent.

I might never know firsthand about raising a child. But having someone supportive to help make better choices was a good thing. Didn't have to be a romantic partner. Just someone that could keep things balanced. A trustworthy friend. A loyal sibling.

"Yeah. Maybe it's part of my religious background. Maybe I've spent so many years knowing I can't enjoy unfettered sex with a man without killing him, that I've shut that part of myself off."

He held my gaze. "You can't kill me."

"That's even worse, Dusty. I can't even consider the idea of sex with a corpse. Sorry. That's what you are. Really."

He let go of me then. One hand ready to catch me if I swooned. Chivalrous despite his resentment. He realized that I didn't need his help anymore and he walked away. I'd hurt him. Badly. But it was the truth. Nothing I said to make him feel better would change that. So I watched him walk.

"Bianca!"

Sandra Tiptree-James, one of my youngest neighbors with pale skin, blue eyes and Nordic blonde hair came rushing into the parking garage. She held a baseball bat in a tight, two-fisted grip. Mrs. Chavez was with her, cellphone at the ready. They saw the blood and studied me. Trying to find out if it was mine.

"They're gone." I smiled, a bittersweet sad twist of my mouth. "Thank you for coming to my aid. You chased them away."

"I called the police," shouted Mrs. Welby from the top of the stairs leading into the garage. As if I couldn't hear her from twenty feet away. Or maybe the way she peered into the corners of the garage, she feared they might be watching. Waiting. The elderly black woman clutched her cane with both hands, ready to swing at the first sign of trouble.

"I would miss you guys."

Mrs. Chavez smiled uncertainly. "You're fine, Bianca. Safe now. We'd miss you, too. Best not let anything happen."

Mr. Huong and his niece Mei stepped around Mrs. Welby. They each had kitchen knives in their hands. Looking fierce and afraid both. Bits of food stained Mr. Huong's apron. I'd interrupted their dinner preparation. Such loyalty among these everyday people. Tears threatened to form.

"Thank you, Mrs. Chavez. Everyone."

She thought that I'd meant, I'd miss them if I'd died. I'd meant, that if I chose to move away to protect them. I'd break their hearts and mine. At least they'd be alive to feel that pain. Tonight had been another close call. And it was going to be the last.

CHAPTER THIRTY-TWO

Janet showed up just as I finished giving my slightly abridged statement to the incident commander. Someone had called her. She waited until the cops and the E.M.T.s finished giving me the once over before approaching me.

"Bee! What happened? Another hate crime?"

"Oh, these guys hated me alright." I put an arm across her thin shoulders and led her to the far side of the garage. Away from the police talking to my neighbors. "But not the way you're thinking."

"The case?"

I nodded. "Werewolves." I saw her horror and bumped her temple with my head. A gentle rebuke. "No! Stop stressing out. This is what I need you to do, since you're here. Call Amperdyne. Tell them I need to hire a security detail for my condo complex. Tell them werewolves are one of the more serious threats to me right now. Not a big detail. Just enough men to handle four or five unarmed lycanthropes."

"Five men attacked you?"

"No. Three." I paused and she saw something in my expression.

"What?"

"Nothing. Just, the reason I'm okay is that one of the vampires happened to stop by."

"He just happened to stop by? On the off chance?"

I tried not to squirm with embarrassment. "He fancies me. Alright? There, you know."

She looked astonished. "You said you'd never date a corpse."

"And that's what I told him. Afterwards. It didn't go over big."

"So the next time he comes back, he might be in the danger category?"

I wrinkled my brows, rubbing my chin. "Honestly, I'd say 'no.' I think he's too innocent for that. Too green. He's upset. But not the way that would make him want to hurt me."

"Small favors," she muttered. "Fine, I'm on it. Anything else?"

"Yeah. Tell me who ratted me out?" I studied my neighbors. They had gathered together in a corner. Talking to the police all at the same time with their anxious renditions of what they saw. Or rather, didn't see.

"Sorry. I'm having a senior moment. It was someone in the complex. That's all I can remember." She gave me a smug grin and I let it go.

"This attack was on me. You're safe. I touched a raw nerve with Killian, it seems. Once the police run the DNA on the blood splattered all over the garage floor, the Feds'll take over."

"That's why the expensive security." Janet nodded unhappily. "Oh! And it's why I had the office locked up. I checked with the tenants. None of them are doing any evening work this week. They didn't complain. What's the next move, Boss?"

"I still have a meeting with Blake Mansfield and some reports to go over." I dangled my housekeys in front of her. "Could you go up and make sure Martini's okay? The attack pretty much put me behind schedule again. I need a shower more than ever, but it'll have to wait."

She patted her purse. "I know I never use it, but you gave me a spare when you bought the place."

"Wasn't sure you had it on you."

I pulled out my phone. Used the Uber app and went to the garage entrance. Two minutes later I was on my way to the office. I didn't wear a watch and glanced at my phone. I was five minutes late. Hopefully Mansfield wouldn't use it as an excuse to take off.

He didn't. As we pulled up, I saw the man leaning against a taxi. Arms folded imperiously across his chest. Dressed in the same suit as before. Or at least the same color. He eyed the car guardedly as I opened my door.

I thanked the Uber driver and brushed off my skirt to make sure it draped properly as I stepped out. I should've changed. Nothing I could do about it now. I approached Mansfield with a smile.

"You're late." He thumped the taxi with a palm. It drove away behind the Uber car. Then he seemed to actually see me. Maybe it was the oil smeared on my jacket. Or the deep scuffing on my boots. Very little blood had made it onto my clothes. "What happened?"

"Unexpected visitors dropped by my place. The police report took longer than I hoped."

"One of the perks of being a P.I.? Angry ex-husbands?"

I eyed him somberly as I unlocked the entrance to the building. "I don't get angry ex-husbands after me. They're too afraid. This was because of Gibraltar."

"Pardon?" He stepped closer. "Vampires did this?"

"They aren't the only preternatural element on offer, Mr. Mansfield."

"Anton wouldn't have attacked you."

"No. Not Anton. Keep trying..I'm sure the brain cells will kick in eventually."

His mouth opened in an ugly snarl. "I didn't come here to be mocked, Miss Savage."

"No. And I'm not very congenial after being attacked by three brutish werewolves, either"

He froze, one hand reaching out as if he needed to touch me. To make sure I was real. A physical response to disbelief. I'd seen it more than once. One of those things that people did that revealed that they were genuinely surprised. Without even knowing they did it.

"Are you alright?"

I unlocked the door and walked inside. He followed. "A few scrapes. And I need a new holster, apparently. Claws are murder on leather straps."

"You shot them? Killed them? Who were they?"

I kept walking. Past the closet with the goat. I reached out my power. Completely under my control. Still full to capacity. My hunger was like a bear slow to wake from hibernation. It grumbled and breathed deeply. I let the goat alone. It had water and food according to Janet. It'd wait until the morning.

Truthfully, it wasn't even appetizing now. I'd eaten something much more substantial. Something powerful enough that I worried it'd be hard to go back to feeding off of livestock and rodents. Well, unless I let myself get hungry again. I hated to do that.

"I didn't kill them."

I hadn't had time to reload the silver-tipped ammo. Not that I was planning on sharing that with anyone. Mansfield might not have known about the werewolf threat, but I liked the element of surprise in case I was jumped again. No telling what he might inadvertently reveal to the wrong person. They weren't afraid of my guns for now. They would be.

I unlocked my office door and pushed it open. The lights were off but there was no one waiting inside. My succubus power would've warned me otherwise. It was safe.

Mansfield touched the back of my shoulder. Fingers on cloth. "Who were they?"

I gave him a withering look, ruined by my sunglasses. "I know you're used to getting your questions answered because of your position in Gibraltar Global. But take a chill pill and have a seat."

He scowled and followed me into the office. I walked back past him and shut the door. Locked it for good measure. He seemed surprised. Definitely not security conscious. Amperdyne always had his back. Maybe he was afraid I was locking him in.

Something else occurred to me then. Why had he taken a taxi here? And why hadn't I seen or sensed any ninjas lurking in the shadows. After what had happened to Thrace, I was becoming a bit more paranoid where the Gibraltars were concerned.

"Where's your security detail?"

"I ditched them." He looked furtive. "I don't know who to trust. They know our real identities. If they turn out to be involved—Maureen and I could be next."

I studied the nervous man. He hardly seemed capable of talking to a judge in court. Much less ditching a highly trained security detail. Maybe they'd let him out of sight because he was bugged in all manner of places.

"What put this bit of paranoia in your bonnet?"

"I called Maureen after the bombing. To make sure she was alright. We talked about things. How nothing was like we'd thought growing up."

"And you both decided your security details were a two-edged sword. Unless they're innocent. Which by my last reckoning they were."

"Their men took Vincent! Isn't it obvious? Someone's paying them more money than even we have to destroy us."

I sat down and detached my beret. Tossing it into the same bowl I usually put my sunglasses in. It's also where my keys wound up half the time. Anything else in my jacket pockets, too.

"The men who disappeared with Vincent are dead. At least, we'll get confirmation soon, I hope. Charred body-bits apparently take longer for forensics work. I hardly think they did it to their own people."

"Charred body-bits? What do you mean?"

"I asked you here to get information, not catch you up." I paused, studying him. Too much white in his eyes again. His hands fidgeting. Playing with the edges of his suit jacket. Sweat forming on his upper lip. I knew a bad case of the jitters when I saw them. "But you're the client. After a fashion. I can spare time."

He paced, eyes never leaving me. I motioned to the chair. "Just sit!"

Reluctantly he dropped into the comfortable seat. I'd made sure that they were comfortable when I bought them. No power play to encourage clients to leave quickly. People who came to me had complex stories to tell. They needed a safe haven while they explained their needs. It was part of the service that most private investigators failed to focus on.

"A pile of charred human parts were found. Faces smashed in to delay or prevent dental comparisons. And when I say parts, they weren't cut into hands and feets and stuff. This was like someone took a butchered chicken and threw it in a woodchipper. Then grilled the pile on high."

He paled, gripping the armrests. "Vincent?"

I shrugged and shook my head. "We don't know for sure. But my gut says 'no.' I think it's just the two Amperdyne men who disappeared with him."

Mansfield was quiet for a few long heartbeats. "That's why you asked me here?"

"No. Not exactly." I leaned forward. "We talked about trust at our first meeting. You didn't seem to trust me. Maybe you still don't."

"I do." He stammered and averted his gaze from my reflective sunglasses.

"Then I think you know more than you've told me. Perhaps even more than you've told your grandfather?"

He looked up. Afraid. "About what?"

"I'm not talking about porn and prostitutes, Blake. If that's what you're afraid of. Or recreational drug use. None of that's relevant to finding Vincent. It's your personal business."

"Then what? I don't know anything about the kidnapping! I swear! Or I'd have said. I like the little shit."

"Why's he a little shit? He's more like a prisoner. Sheltered. Protected from the world. I haven't heard anyone say a bad thing about him."

"That's because there's nothing to say. Not really."

"So you knew he was gay?"

That startled Mansfield. His expression was surprise. Not denial. "How'd you find out?"

"How did you?"

He rubbed his hands together as if the friction would help materialize his words. "Vincent hinted. Asked me questions that let me put two and two together. I'm not as clueless as you seem to think."

"Did he mention anyone specifically?"

"Not really. He was feeling me out about coming out. Without actually coming out. I haven't been the best cousin. It's hard not to be jealous sometimes when your position in the family has been buried beneath ages of paper-trails and misdirection."

"If your mother had lived, you still wouldn't be the heir. Or a Gibraltar."

"I am a Gibraltar! Maybe Maureen and I don't carry the name. But it's our blood. He's our grandfather, too."

"What would be different then? If she were alive?"

"People would know we were his grandchildren! We'd have their respect. Access to Gibraltar resources like members of the family instead of well-paid executives. She'd have fought to make sure we were treated better."

I studied his expression. "So you resent Vincent."

"I did. Growing up. Then he started treating me like his big brother. Turning to me for problems that he couldn't trust to anyone else. And Maureen. He made us his family even if the old man didn't."

"So you were okay with him being gay."

"He's a sweet, innocent kid! How could anyone not be okay with him loving anyone?" Mansfield grew agitated. "If our goddamned grandfather would stop living in the eighteenth century and open his eyes! The son of a son doesn't need to be the heir. A woman shouldn't be on the bottom of the inheritance pile because she doesn't carry the name. She still carries the blood."

"So you and Maureen looked out for Vincent."

"Yes!"

"Could Vincent have told her about a boy?" I didn't say 'man.' It would just muddy the waters and I needed answers.

"Sure. I guess. He was more comfortable opening up to her. The only woman in his life. If you don't count Cook. Cook's a hardass just like Grandfather. But she kept us in line on family holidays."

"You were together for holidays?"

He laughed. "Not in public. Or anywhere that people existed. Tiny chalets in the middle of dense forests. Cement bunkers alongside secluded lakes. Once a year to look over his progeny. Like counting livestock."

"So the three of you had a relationship. You said you hardly knew him."

"I don't. Not really. We had minutes alone together. Occasional haphazard encounters. The family get-togethers stopped about the time Vincent turned eight or nine. He wasn't allowed to call me. But we'd talk when I stopped at the house to deliver legal documents.

Occasionally Maureen would be allowed to visit on the pretense of doing electrical work. She pushed harder for a relationship with Vincent. He remembered our holidays together. Missed us. Otherwise Grandfather would've never let us see each other after that."

"I thought Vincent grew up alone and guarded his whole life. It's helpful to know that he had a relationship with the two of you. Don't underestimate the value of family. Especially family you aren't allowed to know."

He nodded. "Does this help? Did someone take Vincent because he's gay?"

"We've been assuming that this has to do with your grandfather. What if it doesn't. What if all the people we've been questioning are the wrong people. Vincent might've run away to be with a romantic interest."

"He'd have to. Grandfather would never knowingly let him be near someone he loved if they were a guy."

"I figured as much. I appreciate your candor. It's been helpful. Is there anything at all you can think of that Vincent might've said. Hinted at about someone he liked. No matter how vague."

"Well, I suppose he did say something odd. I thought it was about family. But the way he said it. 'You can love someone your whole life and be invisible to them at the same time.' I thought he was talking about Grandfather. But Vinnie's not invisible to Grandfather. Overprotected. Maybe burdened with the responsibilities of being the heir. But that man spends time focused on Vincent every day of his miserable life. Grandfather's. Not Vincent's."

"Sounds like unrequited love."

"It never occurred to me he might've been infatuated with someone. He's homeschooled. The staff are pretty boring. They're paid to keep an arm's length from Vinnie."

"How did Vincent feel about Anton Thrace? Did they get along?"

"The werewolf? He's alright I guess. Never talks about anything personal. Takes his job seriously. Feels a huge amount of gratitude for the old man. Grandfather saved his ass or something when he was in the preternatural prison."

"Assessment facility. It's not a prison. Bad people aren't sent there. People who need to learn to control their urges are."

"Yeah, I know. Sorry. I remember that's the one thing Anton said about the place. It was nice having a high security room to keep you from hurting someone during a full moon."

"But he learned to control it there."

Mansfield shook his head. "No. That's the thing. He never could. He takes these shots that keep him from losing it during the nights around the full moon. A strong enough dose can even keep him human."

"He can control the change with drugs?" I was confused. Thinking about what Chandler had said. Thrace wasn't an alpha, but he could stay human on the full moon.

Werewolves could control their killing urges when they changed. Maybe not at first. During the first few moons, they were dangerous because it was a confusing transition. Took a while to come back to their humanity. Back to self-control.

"More than that. Even if he transforms, he doesn't lose it. He doesn't turn into a wolf up here." He tapped his temple.

"So without those drugs, he's dangerous?"

Mansfield consulted his phone. "Shit. Whoever took him may be in real danger. The full moon's tomorrow."

"And whoever's with him."

"Pardon?" He blinked at me. Confused.

He hadn't connected Thrace and Vincent despite my questions. He didn't have as much upstairs as he thought. Sadly, most men didn't. Even the smart ones overestimated just how much smarter they were than the people around them. It made catching them easier when they turned to crime.

"Nothing. Thank you. Can you arrange for me to talk to Maureen? Now? I'm worried that tomorrow night's our last chance to save Vincent."

"Save him from what?"

"Himself."

CHAPTER THIRTY-THREE

Meeting Maureen was problematic. I had to talk Mansfield out of calling his grandfather first. What could he tell the old man? That Maureen might know which man Vincent fancied? That she might know if they had a relationship? It would kill my investigation as surely as finding his cold, hard corpse.

If Thrace and Vincent had run off together, the boy might be fine. Surely the werewolf would've taken a stash of the drug with him. Keep himself from hurting Vincent. But if Anton had been taken by or because of the boy—that would be very bad.

Maureen didn't want to meet. Not outside of the anonymity of work. Not surprising after that explosion meant to kill me had failed. So we opted for a 'random' encounter in a parking garage that served the boardwalk area of Long Beach.

I found her sitting in the driver's side of a newer silver Lexus. Nice. But not expensive enough to draw undue attention. A car with tinted windows was parked strategically four stalls away. An Asian man in a trench-coat was leaning on the parking structure's exterior half-wall. Smoking a cigarette. Pretending to survey the lights from the boardwalk. Not very stealthily.

I rapped gently on the window and she rolled it down. "Should I come in? Or you going to come out?"

"In, if you don't mind."

I walked around to the passenger side. The door unlocked as I reached for the handle. I slipped inside and shut the door before speaking again.

"Thank you for agreeing to meet."

"You said Vincent's life may depend on it. Or was that an exaggeration?" She glared at me with that Gibraltar imperiousness. Mansfield was right. She didn't need the family name to carry the blood.

"It might."

"Fine. Whatever I can do. Though I'm not sure what I could possibly tell you that Blake didn't already say."

"The fact that we have to meet in person to avoid electronic surveillance is a pain, but I'm hoping you know something. Not about the kidnapping. About Vincent."

"Such as?"

"You're probably the closest person to him in his life?"

She frowned. "I'd think that would be our grandfather. I hardly get to see him."

"Blake hinted that Vincent might've confided in you. On those rare occasions when you find a few minutes to talk?"

"Blake needs to learn discretion. If anyone found out that I even talk to my cousin, it puts everything we've given up at risk."

"I understand that. I'm not planning on sharing this information. I didn't even tell the F.B.I. I was meeting you."

She rolled her eyes theatrically. "They leak like a sieve."

I felt a strange surge of loyalty to defend the agents. Wisniewski and Hardwicke had been more than fair with my involvement in the case. Bigoted first meetings aside. "Hard to contain big news. Important stories. Someone always has to tell a sister or mother that they have the inside track."

"I like you, Miss Savage. Or may I call you Bianca?"

"Bianca's fine. Better actually."

"Then you must call me 'Maureen.' So, what is it I might possibly know to help Vinnie out?"

"I know he's gay."

"Ah. The real family secret. Bigger than our secret identities! The heir will never have heirs of his own. And the Gibraltar name dies despite Grandfather's machinations."

"You don't sound like you like your grandfather."

She turned her face away to hide the bitterness. "He'd never win an award for outstanding parent. Or grandparent. But we're comfortable. If a life inside a box is comfortable."

"Must be hard. Harder still on Vincent."

She jerked back toward me. Defiant. "Vinnie? He has it easy. Just don't make waves and he'll get everything. Make waves and he'll be beaten into submission—figuratively. And he'll still get everything. He's no more sheltered than Blake and I've had to be. He gets to do things with the money. Trips with Grandfather abroad. Nice clothes."

"While you have to show off modest means." I motioned to the car.

"Exactly."

"Alright. Back to Vincent. We know he's gay. Was there someone?"

"Virginal Vinnie? Not a chance. Security never left him alone. Excuse me. Unsurveilled. Even in the toilet."

"I saw. They let me review the video footage."

"Then you know!" She practically shouted her vindication.

I took a few quiet breaths. To study the woman. She was more unhappy with her life than Blake. But it explained his comments. His focus on her not being the heir rather than himself. Sibling loyalty.

"I'm not talking about sex, Maureen. I'm talking about romance. Something that wouldn't have triggered any alarms. Maybe something unrequited?"

She chuckled morosely. "Oh. Figures a woman would notice what the goon-squad there didn't."

"Go on?"

"You noticed how smitten Vinnie was for a certain handsome and athletic werewolf. The aloof and unattainable Anton Thrace."

I nodded. "So it wasn't reciprocated."

"No. And didn't poor Vinnie lament about that. On and on sometimes. I get it. He's a teenage boy. In love for the first time. For a long time, apparently. He stumbled at the top of a landing a few years back. And the strong arms of Anton Thrace scooped him. Kept him from breaking his pretty little neck." She eyed me shrewdly. "Thrace was only doing his job. Didn't realize how my kid cousin reacted to that little chivalrous act."

I nodded again. Back-channeling acknowledgment. Something clients expected from me to confirm I was actually listening. If they took it to mean I agreed with them, all the better.

"Did anyone in your family or the Company have dealings with Thrace's old pack?"

Maureen looked startled. "The ones that threw him out? That threatened to kill him if he showed up again? Not a chance. Grandfather tolerates his pet preternaturals. But that's expedience. Nothing more."

I frowned but let the insult slide. "So there's no chance they ran off together."

She flashed another look of surprise. Not because the werewolf could've run off with the boy. That I thought they might've done so. "You think this was all an elaborate ruse to escape our grandfather?"

"If it was, there might be a problem." My face became a grim mask of warning.

I had her attention. "Such as?"

"Thrace uses medication to keep from hurting people. During the full moon." I paused significantly. "The full moon's tomorrow night. If they're together and he hasn't taken his meds—he might kill Vincent."

"Wouldn't he have taken it with him? He's not a fool."

"I don't know. It's apparently a specialty drug. Turns out that's why he owes your grandfather a huge debt. I had time to research it on the way over here." I felt a pang of guilt. I hated it when men took credit for the women who worked under them. I couldn't do that to Janet. "Well, my secretary did because I was driving. He can't get it anywhere except from your grandfather. And it has a limited shelf life. Has to be made monthly around the time of the moon. The older it is, the less potent."

"Then he wouldn't run off. Not and put Vincent at risk. I think you've got the wrong end of the stick, Bianca."

"Maybe. And you're sure it was unrequited? That's what Blake seemed to think as well. So you agree? Vincent disappears and Thrace's disappearance a few days later isn't part of a plan to escape?"

"I wouldn't think so. I mean, I could be wrong. I don't know that much about werewolves. Anton and I've spoken a couple of times. But it was always professional. He never shared anything personal."

I nodded. "Anything else you think might help? Anyone else have a motive to take the boy and Thrace?"

She shook her head. "I've been racking my brain for days. Everybody loved Vinnie."

"Well, Maureen, if you think of anything, please get word to me through your brother."

"I will. But what're you going to do next? Do you even know where to look?"

I shook my head. "It won't stop me from trying. I'll let Blake know if I learn anything useful. And I appreciate your time. Not sure how it'll help but I needed to be sure that Thrace didn't have a thing for Vincent. Motives get muddy otherwise."

"Good luck, Bianca. And be careful. Werewolf bites can be dangerous. Even to non-humans." She smiled and I got out of the car.

She was right. I had no idea what might happen if a werewolf bit me. Dusty's bite would hurt a werewolf. That had been scientifically documented. Some kind of antibody reaction like in the movies. What either of their bites would do to me was anyone's guess. I intended it to stay that way.

CHAPTER THIRTY-FOUR

I made it back to my office without incident. Drove around twice before parking. Less preoccupied than before. More paranoid. The werewolves would have less difficulty finding out where I worked than they had finding my condo complex. And there was the matter of the mystery woman. No sign of either.

Inside, however, someone was waiting. More than one, someone. I felt the blank spots of undeath like holes in my power. One of the energy voids was slightly different from the others. Chandler.

I rushed inside. Andre was standing near the entrance. He looked shaken. Plaster had scuffed his uniform as if someone had shoved him up against a wall.

"They told me not to call. I'm sorry."

"Nothing to apologize for. Vampires are scary one on one. A coven's enough to make anyone afraid to disobey. Better alive than sorry."

"Should I go?"

"Probably. Yes. No police. They aren't here to hurt me. And I'm not in the mood to press charges for trespassing. Or get a lecture from your mother about endangering her baby boy."

"Yes, Miss Savage." He hesitated. "I can wait outside in case you call for help."

I smiled and turned to him. "You're a good man, Andre. But I'll be fine. I promise. Call it an early night. Go see that girlfriend of yours. Keep her from complaining about the long hours you put in. I doubt anyone else will break in here before sunrise with all the monsters in the neighborhood."

He studied me then chuckled, low and masculine. "I do like working for you, Miss Savage. Even N'awlins had nothing like you."

He disappeared out the front. I locked the door behind him. The vampires were waiting for me in my offices. Chilton stood. Several of the others sat in chairs or on the edge of Janet's desk. No Joseph. No Dusty either.

The MI-6 undercover agent was comfortably settled amongst them. "Now before you go off on us, hear me out," warned Chandler with hands raised. "They're here because I called them. I heard about the werewolf attack through police contacts. Why didn't you call me?"

"Why would I do that?"

He stared at me. Hard. Unspeaking. Trying to figure out if I was playing a game. Maybe I was. Not the way he thought. Finally he gave in. "I don't understand."

"Why would I call you, Chandler? You aren't security. You aren't the police." I wasn't going to out him with the vampires. But it wasn't a lie. MI-6 wasn't jurisdictionally recognized law enforcement in the United States. "You aren't my boyfriend. What category of person are you that I would've thought to call you about a werewolf ambush?"

"I dunno, Miss Savage. Maybe a friend?"

I'd hurt his feelings by not calling. No. Worse. His masculine pride. But my questions were legitimate. We didn't have a relationship. Not one that would make me call him. Or did he think that as MI-6 I should've run to him about the boogeymen?

"I would never put my friends in harm's way with dangerous preternaturals. And we're barely acquainted, Paul. A long ways yet from being friends. I'm not casual about the people I give my trust to."

"Fine. As for us being here, well, as an acquaintance, I had resources. And I reached out for them." He sulked defiantly.

"Chilton's people are your resource?"

He nodded and the Rake bowed at the neck. "We are not above providing security for a fellow preternatural. Dusty said the two of you held your own against three werewolves. I suppose that puts us in the middle anyway."

"They don't know who Dusty is. Or that he's part of your coven. You could walk away without any beef with the werewolves." I kept myself from naming Killian. I didn't want the vampires to run off on their own to avenge the attack just because one of their people had stumbled across it.

Chilton eyed me somberly. "Is it true you've been suggesting to law enforcement that we had nothing to do with the abduction?"

I held his gaze, sunglasses in place. "Yeah. I'm pretty sure you're innocent of that."

He frowned. "But perhaps not other things?"

"Like I told him, my trust isn't easily given. Has to be earned actually."

The Rake forced a smile. "Well then we'd like to earn it. The full moon is tomorrow and werewolves are their most dangerous then. Stronger. Faster. More wild like beasts than men."

"I don't want werewolves killed to protect me. Not unless it's a matter of another's life or death." I knew that vampires were already dead, but I didn't try to explain away my language. Permanently dead was implied. "How do I know your people won't get carried away and make a mess of things?"

He grew chilly. "I don't make a mess of things, as you put it. I'm offering to put my people at your disposal. To follow your instructions, not mine. If you say don't kill, they won't."

I glanced at Chandler. Unlike Chilton, he could hardly hold my gaze. Angry. No, furious with me. Something of an overreaction for someone he barely knew. If I'd used my power on him, if he were smitten with me, that would explain his emotions. But he'd been untouched by my energy. I could feel the numbing emptiness of the totem at his waist.

"I can't have a whole coven of vampires going everywhere I go when the sun goes down tomorrow. It might be safer but more conspicuous. As a P.I., I need to move with stealth sometimes."

Chilton shrugged. "As many or as few as you like."

"Not Dusty," said the redheaded Bonnie, who clearly didn't like me.

"Want to protect him from me?"

She smiled, bitterly. "Oh no. Those were his words. *I won't help her.*"

"Oh." I actually felt bad about that. Not because I wanted him with me. But because he'd fought to protect me and I'd basically treated him like crap. "What if I asked for him specifically?"

"Then he'll do it," replied Chilton without hesitation. "Although I would advise that taking him could put you both in an awkward position."

"I know that he stood up for me once. That bought a bit of trust. Not Rhoda though. She can stay at home or far away from me until you get her on a better leash."

"Into S&M Miss Savage?" The redhead preened at her wit.

"I don't know. The last person to tie me up died. Horribly. What do you think?"

"Enough! This is serious, Bianca." Chandler punched the wall. Not hard enough to break the drywall. "There were three werewolves. Next time there might be more. You need at least five vampires with you. And me."

"You? Who said you get to come to this party? How're you going to protect yourself from werewolves?"

He withdrew his .45 from its hiding place under his jacket. His shoulders were broad. His jack fit more loosely than mine. I hadn't even seen the weight of it in the fabric. I'd have to check out the holster when I wasn't dealing with a preternatural gang-war.

"Silver rounds."

I frowned. "Silver-tipped or silver?"

"Silver."

"Interesting."

"Why?" asked Chilton. He understood the significance of my concern. The look on my face.

"They aren't manufactured in the U.S. Silver-tipped only, domestically. Which means you got them in advance from overseas. Would take at least two days to arrive. How is it that you're armed with full silver bullets before we even went to visit any lycanthropes?"

"I also come prepared."

Chilton frowned. "Does that mean you have wooden bullets?"

Chandler shrugged. "I do. I also have hollow-points and armor-piercing rounds. Doesn't mean I know that I'm going to need them."

It was plausible. MI-6 dealt with all manner of British preternaturals. That would include werewolves. Silver bullets could've been standard issue. He'd have brought them with him.

While all of that might be true, a certain sense of paranoia set in. Just in case it wasn't. I hadn't survived as long as I had by believing in happenstance. Or falling for handsome, sexy men.

"Where are we going tomorrow night?" demanded the redhead.

"I don't know. Not exactly. Wherever I need to go."

She glared at me. Wanted me dead. That was a lot of loathing for someone I barely knew. "You really want to send a handful of us against a full pack?"

Chilton frowned. "I don't believe Miss Savage is foolish enough to confront a werewolf pack without sufficient numbers." He turned his gaze to me. "That's not the plan is it?"

"No. If I have to challenge the pack, your whole coven wouldn't be enough backup."

"There. Your fears have been allayed, Bonnie." Chilton turned to me. "You insist on Dusty?"

"I do. And three of your strongest to boot."

I wondered where Joseph was. Protecting the old man for all he's worth probably. I'd have felt better have him with the other vampires. But they weren't part of the same coven any more. Asking for him would leave Gibraltar vulnerable. No way he'd say 'yes' to that.

"Metaphysically or emotionally?"

I grinned. "Let's call it three of your most dominant and confident."

"Chilton!" snarled the redhead.

"Yes, Bonnie. That includes you. But Miss Savage, why then Dusty? He's one of our must submissive."

"Everyone's gotta start somewhere." I smiled but he didn't. "Fine. I told you, he's earned some trust. And I want at least one of your people I feel would put themselves in harm's way to help me."

"Don't get them killed as cannon fodder."

I shrugged. "With any luck, there won't be any killing involved."

CHAPTER THIRTY-FIVE

The vampires left to ready themselves for the following night. Chandler, however, didn't go. His posture was petulant. Like a child. A man unwilling to be told what to do. .

I remained sitting in my chair, legs on the desk. Staring into his eyes without my sunglasses. Pleased that I could do so with impunity. Waiting for him to speak.

"Why?"

I frowned. "Why what? We're alone. No need to be opaque."

"Why didn't you call me."

I sighed. "We went over this. I didn't lie."

"You said I wasn't a police officer. I'm MI-6. That's better an' police. We train in preternaturals."

"How would that look for your cover? I call Blake Mansfield's personal—what? Hatchet man? Investigator? Because of a werewolf attack? Why would I do that? And honestly, what could you have done if I had?"

"Alright. That's all true. But I went with you to confront them. Drove you home after it went badly. Didn't I earn any trust?" He stared into my eyes. Hard. Full of a familiar emotion.

"You're jealous."

He pursed his lips together. Tensing up. I laughed in surprise which only pissed him off more.

"Is that it, Paul? Are you jealous of Dusty?"

"He's the one you kissed. The one who brought you jewelry. You rejected Joseph. But not him? I don't understand the relationship."

My smile of surprise withered into something ugly. "Neither confirmed nor denied. I thought we'd cleared this up? You can't be interested in me because a life together depends on a totem you can never remove in my presence."

"Would that be so hard?"

"You didn't argue that the first time I asked."

He looked away. Embarrassed. "I needed to process the facts. Didn't want to make a promise I couldn't keep."

Men desired me as an exotic object. Something new and unusual. To challenge their ability to withstand my kiss. The only other time men wanted me was because my power had influenced them. Captured them with obsession. Lust. Never romantic love.

That was something I'd learned decades earlier. I knew it was still true. He couldn't want me as just a woman.

I picked at him. "Why are you so interested in me? Is it a preternatural fetish?"

"Do you really think so little of yourself? That your beauty and character might not impress me?" He gazed earnestly at me. Willing me to hear him. Accept his words.

I frowned. Feeling a different sensation in my gut. Not the cold of hunger. Cold fear. As if he'd exposed something I'd kept hidden.

"Most guys don't react positively to the horns and sunglasses. I know I impress people. But not in a good way." I waved a hand dismissively. "And being beautiful isn't the kind of qualifier every woman wants. I know I'm nice on the eyes. But I don't want to be wanted just because I'm attractive physically. Truthfully, most women don't."

He held my gaze. "I said 'character.'"

"You did." I went quiet for a moment. Watching him watch me. Surprised to believe that he meant it. Or at least, he thought he did. "Two conversations and suddenly I'm the girl of your dreams?"

He stiffened. Breaking our mutual gaze. "You're smart and strong. Being beautiful and stacked are just bonuses."

I laughed. "Wow. Really? Stacked? You'd tell a homely, flat-chested woman you liked her because she was strong and smart, too?"

"Physical attraction counts for something. Sometimes it's the expression on a face. Or something in the noble way a person lives their life that adds to that attraction. How many ugly men have you dated?"

"None. I don't date."

"Sounds like I'm not the one with the problem."

I studied him. Unnerved by his argument. I wanted to believe he was wrong. But it was bad to lie to myself. Worse to want things I could never have. Things I was being offered by someone immune to my charms. At least, while he wore the totem.

I stopped fighting instinctively. Let my higher intellect override my insecurities. I stared at him like a man. Appreciated the breadth of his shoulders again. The firm muscling of his neck. The clean lines of his jaw. Masculine. Strong. There was more than intelligence in his eyes. There was emotion. An openness that his persona faked. This was real.

"Fine. I'll consider it." I fought the words as they came out of my mouth. I think I blushed. That was new. "Slow and steady though. Begin with friendship. Flirtation. Nothing physical until we get to know each other. I'll tell you when. If ever."

He smiled. But it was cautious. "Didn't forget that I like to be dominated did you?"

Now that I'd agreed to get to know him, he was afraid of me. Afraid of being hurt. That I wouldn't find him worthy. The candor on his face made him easy to read. Made me think I'd been wrong to call him shallow.

"I'm a strong woman. I don't let a man tell me what to do. Don't get me wrong. I'm not bossy either. But I know my own mind. I don't compromise on many things. Or for many people."

"There's a differences between being bossy or controlling, and dominating someone. A true alpha knows it. Somewhere in here." He pointed at his chest. Not the heart. Something more encompassing in his gesture. The soul maybe?

I looked for other ways to push him away. To test his resolve. "You know I'm a Christian, right?"

"That for real?"

I laughed, startled. "Hell, yes, it's for real. That a problem?"

"Not for me."

"What're you?"

He shrugged meekly. "A pragmatist. There may be a higher power. But I don't need one to get through life."

"Fair enough. I don't really need you to believe in God to believe in me. As long as you understand, I do. I believe He's real. That He made creatures like me for a reason. Not evil. Not to punish men. Just another predator on the food chain, maybe. Something. Anything but chance."

"Heard and understood." He bobbed his head with a shy smile.

"That's a start. No get out of my office. I have some files to go through and I don't need you here distracting me."

He practically beamed at me. "So I would be a distraction?"

"I'd want to keep smacking that smug grin off of your face. So, yeah. You'd be a huge pain-in-my-ass distraction."

"I'll take it." I didn't think he could grin any broader but he managed it as he left the office with an exaggerated bounce in his step. I heard him chanting down the hallway "She likes me. She likes me."

"Don't think I don't know the little-boy routine is another affectation."

He laughed and it was a nice sound. A warm masculine tone that faded slowly from my mind. Then I was alone with myself.

Usually I liked being alone. This time, with him finally gone, the room felt empty.

I swung my feet off the desk and focused on Killian's financials. Somewhere, there had to be a place they'd hide a prisoner. Whether it was Thrace or Vincent or both of them. I had to figure it out before the sun set tomorrow. I had no time for romantic flights of fancy. Or self-pity. If I couldn't do this, Vincent was dead. I knew it in the core of my soul.

CHAPTER THIRTY-SIX

"Nothing." I growled at the file as I slammed it shut and slid it across the desk.

"Pardon?"

I looked up at the unexpected male voice. "Bob. What're you doing here?"

The wall-clock said three-twenty-one in the morning. I automatically scanned his hands. No weapons. Clenched fists. Anxiety all over his face. It seeped away as he gazed at me.

I cursed, grabbing my sunglasses. I put them snuggly into place. Waited for him to regain control of himself. His anger was the worse for having had thoughts of desire.

Bob was a couple of years older than Janet. Not unattractive, I supposed. He hadn't aged nearly as well as she had. Receding hairline. Bald patch at the center. His remaining hair was still dark. Almost black. Stubble painted a mask on his jaw. His belly sagged from lack of exercise and he was twenty pounds overweight. Fingers doughy. Probably destined for diabetes.

"Janet can't keep doing this." His knuckles were white as he clenched harder.

I tried to keep my expression bland. Professional. Maybe even friendly. "This is a conversation between you and Janet."

"No. It's a conversation between me and you! Cheating husbands and embezzlers are one thing. Even the occasional murderer isn't nearly as terrifying as knowing my wife's being exposed to real monsters!"

I leaned back in my chair and folded my arms behind my head. "I'm not going to mock you by pretending I don't understand what you mean. Vampires and werewolves."

"Yes! Goddamned right, I mean vampires and werewolves! And Jan won't listen to me. She won't abandon you to the dangers of this job. The dangers that come from being what you are!"

"A strong and capable woman?"

I narrowed my gaze. He couldn't see my contempt. My resentment that the woman I loved most in the world loved a man who couldn't stand me. Who treated her with less respect than she deserved. I'd never make Janet choose between us. I wouldn't make her give up one love for the other. But that's why Bob was here. What he was trying to do.

"Don't fucking mess with me, Bianca. I'm not a sexist. I know women are strong and capable. Jan's stronger than me. That's why she's not half as terrified of this job as I am."

"I admire you for acknowledging that. But it's still a conversation between the two of you. I'm not taking away Janet's choices because you're afraid for her."

"So you're willing to risk her life? Get her killed? That's how much you love her? Why she's so goddamned loyal?"

"Will you please stop taking the Lord's name in vain?" I wasn't really upset about it. Linguistically, it had nothing to do with questioning God or calling on His wrath. It was linked to the same part of the brain that people with Tourette's tapped into. Emphasis rather than meaning. But the complaint stopped him.

"I wasn't being disrespectful to God. Or to you. Or to women. For God's sake! Shit. For Pete's sake, Bianca! Please let her go! Don't wait until she's almost killed again before you decide that the life that works for you doesn't work for her."

"Bob. That's just it. I can't take away her choice. I didn't decide that Janet should stay with me. That the risks of the job were anything other than serious. I've told her a hundred times if it gets too rough, she can retire. I've already vested her severance package."

"Y—you have?"

"Yes. She'll get eighty-percent of what I pay her now just to call it a day. Stay at home and be safe for the rest of her life. Play the doting wife. Knit or decoupage or whatever it is modern housewives do these days."

"I never said she had to stay home." He grew defensive. If he'd had a hat in his hands he'd be wringing it. "There are plenty of jobs that are challenging but won't put her in front of a werewolf."

"I was the one attacked. Not her. But fine, talk to her. Tell her you talked to me. Insisted I let her go. Have her come to me and agree. I won't try to change her mind. Won't even tell her how much I'd miss her. Will that make you happy, Bob?" I couldn't keep the anger out of my voice.

He grew agitated, pacing. Small half-steps in either direction as if he couldn't make up his mind. He wanted to come around the desk and stick his fists in my face. But he wasn't the kind of man who threatened women. I suspected he wasn't sure that I fell into the 'woman' category.

"She won't listen to me. You have to be the one. Tell her you don't need her anymore. You want to go solo."

"I can't do that, Bob. It's not only impossible to keep my business running without someone to man the front desk, but it'd be a lie. I do need her. Or at least someone like her." I scowled and ran my nails across the desk in frustration. "I knew her before you, Bob."

"That shouldn't matter. I'm her husband."

I looked up at him harshly. "You mean her owner?"

His face paled, mouth dropping open. "Stop putting words in my mouth."

"You just said her opinion shouldn't matter. That you're her husband and that what you want is all that does."

"Not all! But it should matter. Some! Enough that she could find something safer."

"Bob, you're not hearing yourself. You're not asking her to give up a job. You're asking her to give up a lifelong friendship. You don't think that never stepping foot in my office makes her less of a target than if she's my best friend, do you? Right now people think she's an employee. Hating me doesn't have to involve her. Just a human who works for a preternatural. But if she's my friend first, people can leverage Janet to get to me."

His mind raced. I'd suggested things he'd never considered. The terror in his eyes grew. His fear had become a many tentacled creature. "You're saying someone's more likely to hurt her if she doesn't work here? Unless she stops being your friend?"

"Yep. That's the short and sweet of it."

His voice grew hoarse with emotion. "She'd never do that. She'd give me up before she'd let you go."

"Would you want her to do that? Give me up? Never see me or hear from me? Honestly, Bob? Would you want what that would do to her?"

"No. Goddamn you, Bianca Savage! You are a bigger bitch than I thought." He stormed out and I simply stared at his back.

I didn't like Bob. But it wasn't my call. Janet did. Hell, she loved him with all of her enormous heart. His name-calling didn't faze me. What bothered me was that he'd created a need for me to lie to Janet. Or at least, not tell her that he'd stopped by.

The man complicated my relationship with her because he was afraid. Didn't trust her to know her own mind. I understood one thing that Bob didn't. Janet would be just as devasted at losing him if he forced her to choose, as she'd be giving up me.

I glanced back down at the pack financials. I rewound my thoughts. Nothing. Right. There was nothing in the documents to suggest a physical location besides their Joshua Tree commune. No payments going out that could be rent or property taxes. Nothing recorded with any county on the West Coast. Not just California. The F.B.I. had even added Nevada, New Mexico and Oregon for safe-measure.

I started to call Janet. Remembered the time and held the phone to my chest. Thinking. I went to her desk and found the number for Yuri Kamaguchi. Dialed it myself.

"Do you know what damnedable hour it is?" His accent was thick with annoyance.

"Yep. But security never sleeps does it?"

He muttered. I heard fabric rustling. "No. No it does not. Good news or bad?"

"I need your help."

He grew interested. "Another werewolf attack?"

"No. Not yet. Something related, though. Do you have men you could spare to watch Killian's pack? Follow anyone who leaves their compound without being noticed?"

He didn't answer right away. I listened to his breathing. A rattle from something wrong with his lungs. Chain smoking maybe. Or allergies.

"You want them now I take it?"

"Only reason I'm calling. The pack lives in Joshua Tree."

"I know. We vetted the gay werewolf's connected to them. See, I can use proper language like an American."

"Never said you were dumb, Yuri. Can you arrange it?"

He grunted. Pleased or annoyed, I couldn't tell. "What are you looking for? Why follow them?"

"I'm looking for someplace they might store something."

Now I had his attention. I could hear excitement in his words. "Like a kidnapped boy?"

"That, too. But I don't want your people to move in if they find a place. They can be there when I go in. But I'm the one leading the way. You understand me?"

"*Da*. Can do. See, now I sound like Russian immigrant."

"Why the performance? Mocking me because I woke you up so early?"

"No. Just showing you that Paul Chandler is not only one who can hide where he comes from. I'll see to it that you're called the moment someone leaves Joshua Tree and arrives someplace else."

He hung up abruptly. I was too stunned that he knew Chandler was MI-6 to respond. Then I dialed Paul. He answered on the first ring.

"Miss me already?"

"Just a friendly warning. Amperdyne knows you're MI-6. Kamaguchi just dropped that tidbit on me a minute ago."

"Shit. My cover's supposed to be too deep for their connections."

"Or someone's talked." I paused, asked a question I really wanted answered. "What's the real purpose of watching Chilton?"

His voice tightened. "Can't say. Won't tell."

"That's not how it goes."

"I know. Doesn't change the facts."

"Fine. I respect your discretion. Doesn't mean I like not knowing."

"If it would put you at risk, I'd warn you. Thanks for the head's up. I'll have my people look into it from our end. He gonna take action on that knowledge?"

"Don't think so. Just trying to rattle me. Pissed that I woke him up with demands."

"Demands for what?"

"Surveillance. More eyes on the pack than we have access to between us."

"Us as in you and me?"

He sounded happy. That pissed me off for some reason. "Not if you put it like that."

"I do like the sound of 'us.'" He went silent. Then I heard a rush of air. "You're giving Amperdyne the case? Why?"

"I'm not. That's the other reason he wanted to rattle me. I told him that I get to be there when anyone goes in. That I'm in charge."

"Bet he wasn't happy about that. Not like I'd have been."

"He wasn't. So telling me my new acquaintance was a spy was his way of paying me back."

I could hear his playful frown. "Now see, you're going backwards. Acquaintance is such an ugly word."

"Good night, Paul."

"Night, Bianca."

CHAPTER THIRTY-SEVEN

I made it back to my condo before dawn. In retrospect, that was probably a mistake. I was tired. Sloppy. The shadows were darker than usual.

The nightlight that I always left plugged in for Martini was burned out. She didn't greet me as I tossed my keys on the counter. I hadn't bothered hitting the lights. I hesitated. Unable to see well enough to navigate the condo. I just wanted to fall into bed. Fully clothed. I was that tired.

I saw movement in the blackness. There was no time to pull the gun from my thigh holster. Someone struck me. Wrapped their boney hands around my throat and carried me to the ground. An inarticulate keening of rage filled the room. It almost sounded inhuman. Not a werewolf though.

My stomach grew icy cold. My arms shivered with goosebumps as energy flowed along my skin. I lashed out with my power. Finding nothing. No testosterone. No warmth. The cold blankness of the undead.

I punched blindly at my attacker. There was a crack of bone on bone. I'd connected with the jaw. It hurt my knuckles. But had to hurt their face more.

The hands loosened. The vampire didn't speak. Fingernails dug into my skin as they tried to grab hold of me. Clawing at my flesh.

I ignored the pain and reached for my Glock, again. Thankfully, it was the one with wood-tipped bullets. I couldn't see to aim. But at this range, there was little chance I'd miss. I only hoped whoever it was, wasn't someone I'd regret killing. If I hit them in the heart by accident.

I aimed lower in the ribcage. Squeezed the trigger. This time there was a scream of pain and rage. Female. Feral and hateful but definitely a woman. Not Dusty, then. I had an idea who, though.

The vampire withdrew back into the shadows. I glanced at the microwave. No LED. Same for the oven. The power had been turned off. The curtains pulled tight as always. I was at a serious disadvantage. Night vision wasn't one of my preternatural abilities.

I threatened the darkness. "Stay back if you don't want me to unload the entire clip into you!"

"He was mine! I warned you! Begged you to leave him alone! But no! You ask for him personally!"

I knew who it was for certain then. "Rhoda, you need to stop. I'll kill you if I have to. And I won't lose a wink of sleep over it."

"Kill me! Go on. Then he'll see you for the monster you are."

I sighed. When other monsters started calling me a monster, I took it personally. "He'll understand it was self-defense. That you lost your mind at his rejection of you. He won't blame me. But he'll blame himself. Is that what you want?"

"No. That's not right!" I heard doubt in her declaration. She was moving. Back and forth. Making herself a difficult target. She could see my uncertainty. The one thing vampires had that I wished I did. At least at the moment. Night vision.

"It is, Rhoda. You've already threatened me in front of him before. This is my apartment. There's no reason he won't believe the police report. You have no other reason to be here."

"I don't care if I die! As long as he hates you!"

"Then maybe you better not die. Try something else."

She lunged again. I heard her sobbing. The air moved in front of me. I raised the gun and fired.

The flash from the muzzle revealed her position and I adjusted. Up eight more inches. Not her heart. Her shoulder. The first shot had hit her below the ribs. It wasn't enough to slow her down

I squeezed the trigger. She spun backwards as the bullet connected at the clavicle. Screaming again. Shouting like a madwoman.

My neighbors would've already called the police. I wasn't going to cover for her. If I didn't have to kill her, she could serve time. Cool off.

Then I realized what I was thinking. Or wasn't thinking. That's how tired I was. She was a vampire. Preternaturals didn't get simple sentences for attempted murder. It was the death penalty. No chance to appeal. If I didn't kill her, the State would.

"Rhoda, if the police come, it's death for you. You keep coming at me, I'll stop aiming for the areas around your heart and target it exclusively. Also death. I'm giving you one last chance." I'd been giving a lot of people one last chance lately. One of these days I was going to regret it.

"Doesn't matter! You came too late."

I didn't lower my gun. But I hesitated. "What does that mean?"

"The sun's rising. I can feel it in my blood. I can't go home. The light will kill me."

"Did you intend on this being a suicide mission all along?"

"No. I wanted you dead." She sobbed. Defeated. Then her resolved returned. "It's still not too late for that."

She moved toward me. Keening like a demon. Didn't matter that vampires weren't superfast. I couldn't see her. Couldn't track her with my eyes. So I used my power. Felt her emptiness like a shadow in my mind and squeezed the rest of the rounds into its center.

She landed on top of me. Her dead weight knocking me backwards. I let the gun go. I was out of ammo anyway.

The flashes from the muzzle had told me all I needed to know. She was dead. No. I hadn't killed her. Daylight had worked it's magic. Even behind the heavy curtains and in the dark, the first rays of daylight had turned her once more into a corpse.

My bullets had taken out most of her belly. Intestines were splattered like bits of gooey plastic on the carpeting behind her. Neater than a human kill. Definitely less deadly.

I heard sirens. Shouting in the hallway. Someone banged on my door. An Asian accent. Not one of my neighbors.

I opened the door. Enough that the Amperdyne guard could see my face. "First, how'd she get past you?"

"Who?"

"The vampire." I stopped myself from saying 'the woman.' Yes, she was a woman. But that wasn't relevant. Man or woman, she would've killed an ordinary person.

"We were told to stop werewolves."

I sighed. How had Amperdyne become an industry standard if the agents took their protective duties so literally? "So you thought a vampire coming up unannounced is okay?"

He frowned. Annoyed. Angry. A little afraid. The fear intrigued me. What had his screwup cost him? Would he be fired? "Infrared scanners showed you alone up here. We were contracted to keep out werewolves."

"Why didn't you come in when you heard the first gunshots?"

"We weren't allowed to bug your apartment. The noise could've come from any of the rooms."

I stared at him. "Tell the police someone had their TV on too loudly. One of the older residents mistook it for gunfire."

He nodded. No hesitation. Relieved even. I shut the door and tried to figure out how she'd cut off my electricity. Finally, I scrambled around in the dark to find my landline. Autodialed maintenance. Thank heaven for batteries.

"Maxine? Bianca here. Yes, I know what time it is. I think my breaker got flipped. Can you see about getting my power back on? Thanks."

Maxine Odessa lived in a first floor apartment with her younger siblings. Their parents had died in a car accident. No life insurance to speak of.

She'd come to me about investigating the accident. Find out why she hadn't been offered a settlement. Turned out that her father had been drinking. The other party survived mostly intact. Didn't want to destroy the children's lives. So he'd asked for the matter to be dropped.

I didn't have the heart to tell her. Instead, I explained that due to mistakes on both drivers' parts, there would be no damages. She'd believed me. But the way she'd stared at her two little brothers and baby sister was miserable. Broke my heart.

Maybe I couldn't save everyone but I'd help where I could. I set up a trust fund and made her a deal. She kept going to school. Made sure the kids went to school. Working in the complex as needed. In exchange, they'd get free rent and enough for food and basic clothing until the last one was eighteen. She was good with her hands. And the siblings didn't mind scrubbing the garage once a month top to bottom.

She'd been grateful at first. Still worked hard to keep her family together. But somewhere along the way she'd figured out that I'd lied. She wasn't sure what I'd lied about. But someone had said something.

She kept her word and accepted my help. But I almost never saw any of the family. None of the other tenants talked about Maxine either. Shame or anger, I'd become the enemy. The rest of the tenants tried to protect me. Took my side. I'd asked them not to treat her badly for it. As far as I knew, they hadn't.

The lights came on while I was thinking about the children. I could see Rhoda sprawled awkwardly on the ground. In a pose only possible with the dead. Or the sleeping undead I supposed.

"What to do with you?"

I called the Atlantic Street Revenants hotline. The man who answered sounded pleasant but cautious. With the vampires out-cold for the day, it had to be a human employee. Unhappy enough with vampires to be paranoid. But a job was a job. Especially in this economy.

"Are you just a messenger service or can you actually help me?"

He hesitated. "Depends. I guess I'm mostly a messenger service."

"What happens if one of your clients gets stuck someplace away from home when dawn breaks?"

"That fool girl! You talking about Rhoda, aren't you?"

"Nailed that. How'd you guess?"

"We do bed checks. Chilton was pissed. She with you? Or did it happen?"

"Happen?"

"The flame and burst? Was she caught outdoors?"

I grinned ruefully at the expression. "No. She was visiting me when she collapsed."

"I can send someone to get her, if that's what you meant by can I help."

"It is."

"Give me the address. We'll send a windowless van around. And a spare coffin."

I raised my brows. "Vampires really sleep in coffins?"

"Naw. It's what we call their pods. They have to be light-proof and hold a human body. Close enough to a coffin for me."

"I suppose so." I gave him my address and the parking instructions. I didn't mention the bullet wounds that had taken out her guts. Figured no sense in stirring the pot before I had to. "You coming personally? Or who should I expect?"

"Pickup crew'll do it. I gotta stay by the phones."

"Alrighty then. Thanks for your help—?"

"Gabe."

"Thanks, Gabe. I'm Bianca."

"The one Dusty's got it bad for?"

"You sure know a lot for just the messenger service."

"Me and Dusty are pals. From before he, you know."

"Dusty didn't strike me as being from L.A."

"He was a runaway. Like me. When he decided to become a vamp, he got me this gig. Better than selling myself on the streets." He tried to sound playful but there was pain in that last comment.

"Did Dusty?"

"Him? That boy's so tightly wound he'd probably punch the first person that touched his knee, much less his wee willie winkie."

"Wee willie—never mind. Thanks, Gabe. I'll wait up until they arrive."

"Kinda have to don't you?"

I laughed and hung up. He was right. What else could I do?

CHAPTER THIRTY-EIGHT

"What happened?"

I studied the young man's gang tattoos. Most of his neck and arms were covered in ink. Some of it done in prison. We didn't exchange names. For obvious reasons. "She had a beef with me. Wouldn't stop."

"You know guns won't kill a bloodsucker, right?"

"Wood-tipped bullets to the heart will."

His gaze jerked up to my lips. "For reals?"

"But I didn't take out her heart."

"Sure made a mess of her guts though. Why'd you spare her?"

"I'd never kill a woman over a man. Especially a man I didn't have eyes on."

"Wish my old lady felt that way. She's serving eight in Lompoc."

"That's rough."

His expression softened. Somber with responsibility and love. "Yeah. I gotta look out for my twins. At least she wasn't using when she had them this time."

I nodded, sagely keeping my mouth shut.

"Need us to clean up the bits?" He motioned to the carpet.

I didn't want them around any longer than necessary. I wasn't hungry, but I couldn't recall being this tired. "I think I can manage that. If you'll take her back to Chilton."

"That's what we get paid for." He motioned to his crew the same way he'd motioned to the carpet. They brought the pod to my doorway. "No windows in the hall. We can load her up out there."

"Thanks." I watched quietly as they picked her up. Limp. No sign of rigor as they put her in what looked like a human-sized Easter-egg. Black lacquered glass or something similar. An opaque plastic seal dropped into place once the top was closed. She'd be safe from the sun as long as they didn't crack it open. And no one would suspect it of containing a corpse of any flavor.

"You can, you know, leave a review on Yelp if you want." He looked at me hopefully.

"For vampire retrieval?"

He grinned. "No, Woman! We do all sorts of pickup and delivery. Discrete, you know? Here's our card if you ever need anything."

I took the card. Neat. Professional. Just the business name, website and phone number. Gabe was clearly the brains behind the business. Or one of the brains. "I'll see about leaving a review."

"Great. We, you know, work hard on personal communication skills. A happy customer, they come back, see?"

He was being sincere. I tried not to mock him. "If I need something discretely disposed of, I will definitely think of you first."

He grinned and started ordering his people to take the pod down to the stairwell. I watched as they picked Rhoda up with relative ease. Strong backs and muscular arms. Nice tight butts. I sighed. A little time around Paul Chandler and I was thinking of men as potential sex partners. I was far too old to start puberty now.

I went back inside and shut the door, staring at the gooey bits. I wished I'd let them clean up after all. Not because it bothered me. I was worried Martini might take an interest in it. The thought of her eating undead flesh made me shiver.

"Martini?" I went to the bedroom and peered underneath the mattress. I saw her eyes reflect the light. She didn't come when I tried to coax her out. Unlike me, gunshots scared her badly.

"It's all right, Little One." She hissed and I frowned. "Bad kitty. But I get your point. Give you your space."

I stood and went back into the kitchen. Alcohol didn't get me drunk. But surprisingly, valerian root put me to sleep. I popped two capsules with water and curled up on the couch. I realized that Martini wasn't the only one who wanted her space. I dozed off, forgetting all about bits of vampire entrails and attractive male parts. Thankfully, I didn't have to worry about dreams on either subject.

CHAPTER THIRTY-NINE

I woke up on my side. Opened my eyes without moving. The clock said it was mid-afternoon. Shit. Most of the day was already gone. Then I saw the dried bits of vampire. Dark spots on the light carpet.

I cursed aloud and reluctantly got up. I poked the nearest glob with a fingertip. It exploded into dust. Not solid or stuck to the carpet like I'd feared. Martini would definitely not be tempted by that.

I hunted her down. She was still under the bed. Still unhappy. I left her alone and showered.

The hot water relaxed my aching neck and shoulders. I'd slept deeply but not comfortably. My stomach was warm. It tingled with a release of heat that emulated the water. Still feeding on the werewolf energy. Processing it.

Maybe I could find a way to make access to werewolves a regular thing. No more killing innocent critters. Janet would be grateful.

The heat in my belly spiked and became an agonizing pain. It shot up along my nerves. I fell, grabbing at the shower stall walls. Slipping down to the floor. Scratching a line through the tiles with one horn.

I couldn't stand. The pain was that great. Like my nerves were being pulled out of my flesh. My muscles stretched. Ripped from the bones.

The phone rang but I ignored it. Not that I had much choice. I was curled into a ball. My tail wrapped forward between my thighs. Bunched up against my belly. Water pouring down into my face.

I couldn't do anything as wave after wave of agony pulsed through me. Into the nerves of my womb. My groin. Burning inside my womanhood. Something my tail couldn't protect me from.

I gasped. Trying not to make a noise. Seconds passed. The pain briefly ebbed. Like it was over. Then it pulsed again. Deceptively. Repeatedly. Stronger. And stronger still. My flesh burned. The nerves in my fingertips felt raw at any slight contact with the shower. The pain pounded behind my closed eyes as I wept. Trying to hold it back.

Finally I cried out, mouth muffled against my shoulder. I screamed in combined rage and pain. I didn't want to scare my neighbors again. Didn't want the cops to break down my door and find me like this.

Time seemed to slow down, every second of pain more like minutes. Then the agony eased. Abruptly. My skin grew cool and clammy. Except where the hot water continued to spray me.

I tried to stand. Using my hands for leverage. My legs worked. My muscles weak. Wobbly. But they held me upright.

I ran a finger along the damaged tile. My horns were sharp. I hadn't realized they could cut through ceramic. Good to know I supposed.

"What the fuck was that?" I spoke aloud. Needing to hear my voice. Something to mask a sudden fear of my own body.

I stood under the stream of hot water. Rotating slowly until my skin felt clean again. The clamminess washed away. I kept one hand against the wall. In case. Ignoring the steam building up along the glass and mirrors. Filling my lungs.

I felt my heartbeat beneath the rush of water. Racing. My pulse in my throat. I counted to three, fighting fear this time. Not anger. My stomach grew cooler than the water. Like I'd used up most of Killian's energy in that unexpected fit of pain.

The phone rang again. Not the temporary disposable for dealing with Amperdyne's spyware. My regular phone. Sitting on the vanity.

I reached for the towel. Shutting off the shower and cursing. I grabbed the phone, held it up. Avoiding the water dripping from my arms.

"Hello?"

"He's dead, isn't he?"

I recognized Henry Gibraltar's voice. If not the emotion in it. "Pardon?"

My mind was spinning. Blake? Anton? I refused to believe he was asking about Vincent. I couldn't have failed the teenager. Not yet.

"He's dead and no one has the balls to tell me to my face."

I nodded, dripping naked. Distracted by the call. The towel slipped down to dangle from one hand. The steamy bathroom was too warm anyway. "No, Mr. Gibraltar. I believe Vincent's still alive. Until tonight."

His breath caught. A gasp of hope. Or something else. "Why? Why tonight? How do you know?"

"I believe that this entire thing is about the full moon."

"What the hell are you going on about? What would the full moon have to do with Vincent?"

An idea finally settled into my head. I almost didn't answer the man. Could it be that simple? Machiavellian. But simple. "I think whoever has Vincent wants him dead. But they can't do it themselves."

"What? Why would anyone want Vincent dead?"

"Because it would hurt you more than anything else could."

"Then why not kill him and get it over with? Or is making me wait part of the torture?"

"Because they don't have the heart for it. Not really." I didn't explain. Didn't tell him the mad idea that had gelled into my mind in that second. That I believed it was someone who knew Vincent. Who cared enough that they couldn't do it themselves. Not even ordering it done the way that the two guards were killed.

"You're being intentionally cryptic! What does this have to do with the full moon?"

"There's no time for this, Mr. Gibraltar. You said you trust me. Do you, still? I can find him. Save him."

He was silent for several long heartbeats. The water puddled at my feet. Martini appeared and lapped at the warm liquid. I frowned. It was almost like she was tasting me.

She raised her feline head. Glanced into my eyes and meowed inquisitively. No longer scared or angry. Atypically fickle with her moods. That disturbed me on some level I couldn't name.

"Yes, Miss Savage. I have no one else. What can I give you to bring my boy home safely?"

He'd never called Vincent 'his boy' before. Maureen had said that Henry was an awful guardian. Maybe that was simply because he didn't know how to be anything else. I heard the love in his voice. It made me dislike the man just a smidgen less.

"For now, let me get off the phone. I'll call you the moment I know anything. Anything at all."

"Thank you."

His gratitude sounded almost sincere. But it lacked hope. I was his only chance at finding Vincent alive. And he honestly didn't think I'd do it. This was one of those times I really hoped I could prove someone wrong.

CHAPTER FORTY

"Two hours to dark." Paul Chandler sat on the edge of my desk. Closer to me than I'd like. Only because we weren't alone.

"What are we waiting on?" demanded Olivia Wisniewski.

Abigail Hardwicke leaned with her back against the wall. Comfortable on her feet. Still too beautiful to be a Fed. Smart enough. Tough enough. Maybe I was being sexist. I just hated to see how working with the worst of the worst could age a human. It would take away that phenomenal beauty. Leave cynicism and mistrust in its place.

"That would be me." Yuri Kamaguchi slipped into the office fully loaded. Black body armor. Two handguns. And a rifle over his shoulder. At least, those were all the weapons I could see without patting him down.

"This is a Federal matter, Bianca."

"It is," I nodded to Wisniewski. "But it's also about saving a boy's life."

"If we're all here?" prompted Chandler.

"Mr. Chandler's right. We need to start."

"Why him?" asked Hardwicke. She'd been watching the MI-6 agent silently the entire time she'd been there. I admired her patience. And instincts.

"He works with Blake Mansfield. I wanted an inside man, as it were, on this. An inside man on our side." I glanced at Janet. She stood in the opening between our offices. Fretting. "Oh. I should warn you all that not only do I have Gibraltar's full cooperation and authority in this, but I have backup ready to help at dusk."

"Vampires? Hell no!" Wisniewski stood up.

"Sit, Partner. The lab confirmed that Bianca was attacked by werewolves. We don't have the manpower for a full preternatural onslaught."

"Onslaught," repeated Kamaguchi with a grin. "I like this word. It's meaning something about slaughter?"

Hardwicke nodded politely. "Yes, they're related."

"Fine." The Ukrainian-American agent knew she was beat. That didn't make her happy. "Why the Dirty Dozen scenario? A way to even the odds against werewolves?"

"Yes, Agent Wisniewski. After a fashion. But it's not just about battle." I pushed the folder in front of me away. "We've triple checked. And by 'we,' I mean all participating agencies. Including Amperdyne. The werewolves don't have any connection with any real estate holdings of any kind."

"But they have Vincent?" asked Kamaguchi.

"Yes. I mean, I'm almost positive. But they're working for someone else." I nodded to Paul. "Make the call."

Chandler smiled and pulled out his phone. "Blake? Chandler here. Yeah, good news! The Feds found out where Vincent's being held.

They're gonna take about an hour to get a team together. Get them into place. Federal warrants aren't as quick as the local judges on Hank's payroll. No, I don't know where. Look, I gotta run. Don't tell the Old Man until it's a done deal. Oh, I know. You're welcome." He hung up. Beaming. "Balls in play."

"Whose balls?" asked Hardwicke with a wry grin. "Who exactly are you, Mr. Chandler?"

"A reprobate!" I laughed. "Or whatever word replaced that in the twenty-first century. We set things into motion. Kamaguchi, you should be getting a call any time."

The Russian-Asian frowned at me. Studied my mouth. Glanced at my hands which were folded neatly on the desk. "Mansfield is working with the werewolves?" He looked to Chandler for confirmation.

"Someone who cares about Vincent, who couldn't even order his execution is working with them. I don't think Gibraltar employees fit the bill. And Anton Thrace isn't the bad guy here. Who do you think that leaves?"

"Family," said Wisniewski. "Are you telling me that Blake Mansfield is related to Vincent Gibraltar? Wait! The missing grandson. They're alive? What about the granddaughter?"

"I didn't reveal that information to you. I cannot expressly tell you anything about the family per my contract. Not unless it's relevant to law enforcement needs. This isn't that." I stared the Ukrainian-American agent down.

"Fine. But I'm right about the grandson."

I shrugged. "I can only say I'm not happy. I'd like to be wrong. That Yuri Kamaguchi's phone doesn't ring. But if it doesn't—then Vincent dies."

As if on cue, a strange Russian melody came from the man's vest pocket. He pulled it out. "*Da. Da, horosho!*" He put the phone away. "You're right. The balls are on the move."

"That's not quite how that works. But good. As unhappy as it is, we know that Blake's involved. Hardwicke, you should probably pick him up. Kamaguchi's people are following the werewolves. Apparently a group of them are having lunch in a café just off the Ten in West Covina. We set a fire under their ass. His men will let us know when the werewolves reach their destination. Keep an eye on things for us. We'll be mobile before they get there. Tracking the team via satellite surveillance. You can join us once we know the location."

"One of us should go with you." Wisniewski glanced at her partner. "I think it should be me."

"Fine. I don't need to go face to face with werewolves without more backup than a succubus, a reprobate and an Amperdyne security team. The silver-tipped bullets haven't even been issued yet." Hardwicke wasn't happy but she knew there weren't other options.

I nodded. "Chandler's driving. It leaves the rest of us free to focus on a plan of attack."

"To the Batmobile!" exclaimed Chandler.

"You have Batmobile?" demanded Kamaguchi in awe.

"Er, no. Just an expression. Sorry."

Disgruntled the Russian-Asian stood. "Always with the funny talk, you Americans. Then we take Amperdyne van. My people drive."

I glanced at Chandler. He shrugged. "My gear is easy enough to move."

"Fine. Janet, you have one last task."

"I know what to do. Call the hotline. Tell them you need the backup portable and with you. I'm on it." She disappeared back to her desk to make the call.

"Any other questions?"

"Can we get a Batmobile?" asked Kamaguchi.

"No. Besides, it's a two-seater. Where would the rest of us sit?"

"With Batmobile, you and me could defeat whole pack of werewolves."

"Is he serious?" asked Hardwicke as she pulled out her phone, walking toward the exit.

"I'm afraid he probably is."

"Definitely not the backup you need for werewolves." She disappeared shaking her head.

Wisniewski frowned. "I don't have werewolf gear."

"No worries. Amperdyne comes prepared." Kamaguchi followed Hardwicke outside. The blonde agent followed him.

Chandler touched my bare arm as I started to move past. I paused, looking into his eyes. He had to settle for his own reflection in my sunglasses. "I'm not happy about it. But you're good."

"Pardon?"

"I can't believe Blake would want to kill Vinnie. But the evidence is hard to refute. Just want you to know. I'm glad they called you in on the case. Glad we met."

"Stop being so maudlin. No we're-gonna-die confessions of love."

He laughed. "You are so full of yourself."

He pulled me close and kissed my mouth hard. It felt warm and my power surged. But the totem protected him. A blank spot in my heart. It felt like kissing a warm piece of plastic. No testosterone to make my loins tighten. I pulled away. He sensed something but from the puzzlement in his eyes, he didn't know what he'd felt. Or what I hadn't.

"You get one."

"One what?"

"One stolen kiss. Now get your perky ass out the door. Time to go."

I glanced over his shoulder. Janet was watching. Disapproval all over her face. And worry. She'd seen my expression. Knew what it meant. A conversation for after we'd saved Vincent. And I was determined to do just that. He'd get saved. Even if I had to kill every werewolf in Killian's pack to make it so.

CHAPTER FORTY-ONE

The back of the Amperdyne van was windowless as predicted. And crowded. It would've held three of us comfortably. Not so much the additional eight Amperdyne men. Four black glossy vampire carryalls. And the tattooed man from the previous night. The vampires didn't trust their sleeping bodies with strangers. Not even me.

"Are you sure Chilton's not gonna shit a brick when he finds out what you did?" Chandler stared at me.

"It wasn't my idea. Blame Rico, there."

"Name's Cesar. Not Rico."

"Sorry." I didn't explain that 'Rico' had been slang for someone Hispanic long before 'Juan' or 'Jose' became popular replacements. "It makes sense though."

"As long as we don't confront the werewolves before dawn." Wisniewski wasn't happy with vampires being in the van. Even sleeping ones.

"We'll park far enough away that Killian's people won't know that they're here. When the vamps wake, Cesar will fill them in and they'll move out."

Kamaguchi peered at a device. "The werewolves are moving toward an industrial area off the 705. We'll intercept them soon at this rate. But we're cutting daylight a little close."

"We needed the time. If they thought we'd get there before their plan could go off, they might've killed the hostages just to be sure. This way, they'll wait. At least, I hope they will." I glanced at the black clad security detail. "Everyone's loaded with silver bullets, only, right? No wood-tipped ammo. It won't hurt a werewolf but our vampire friends might become collateral damage."

"*Da, da.* You already say this."

"Just repeating. Once we find out where they're holding Vincent, we go in together. Amperdyne teams circle the building to keep people from escaping with Vincent. I take the lead because I can use my unfettered power against the werewolves. Wisniewski calls in our location to her people who will be at least twenty minutes out. How's that warrant coming?"

"Stop asking. Hardwicke's pushing all the buttons she can. Expedience will allow me to go in without the warrant." She grumbled. "We can't wait for back up anyway."

"Exactly. When that sun sets, I think they're counting on Anton Thrace transforming. That he'll lose control and kill Vincent."

"Shit. You didn't mention that part." Chandler stared at me. "What if the werewolves hold us off long enough for that to happen?"

"They won't. My men shoot to kill." Kamaguchi looked at me.

I nodded. "Damned straight. I hate the idea of senseless killings. But if it's a choice between them and the boy? I'm choosing Vincent Gibraltar all the way."

"What about Thrace?" Wisniewski eyed me. "He's potentially a victim, too."

I eyed her bitterly. "I know. But if he's transforming. About to attack Vincent? Shoot to disable if you can. Vincent's the one we save. Be smart. But save the boy."

"Understood." Chandler nodded, eyeing Kamaguchi. "Your men understand?"

"*Da.* They all speak English. Maybe not so good as me. But they understand."

"Would you mind repeating all that in Russian, just to be safe?" asked Wisniewski.

"Fine. Yes." Kamaguchi rambled off enough Russian that the men nodded, gripping their weapons firmly.

"Don't suppose you have silver nitrate cannisters in all this stuff?" I asked.

"It's illegal." Wisniewski eyed Kamaguchi. "Although it would be useful."

"No. Company's too important. We don't break the law like that."

I smiled. He'd practically admitted that they broke the law in other ways. Such as trying to kill me. I'd gotten past that. Not that I didn't hold a grudge. It was more practical to use it as future leverage. Never knew when I'd need them again.

A man from the front interrupted. "They've stopped."

"Close the distance." Kamaguchi glanced at me. "If that's what you want us to do."

"Hard letting a woman lead?" Chandler held the man's gaze and grinned. It was a secret smile. Because he liked to be dominated by a woman. Wanted to be dominated by me. All I could do was remember the dead feeling of his kiss. Human warmth without human energy.

"I am not used to letting anyone lead me. I am in charge of Gibraltar's team."

"Who's your boss then?" I hadn't seen anything in the files about Amperdyne's overall structure.

"Need to know. For security purposes." He motioned to the driver. "We go now. Quickly."

"Where did they stop?" Wisniewski leaned forward to look at the man's tablet. "An empty bakery at the edge of that industrial area. Real close to the 705. We'll make good time." She glanced at the Russian. "Does it have any connection to Gibraltar?"

Kamaguchi did a search on his laptop. "*Da.* It is owned by a subsidiary of Gibraltar. Paperwork just recorded."

"Too recent to be a casual choice. Someone leveraged the purchase for this purpose." I shook my head. Blake had convinced me he cared about Vincent. I hated to think my own desperate longing for family had clouded my judgement. "Who signed the purchase order?"

Kamaguchi looked up. "Mansfield."

"Damn it." I checked my guns, making sure the replacement holster was properly adjusted. Fighting anger. I hated to be made the fool. "How long till sundown?"

"Too long for vampire help." Chandler touched my arm. Everyone noticed.

I shrugged it off. "Don't get too familiar, Mr. Chandler."

"Sorry. Just, are you sure we don't wait until the Feds get here? While there's sunlight, Vincent's not in danger. Right?"

"And how long will it take for them to set up a perimeter? Use official means to make demands on the werewolves? Time wasted and

Vincent's life is over. No. We go in. Kamaguchi, your men are excellent marksmen, correct?"

"Normally." He eyed me. I could tell what he was thinking. The sniper missed me. But he'd hit Rhoda. The difficulty hadn't been his shooting skills. Just misdirection.

"Then they shoot to kill. Every last werewolf except Anton. We move quickly and without mercy."

"Wow. I'd have thought you'd feel differently." Wisniewski studied me. Her expression almost sad. Like I was willing to betray my own. Only they weren't my own. Having a preternatural origin didn't make me the same as monsters that killed for profit.

"Lives matter, Wisniewski. Young or old. Black or white. Blue lives. But when you're weighing murderers against a single innocent? Vincent's life is the one worth protecting."

"Maybe you get tired of being P.I., want to work for real company." Kamaguchi nodded respectfully.

"My company is a real company. Small doesn't make it any less so."

I looked away from them all. My stomach had been starting to cramp. Not hunger. That same pain from the shower. Reminding me I'd used up all the previous feedings.

My belly grew cool at the thought. Hunger stirred alongside the pain. It would help me weaken any werewolves I got close to. Let the gunmen pick them off. Chandler would have my back. I didn't have to ask.

"Our people are twenty minutes out. The court order went through. If I'm inside with you, they won't waste time trying to negotiate. They'll come in guns blazing."

"How much silver-tipped ammo they have?"

"Just what we stock. Probably enough for five handguns. One rifle. We've never had an entire pack go rogue at once." Wisniewski gave me a dire look. "This is the end of Killian's group."

"There are children in his pack. Innocent women and teenagers. They can't all be held accountable for their leader's actions."

She shrugged, unhappy. "Not my call."

I cursed again. "One thing at a time. Stop here. The bakery's around the corner. There's an alleyway—." I studied the digital map Kamaguchi held up for me. Got my orientation. "There. It leads to the back of the building. Roof access from the adjacent cement factory. Zoom in that aerial map?"

I saw a door leading onto the roof. "Is that live?"

"*Da*. Why?"

"The door cracked open. They're already expecting an attack."

"They can't know we'd be here this fast." Wisniewski shook her head. "You must've imagined it."

"No. Look, I don't think they know we're here specifically. I think they're just being careful. Whoever goes up there will have to be better than stealthy. Werewolves have super-hearing."

"We know this. Amperdyne have special drones that play ice-cream music." He spoke Russian to one of the men. The man hopped out of the van carrying a large plastic case. "Pattern set to go up and down streets, playing music very loudly. Also is static with special noise generator. Masks footsteps. Breathing."

"Werewolves are the only preternaturals I know of with superhuman hearing. How is it Amperdyne has these?" I watched him suspiciously.

"We have full division working on preternatural problems. Amperdyne is international agency. Music changes for country."

I stared at him a few seconds longer than was polite. Trying to determine if he was telling the truth. Not that it mattered. "How long before the drones are in place?"

"Two minutes. Must start from three separate points to create proper web of interference."

"Web of interference. I like that." Chandler was taking mental notes. MI-6 would be given lots of ideas about their future dealings with preternaturals after this. If he lived to pass those ideas along.

Kamaguchi motioned to the back of the van. "We can get out. Start moving toward the buildings."

"How many of your men are coming inside with us?"

"Five. The one on drones will go roof. Two will watch back. The rest come inside the front with us."

"Make sure if they spot Vincent that we're told immediately. No wasting time trying to find him inside or being careful with the shooting through walls otherwise."

"Of course. Not my first rodeo."

Chandler couldn't resist poking Kamaguchi. "Rodeo. Not rodeo. That's only for Rodeo Drive in L.A."

Oddly, it felt like I was the source of their rivalry. But Kamaguchi wasn't romantically interested in me. He only wanted to hire me.

I stretched my legs outside the van, adjusting my clothes so that the weapons weren't visible. I wore black jeans and a burgundy leather jacket. Tougher than cotton and padded with mesh-wire. The mesh was meant to be body armor. Protection from knives and low caliber bullets. Hopefully it'd help slow down werewolf claws, too.

The Amperdyne men slipped off into the nearby alleyway. I walked toward the corner that led to the front of the bakery. No other foot traffic. I thanked God for that small favor. Praying silently that He'd let me recover Vincent alive. I paused and glanced around the corner using a handheld mirror. Music started. Loud. I jumped with annoyance. It was like having an ice-cream truck in my ear.

"I don't know if that's gonna pass as normal." I looked again. No one visible. They were keeping a watch from inside. We could get to the front before they saw us.

"Wait." Chandler pulled me back. "Security camera. New. Hard to see."

I glanced at him. He was staring at his phone. Or whatever the device really was. A red light flashed on a strange x-ray or infra-red image of the street.

"Can we block it?"

"That's almost as good as announcing us." He eyed me. "I can if you say so."

"If we had time I'd suggest trying to loop a few seconds. If it could be accessed remotely."

"That I can't do. The cameras are set up for wi-fi but the encryption is top-notch. Probably stolen from Amperdyne. Or purchased."

"Then we disable them and run like hell."

He nodded. "On the count of three. One. Two. Three."

We ran. I stayed in the front. Holding back my energy until I was almost at the door. The windows were boarded. Out of business signs plastered across everything. I didn't test the wood, smashing through it with ease. My strength tore the deadbolt out of the metal frame. It clattered loudly into the bakery.

"Shit! The Feds are here!" A man's voice. Vaguely familiar. Not Killian. One of my attackers from before.

I poured my power outwards. Felt three male werewolves just on the other side of an interior wall. Moving toward us. Not away. They appeared through a doorway.

I picked one. Let my hunger flow into him. He cried out. Crumpled to his knees.

Guns went off on either side of me. The other two werewolves dropped. Dead. That left the one I was feeding from.

"Shoot the bastard!" I said through gritted teeth. Filling myself up on one of them would make the others harder to stop.

Chandler stepped beside me. Aimed and fired. Middle of the forehead. A killing shot. I pulled my energy back. My stomach cold with delight at the heady food.

"How many more?" he asked.

I walked slowly, spreading my energy ahead of me. Through the building. Too slowly. They were crawling above us. Through ventilation shafts. Ready to drop behind us. "Watch out!"

I spun but two of Kamaguchi's men died as quickly as the werewolves had. Their guns went off wildly. Chandler fired his weapon, still facing forward. They'd surrounded us.

I felt the cramps return. Feeding had triggered it. It was a pain that wasn't hunger or anything else I'd ever felt. Like I was dying.

"How many, Bianca?" Chandler fired until his clip was empty.

I concentrated past my pain. "Ei—eight. With us anyways."

"Why aren't they dying?" snarled Kamaguchi. He fired two weapons, one in each hand with semiautomatic speed.

"Body armor!" Wisniewski had her back to a wall. "Aim for the heads."

I cursed. "Damn it. Just because they're werewolves!"

I was angry at myself. I'd fallen into another trap of prejudice. Lycanthropes were classified as wild and feral. It had never occurred me that they'd prepare for our assault like actual thinking and clever human criminals.

My anger helped me stand upright. Helped me ignore the cramps as I drew my guns. The fact that I'd waited so long to do it was worrisome. Relying on the men and woman behind me had relaxed my vigil. Not something I'd do again.

A shape lunged at me from the left. I dropped to one knee. Lashed out with my power. Firing in the second's hesitation it bought me. My energy flared unexpectedly then. The cramps intensifying. My hunger pulsed like a biological E.M.P. All directions at once.

I was aware of everyone in the room. Tasted their lifeforce without hurting them. Even Wisniewski. Only Chandler's totem kept him a blank spot of nothingness.

"What the fuck was that?" hissed the F.B.I. agent.

"Sorry. Something's wrong. I can't control my energy."

"Thankfully it hit the werewolves as hard as the rest of us."

The remaining lycanthropes—six in total—circled us warily. Some had guns in their hands. Taken from the Amperdyne guards. Only Kamaguchi and one other black clad ninja remained alive. We formed a circle with our backs to each other. No one fired.

"So, the bitch figured out where we had the kid." Killian stepped into the room. "Your power ain't nothing against this many. And it's still daylight. No vampires to come to your rescue this time."

"Why, Killian? How much money are they paying you to destroy your whole pack?"

"I'm doing this for my pack! With the payday from this job, we're set for life. Guaranteed income for twenty years. No more trailers and mangy animals to hunt."

"The Feds won't leave your people alone. They know you're involved in the kidnapping."

"What's she talking about, Kill?" One of them men shuffled nervously toward the alpha. "You said no one would trace this back to us."

"They won't! Once they're dead, it'll all fall onto Anton's faggoty little ass."

I smiled bitterly. "How will Thrace explain your blood being present at the crime scene?"

"We got a clean up crew just waiting for us to leave." Killian made some gesture and a gun went off. Wisniewski screamed in rage and pain. "Not that my guys shoot as well as they snap necks."

The agent held her thigh. Blood spilling between her fingers. "My people know Thrace isn't the one behind the kidnapping. I've been on the radio telling them."

"No you haven't. Radio blockers." He held up a device.

"It's one of ours. Damn that Mansfield!" Kamaguchi was furious. Watching the werewolves for another attack.

"Mansfield?" Killian roared with laughter. "Kill them. We're running out of time."

People fired. I was one of them. I hit Killian in the arm. A glancing blow before he disappeared into the rear of the building.

Another cramp tore through me. I screamed and my power flowed out in a torrent. Blinding me. I'd never experienced so much energy. My hunger consumed everything it touched. Seeking testosterone. Focusing on the strongest sources of sustenance.

Men cried out. Bodies hit the ground. A gun went off near my head. I winced. Partially deaf. My belly filled with fire. It drove back the cold spikes of hunger. My nerves burned and tingled with raw sensitivity. I screamed again, one final loud cry of agony.

Then the cramps subsided as unexpectedly as they'd started. My power came back into me. I realized hands held me. Chandler helped me stay on my feet. Everyone else was on the ground.

"What did you do, Bianca?"

I glanced at Wisniewski. Kamaguchi. They stirred. Not dead. I sighed with relief. "We can't worry about them. The sun's close to setting. We've got to find Vincent."

I struggled to walk. Sagging against him. For a change, I didn't fight his touch. Together, we went into the back of the abandoned building. It looked very different from the front.

"That's a vault."

"Used to be a bank." Killian was getting back to his feet. My energy hadn't done as much damage back here. Or he was just that powerful. Nope. Distance had made the difference. A figure stepped into the room. Features obscured by shadows. A woman. Somehow familiar. I thought about Killian's woman. The one who'd begged me to spare him. Only, the build was wrong.

The woman was flanked by another werewolf. Another muscular brute. She took a step closer. The shadows bled away. It took me several seconds to process the truth. "Maureen?" I shook my head. "Not Blake. He called you."

She smiled hatefully. "Yes. My sniveling brother called me. So excited that poor little Vinnie had been located."

"Damn. I should've realized. You warned me about werewolf bites. But you shouldn't've have known I'd been attacked. I thought it was just a general warning for the future."

She smiled with a shrug. "You've proven a formidable adversary. I suppose I'm glad you're a woman. Men are the cause of all this."

Chandler wanted to move forward. Reach for his weapon. But both hands were supporting me. Keeping me on my feet. It probably saved his life. The werewolves were waiting for a reason to attack. The only reason they didn't was because Maureen and I were talking.

"This is about your grandfather?"

"Yes."

"And what, Vincent is collateral damage?"

"Unfortunately. Not that he's entirely innocent. He never stood up to Grandfather. Never fought for me to have my place as heir."

"He's a boy. You're the grownup. Maybe not by much, but—."

"But nothing!" She aimed a small handgun directly at my chest. I hadn't seen it in her hands. Even a bad shot couldn't miss at this range. "There's no way you'll get the vault open in time. Vinnie's dinner."

"You pretend not to care. But you didn't just shoot him. Didn't even order Killian to do it. You don't want him dead. You aren't that heartless."

"Stop telling me what I am and am not! People have been doing that my whole life." She laughed bitterly. "Even Vinnie told me I could do whatever I wanted. That I didn't have to be stuck working for Grandfather. He wanted me to leave. To run away from my inheritance. Said he'd come, too. And that's when I came up with this glorious plan. Vinnie was a willing participant. I told him Anton felt the same way."

"The origami wolf."

She nodded, pleased. "A love token from Anton that I was asked to deliver. Because the werewolf could never express it on camera. Vinnie believed every word."

"And the E.M.P.?" I pictured the video over and over. "It was in the hippo!?"

She grinned, bowing at the neck graciously. "No one suspected a thing even afterwards. Some security!"

"Drop your weapon, Maureen." Chandler held his gun pointed at the woman. He'd managed to slip it into his hand without dislodging me. "Tell Killian to stay back. You'll be dead before he reaches us."

"Oh, I think you should drop your weapons. One squeeze of the trigger and she's dead, too. Even if I die, Killian will rip you apart. He'll get paid for doing the job regardless."

"This is what they call a stalemate." Killian preened with his imagined wit.

"No. We have the advantage." Maureen took another step out of the shadows. "Grandfather always failed to realize that I was the smart one in the family. I prepared for all sorts of contingencies."

"What do you mean?" Killian took his eyes off of us for a moment.

"I knew the Feds might find this place. If they figured out your connection to Vinnie's abduction. Once Bianca confirmed that you were in the frame, I decided better to just take care of all witnesses at once."

"What's she saying, Kill?" The other werewolf stepped away from her. As if she were suddenly dangerous.

"Amperdyne has so many great gadgets. It was easy to adapt them to my specific needs."

Maureen did something because there was an electric hum. She fired her gun at me. I felt the bullet snag in the jacket. Punching into my shoulder with enough force to make me scream. Chandler had to drop his to catch me.

The Glock was wrenched out of my hand. It flew across the room as if by magic. The same force caught my jacket and jerked me off of my feet. I was dragged out Chandler's arms and across the room. I slammed against a panel built into a wall. Hard. Stunning me for a moment. Some kind of super-magnetic device. Reacting to the wire mesh. Attracting the guns in the room.

I struggled out of the jacket. Dropped to my feet but it took precious seconds. Killian held Chandler up in the air by one fist. His other hand had formed into claws. Drawn back to slice into the MI-6 agent's handsome face.

Maureen stepped back and dropped a cannister at the alpha's feet.

Killian snarled with confusion. Hesitating mid-strike. "What the fuck is that?"

"Silver nitrate!" cried Maureen gleefully. "No loose ends I'm afraid."

The room clouded with the gas. Lethal to werewolves. Only painful to me. Probably nothing more than annoying to humans.

Killian released Chandler. Staggering after Maureen who fled. The alpha didn't make it more than a couple of steps before he collapsed onto all fours. The other werewolf had hesitated. Waiting for Killian's instructions. Breathing in the fumes instead of holding his breath. I watched him fall face-first onto the cement floor before the smoke obscured him. Dead.

I heard the sound of crackling. Fires had been ignited along all the outer walls. Front and back. Maureen had set the place up to become a death trap. She'd always planned on eliminating the werewolves. Chandler and I were the only ones who knew Maureen was involved. Even if Kamaguchi and Wisniewski managed to escape the fires through the front.

I had to stop her. But Chandler had dropped to one knee. Choking. Clawing at his throat.

"Paul?"

"Not just silver." He crawled toward me. "Get out, Bianca."

"No." I closed my eyes. Felt the fire like a living creature that my power could taste. Could touch. The cramps in my gut returned. Daggers of pain rode along my spine. I moved toward Chandler. Fell onto him. Carrying us both the rest of the way to the floor. He kissed me. Cold, without any humanity. That blasted totem. I kissed him back. Trying to reassure him.

I screamed into his mouth. My back exploded with agony and my power spiked again. It even drank in the heat of the fire blazing all around us. Soaked up any energy it could find.

The smoke grew thick. Not just from the cannister. From the fire as well. It overwhelmed me. I felt Chandler grow still. My heart burst with unfamiliar grief as I imagined him dead. Then I felt myself slip into darkness. A lack of oxygen. Or caused by whatever was in the cannister.

I passed out. Which meant the smoke would kill me. I prayed to God that Chandler would live. But I wouldn't know if it worked because I'd never wake again.

CHAPTER FORTY-TWO

Cool hands lifted me off of the ground. "Bianca?"

I opened my eyes. Blinking. "Paul?"

"No. Dusty."

I shook my head. "I'm not dead?"

"No. Neither is your boyfriend."

"What're you talking about?"

"Chandler. He's alive. You protected him somehow."

"The gas?"

"Expelled from the building." Chilton stood beside Dusty, surveying the charred building. Then he pointed at me. "Probably by those."

"By what?" I stared down at myself. My blouse was ripped at my shoulders. Leaving me covered in only a bra and tatters of silk.

"Your wings." Dusty stared at me sadly.

"I don't have wings!" I laughed but reached involuntarily around at my side. Felt a thick flap of something leathery. "What the blazes?"

"You do now."

The cramps were gone. So was the energy I'd soaked up from the werewolves. And the fire. My mind reeled. Stunned to be alive. Even more stunned at this!

"Is Agent Wisniewski okay? Kamaguchi?"

"Alive. Barely." Bonnie, the redhead came into the room. "The Feds are almost here. Someone gave them the wrong address. A radio intercept."

"Killian?"

Bonnie shook her head. "A woman."

I nodded. Maureen. "What happened to him? Killian?"

"Don't know. Which one is he?"

"Set me down."

Dusty was reluctant. "Can you walk?"

"If I can't, then help me. Otherwise—."

He put my feet on the ground and I stumbled forward. He held my elbow. Balanced me. I walked toward the exit. There weren't any bodies there. Killian had made it out.

"What about the boy?" Chilton touched my arm tentatively. Then he removed it as if remembering I was dangerous.

"The vault. Oh shit. It's after sundown. I need the vault opened now!"

The vampires worked together as a team. Even Bonnie. They tore the vault door open after a few moments of straining. The metal ripped easily in their powerful hands.

I went in first. Just in case. Anton was huddled in a corner. Furry. Looking up at me. Another smaller shape was curled into a ball, arms over his face in the opposite corner.

"Get him out." The werewolf's shout was animalistic. Urgent. "Out!"

I went to the boy. He screamed when I touched him. Calmed when he heard my voice. "Vincent, you're safe. Your grandfather sent us."

Dusty helped me get him to his feet. Vincent pulled his shirt down, sobbing. As if embarrassed to show skin. Hiding a scratch. Or a bite. I wasn't sure which I'd seen, but he was alive.

"Are you alright, Vincent?"

He nodded and threw himself into my arms, weeping. I pushed him off. "Can't!"

I fell backwards onto my ass. Dusty chose to catch the boy instead of me. I couldn't blame him.

I waited to feel the intangible drain on the boy's life from that touch. But I'd jerked away fast enough. That and the fact that I didn't feel hungry at the moment.

"You did it, Bianca. You saved him." Chandler leaned against the torn frame of the vault door.

"We did. Everyone gets the credit." I smiled at Chilton. "Maybe there's a way Amperdyne and the Atlantic Street Revenants could work together on Gibraltar's security."

"With all that's happened, we gave up on that idea. Especially not with Joseph in charge. We're trying an alternative approach."

He reached out and I took his hand with my gloved fingers. He pulled me gently to my feet. "Thanks."

"I want everyone isolated for questioning." Hardwicke came into the building with a swarm of helmeted F.B.I. agents. Weapons drawn. I glanced at the wall panel. Nothing happened. The magnet had been deactivated. My jacket and the guns were piled on the floor beneath it. She looked to me for answers. "What the hell happened to Wisniewski?"

I glanced at Chilton, anxious. "They said she's alive."

"Barely!" snarled Hardwicke.

"We've got the boy. Thanks to Bianca and the vampires." Chandler folded his arms defiantly at the F.B.I. agent. "Don't need any trigger happy Feds killing one of the good guys."

"Yeah? Well, all the werewolves are dead. And so are most of the Amperdyne ninjas. Care to explain that?"

"Self-defense."

Hardwicke glared at me. Trembling. I'd never seen her that angry. Like me, she took a moment to pull herself together before speaking again. "We couldn't find Blake Mansfield. Anyone else get away?"

I shook my head. Without emotion. I was too drained. Family betrayal cut deeper for me than other cases. Because I didn't have one. "It wasn't Mansfield. Maureen Edwards was behind it. She and Killian plotted it all."

"Shit. Why Maureen Edwards?" The penny dropped. "Oh! The missing granddaughter. They were here?"

"She set the building on fire. Tried to burn down the evidence."

"She may be related to the billionaire but she doesn't have Gibraltar's money. We'll find her." Hardwicke moved toward the vault, then froze. Staring at me. "What the hell are those?"

I stood taller. Tried to flex my shoulders. Felt the wings flare out, like new limbs. My brain and body were still trying to adjust to them.

"Apparently I have wings."

CHAPTER FORTY-THREE

I stood beside Agent Wisniewski's hospital bed. Anxious. The doctor's said she'd be fine. Depleted of electrolytes was the only official diagnosis they could give to what I'd done. Being a woman had saved her. She opened her eyes.

"How long you been hovering over me?"

"Not long."

"Two hours." Hardwicke pushed herself out of the chair on the opposite side of the bed. "How you feel?"

"Like a Mack truck ran me over." She laughed, coughing as she did. "Need something to drink."

"Here." Hardwicke handed her a juice the nurses had left.

It had a bent straw and Wisniewski sipped from it before she tried to talk again. "We're alive. Does that mean we saved the boy?"

"It does." I didn't have to force a smile.

She eyed me hopefully. "And Mansfield? We have him?"

"He wasn't the one behind it. His sister was. Maureen Edwards."

Her astonishment was eloquent. "Tell me we got her?"

"No. Killian did though." Hardwicke grunted with approval.

I couldn't hide my surprise. "You didn't say."

"Not any of your business. My bosses made sure to let me know that in no uncertain terms. But I can't help it if you overhear me explain to my partner." She smiled and took Wisniewski's pale hand. "Found her strung up and gutted in her apartment. Killian's blood was at the scene. We sent people to their territory but he wasn't there. They claim he never made it back."

"You believe them?"

"He knew he'd be made for killing Maureen. For what they tried to do to Vincent. If it wasn't for that blood, we'd have never known for sure."

"When you winged him I was thinking, what a lousy shot you were." Wisniewski laughed which made her cough again. "Guess it was just as well."

"It was a lousy shot. My body was too busy giving me shit over these. I did a little spin and unfurled my wings. They nearly filled the room.

"Holy shit!" The Ukrainian-American agent made the sign of the cross before she could stop herself. "Sorry. Habits."

"If I didn't look like the Devil before, I do now." I pulled them tightly against my back. Made them barely visible from the front. "Thankfully an oversized trench-coat will hide them."

"So what happened to me?" She eyed me shrewdly. Not exactly unhappy. Suspicious. "I mean, I take it that it was you that kayoed us."

"It was. But not on purpose. My power sort of went out of control. Probably to grow these. I don't know exactly. I don't normally have that effect on women."

She fought a smile. Changed the subject to help hide a laugh. "How's Vincent. Did you have to shoot Thrace?"

"No. He held it together by sheer force of will. Long enough to get to them anyway." I left out the part about him nipping Vincent. Barely broke the skin. Of course, barely was enough. "The doctors are still running tests on the boy before they'll let the old man see him."

"Aren't you supposed to be there when that happens?" asked Hardwicke, giving me a look. She wanted to be alone with her partner.

"I am. I just wanted to say, I'm sorry. And that I'm glad you're okay."

Wisniewski let her chin drop to her chest. I could barely hear her reply. "Thanks."

I started to the door and heard her clear her throat. I glanced back and she was watching me. "Something wrong?"

"No." She cleared her throat, again. Actually smiled all the way to her eyes. "Just the opposite. Nice working with you. Sorry for being such a judgmental bitch."

I laughed and waved as I left. It was a good laugh. I felt it to my core. Like I'd made a new friend. Made up for being such a bad one. Only time would tell, but I was optimistic. I'd helped save the boy. That had made it all worthwhile.

Vincent Gibraltar was five rooms away. The doctors had promised to get me before they let anyone else see him. The only credit I got for keeping him alive. Chandler was watching the door just to be sure.

I paused halfway and went into Yuri Kamaguchi's room. The Feds had brought us all to the same place. I'd just recovered faster than the rest.

The Amperdyne security chief hadn't done as well as the others. But he'd awoken sooner. Some quirk about his body chemistry and what I'd done to him.

"There she is. The woman who almost killed me." His eyes glinted with humor. "Gibraltar called. Said you gave us credit for keeping Vincent alive. Keeping you alive to rescue the boy."

"It was a team effort. No sense in you losing your livelihood because of what Maureen Edwards did."

"What is this livelihood. Some kind of jacket?"

I tilted my head and frowned at him. "Now I think you're punking me."

He grinned broadly. His color bad. "Hah. She's smart and beautiful. The job offer is still on the floor."

"Table."

"Yes. The table is also on the floor." He laughed at me. Still making fun. "Thank you for not making problem for our earlier mistake."

"I haven't forgotten you tried to kill me. But I can overlook it. For future favors."

"We must all pay the price for our mistakes." He closed his eyes. Suddenly tired. "They say I almost died. Why did I not?"

"Your high-tech body-armor. The electromagnetic fibers woven in to disrupt electrical charges or whatever its purpose. It deflected some of my power." I touched his arm with my gloved hand. "I'm glad."

"Me, also! Dead isn't so much fun!" He sighed, dozing off. Then his eyes opened briefly. "We will meet again, Bianca Savage. Now let me sleep."

I slipped out of the room as his snoring began. The next room was Anton Thrace. I was reluctant to go in. I wasn't sure what to tell him. I hadn't made up my mind about telling the F.B.I. about the bite. The doctors weren't testing for lycanthropy. As long as Vincent wasn't a vampire, and alive, Henry Gibraltar was happy. Honestly, I think he'd forgotten what I'd told him about using the werewolf to kill his grandson. Or maybe I'd only said 'full moon.' He hadn't put it together.

"Anton." I pulled the curtain back and stared down at him on the bed. He was fully recovered. The I.V. on his arm merely a precaution. Mood stabilizers and Gibraltar's drug forced him to remain a man. There were at least four more hours of the full moon to worry about.

"Miss Savage."

"Bianca. Please."

"Is Vincent okay? No one will tell me. My memories are muddy. But I thought—I thought—is he okay?"

I nodded. "He's alive. I haven't seen him yet. But you kept control of your beast better than they hoped."

"So I didn't bite him?"

I shrugged. "I didn't say that. I think that he might need your guidance over the next few years."

"A relationship? He's only seventeen. A boy." He looked terrified of the prospect.

"I didn't say sleep with him. Teach him how to deal with what he is."

He grew sad. "So I did bite him."

"You also have more experience being gay than he does."

"That was real? I thought I dreamt it in my fever. He said I'd invited him to run away with me. That I felt the same. I didn't have a clue what he was talking about."

"He's been smitten with you for some time."

He grunted. "Killian said I'd finally do something good for the pack. Just before they locked me up with Vincent. What did he mean? Was I supposed to convert the boy?"

"No. You were supposed to kill him."

He jerked his gaze upward. Stared at my glasses. Stunned. "Why?"

"Maureen Edwards. The firstborn cousin who should've inherited instead of Vincent."

"That's messed up."

"Yeah, it is. She's dead now. Killian killed her. He got away." I studied the man's expression. "Will he come for you again?"

"No. He's too smart for that. And there's no profit. He'll run. You won't catch him."

"Not my job. I did my job. Vincent's alive. That's what matters."

He grinned sheepishly. "Save the boy, save the world."

"And the werewolf."

He laughed softly. Sadly. "I don't know if I can be what Vincent needs. Not if he's in love with me."

"Who else does he have?"

I left the man with those thoughts. A nurse stood at the doorway, motioning. Vincent was ready to talk. Which meant I had about ten minutes before Henry Gibraltar would barge his way in. And with him, Joseph.

CHAPTER FORTY-FOUR

Chandler opened the door for me, watching the hallway like real security. "I'll rap on the door the moment Gibraltar appears. But, Bianca, why do you need to talk to him first? And alone?"

"It's private."

I stepped inside, hearing the sounds of machines tracking his vitals. Another I.V. drip for dehydration. He was on the bed shirtless. No bite mark or scar visible.

"It's you."

I moved my gaze to his face. He watched me with eyes as big as saucers. Maybe it was the horns. Or the wings. No point in hiding them until I'd updated my wardrobe.

"It is. It's me."

"They said you saved me. That you're—."

"A succubus. Yes. Don't worry. As long as I don't touch you skin on skin and you don't look into my eyes, you're golden."

"Is Anton okay? Is he mad at me?"

"Why would he be mad at you?"

He grew shy. Embarrassed. "I thought he was in on it. I thought he wanted me to come. The F.B.I. said Maureen tricked me before the doctors took over."

"She did. He cares about you." I made my voice as gentle as I could. "But he's not in love with you. You're a little young."

He didn't look up. Instead, he stared at the blanket gathered in rows at his narrow hips. "I know. Everyone keeps telling me that."

"Not too young to be loved. But he's been looking out for your grandfather for years. You were a little boy. In his mind, you still are. But he can help you."

"Help me how? My grandfather will ground me for life once he finds out I'm gay."

I smiled. Teenage priorities. Being gay was worse than becoming a werewolf. "Well, he should probably learn about that from you. But he doesn't have to know about the other."

"The other?" He eyed me cautiously. Shrewdly.

"You aren't as foolish as people think. The bite healed awfully fast."

"What bite?" He stared at me defiantly. "Anton didn't do anything."

"I'm not gonna narc. I'm just telling you, Thrace knows what happened. He'll try to help. If you don't try to get into his pants while he's doing it."

Vincent blushed and grinned sheepishly. "I'd settle for cuddling in front of the TV."

"That might be a bit much as well. But that's between the two of you. Legally, I'm supposed to report anything that might endanger you. I must've been mistaken when I thought I saw a bite. The blood could've been from anything."

"Right." He blinked. Then his face lit up. "Right!!! Nothing happened. Vincent kept it together without his meds and didn't hurt me. Grandfather can't fire him, right?"

"I'll put in a good word. A very good one."

"What happened to Cousin Maureen? No one will tell me."

I hesitated. Saw the earnest, needy expression on his young face and nodded. He deserved the truth from someone. He'd been sheltered too much already.

"She's dead. Killed by the werewolf she hired to kill you."

He went silent. Tears welling in his eyes. "I'm tired. I'd like to be alone if you don't mind."

I nodded and went outside. Chandler closed the door, surprised. "That was fast. You get what you needed?"

"It was more about giving. I think the matter's resolved."

"Speak of the Devil." Chandler motioned. Henry Gibraltar was walking stiffly toward us. Joseph close behind.

The vampire caught my eyes. Glanced at Chandler. His expression disappointed. Somehow he knew about me and the human. Maybe some of the coven vampires still talked to him.

"I want to see my grandson!" Gibraltar shouted as if addressing us. But there was a nurse trying to slow him down.

"We need to talk before you go in." I unfurled my wings which froze him in his tracks. Joseph didn't blink. Yep, someone had already filled him in. I smiled reassuringly at the old man. "Yeah. I was surprised at first, too. Let's step into an empty room."

He reluctantly let me steer him to the closest available doorway. It hadn't been cleaned yet and smelled of urine and blood. Joseph stood watch outside. Didn't try to speak to me. Unhappy with my choice. That made things easier for me. I didn't have to explain.

"I'm grateful you saved him, but I want to see for myself that he's not a bloodsucker!"

I glanced at Joseph. The vampire didn't react to Gibraltar's derogatory remark. "He's not. The doctors confirmed it. But he is upset. He knows that Maureen's dead. And why."

The man snarled with pain. "She tried to kill him! Why should he be sad she's dead?"

"She was your granddaughter, too. Don't you care?"

He grumbled and glanced around the room to avoid his reflection in my glasses. "She was always aloof. Independent. Argued about her rights. Wouldn't listen to logic or reason."

"It's logical for a girl not to inherit?"

That drew his gaze back to me. Angry. "To preserve the name? Absolutely!"

"Why not just keep the name. Even if she married. She was the first born. 'Gibraltar' is just as good as 'Edwards.'"

"It's not done that way."

"Better to have a—a grandson who might not meet your expectations?"

"Vincent's a good child. He'll do fine. Once he grows a backbone. That comes with age and experience."

I wanted to prepare him for the fact that Vincent was gay. But it wasn't my place. It might backfire. I'd done enough to save the boy. The rest was really up to him.

"Two things before I let you see Vincent."

He glared but I'd already broken him once. He nodded reluctantly. "Go on."

"First, Anton Thrace proved his loyalty to you. Again. By keeping Vincent from harm. I think he should get a raise. Maybe extend his job to protecting Vincent, as well as you."

"Fine. I wasn't going to fire him for being kidnapped. I know how hard it is for him without the drugs we developed. He put my grandson's welfare above his own. It might be good for Vincent to understand preternaturals. Since werewolves almost killed him." He was impatient. But I could see he was trying to listen. "What's the other thing?"

"Killian's pack is going to be held accountable for his actions. Most of them didn't know what he was up to. There are children among them. Infants. I need you to use your considerable resources to make sure the innocent aren't blamed."

He rubbed his chin. Grunting and breathing loudly. "Can't make any promises."

"I want a promise. I promised I'd do everything I could to get Vincent back and I did. My two requests aren't that much considering what was at risk."

"Fine. I give my word. Now can I go see my grandson?"

"Be my guest." I motioned with a flourish.

He took a final glance at my wings and rushed out the door. Joseph marched off after him. Not even a glance my way. I hated being contrary but it bothered me. Just a smidgeon. I sighed and shook it off.

I had one more difficult task. To talk to Chandler. Make sure he still wanted to try this dating thing. I hadn't found a way to tell him how the totem made me feel. Like kissing a boy instead of a man. He didn't stir my passion. No more than Joseph would've.

I stopped beside the full-length mirror on the outside of the bathroom door. Stared at myself. "No, Bianca Savage. You've taken care of enough people for one day. The rest of the night is for you."

I stepped into the hospital hallway. "Good night, Paul."

I walked away without waiting for his response. Left him staring at my back in the hall as confused as I was.

CHAPTER FORTY-FIVE

It was an hour before dawn when someone rapped at my door. I was still awake. Lying in bed hadn't put me to sleep. I was fretting over Vincent's fate. Wondering what would happen to Killian's pack. And hungry. Almost enough to go to the office for that goat.

I opened the door cautiously. It was too late or too early for anyone casual to show up. And I didn't want to deal with Chandler until I'd had a decent night's sleep.

Blake Mansfield stood there. Pale. Nervous. No. Anxious. "May I come in?"

"Certainly. Where have you been?"

He didn't answer right away. He scanned my apartment looking for other people. Windows. I wasn't exactly sure.

"Are you alright, Mansfield?"

He turned to watch me as I shut the door. I faced him and leaned against the kitchen counter.

"Is it true? Maureen did all this?" He sounded defeated. He'd lost his parents. Now a sister. I felt a wave of compassion.

"It is. What's going on?" My power slipped outward, just for a taste of his nervousness. My body reacting to his emotional state. Only there was nothing. A familiar emptiness. "Blake. What happened? What did you do?"

He laughed. A strangled maniacal bark. "You can tell. They told me you could." He continued to pace, wringing his hands together. "It was the only way, you see. I needed to be free. Empowered to take back my life. The way Vincent decided to run off with Anton." He strangled another sound. I thought it was a sob. Or a twisted bark of laughter. "The way Maureen tried to take back her power from Grandfather. All of us foolish."

"Did the vampires force this on you?"

"No. No. Lots of talking. Discussion. Chandler pointed out all the benefits. Losing daytime was the only real downside."

I held my breath. Counted to three. Then to five. Mind racing. Chandler had been involved? My stomach knotted for reasons that had nothing to do with hunger.

"Not the only one." I shook my head. Realizing what he'd given up even if he hadn't. "You can't be an attorney if you only come out at night. And people will figure it out."

"I know. Only. They won't. I mean, I have the authority to set my own schedule. Grandfather only calls on me occasionally. It'll be a long while before he realizes. I haven't set foot in a courtroom in months."

"And what happens in the meanwhile?"

He wanted to smile. It wasn't convincing. "I get to be free. Experience life without fear of being discovered."

"But you hate vampires." I watched him. Trying to catch the lie.

"Still do, I guess. I've always been full of self-loathing. What's a bit more?" He stared at the floor. Lost.

"I see. And why are you here?"

His apprehension spiked but he jerked his head up. Held my gaze. "You helped my family. Helped rescue Vinnie. I figured I should repay the favor. Watch out for Chandler. He's not what he seems."

I nodded. "I kind of figured that out. Definitely more than he seemed."

"Not 'more.' Dangerous. Don't trust him."

I frowned. This wasn't the same recommendation I'd heard from him before. "What do you mean?"

"I have to go. Just be careful." He pushed past me. I was too astonished to hold him back. Then he was gone.

"What the hell did that mean?"

CHAPTER FORTY-SIX

Blake Mansfield wasn't my last visitor of the night. Dusty showed up twenty minutes later. Awfully close to dawn. And I was incredibly tired. My body finally taking control away from my mind. Feeling the day's trials.

He stood in the doorway. Helpless. Lost. Just like Mansfield. I was starting to feel like social services.

"Dusty. Shouldn't you be tucked away in a coffin somewhere?"

"I had to see you one last time."

"One last—what do you mean?" I couldn't hide the worry in my voice. I wasn't attracted to the vampire. But I'd grown to like him. He was as much an innocent as Vincent Gibraltar. In his own way.

"Chilton's sending some of us out of town. On a project. Can't say more than that."

"For your own good I presume?"

"What, because I like you? Don't flatter yourself. He doesn't care enough about you or me for that. It's strictly business."

"So you just wanted to say 'goodbye?'"

"I know you think I'm nothing but a corpse. We can't help how we feel. No hard feelings. Just—I really thought, you know, you might be as tired of being lonely as I am."

"Does Rhoda know that's how you feel?"

"What, and make her feel worse than she does? I'm stupid maybe. But not a monster." He laughed morosely. He tapped his chest. "Not in here."

"I am sorry, Dusty."

"Yeah. I know. Everyone's sorry. I'm sorry that I can't love Rhoda back. You're sorry you can't love me back. Blake's sorry his sister turned out to be a nutjob." He turned to leave. Short and sweet.

"Why's Chandler involved with your coven?"

He glanced back at me. Shrugging. "Dunno. He and Chilton are thick as thieves. I always figured it's the shared English thing."

"Chandler's English?" It wasn't a lie. I wasn't saying I didn't know. It was a question. I needed to understand how Dusty knew.

"He drops the fake American whenever they're together." He smiled. His eyes full of pain. "Guess you don't know your boyfriend as well as you think."

"He's not my boyfriend."

He made a face that said he didn't believe me. Then he shrugged. "I wish you well, Bianca."

Then he was gone. Not superfast. Vampires didn't have superspeed. But it felt like it. By the time I stepped into the hall after thinking about my reply, he was already out of sight.

CHAPTER FORTY-SEVEN

I went into the office late the next day. It was almost closing time. I'd slept longer than usual. Growing wings will do that, apparently.

Janet looked up. Gasped. I'd forgotten to warn her. "What happened to you!? Are—are those real?"

"Yes, they're real. As far as what happened. I haven't a clue."

She came over and hugged me. Skin on skin. To my surprise, my hunger ignored her completely. It was more interested in the goat in the hall closet. A refinement in control. Only interested in things with testosterone. I suddenly wondered if the wings were responsible.

Janet released me. Keeping one hand on my covered shoulder. "I saw that you saved the kid. It was all over the internet. Then the check came in."

"That was fast. Gibraltar must've wanted to be sure I didn't come around to collect it personally."

"I don't know. It's twice our fee."

I raised my brows. "Any note?"

"Something from Vincent Gibraltar. I didn't understand it."

"Let me see."

She handed me the paper. A young man's handwriting. But with a flourish. '*He promises to show me a wild time. I owe you everything.*'

"What's it mean?"

"It means that a certain older man is going to give young Mr. Gibraltar the guidance he needs to navigate the real world."

"Sounds naughty to me. A wild time? Drinking? Sex?" She watched me disapprovingly.

"Wild, in this case, simply hints at living large under the open sky."

She shook her head. "What aren't you saying?"

"The less you know, the less likely you'll have culpability."

"I knew it! You did something wrong! And you're right! I don't want to know."

I laughed and went into my office, happy. Vincent was no longer a prisoner. As a werewolf, he could risk himself in ways he never could before. Anton would teach him how to control his beast. And maybe how to be a man independent of his grandfather. Happily ever after. My favorite kinds of stories. Even without reciprocated romance.

There was a white box on my desk. No bow. Something a hat might come in. Janet had forgot to mention it. I raised the lid. Found another note in that strange writing. A cluster of yellow flowers beneath it, wreathed for a small head. A gift? It felt like something more.

The first time had been an invitation. A greeting of some kind. This message was less straightforward. Someone with powers that rivaled mine was asking or telling me something. And I had no clue where to start. I had a feeling, the wings weren't the only thing I'd be spending the next few weeks figuring out.

The End

ABOUT THE AUTHOR

MICHAEL DON ANDERSON was born and raised in Fresno County, California. His first professional publication was in *Marion Zimmer Bradley's Fantasy Magazine* with a short story called '*The Lamp*,' although his writings have appeared in school-related newspapers, journals and competitions since his early teens. His published books include *The Pride of the Pard* (teen fantasy series), *Dragon's Reach* (family focused traditional fantasy series), *Murder at the Undead Comedy Club* (fey urban crime fantasy); *Werewolf Incorporated* (lycanthrope and fey urban crime fantasy); and *The Fey Adventures of Devon Mosteller* (his popular gay-themed adult contemporary fantasy series); and now *Succubus for Hire* (urban crime fantasy).

His educational background includes two B.A.s (Anthropology and Linguistics) and an M.A. (Linguistics) from the California State University at Fresno, as well as an M.A. and Ph.D. (Linguistics) from the University of Arizona.

To contact Michael Don Anderson, please write him in care of the publisher CRIMSON WEREWOLF LIMITED, at 7260 W. Azure Dr., Ste 140-798, Las Vegas, NV 89130-7999.

For more information about our books, please visit our website at *www.crimsonwerewolf.com*